# TARBIN'S FALSE PROPHET

# TARBIN'S FALSE PROPHET

## THE RECHARGING BOOK TWO

### KELLY LYNN COLBY

**Cursed Dragon Ship**
PUBLISHING

Copyright © 2019 by Kelly Lynn Colby

First Edition by Inklings Publishing

Second Edition 2020

Cursed Dragon Ship Publishing, LLC

4606 FM 1960 Rd W, Suite 400, Houston, TX 77069

captwyvern@curseddragonship.com

Cover © 2019 by Stefanie Saw

Copyediting by Dorothy Tinker

ISBN 978-1-951445-09-6

ISBN (ebook) 978-1-951445-08-9

*To the inclusive people who believe there is room on this planet for all of us.*

# CHAPTER ONE

Talia Winterlaus adjusted the bejeweled Tarbin crown atop her carefully coifed curls. She felt silly wearing the thing. After finding out she wasn't the child of the king of Tarbin, she had no right to claim the title True Heir. Nevertheless, the astropriests insisted she was the one.

Within the stone walls of Astropriest Tower, somber music announced the beginning of the ceremony. The home of the astropriests vibrated with excitement as priests, acolytes, and servants awaited Talia's march up the spiral stairway into the Star Chamber. This moment had to be important based on the number of shining rubies lining the walls. Nomyra had explained how torches blinded the eye to the Stars. The red preserved night vision, allowing their message to be seen above the open top floor of the tower. The blatantly limited use of magic showed the confidence the astropriests had in Talia's success. The Recharging would fill the planet with an enormous amount of energy, easily replacing the minuscule investment.

Talia scuffed her feet against the floor. Her sequined shoes reflected the red light, even as her matching dress danced with the moon's glow filtering through the side windows. She lifted her head to share a funny thought with her guardians before she remembered they weren't beside her. She had insisted that they wait for her above. No danger could penetrate the island and assault her with all the protections placed on the seat of astropriest power.

The way Talia saw it, she didn't deserve guardians since she's wasn't heir to the Tarbin throne. The first thing she had done once she shared the news of her sketchy parentage was free her guardians from their vows. Talia might not have any choice, but that didn't mean her closest companions had to share the same fate. Though it still took a great deal of convincing, she needed them to get used to making decisions for their own benefit, without worrying about her safety.

Though she had professed her independence, Talia was relieved that each of them had refused to leave altogether. Her journey wasn't over yet, what with the impending Recharging. She couldn't do it without them. But their roles remained in flux.

The overt difference due to their change of status seemed to be their romantic involvements. Though it had been forbidden, Ial and Nyna had always had affection for each other. Now they were allowed to explore it. Naul found a few acolytes more than willing to give him a taste of physical pleasure. Dew, on the other hand, found more interest in studying the ancient texts that weren't in the library in Tarbinulus.

An acolyte bent around the corner of the spiral steps and waved Talia forward. She gathered her skirt in her hand and hurried up the first few steps. A different acolyte higher up gestured for her to slow down. Talia took a deep breath and forced herself to assume a statelier pace. It wouldn't do for her to be dizzy from the journey up the tightly turned staircase when she presented herself to the Stars above.

Nomyra hadn't explained the details of her role today, but Dew had discovered another title the True Heir usually took on at the time of the Recharging. However, the cultural guardian hadn't been able to translate the term, and Nomyra had insisted it would all become clear during the ceremony.

Talia hit the top floor and bowed slightly to the astropriests acting as formal guards at the entrance. She could make out the audience on the other side, all standing. The dark blue of the acolytes' robes contrasted with the pristine white of the fully ordained astropriests. Splashes of muted color along the outer walls were all Talia could see of the servants who had earned the chance to bear witness. All four of her guardians stood on the bottom step of a raised dais, which climbed higher than the top of the tower's crenellations. Talia wasn't afraid of heights, but that elevation looked daunting.

One of the guard astropriests cleared her throat to garner Talia's attention. The second astropriest proffered a shiny needle. At least Talia had been prepared for the blood offering. These learned people had been anxious to test her blood since she arrived at Astropriest Tower. Nomyra had forced them to wait until the formal ceremony.

Though Nomyra had been disgraced and stripped of her title in Tarbin, the astropriests here practically worshipped her for fulfilling the prophecy and discovering the True Heir.

Talia offered the crown to the first astropriest and her hand to the second. A quick prick of pain later, her blood was smeared on the Holy Diamond, the central of the five gemstones that adorned the crown. For a moment, Talia was afraid nothing would happen. Would she be disappointed or relieved? She had never asked for more than control of her own life and a chance to serve her people. Now she wasn't sure who her people were, and she had less control than ever in the hands of the astropriests and their prophecies.

The Holy Diamond soaked up her blood and shone a bright blue that cut through the subtle red of the wall-mounted rubies.

The astropriestess held up the crown as her companion announced, "The Key acknowledges the True Heir of ancient Raqmu, the city of Light and Dark."

Talia's mind whirled as they tucked the darkening crown back atop her curls. She'd never heard of Raqmu. She tried to catch Dew's eye to see if her research had turned up anything under that name, but she couldn't see the cultural guardian; the gem's reaction had temporarily blinded her. So much for the protective red light of the corridors.

Nomyra's full, almost white hair flowed down her sparkling, white robes as she joined Talia at the entrance. The two walked shoulder-to-shoulder down the center aisle. Each row of attendants bowed as they passed.

Talia mirrored Nomyra's straight-backed posture, though her insides swam with doubt. Matching her footsteps to the rhythm of the slow music and hoping it would drown out her voice, Talia asked, "Raqmu? You didn't mention anything about some random city I was to be the True Heir of."

Nomyra raised an eyebrow but didn't turn her head. "You didn't think the Machine lay somewhere in Tarbin, did you?"

*So this oddly named city is the location of the Recharging. Why couldn't Nomyra have just said that earlier?*

The continued dependence on secrecy drove Talia crazy. She wished Aleck were here. She could use a bit of his naive bravery around the priestess. Unfortunately, he'd had to miss the formalities to travel home and inform Dragick's and Gallick's families of their sacrifice. A heavy swallow forced down her grief for the loss of the dwarven guards.

She moved the crown a bit to the right of her head to free a strand of hair that pulled at her scalp. She wondered how Prince Aleck's father would take the news that they would need the Holy Diamond for another year.

Luckily, he hadn't had to go alone. Lordling Gregor Rivenwood had to visit *his* father to check in on their holdings. Talia's stomach tingled at the thought of his deep brown, expressive eyes. He had attended every formal ceremony since she was a child. She would miss Gregor's easygoing take on the stressful event. He always made her smile when all she wanted to do was scream. Now that she wasn't stuck in a role of her father's choosing, maybe Talia could make her own romantic choices.

At the foot of the dais, Talia's companions bowed. Naul had to bend almost in half to match Dew's slight head tilt. Nyna's long, dark hair fell over her face as Ial's hand twitched next to her. Talia hadn't seen the two not holding hands for days. She wondered if their hands felt cold.

Nomyra turned sideways and gestured toward the rise. "The True Heir must ask the Stars to judge her worthiness to act as Bright One for the Recharging."

Talia almost tripped on the first step at the mention of the new title. A quick glance at Dew's huge eyes told Talia she was just as fascinated with the clue. She'd leave that worry to the studious cultural guardian. Instead, Talia climbed the steps at a determined pace as she contemplated how she'd prove her worthiness to the Light above when she was surrounded by the Dark.

Nyna and Ial fell in line below and on either side of her. Naul and Dew came last, matching their footfalls to Talia's rhythm. The V-shaped entourage made it to the top of the dais just as the music ended.

So far above the ground and elevated beyond the solid footing of Astropriest Tower, the night sky enveloped Talia. Oppressive Dark squeezed against her as if it were a true physical presence. She felt her confidence wan as the moonlight seemed to flee from her. How was she to seek approval of the Light when she couldn't escape the Dark?

Panic gripped her thoughts. She wrapped her arms around her stomach like a barrier against the negative influence. Tearing her gaze from above, she sought comfort in the green landscape of the island. Instead, the ground reflected the moon's Light with a cold indifference. The surrounding lake absorbed every bit of energy, morphing into a black abyss.

Talia would fail. Why did she keep pretending she was worthy of these titles, of this responsibility? What made her think she could

Recharge the planet? She was nothing but a girl who didn't even know who her father was, let alone where she belonged. She closed her eyes as a bout of nausea whipped through her.

A warm hand gripped her shoulder while a smaller one gripped her elbow. A third hand fell on her second shoulder at the same time as a gentle tug on her chin made her open her eyes. Her guardians, her true companions, stood around her, driving back the Dark with their inner Light.

Dew gestured at the sky. "Look, Talia."

Five celestial bodies shone with increased intensity as they approached one another overhead. The trajectory of the flawlessly round points of pure-white brilliance didn't quite align, but close.

"They're beautiful," Talia said, as she felt Dark's grip loosen and crumble away. A breeze blew off Lightndark Lake and whipped Talia's hair around her head. She held the crown on with one hand as she stared at the hope offered by the blessed Light.

Below, Nomyra's voice rose as if amplified by the wind, instead of stifled by it. "The Great Conjunction is but a year away. Tonight, the Stars step aside and allow the Planets to choose their own champion, to anoint the Bright One of their choosing."

With chins straining against their necks to look as far up as they could, the witnesses chanted their love for the Light in complex harmony. The sweet sound of the music drove tears down Talia's cheeks before she even realized she was crying.

Maybe, just maybe, she was worthy. If she was chosen, nothing would stop her from ensuring the Recharging. She swore her pledge to the focused Planets, the emissaries of the Light. Nothing short of her own death would prevent Talia from bringing back the hibernating magicals. She wouldn't see them die in their sleep, never setting eyes on the beauty of this world once more.

Talia squeezed the hand of each of her companions in turn. "I'm good. Thank you."

Naul stepped down first. The loss of his comforting hand chilled her shoulder. Her whole body went cold as her companions gave her room once more. But the feeling was temporary as exhilaration took its place.

With her arms outstretched, as if the music of the chanting astropriests would lift her into flight, Talia offered herself to the lesser conjunction. Four Planets seemed to click into place. The fifth rested slightly above the others.

Buzzing filled the air and overtook all of Talia's other senses. The gentle wind from the lake whipped into a frenzy as waves formed on the once-calm surface. Gentle rain fell from the cloudless sky, reflecting the Light's love more brightly than the moon. Shining water droplets passed through the stone at Talia's feet.

*Wait. That can't be right. There are no clouds in the sky.* She squatted to brush the stone and felt no moisture. But her hands shimmered. That wasn't water. It was magic.

She stood, almost losing her balance in her haste, and splayed her fingers like they would bite her if she brought them close. Another drop the size of a lightning bug hit her hand and was absorbed, much like her blood by the Holy Gemstones.

Nomyra's voice rang above the chants, but Talia couldn't understand the words.

Naul's hands clenched and unclenched as if he wanted to help but didn't know how. "Uh, Talia, you're glowing."

Ial whistled.

Nyna chewed on her bottom lip as her normal, mundane fingers touched Talia's brightly luminous skin. "I don't feel anything."

"I do," Talia said. Every hair stood on end while every nerve vibrated. Though it wasn't painful, the sensation was certainly unpleasant.

Dew's head swayed side to side. "You really are the Bright One, Talia."

Naul pointed at her head. "The crown!"

Talia snatched the Key from her curls as if it were a snake. She stared into the Holy Gemstones, all of which pulsed with energy. Inside the facets loomed the face of the wizard.

# CHAPTER TWO

FOR JUST A MOMENT, Talia couldn't breathe. Her recently pricked finger brushed the surface of the Holy Black Opal and stuck.

*No, no, no, no!* Talia cried in her head as the Key tugged at her very soul.

The world of glittering magic droplets and chanting astropriests faded as Talia tumbled into the crown.

"My child, you've done it. You are the Bright One." Wizard Maitliin's voice swirled from the mists in the colors of the gemstones.

His body manifested as Talia's feet hit a solid surface. She had been told, last time she communed with Maitliin, that her body remained outside the crown while her face went blank. Yet the chill in the air and the firmness of the ground under her feet made her feel like she stood in a real place.

Like before, his robes twisted around his thin frame as if they were made of the mists filling the crown chamber. He paced around Talia. His expression danced with glee. "I must say, I prefer your modest ceremony over the extravagant shindig they threw for mine in Raqmu."

Talia's mouth dropped open. "Of course. You were the Bright

One at the last Recharging. You had to be. Otherwise, we wouldn't have to . . ." She stopped herself before she blamed him for messing up the last one. She didn't actually know what had happened, only that Nomyra had told her that Maitliin had failed.

His laugh vibrated the clouds, like a wave of sound over water. Talia remembered nightmares filled with that laugh.

"Oh, Granddaughter, they lied to me as I know they will lie to you. They want you to sacrifice as the Bright One, but they offer nothing in return." He disappeared and then reappeared directly in front of Talia.

She took a step back, sending misty spirals around her ankles. The last time she'd been faced with Maitliin, Nomyra had been with her. Talia had never thought she would miss the presence of the priestess. She didn't know how to act or how she'd get out of there without Nomyra's help. Talia would have to talk her way out. She focused on Maitliin's words.

The wizard grabbed both her shoulders. "My granddaughter will finish what I started, not fix what I ruined. I was only trying to correct a corrupt system. I was so close. This time, we'll work together and get it right."

That was the second time he had used that title. "Granddaughter? Are we related?"

Talia cringed as he laughed again. "Yes, you are my descendant: a Highwind. I'm surprised Nomyra hasn't filled you in."

Talia's face burned as blood flowed to her cheeks. Who did Nomyra think she was? Talia would have to force the priestess to confess what she knew.

Maitliin squeezed her shoulders tighter. Talia had almost forgotten he was there. She took a deep breath to get control of her emotions.

She firmly brushed Maitliin's hands off her. "Don't touch me. If we are both Highwinds, it's been a thousand years. I am not your granddaughter."

"Feisty." Maitliin tucked his hands in his ethereal robe sleeves. "Good. You're going to need that fight for what comes next."

Behind him, the mist parted, revealing a contraption completely outside of Talia's experience. It had gears like those from a children's toy and levers attached to pulleys. It was foreign and beautiful.

Talia walked around Maitliin to get a closer look. "That's it, isn't it? The Machine?"

The wizard popped to the other side of the mechanism. Talia was getting used to his abrupt change in positions. She didn't startle at all this time.

"Yes. Reloian of the Before Time invented this beast to focus and capture the bits of dissipated magic that naturally fall to the planet from the Great Conjunction." He took a deep breath through his nose, like a starving man smelling fresh-baked bread. "You are getting a taste of the real thing. I can feel it."

Talia's body still tingled, though it felt more like a memory than a current event. "Four planets have aligned. The real thing occurs one year from today."

Maitliin clapped his hands, the sound startling Talia from her musings. "Good. We have time for me to show you how the Machine works and what you need to do to fulfill your destiny. A year is more than sufficient to travel to Raqmu and get everything ready."

The ground trembled, shaking the image of the Machine and the manifestation of Maitliin. "What is that?" Talia asked.

Maitliin's face contorted. His hands clenched into fists. "Begone, dwarf. You have caused your damage. Let me fix this."

"Noooo!" cried a female voice, reverberating inside the crown chamber. A dark shape, no taller than Talia's waist, whipped through the darker mist and rammed into Maitliin's ethereal form.

He evaporated with a whoosh.

Clothed in the same misty robes Maitliin had worn, a female dwarf slid to a stop at Talia's feet. "You must go now. Quickly. And don't return."

It was the same wizardess who had helped Nomyra and Talia escape from Maitliin's grip the first time.

"But I don't know what I'm supposed to do or how the Machine works or what is required of me for the Recharging." *And I can't depend on Nomyra to tell me a thing.*

"All you need to know you will find in the Library." Her gaze roamed the swirling interior. "He could be back at any moment. You must go."

"The library? The one in Tarbinulus?" There was no way Talia could get back to that library without facing her king. She wasn't ready to answer any of his questions.

"If that is the closest entrance, then yes." She grabbed Talia's hands and held them up. "You have extra magic from the mini-charging. I can feel it in your soul. I siphoned a bit to drive Maitliin into the mist. My disruption won't keep him away for long."

Talia concentrated on her own body. She could feel the cooling clouds at her feet, but she also felt the crown in her hand on the outside. She could return. She saw the way through the facets of the gems.

"Wait," she said. "Who are you?"

The dwarf sighed. "What is it with you Highwinds and your never-ending curiosity? I am Wizardess Billivin. I partnered with Maitliin until I discovered his plans to take all the magic for himself instead of allowing the Recharging to restore the planet's supply."

She pushed Talia, as if there were a door she could force her through. "Now go. He is stronger than I. If he didn't like the sound of his own voice so much, I never would get the upper hand."

Talia's lips twitched. "What if I can't get to the Tarbinulus library?"

"Then go to whichever entrance is closest."

A deep rumbling shook the mist into particles that cascaded to the ground like a waterfall. Talia obeyed Billivin's pleading look. She closed her eyes and ignored the tugging on her core that tried to anchor her to the crown.

The image of her fancy shoes on the elevated dais formed solidly in her mind. Talia thought of Dew, Naul, Nyna, and Ial gathered around her, worried. She clung to their friendship and the comfort it brought her, as her body vibrated with energy. With a mighty snap, Talia's consciousness returned to her body.

She yanked her finger off the Key and stuck the bejeweled item back on her head, as though her hair could insulate her from being sucked back in. The pale faces of her guardians stared back at her.

"I'm all right," she whispered, though they didn't look reassured by her words. "I'll tell you later."

At the bottom of the dais, Nomyra cleared her throat. Talia noticed the entire viewing area had grown quiet. Even the wind had settled to a gentle breeze. Talia straightened her back and stared up at the conjunction. The planets had moved out of alignment while Talia was in the crown. The magic droplets had dissipated to an occasional flash, which Talia couldn't discern from the usual bug activity.

She lifted her hands. Her skin pulsed still, but the glowing had stopped. Unsure where to go from there, Talia only knew she didn't want to remain at the top of the dais, exposed to the judgment of everyone below.

With a tug on her skirt to clear her feet, Talia took the first step down. Nyna and Ial made way for her, then followed as before. Naul's clunky steps told Talia he and Dew were bringing up the rear.

Nomyra's expression tensed, and she quickly climbed up the last few steps to block Talia's final descent. The priestess turned around and flung out her arms.

"I present the True Heir of Raqmu and the Bright One of the Recharging: Talia Winterlaus of Tarbin."

The servants erupted in cheers, garnering disapproving stares from the astropriests and acolytes. The small orchestra started an upbeat tune. The more dignified attendees joined their voices in praise to the Light.

All Talia saw was red, and it had nothing to do with the rubies gently shining on the surrounding stone walls. She leaned forward until her mouth was at the back of Nomyra's ear. "I think you mean Talia Highwind."

Nomyra's arms dropped to her sides. Her face became paler than her white robes as the priestess moved aside.

Talia smiled for the first time all evening. She finally had something on Nomyra. Maybe she could get her to spill more about Raqmu and what her sacrifice was supposed to be. Meanwhile, she had to find access to a library that might or might not have information about the Machine.

As she passed through the elated crowd, Talia shivered at the weight on her head. Maitliin was in there. She hadn't imagined him at her Forging Ceremony; he was real. She had to keep the Key close but had no desire to encounter the wizard again. He talked of helping her, but she had felt his dark designs before Billivin verified them.

She hurried her pace. With the Recharging a year away, she had a lot to learn and so few resources to depend on.

# CHAPTER THREE

In Tarbinulus Castle, Prince Tanin Winterlaus paced before the desk of his father, King Roland. The heir apparent chewed on his anger over his sister's betrayal. She had stolen the crown and the title True Heir right out from under him.

"We have to get it back, Father." Tanin stomped a spider who was in the wrong place at the wrong time. "The crown belongs to you, the leader of the kingdom of Tarbin. She has no right."

King Roland looked up from the paperwork he was reading. Tanin had watched his father slice the throat of his secretary because the old man had been spying for the treacherous Priestess Nomyra. The king hadn't had a chance to find a new person yet. Tanin hadn't gotten used to his father being so preoccupied with the drudgery of his position.

"It's not your sister's fault. She fell under the influence of that conniving witch and the rest of the magicals." He scratched the beard under his chin. "She could have been under their spell. We'll get her back. I promise."

Tanin planted both hands on the edge of the heavy granite desk. He had no intention of getting Talia back, unless she were to be tried for treason. "How can you still defend her after everything she's done?"

King Roland rolled up the scroll he'd just signed. "You are the True Heir, regardless of what the witch said. There was never a question." He took a moment to meet his son's eyes. "Tanin, you were always going to be the next king of Tarbin. The Light would not have brought you into this world only to abandon you to the whims of a religious zealot."

Slumping into a chair meant for dignitaries, Tanin flung one leg over the padded arm. His father's words brought him little comfort when the king insisted on defending his sister. "We have to get the crown back."

"On that, we can agree. I have the latest report from the royal network. They've sent back every sighting of Talia as she crossed the kingdom." King Roland pulled out another scroll from the pile and flattened it across his desk. "They were last seen flying over Lightndark Lake."

Tanin shivered as he remembered the huge red dragon crashing through the ceiling of the great hall. It still wasn't fully repaired. At least the beast made Talia easy to track. "Astropriest Tower."

Roland nodded. "High Priest Seamus assures me they will bide their time until just before some sort of Recharging ritual that takes place almost a year from now."

"I'll get the army set to travel. We'll retrieve the Tarbin Crown long before they set off." Tanin motioned for his weapons guardian, Rory, to open the door.

His medicinal guardian, Orui, pushed up from the wall he'd been leaning against to follow.

"Wait." His father's command stopped Tanin in his tracks.

Rory had one hand on the cast-iron handle. He didn't drop it until Tanin nodded his approval. Orui slumped back against the wall.

"We'll need more than our army to breach the tower. You heard Seamus. That crown is terribly important to the astropriests. They're not likely to give it up without a fight."

"It has to do with that weird glowing sky the other night, doesn't it?" Tanin shivered at the memory of the entire night sky lit with a shimmering haze. Luckily, it had only lasted a few minutes, but Tanin knew it was a portent of something nasty and unnatural.

"I'm not sure. And neither is High Priest Seamus. I never thought I'd miss that Nomyra, but she at least knew what the Stars were trying to tell us." King Roland sat back in his chair and rubbed his eyes. "What I do know is that the astropriests have ways beyond swords and shields. Their island, sitting in that vast lake as treacherous as the ocean, is formidable enough. Our army on boats won't make a dent."

Tanin's eyes lit up as he remembered Ngaro ships armed with cannons. It was a technology he would have considered impossible, but the pirates had pulled it off with expertise and deadly precision. "What if we had something more powerful than swords and shields?"

"If you mean magic . . ." Roland's brows shadowed his eyes.

"Magic?" The memory of being flung to the ground, completely helpless, by a mad elf assaulted Tanin. He closed his eyes and forced his breathing to regulate. Magic would be banned from his kingdom as soon as he was crowned. He straightened his shoulders. "I would never sully myself with the trickery of lesser races."

King Roland met his eyes, the reflected blue identical. "Good." Leaning back in his chair, Roland cracked his neck. "The Dark-cursed power of magic somehow corrupted your sister. I don't want to lose my heir as well."

Tanin swallowed a growl. His father refused to see the truth in Talia's actions. Even after everything she had done, Roland still supported her.

Tanin beat his fists against his thighs. There had to be a way. But first he needed a technological advantage to defeat her allies. "Remember how I told you about the cannons on the Ngaro ships?"

Roland laughed. "Yes, you've spoken of little else about your trip across the continent. But I don't think now is a good time to broker a deal with our northern neighbors. We still have Darvis to deal with, and our spies have found their trading to be more far-reaching than I first feared."

Tanin wouldn't give up so easily. "No, Father, that technology is exactly what we need to fight Darvis and their impressive navy. Plus, if we could get the warships into Lightndark Lake, we could easily bring down their defenses and get the Tarbin crown back."

Orui spoke up from the corner. "The Ngaroans would probably be up for a treaty. They kicked the astropriests out of their kingdom a few years ago."

King Roland's lip curled at the interruption by a servant. Tanin mirrored the same annoyance, but disciplining his guardians was Tanin's job.

He jumped in before King Roland could order Orui beaten or worse. "How do you know this?"

Orui shrugged in his usual casual manner. "I hear rumors. I go to town more than most."

Rory curled his lip, much like the king. "He means his whore, my Prince. She's from North Port and still has family up there."

Quicker than Tanin could stop him, Orui pulled a thin knife from his belt and threw it at Rory. The thunk in the wood of the door propelled the king's guardians to move protectively to his side. Rory growled at Orui as his hand flew to the hilt of his sword.

Orui's deep voice sounded more threatening than a shout. "She's not a whore."

"You pay her, do you not?" Rory was not backing down.

"Marianda shares her bed with only me." Orui's hand moved to his dagger.

Tanin's face flushed as his anger rose. He didn't mind the bickering. He'd sometimes encourage it to keep the men on their toes. But now was not the time.

King Roland folded his hands on his desk and addressed his son. "If you don't have control of your companions, how do you expect to rule Tarbin?"

Tanin stormed to the door and yanked the knife out. He placed its blade against Orui's palm and squeezed his hand closed until a trickle of blood dripped to the floor. Orui's face tensed, but he made no other outward sign of pain. The guardian lowered his head in obeisance, making no other aggressive move.

"Aren't sworn guardians forbidden to date? Something about split loyalties?" King Roland's voice was calm, but the threat was eminent.

"Whores don't count, Father." Tanin flashed a glance at Orui, who wrapped a cloth around his hand. The guardian didn't argue the point.

The king laughed and gulped down a huge swallow from his beer mug. "They certainly don't, right?" Roland's guardians joined in their charge's mirth, completely duty bound without a single free thought between them, just the way Tanin liked them.

He frowned. Maybe he did need to get a better hold on his companions. They existed only to protect him and support him in all his endeavors. He had to do something about discipline. But for now, he had to get his father to agree to this mission.

"About the cannons . . ." Tanin pulled the king back to the matter at hand.

"All right. I say give it a try. I have repairs to get to here and a declaration of war to dictate against Darvis." King Roland stood and leaned across his desk toward Tanin. "If you come back with a treaty and new technology, the Tarbin flag could very well fly across the continent as Nomyra predicted."

"But without her unnatural magic to sully its name." Tanin lifted his mug to his father.

The king raised his own. "To Light-Blessed Tarbin."

"To Light-Blessed Tarbin," Tanin repeated, clinking his mug to his father's.

They both took a long drink.

Roland dropped his mug to the desk, empty. He wiped his mouth. "If you could get one of those Ngaro pirate ships to steal a load of Darvis mead while you're there . . . ?"

Tanin bowed to his father. "I'm sure that could be arranged."

# CHAPTER FOUR

A FEW DAYS after the naming ceremony, not much had happened. Talia and Dew sat in the guest chambers, scouring Master Overstone's book for Raqmu's location.

Dew slammed the volume on the table. "It's no use. It says it's located in the Renquist Desert but gives no other landmarks."

Talia fell back on her bed, arms outstretched. "It's not like that part of the continent is small. We couldn't search it in a year's time."

"Which is all we have." Dew drummed her fingers on the tome she'd been gifted by one of the elder astropriests. "And this thing is impossible to read. If 'Bright One' is how you translate *Milen a Hoira*, then I'm completely confused. I thought the *-en* at the end meant it was plural." She dropped the book next to the first one. "I miss our Tarbin library."

Talia hadn't told Dew about the conversation she had with Billivin. She still wasn't sure whose side the dwarf was on.

"He's here. He made it." Nyna grabbed the doorjamb before she could slide past the opening. The acolytes of Astropriest Tower kept the marble shiny, creating a beautiful but dangerous walk.

"Finally." Talia was relieved that something was happening. She welcomed the break to head outside and greet a friend. There was a year until the Recharging. She had plenty of time to travel to the south desert and work it out.

As she hit the steps leading to the gardens, Talia bounded down the large slabs like a child on solstice break. Dew jumped in front of her to push the door open to the courtyard.

Talia almost ran headlong into Ial and Naul.

"What's with all the excitement?" Naul held a torch high to fight the gloom of the early night.

Talia pulled all four of her companions in for a big hug. "He's here."

Naul looked down at her. "We've been watching his progress as he's floated across the lake. He was bound to hit land eventually."

Talia laughed. "It's still exciting that we can finally talk to him."

"To the garden." Dew lead the way to the courtyard behind Astropriest Tower.

When Talia had first toured the meticulously manicured garden, a huge patch of mossy mud in one corner had shocked her. She hadn't been able to figure out why everything else was perfectly weeded, trimmed, and cultivated, while this section was left to rot.

Now she knew why. With his roots sunk deep in the soft mud, the huge nadph from the royal Tarbinulus gardens shook its branches of excess water from its long journey across Lightndark Lake.

Talia ignored the mud sucking at her shoes and embraced the trunk of her beloved tree, which had brought her comfort since early childhood. Of course, all those years ago, she hadn't known her inanimate friend was a nadph, a sentient treeling of another age.

Torchlight reflected off a forty-foot-tall tree with vertical bark leading up to thick full branches covered in bright green leaves. As Talia backed off, the bark shifted until it formed a face with two eyes, a nose, a mouth, and eyebrows. Two limbs reached down like arms, welcoming Talia into his embrace.

Talia squeezed the bark under the makeshift face. "I'm so glad you're here. I was terrified you wouldn't make it out unharmed." Her body tingled at the touch, as it had her entire life, but now she knew why. Her blood sensed the magic in the tree. After the mini-charging a few nights ago, she'd been even more sensitive to its presence.

A little ball of light flitted from the branches. The fairy, Philomena, hovered long enough to plant a kiss on Talia's forehead, then returned to her roost.

The princess pulled back. "You never told me your name."

"Names. We've never understood why so many animal sentients insist on names. Your role in life is all that matters." The nadph adjusted his roots deep into the ground. A rumbling purr resonated from inside his trunk. "The filtered water is much fresher here than in Tarbinulus. The reservoir there gets a bit brackish sometimes."

Talia loved that the nadph could feel like her, but she had to call him something. "I don't want to call you my naddle tree, especially if you don't like that bastardized form of your people's name."

"You may certainly use my role, Second Emissary to New Tarbin."

Dew's confused expression mirrored Talia's. "New Tarbin?"

The tree nodded again, sending a few damp leaves to the ground. "The astropriestess did not get everything wrong. Tarbin used to be a much more powerful nation. It collapsed, leaving only a fraction of its former self. Since the Winterlaus family chose to keep the ancient name, we of much longer memories had to discern the original from the current."

Talia nodded. "Second Emissary to New Tarbin it is, then."

Ial whistled.

Nyna squeezed his hand. "And we thought Talia's titles were getting out of hand."

With a scuff of her foot against the ground, Dew snarked, "Prince Tanin's going to have to make some up to compete."

"How is my brother?" Talia wasn't sure what she wanted to hear.

"Unhappy. But he was always unhappy." The nadph bent a branch into his thick growth. "There is something I need to give you."

He pulled out a speck of green that flashed in the torchlight. A filigree of silver twisted like branches in a circle. Where the branches connected, an emerald the size of a human eye glimmered.

Talia reached for the ring. Its cold touch sent a tingle through her arm. She'd seen it somewhere before.

She put it on as if it had always belonged to her. An image of Nyna and Dew bickering over her cut hand while Talia admired her beloved naddle filled Talia's memory. "The hunt. On the day of my graduation ceremony. You dropped the ring?"

"We had to test your blood to make sure. There was a bit of panic among the remaining magicals when your brother's blood didn't work."

"You tested him too."

The nadph flattened his eyebrows and his mouth. "There was too much at risk for us not to be sure. Nomyra seemed convinced Tanin was the True Heir. We tried to verify and found it was not him. You were the next logical possibility."

Talia rubbed the emerald, feeling each facet of its cut. From inside, power vibrated. "Does it have a name?"

Second Emissary to New Tarbin shook his whole trunk, his laugh contrasting with his serious expression. "Always curious about what to call things."

Ial pushed up the corners of his lips. Second Emissary must have understood, for he fixed the dichotomy of his mood compared to his expression and broke into a huge smile.

Talia blushed. "I just meant, Priestess Nomyra has a similar piece with a ruby. She calls it the Krag ring."

"Ah, yes, of course. This one is called Windall," the nadph continued. "Two dozen Unity rings were forged and charged millennia ago. They were spread among the races as a sign of cama-raderie between the magical and the mundane. Each has a precious gem that can store magical energy."

That was why Talia could feel it tingling. She wondered if she could access the magic.

Nyna adjusted the strap of her ever-present shoulder bag of herbs. "You missed the mini-charging. It was something to see."

The nadph's trunk expanded and contracted as if he were taking a deep breath. Whether that was an imitation of the human motion or he did breathe to some degree, Talia could only guess. "We felt the power as Philomena helped me across the lake. It made our arrival much quicker. It was only a taste of what is to come."

"The Recharging." Talia studied the planets above, still visible, though farther apart than a few days ago. "I don't understand why we need the Machine and all this ceremony when the planets align themselves without any interference from us."

Second Emissary shook his branches. "It is true the conjunction is natural. It was enough to create a few magical races: elves, dragons, unicorns, griffins, and some others."

Ial's eyes scrunched up. "Your people aren't magical?"

"Oh, we are. But only after the invention of the Machine." Second Emissary to New Tarbin rustled his leaves. "The amount of magic fed into the core of the world multiplied by hundreds, which lead to the creation of more sentient magicals: the nadph, mermaids, manticores, centaurs . . ."

Dew's curls bounced, as though her mind solving the riddle gave them life instead of the wind off the water. "So when the Machine didn't work at the last conjunction a millennium ago, only the natural magic rained down from above. It just wasn't enough for a world accustomed to the multiplied supply."

Ial rocked on his feet. "That's why the elves sleep?"

Talia cringed as she remembered Lord Thilphiliari, the last awake elf. Intellectually, she knew she'd only been defending herself and her companions, but emotionally, she couldn't dampen the guilt over his death.

Second Emissary agreed. "Yes, quiet one, as do most of my people and all the mermaids. We will have a Great Awakening along with the Recharging."

Naul rubbed his bald head. "I still can't swallow this magic stuff. Wasn't it a year ago when it was make-believe and fairy tales?"

Philomena dropped from a high branch to hover in front of the weapons guardian. Her hands were on her hips as she yelled at Naul in a high-pitched voice using words none of them had heard before.

Talia nudged Dew; the cultural guardian she spoke the most languages. Dew shrugged. No help at all. Talia tensed, not sure what had sparked the temper tantrum.

Second Emissary shook and swayed back and forth. "I haven't seen her in a right fury in some time. It's kind of cute."

As if afraid to say it out loud, Nyna mouthed "Fairy" at Talia.

Her eyes widened as she figured out why Philomena was so upset. Talia placed a hand on Naul's shoulder, which was quite a feat with his height. "I don't think Philomena liked the term 'fairy tale.' I'd apologize if I were you."

Naul bowed to the tiny hovering being. "I'm sorry for the offense."

Silence overtook the clearing. Talia hadn't realized the volume of Philomena's screeching until it was gone. Everyone turned to Talia as if they couldn't act without her direction. And she didn't even know which way to go. She almost wished the fairy would start yelling at Naul again.

Though maybe Second Emissary had some answers. "Do you know where Raqmu is? We can't find a map that gives more details than the Renquist Desert."

"You must travel south of the Eckerd Mountains and follow the river through the desert. You will know when you arrive. At least, that is what I've been told. I have never been."

Dew shook her head. "But there is no river that flows south from the Eckerd Mountains. That's why the dwarves travel the eastern sea to trade with the southern Kiwa Islands."

"Land can transform over time. I have been rooted in the Tarbin Royal Forest for many centuries." The giant tree scratched the bark above a fake eyebrow. He was getting creative with the human expressions, or maybe he just itched. "The information you seek must be in the Library."

Talia brushed her side where she used to carry the crown. It now stayed in a chest in her room, as she was afraid to accidentally get sucked in again. Still, she remembered what Billivin had said. "We can't get to the library in Tarbinulus without a fight with my brother. I have no doubt he would do all in his power to stop me from completing this mission."

"Then use the entrance in Astropriest Tower."

Nyna leaned her head on Ial's shoulder. "I'm so confused."

Talia agreed. "Me too. We searched the modest collection they have here, but it wasn't any use." They didn't have a single volume that mentioned the workings of the Machine or its exact location. Only religious texts spouting its divine purpose.

"Since you chose the difficult path, the least I can do is give you a few more hints."

The voice was familiar, but Talia couldn't quite place it. She took a few steps back from the nadph to get a wider view of the garden.

On the path stood Librarian Giddeona Feltwith.

# CHAPTER FIVE

GIDDEONA FELTWITH HAD MORE pink in her cheeks than Talia remembered. Getting out of her stuffy library, where she appeared completely gray and ghostlike, had done her some good.

Dew crossed her arms. "We've been here for weeks and haven't seen you once."

Talia agreed with Dew. "That's a good point. Why weren't you at the ceremony? I have so many questions."

"My dear child." Giddeona squeezed Talia's upper arms as though they'd been close once. Which was odd, considering they'd only met twice. She held up Talia's ringed hand. "Well, well, well. Looks like you're moving up in the world."

Second Emissary's leaves rustled. "She earned it."

Without a second glance at the talking tree, Giddeona squeezed her lips together and nodded. "I suppose she has."

Giddeona turned to head toward the tower.

Talia exchanged looks with her companions but didn't move. The librarian wasn't any more forward with answers than her sister, Nomyra.

When no one followed her, Giddeona waved them on impatiently. "Come, come, before I'm discovered."

As the librarian's frequent visitor in Tarbinulus, Dew had been closer to Giddeona than anyone else. "Have you been here the whole time?" Talia swore Dew's words were laced with pain. "Why didn't you seek me out? Help me find resources?"

Giddeona tucked a stray hair behind her ear and stared at the ground. "I have a great deal to share with you, student. But there is no time. I discovered something that must be remedied before Raqmu can be entered."

Nyna squeezed Dew's hand. "We also don't know where Raqmu is."

Giddeona swiped the air as if she were swatting at an annoying insect. "Just follow the water. That's the easy part."

Second Emissary laughed. "That's what I said."

Philomena swooped down from a branch, hands on her hips, squeaking some sort of complaint.

Giddeona laughed with a deep, hearty sound. "Yes, Phi, quite right. The young hear, but they certainly don't listen."

Talia's head throbbed. "But . . ."

"No buts," Giddeona said, her annoyance on full display. "Now come with me, please. I have risked a great deal to leave the Library."

Talia shook her head but didn't see that she had much choice.

As soon as Giddeona entered the garden door into the main hall, she took a quick right down a sconce-lit hallway. If Talia hadn't been right behind her, she would have missed the turn.

At the next intersection, Giddeona glanced around the next corridor, then ducked into a doorway.

Before Talia could question the odd action, two acolytes walked down the cross corridor.

"Bright One." They bowed simultaneously without changing their pace.

Talia returned the bow as she elbowed Naul for snickering.

As soon as the acolytes had moved on, Giddeona bounced from

the doorway. "After you were crowned True Heir, I discovered you had escaped to this prison. I suppose this was as safe a place as any to anoint you Bright One, even if it's not quite right."

Talia exchanged a concerned look with her companions. Dew shrugged and rushed after the fleet old woman.

Giddeona turned two more corners in quick succession.

Naul cursed as his knee hit a corner in his rush to keep up. "Is it wise to trust the crazy old librarian? Working with her sister is bad enough."

Talia twisted Windall on her finger. She forced her hands to her sides as soon as she realized she'd seen Nomyra do the same dozens of times. "Without Giddeona, I wouldn't have known I could participate in the Forging Quest. I don't know what her agenda is, but I believe her intentions are good."

The old woman stopped abruptly by a hanging sconce, one of many identical light fixtures spread throughout every hallway in Astropriest Tower. With a push from Giddeona, the metal bottom scraped aside like a pendulum and moved aside. The light flickered as wax dripped down the wall.

Ial pulled on a sconce a few feet down. It didn't move.

Nyna asked, "How did you know it was this one, Librarian Feltwith?"

"For centuries, the entries were available to all. No lock necessary." Giddeona pointed to a tiny carved key on the bottom of the light fixture as she pulled a metal key from her tight bun. "A change in religious temperament forced a security increase."

She inserted the key into a small hole and twisted. Talia jumped as Giddeona grabbed her ring-adorned finger and closed her eyes.

Talia's hand tingled as a wisp of smoke weaved its way from the emerald to the stone wall. It split in two as it snaked its way around the perimeter of a camouflaged door. The stones creaked and moaned and swung forward with a whiff of dust.

An aged mildew smell wafted into the breezy hallway. Giddeona dropped Talia's hand, Windall still vibrating.

Dew leaned toward the opening. "It smells like . . . books." Her eyes opened wide, and she rushed through the opening. "By the Light, it can't be."

Naul cocked an eyebrow as he followed behind her. "Books have a smell?"

Giddeona laughed as she ushered the rest of the group beyond the wall.

Talia motioned for Ial to retrieve the candle from the sconce. She couldn't see Dew from the well-lit hallway and didn't want to go blindly into the room.

Ial removed the candle from the sconce and carried it tilted to the side so the wax wouldn't drip on his trousers.

As soon as Giddeona's foot crossed the threshold, the door slammed shut with a resounding echo. Talia froze as the rush of wind whipped the flame. Talia twisted the ring on her finger. She really needed to figure out how to use the magic within it. It could come in handy in dark tunnels, which seemed to be a regular part of her life now. Maybe that's why Giddeona had come, to show her how to use her innate abilities.

Giddeona pushed Talia's shoulder. "Well, are you going to stand here forever? The magicals won't last another thousand years. If you want the Recharging to be at full capacity, there are a few more things you need to know." Giddeona weaved around the frozen group, apparently undisturbed by the darkness ahead.

Dew and Naul were nowhere to be seen.

Talia followed the older woman's footsteps. The candle barely lit a few steps ahead. Luckily, the bricks of the floor were even and looked well kept, though the heavy layer of dust disturbed only by a few delicate footprints told a different story. Talia tried not to think that the corridor was maintained by magic. Now that she knew that kind of power was real, it was hard not to give it credit for everything she couldn't explain.

A soft light ahead illuminated an archway. Talia passed underneath it into a room much too large to be hidden, underground or otherwise.

Shelves stacked double with heavy tomes lined the walls, forming a maze of the interior. An eerie blue glow emanated from the ceiling high above, but Talia couldn't see where it came from. The color didn't lend itself to anything natural. She didn't spot any sconces with torches either.

Talia couldn't shake the feeling that she'd been here before, though this was her first sojourn at Astropriest Tower. Why was it so familiar?

Dew rushed from one of the book-constructed walls. She hugged Talia and whispered, "The library. I don't know how, but we're definitely in the Tarbinulus library. I've walked this hallway repeatedly and never saw a corridor under that arch."

Talia pushed Dew at arm's length and witnessed the awkwardly stacked books, the eerie light, and the dust-covered surfaces.

"It's the same. How's that possible?" Talia blinked too quickly. She could swear her footprints marked a winding path to the back wall where Giddeona had given her a volume from the Articles of Royal Deference, the book that had allowed her to join her twin in the quest for the Holy Gemstones.

Ial's hand shook on the candle. "That's impossible. We're many days away from home."

Naul shrugged as he pointed at a neatly stacked pile of books that stuck out among the haphazard assortment surrounding it. "I didn't believe it either, but then this. Remember?"

Talia touched the top like it was an illusion. "Is this the pile you knocked over and Nyna straightened into a neat column?"

Nyna shook her head. "It can't be."

"How many 'can't bes' have we seen with our own eyes this past year?" Dew flung her arms wide and twirled in a graceful circle. "This *is* our library. I know it as well as you know the Siren Tavern at the port."

Rubbing his bald head, Naul let out a long breath. "I could use a visit to the Siren right about now. Is there a magic door for my dream spot as well?"

Giddeona appeared from behind a crowded shelf, startling the companions. She leaned toward Ial, who leaned away. Giddeona blew out the candle he held. As Talia's eyes adjusted, the blue light seemed to brighten.

"No fire in here, young man. The knowledge contained in these volumes is the most valuable treasure under the Stars. Irreplaceable."

"Wait." Talia moved in front of her companions. "How is this library identical to the one in Tarbinulus Castle?"

"Oh, it's not identical."

Talia sighed. Finally, something made sense.

Giddeona led the group through a labyrinth of stacks. "It's the *same.*"

Naul cursed as he bumped into a small case and toppled its contents. Nyna shook her head and bent to help him pick it up. Talia wanted to kick something as well. The librarian wasn't making any sense.

Giddeona ignored their reactions. "During the disastrous wars and upheaval after the failure of the last Recharging, the astropriests banded together to protect the collected knowledge. They gathered every tome, every scroll, and every book. Entire branches of priests dedicated themselves to learning and preserving what they could to stave off the dark ages they knew were inevitable. All of it was placed here."

Talia coughed into her tunic. She still didn't understand. "So everything was collected into one room. How is the library in two places at once?"

Giddeona strolled toward a precarious pile of scrolls. "Oh, it isn't. That would be impossible. Don't they teach you anything at those fancy schools?"

Dew grabbed Talia as she lunged to strangle the frustrating librarian.

"The intention was to make copies and get them distributed, but the astropriests were running out of time. The magical races were furious and hunted them for a couple centuries. Which I suppose was justified. We were responsible for their rise, but also their fall."

Giddeona pulled a book from a nearby pile. The brown leather was shiny, as if someone had just cleaned it. The dichotomy between that and the dusty pile she took it from made Talia think the librarian had placed it there in preparation. Talia's wonder turned to annoyance. Why did everyone who knew something about magic have to be so cryptic?

The librarian tucked the tome into Talia's hands. "You cannot simply go to the Machine, place the Key and the blood into their spots, and sit back and enjoy the show."

Naul groaned. "Here we go again."

Giddeona retied her loose hair into a tight bun. "Anything simple is a lie."

Dew took it from Talia and read the title. "*The Unlocking of the Dome to Gain Entry into the Ancient City of Raqmu and the Testing of the Bright Ones.*"

Talia bit her lip. "What test?"

Giddeona explained, "It's really quite simple, though this author liked to hear herself talk. She fills the majority of the pages with explanations on why all of this is necessary and why some races were included and some were left out. It's a fascinating read that delves into the cultural differences between the sentient races. When I think about—"

There was still something odd. "What dome?" Talia crossed her arms. She was tired of not knowing what was going on and didn't want to filter through an old woman's ramblings. Though without this old woman, Talia wouldn't have a destiny to speak of. She lightened her expression and put her arms down. "I'm sorry for interrupting. I only want to make sure I'm better prepared this time. I don't want to mess up."

"My child, I can only guide, not instruct. You must choose to sacrifice. I will tell you that the dome protects the ancient city of

Raqmu. You must unlock it first to enter." Giddeona Feltwith ushered Talia and her companions toward the exit, much as she had done a year ago. "You will need a living individual from each of the sentient races: humans, dwarves, nadph, dragons, elves, and mermaids. You all must gather simultaneously to successfully release the gatekeeper."

"Elves?" Dew blanched.

"Mermaids?" Ial's color matched his companion's.

Talia slid to a halt at the arch before the librarian could lock them out again. "What if there aren't any living ones left?"

"Of course there are. Everything was planned before the races slumbered." Giddeona moved them through the unlit corridor like a force of nature.

Talia refused to move any farther. "I'm actually quite certain that the last living elf is no more." She could still feel the slide of the sword into Lord Thilphiliari's flesh. She awoke from the nightmare too frequently to ever forget the sensation.

"Well, if you are certain, then you'll just have to wake one."

"Wake one?" Dew repeated.

The mutilated bodies of tortured elves half-removed from the trunks of aspens flashed through Talia's mind. Decay mixed in with fresh greenery had forever spoiled the smell of grass for her. "How?"

"How should I know?" Giddeona waved her arms, moving them forward once more.

"Wait." One more thing bothered Talia. She had to ask. "I know I'm a Highwind. That means we're related."

Giddeona froze. "I am no longer a Highwind."

"I am called Winterlaus, but that is not my ancestor's name." Talia swallowed. "Do you know who my father is?"

"Nomyra is the manipulator. She is the one obsessed with heritage and family curses." Giddeona's helpful clues abruptly ended as she snapped and the group slid out into the Astropriest Tower hallway. "I am a librarian."

She slammed the camouflaged door, locking them out.

# CHAPTER SIX

Contentment buoyed Priestess Nomyra's steps as she walked the familiar path to her old room. She had slipped into her routine of study and prayer so seamlessly, it was like she'd never left.

Now, she had to finish what she had started. Maitliin had been instructing her on how the Machine worked, just in case it needed repair. Even though she had met with him frequently inside the crown, Nomyra couldn't wait to meet him in person.

Nomyra closed her door and held up Krag. She was annoyed that Talia had been given a ring of her own. She wished the sentimental tree had asked her first. The spoiled child didn't have the right to wear the earned magic. They were reserved for High Priests and Priestesses appointed by the council. The child wouldn't even know how to manipulate the power contained within it. Such a waste.

As she rubbed the ruby held by steel filigree, a surge of magic flowed through her body. Nomyra directed the energy to the ceiling, where the domed roof disappeared, giving her a full view of the heavens. The Stars winked at her, fully approving her progress.

She ran her hands along an ornate chest on her desk. Krag glowed as she whispered to the lock. The mechanism snapped open. Nomyra warmed to her free use of magic. With the gentle influx a few days ago and the massive Recharging a year away, Nomyra was magic rich. She no longer needed to hoard what little was left.

With a flip of her wrist, the lid swung open. Inside, the Tarbin crown lay tucked in the velvet lining. Talia believed it safe in a locked chest in her sole possession halfway across the tower, but Nomyra had enchanted the Key to come to her whenever she needed to commune with it. The clueless Bright One didn't need all the wisdom Maitliin had to offer. Nomyra would tell her what she needed to know.

Like a mother handling her newborn, Nomyra lifted the crown with loving care. The Key to the Machine fit perfectly within her grasp.

The golden metal contrasted with the warmth of the Holy Gemstones mounted on its surface. The five stones—diamond, ruby, emerald, black opal, and sapphire—had been collected by the Tarbin twins during the Forging Quest. Though things hadn't gone as planned, which still irked Nomyra, the crown was whole again and ready to become the Key it was meant to be.

More importantly, the priestess had her mentor, her many-greats-grandfather, to guide her through the next journey.

With practiced ease, Nomyra cut her palm with her belt dagger. After she applied her bleeding hand to the crown, her body froze as her mind drifted into the mist.

The world inside was somewhere between life and death. Maitliin's soul was stuck until the Recharging, which would provide enough magic to free him.

As long as there was a freshly dead body available for him to inhabit.

Nomyra smirked. After Talia provided the quantity of blood necessary to activate the Machine, there would be.

Through the swirling colors, a dark shadow materialized. The line of his robe remained impossible to distinguish from the smoke, for a bit of him never fully separated from his magical prison.

His voice, however, was as clear as if he spoke in her ear. "You smell refreshed." He raised his head in an exaggerated inhalation. "It's intoxicating."

Nomyra stood tall. "The Stars gave us a taste of the power to come. You are much more defined than normal. You felt it as well?"

He steepled his fingers, his anticipation manifesting as slight movements. "Oh, I did. Talia gave me a taste when she visited me during her naming ceremony."

Nomyra's fingers twitched as she fought down her jealousy. "You spoke with her?"

A short figure dashed between the two, not nearly as corporeal as Maitliin. The waves in the smoke as she darted by were the only indication of her presence.

"Not for as long as I would have liked. Thanks to Billivin." He almost growled.

"She's still here as well?" Nomyra was shocked that the second sentient was also trapped within.

"I punished her. She won't interfere again." He tucked his fingers into his ethereal sleeves to hide the sparks at his fingertips.

Nomyra furrowed her brow. "Shall we continue?"

Maitliin's face lightened as he conjured a model of the Machine from the clouds. "Yes. Show me where the Key goes."

With complete confidence, Nomyra leaned forward and pointed to the upraised dome on an attached platform above the ground. She was good at memorizing the workings of the complicated apparatus. When the time came, she would be prepared to sink the energy from the conjunction into the Great Diamond below the city.

Maitliin had attempted the same move a millennium ago when he discovered the astropriests had planned on sacrificing his life's blood—not just a sample—to ensure the full Recharging to benefit magical creatures he barely tolerated.

Unfortunately, he had failed after the treachery of his trusted mundane companion, Wizardess Billivin. Nomyra wouldn't make the same mistake. She didn't trust anyone.

At the end of the Recharging, Nomyra and the resurrected Maitliin would control the magic of the Recharging, as well as the ancient city of Raqmu. The world would be theirs to dedicate to the worship of the Light. Finally, the Dark would be defeated and the astropriests would take their true place as rulers of all, with the Highwinds as their leaders.

Nomyra cleared her throat to focus her mind on the task at hand. "Now, which wire do I attach to the sunken metal rod?"

# CHAPTER SEVEN

Lightndark Lake spanned as far as the eye could see. The first day Talia freed herself from the hovering astropriests, about a week after arriving, she had walked the perimeter of the island. She had marveled at the vastness of the lake that perfectly imitated the ocean she had grown up alongside. While appreciating the defensibility of Astropriest Tower, Talia cringed at the utter isolation.

As Talia again looked across the lake, even the smells threw her off. Given the size, Talia expected the briny fish odor she associated with the coast. Instead, the breeze brought only fresh air with a bit of a mineral undertone.

The docks bustled with servants as a sailing vessel approached the shore. Smaller than the ocean vessels she was accustomed to, this boat was nevertheless massive, with a modest keel to cut through the fresh-water lake. The oarsmen controlled the speed as the tiller expertly directed the boat beside the floating dock. Hands caught tossed ropes and pulled to properly angle the vessel.

At the railing, the shiny dark hair of Lordling Gregor Rivenwood blew in the wind as his laughter rolled over the side of the boat.

Talia's body warmed at the sound of his voice. She raised her hand to wave, the smile on her face almost painful as every muscle stretched.

Her glee was cut short by the sight of a beautiful young woman clinging to the lordling's arm. Talia's stomach fell to her feet. She tried to squash her biting jealousy, for it wasn't fair. She had turned down his advances before he left on this mission. How could she begin a romantic relationship when she had no concept of what her future held? She had no right to demand his attention now.

Gregor spotted Talia on the shore and gave her a wave. When his companion caught sight of Talia, the young woman frowned. Talia waved back, a bit less enthusiastically than she had started. Regardless of what little future they had together as lovers, she would still enjoy any time she got to spend with Gregor before he had to return home and take over the running of the farms and mills his father managed.

The ramp hit the wooden dock with a slam. Staying low to maintain their balance, the workers secured the vessel. Prince Aleck Stoneworth bounced onto the slanted wood as the floating dock rocked back and forth. His contagious happiness reminded Talia how much joy the dwarf had brought into her life. She'd missed him and was pleased to see him return.

Aleck led two uniformed dwarves down the ramp. Talia bit her lip. It made sense that King Greleck would insist on his son having new guards to replace the fallen. Talia should be grateful he had allowed his son to come back at all. Though knowing Aleck, the prince probably didn't give his father the chance to ground him.

Talia held out her hand as Aleck hit solid ground. He pushed aside her proffered hand and leaned in for a tight hug.

She embraced him back as she fought her tears. The emotion hit her at once, and she wasn't sure where it came from. "It is so good to see you, my friend. We were unsure if you planned on coming back."

Aleck released her. "And miss the Recharging? That was never going to happen."

His enthusiasm filled her with peace. He was much more like

the Aleck from before he adventured with Talia: happy, curious, and overtly friendly. After the death of his guards by order of Talia's ex-fiancé, Bello Hilderamn, she hadn't known if Aleck would ever be the same. Apparently, a trip home was what his soul had needed.

Talia smiled as Naul grabbed Aleck in a bear hug and spun around. The dwarf guards, however, banged their pikes on the ground and moved into attack mode.

Naul almost dropped Aleck in his haste to step back. Ial and Dew stood in front of Talia but remained calm.

Aleck's thick eyebrows seemed to grow bushier as he scowled at his guards. "Parnim. Traneck. Stand down. These are my friends."

In unison, the uniformed guards obediently pointed their pikes to the sky and folded their free arms behind their backs. Talia remembered how stoic Gallick and Dragick had been when they first joined her traveling party. But she didn't remember them being this aggressive.

She cleared her throat and moved between her guardians. She extended her hand. "I'm Talia."

The younger-looking dwarf with a thinner brown beard slanted his blue eyes at the proffered hand.

"Parnim," Aleck ordered over his shoulder as he shook Nyna's hand. "I already told you about this custom."

Parnim leaned his pike against his shoulder and accepted Talia's hand.

As Talia turned to the second guard, he already had his hand out, though his stiff elbow made it difficult to shake. "You must be Traneck?"

A curt nod of his heavily bearded chin was all she received. She couldn't even make out his lips through the brown curls. His eyes were so shadowed by billows of eyebrow, Talia couldn't tell what color they were, nor could she properly read his expression.

Gregor came down the gangplank alone. Talia wanted to run into his arms but couldn't erase the image of the random servant drooling on him. She wondered how much female companionship he had enjoyed while she was stuck on this island with a destiny to fulfill.

"They're going to need some breaking in." He tapped both guards on the shoulder as he walked by.

Parnim tensed and Traneck bared his teeth, but neither moved.

Gregor broke into his crooked smile. Talia took in a sharp breath as her cheeks flushed. He leaned forward, and she knew she'd lose it if he hugged her. With a determined step, she thrust her hand out to stop his momentum. The lordling stopped short and tilted his head. But his smile never faltered as he grasped her hand in both of his.

"It's a pleasure to see you again, Princess Talia."

She offered a tight squeeze before releasing his hand. "And you. But it's just Talia now."

This time his smile fell. The scrunched, serious expression on his chiseled features made Talia bite her lower lip. Somehow, his look of concern was even more attractive than his grin.

Talia let out the breath she hadn't realized she'd been holding. "Too much to go into right now. Just Talia is fine. At least between us."

Gregor lifted an eyebrow.

"The party, that is." She indicated the gathered companions on the shore. "Like all of us." Talia was messing everything up. She decided to change the subject and addressed Aleck instead.

"How's your father?" She wanted to ask about Dragick's and Gallick's families but didn't have the heart to broach the subject.

"He is coping the best he can with the world changing around him. I sent an emissary to the Krimmel Hatchery to establish our first trade agreement. My father, as king of the Krimmel Dwarves, had to pretend it was his idea since I did it before he could say no."

Aleck's enthusiasm for all things outside his underground kingdom enthralled Talia. She loved discovering new lands and new people as well. That's probably why the two got along so well.

"I'm sure he'll forgive you as soon as he sees the goods Penelope exchanges for your procapras."

Talia felt grounded enough to address Gregor again. "How did the wheat crop deal go, Lordling?"

"Completely failed. And it's just Gregor now." He tugged at his ear. "My father disowned me. My younger brother is now the lordling and future lord to the Kenia township and all our wheat fields and mills."

"Why would he do that?" Talia wasn't sure she wanted the answer.

Gregor winked at her. "Something about treason."

"King Roland." Talia closed her eyes and released her breath slowly. Was everyone who supported her to be outcast? "I'm sorry, Gregor."

"Why? I happen to be well acquainted with the True Heir. I'm sure the Light will guide me to a new place and title." Gregor moved to fling his arm across Talia's shoulder.

She skirted around Ial and Nyna to avoid Gregor's touch. She was angry at him again. Apparently, he only stuck around in the hope of whatever power Talia could give him. How could she imagine he'd be interested in her as a woman? She could be so naive sometimes.

Gregor looked at her with deep brown eyes that sparkled in the cloud-filtered light. Why did he have to be so handsome?

Nyna drew Gregor's attention. "Talia has a new title. Maybe the astropriests can find one for you."

"The Bright One," Dew said.

Gregor burst out laughing. "The Bright One?"

Aleck hopped beside Talia. "The Bright One is perfect. That's exactly what you are with the way your skin glowed every time the Holy Gemstones confirmed you as the chosen one."

Talia shrugged. "I suppose that's what it looks like on the outside, but there's so much we don't know." Like how the entire fate of the planet can be placed on the shoulders of one person. It seemed to Talia that someone didn't do enough planning.

Dew clapped her hands together. "We also found out there is a barrier protecting Raqmu and we'll need a sample of blood from each sentient race to get it open."

Aleck's bushy eyebrows shot up and buried themselves in his thick hair. "You mean, the Light needs my blood for the Recharging as well?"

Talia nodded. His need to serve was what she used to feel. Maybe she could rediscover it on this journey. "To enter the city, at least. So thank you for returning. You've saved us a trip. Are you ready to go on another journey with us?"

Aleck took both Talia's hands and twirled her in a circle. "By Thoretick's beard, I'm ready. Let's go."

# CHAPTER EIGHT

AFTER THE WEEKS-LONG SEA VOYAGE, Tanin was relieved to be on solid ground again. He had drooled over the cannoned ships when they entered the port, but nothing else had impressed him, from the dock to this modest royal dwelling. Ngaro Palace was half the size of Tarbinulus Castle. How could such simple people have developed such an incredible weapon?

Prince Tanin rolled onto his toes, then his heels, back and forth, trying not to pace like an impatient tutor. "What is taking so long?" he said, pestering the guards who stood before the double doors leading into the Ngaro king's throne room.

They stared straight ahead, completely unreactive. Tanin's fingers twitched, wishing they held his sword hilt. He had already endured the humility of he and his guardians being disarmed. He had thought Rory would take the head of the master of arms before relinquishing his weapon. Tanin had ordered him to stand down. The king was not going to attack him in front of the royal court. If he had wanted Tanin dead, he wouldn't have sent a pilot to guide the Tarbin warship through the death traps of the well-protected harbor.

Besides, Tutor Grayson's skill at hand-to-hand combat was

unmatched. His deadly feet and hands were why he had been chosen as teacher for Hodan, Tanin's new cultural guardian, not his gift for reading long, boring passages. Though he did that too. For the entire voyage north, Tanin and his guardians had spent hours training with Hodan, expanding their fighting skills without swords or staffs. If necessary, Tanin had confidence that his men could hold their own, armed or unarmed.

As Tanin waited for admittance to the foreign ruler's court, he hoped they wouldn't have to use their new skills. Mostly hoped. Another part of him prayed to the Light above that his guardians would get the chance to show King Juarim Deurwhill how powerful they were without advanced weaponry. The ship-mounted cannons were an excuse to open trade with Ngaro so the risk of piracy could be curbed with legal exchange.

Tanin smirked at his own creative interpretation of the facts. He'd make a great king. He just needed the crown to complete the picture.

The thought of revenge on his sister straightened Tanin's shoulders. He stopped rocking and focused on the door. It was a common practice to put a foreign dignitary on the defensive by making him wait for hours. Tanin wouldn't let this king of a small city state put him on edge. The continent of Ngaro was reportedly as big as Renquist itself, but most cities acted independently, with little camaraderie between them. If this king couldn't conquer his neighbors to unite his lands, Tanin wasn't sure how much power he actually had.

Maybe he should promise King Juarim some of Tarbin's men to fight for him. If they became allies, Tanin might be able to rule land across the sea as well. He really liked that plan. His father would be so proud if he expanded Tarbin from a mighty kingdom into a great empire.

The doors opened, and two men dressed in Darvis formal wear exited. Tanin's stomach tightened as anger swept through his nerves. He had to conquer his own continent first. That traitorous country would pay for murdering his sister's fiancé. If she had been married as planned, the crown would be in Tarbinulus as it should be and Tanin would be called True Heir.

The herald stepped forward with a staff twice as tall as his square-shouldered form. "King Juarim Deurwhill will see you now."

Orui grumbled under his breath. "It's about time."

Tanin pulled his tunic down, straightening any wrinkles that had appeared as he swayed on his feet. With his head held high, Tanin marched through the doors, his guardians behind him.

The throne room's ceiling rose to a great height, drawing Tanin's eyes upward. Every inch of its surface was painted with colorful scenes. One had a man galloping on a horse, his long gray beard blowing over his shoulder. A beautiful maiden, brighter and cleaner than the farmers in her scene, proffered a bushel of wheat to the people bowed before her. Each section featured one person doing something to or for the common people.

The imagery came alive in Tanin's mind. Powerful people raining down gifts upon their subordinates. The adoring faces raised up to their kings and queens was everything Tanin imagined.

He forced himself to look away. He had to present himself as a powerful ruler with much to offer, not a distracted schoolboy awed by a painting. Rory and Kettlor struggled with a large chest between them. Their normally graceful steps sounded clunky as they echoed across the stone floor. The prince decided he liked the sound. There was no reason to tiptoe like he was doing something wrong. Let his arrival echo through Ngaro.

King Juarim sat upon a throne that was modest by Tarbin standards. But the steps leading up to it were steep and would take quite an act of acrobatics to top. A guard with a well-aimed spear could stop any would-be assassin before he posed a serious threat. Upon the king's head rested a crown built of shells, the design iridescent where the inside of oyster shells reflected the filtered light. Pearls formed layers of half circles from the ears to the middle of the forehead, like ocean waves approaching the shore. The crest broke over the king's eyes, giving him the appearance of the rock that stopped the movement.

Kettlor whispered over Tanin's shoulder, "Embracing the whole 'king of the sea' image, isn't he?"

Orui scoffed. "He needs to punish his steward for letting the public see him dressed like that."

Tanin stopped far enough from the foot of the steps to see the king without having to angle his neck back. He didn't want to appear an underling.

Young Hodan pointed from Tanin's other side. "Look at his cape."

King Juarim rose from his throne, which was woven from pieces of driftwood. The tan cloth draped over his back wasn't cloth at all.

Tanin's face tightened. "Fishnet? To meet the crown prince of Tarbin, he chooses fishnet?"

The king cleared his throat. "Sound carries along these stone walls almost as well as across water, Prince of Tarbin."

Tanin tightened his fist at the embarrassing revelation. Bowing in apology, Tanin prayed to the Light that he hadn't already botched his first diplomatic mission. "Please forgive me, Your Highness. I meant no offense. We were just surprised."

King Juarim refused to lower his head as Tanin refused to lift his. The king's gaze fell down his nose as he considered a response. "Your ignorance is not unwarranted. Too many of our world have forgotten the Gods, but they have not forsaken us. I wear the attire that Vinta, God of the Ocean, demands."

He lifted his meaty arm to the ceiling, indicating a scene directly overhead. A bearded dark-skinned man with a human torso attached to a large fish-scaled tail rose from the waves of a violent storm. He brandished a barbed spear in one hand and swung a fishing net in the other. A tentacled monster, bright orange like the squid Tanin's party had killed in Kiwa, threatened a ship, but the man-fish protected the vessel.

"I thought mermaids were a myth," Hodan said before Tutor

Grayson could stop him.

King Juarim scrutinized the boy. "In Ngaro, servants do not speak before the king, regardless of their fancy titles or allegiances. The God Vinta created the mermaids to help mankind survive travel along the surface of His majestic seas. He grants us safe passage as long as we worship Him to His satisfaction."

Tanin bowed again. "There was no mention of a Vinta in the culture of Ngaro on the voyage over. We follow the Light to guide our way through the Dark."

King Juarim waved a dismissive hand at the Tarbin prince. "A primitive religion. No wonder you covet our technology. It must all seem like magic to you."

Mere months ago, Tanin would have scoffed at the mention of magic. At this point, he'd seen too much to deny its existence. "What of the connected Planets and raining Light a couple weeks ago? How could that not be the work of the all-knowing Light?"

"The Goddess Ydiny, Creator of Magic, controls the Recharging, after Lagaw, God of Man, allows it to occur. The brightening of the night sky was a sign that Lagaw will allow Ydiny to have Her Recharging. The light and dark are but energy, like magic, that are used by the Gods to create or destroy, whichever we deserve." King Juarim smiled. Tanin suspected he enjoyed lecturing them.

Rory touched Tanin's shaking hands. The weapons guardian whispered, "How badly do we want the ship cannons?"

Tanin closed his eyes and took a deep breath. He had to have them. It wouldn't be the first time he had humored a crazy ruler. "I see. Your gods seem very powerful, indeed. I have . . ."

Before Kettlor could get the chest fully open, Juarim interrupted. "They are not just my gods. They are yours as well."

Tanin drummed his fingers on the wooden lid. He wasn't sure where to go from there. He decided to just continue. "Tarbin wishes to gift the great Ngaro with this chest full of iron and wheat as a symbol of our renewed friendship. Iron to keep your weapons strong and plentiful. Wheat to keep your sailors fed and multiplying."

King Juarim flung his fishnet cape over his arm and marched down the steep steps with complete confidence. Tanin's guardians fell in formation around their prince. Juarim's guards did the same around their king, though their barbed spears looked much more menacing.

The king waved down his men. "I wish to speak to Prince Tanin Winterlaus, royal to royal. You need to stand down and trust Vinta."

They bowed and let him pass, though the two in the center held their spears ready to throw if necessary. Tanin shook his head at his guardians. He didn't want them to give the itchy guards a reason to attack.

"You wish to trade iron and wheat for our ship cannon technology? I could use a steady supply of both. We can make an arrangement." Juarim dropped his cape and put his hands over Tanin's on the lid of the open box. "But I cannot allow the technology into the hands of nonbelievers. I have already sent away the Darvis representative. He refuses to worship the true Gods, and I cannot risk Their wrath."

Tanin couldn't stop his lip from twitching slightly at the absurdity. But he wouldn't make the same mistake as Darvis. "The Light did not serve me well last year. Maybe I could learn a bit from your— the Gods."

"Excellent." Juarim clapped his fleshy hands, eager to have a possible convert. "You must attend the gathering tonight outside of town when the red of the sun God's cape covers the horizon."

"I look forward to it." Tanin managed to bow without snickering. He was proud of himself.

Kettlor started to lift the wooden chest when Juarim grabbed the lid. "You can leave that here. I'm sure we will work out a deal, and there's no need to haul it back and forth."

The husbandry guardian chanced a sideways glance at his prince. Tanin pursed his lips and added a slight nod. There was more where that came from.

# CHAPTER NINE

Tanin tried to slow his breathing. He'd never climbed that many steps to attend a grand performance. He had no idea why King Juarim had invited him to the large arena. As impressive as it was, Tanin had thought they were headed to a religious ceremony, not a sporting event.

Parted by servants, the curtains that blocked off the private viewing box were as soft as the most delicate fabric Tanin had ever known. On the other side, three rows of stepped seating somehow fit inside. Based on the unobstructed view of the sand-covered arena below, this was certainly the best seat in the house.

King Juarim sat in the central chair on the top row in his full Vinta gear, a spiked spear leaning against the back of his chair. At least Tanin didn't have to wear a crazy costume to conform to the king's request. That might have crossed a line for him.

With an audible grunt, the king rose to his feet. His jiggling gut made Tanin wonder how he managed to climb the stairs without having a heart attack. "Welcome, Prince Tanin, to the Ocean Amphitheater. You and your guardians may take whichever seats appeal to you. Except for the two at my sides, which are reserved for my brides."

Tanin hid his surprise that a ruler of his age wasn't already married. "I'm impressed with the arena, King Juarim." Tanin leaned backward over the balcony railing to see the rows of seats above the royal box. "How many people does it hold?"

"Only twelve thousand." The king's lips twitched like he was keeping a secret. "It's a proof of concept. We are building a colossal amphitheater dedicated to the unification of the three kingdoms: Ngaro, Palawa, and Kani. Lagaw, God of us all, demands it."

A light feminine voice interrupted Tanin's next question. "May He honor us with His knowledge."

Two servants rushed to the wall of curtains. Each bowed as they pulled back the fabric. Through the opening stepped the most gorgeous woman Tanin had ever seen. His usual swagger around the opposite sex melted as he stared, slack-jawed, at the brightly colored dress that hugged svelte lines. As if on cue, the ocean breeze blew through the viewing box, whipping back her black hair and exposing high cheekbones under oval eyes.

The king practically jumped down the steps to kiss the newcomer on both cheeks. He grasped one of her hands and held it against his chest. "Prince Tanin Winterlaus of Tarbin, please meet Princess Augusta Maywin of Palawa, my fiancée."

Tanin bowed but kept his eyes focused on her beauty. "It is a pleasure to make your acquaintance," he managed to squeak out.

Augusta took her seat beside the king. "My father, king of Palawa, allows any deals made with Ngaro to be upheld by Palawa as well. We shall be one before long, as the almighty Lagaw decrees."

"As will Kani," said another female voice from the opposite side of the awning.

The curtain servants exchanged a panicked look, then scrambled to the opposite fabric wall. It burst open and covered the distraught servants in its folds.

A woman so short that Tanin first thought her a dwarf strode through the opening, her arms held straight out, daring any barriers to block her path. "Sorry, I'm late. I had to oil the lift one more time to make sure it ran smoothly for the sermon."

The king kissed her on both cheeks with less enthusiasm, though no less affection, than he'd shown Augusta. "This is Princess Meerin Cragforth of Kani, my fiancée. Please meet Prince Tanin Winterlaus of Tarbin."

Meerin's face lit up, excitement shining in her gray eyes. She smacked Tanin on the shoulder like a drinking buddy. "Good to meet you, Prince Tanin. I've been eager to explore the dwarven architecture school affiliated with your kingdom. Maybe we could work out a deal."

Tanin shook her hand awkwardly, confused by the dual fiancées. Meerin's iron grip cramped his fingers. "I'm sure we can arrange an exchange of some sort."

She released Tanin's hand, allowing him to shake it to get the feeling back.

Her servants whisked her into her chair on the other side of the king's and attempted to tame her waves of unkempt hair. Meerin tilted her head as one of the servant girls scrubbed grease from her face.

Augusta uncrossed and recrossed her legs, arranging her skirt in perfect folds. The contrast between the two princesses distracted Tanin.

The king took his seat in between his future wives, two completely different women.

As tantalizing as the arrangement might appear, Tanin didn't envy the king his two brides. One queen would be more than enough for him. Anything else he needed could be provided for by less permanent relationships. Though Tanin could think of worse ways to unite a nation than by marrying the royal families into one line. But at this point, he believed Talia was too tainted to aid his power by any marriage.

Hodan guided the prince to a seat one row below King Juarim.

Tutor Grayson gave the young cultural guardian a nod of approval. Tanin pulled on his collar. The tight neck of his formal wear held sweat against his skin. He wasn't used to the smoldering heat, especially after the sun had gone down. Without the breeze off the ocean, the temperature would have been unbearable.

The crowd grew quiet at a sign Tanin must have missed. Flickering torches lined the ground of the arena, casting the audience in an eerie shadow.

Rory's fingers twitched, looking for his sword. Tanin's body mirrored his tension. Twelve thousand people should not be that quiet. He wanted to ask more questions but couldn't make himself disturb the silence.

Tanin jumped as a booming male voice sounded just outside the curtain where Meerin had entered. "All heed and absorb, as Prophet Salvo teaches us of the ways of Lagaw."

The announcer's voice carried across the theater by magic or technology; Tanin couldn't discern. But he clearly heard the words echoed back from the other side of the stadium.

The scraping of something massive rubbing together rumbled through the stone columns of the arena.

Tanin gripped the arms of his chair until his knuckles ached. "What is that?"

Rory bent low over his shoulder. "Lift, like with the giant clam."

Tanin relaxed. Of course. There must be mechanisms below the surface. That explained the grease on Meerin's face.

Tanin focused on the center stage. A black-robed figure rose from the very center as if hovering above the ground. Tanin could only pick out an outline as the light in the stadium seating was too far away to reach the center of the stage. Though Tanin knew the figure must be standing on something, the lift was shrouded by darkness and sifting sand.

The man threw back his hood and slammed the butt of a tall staff down on the center of the dais. Torches flamed to life around the raised platform. The audience roared with applause. Even the king and princesses seemed awed and impressed.

Tanin folded his arms. The man's flare reminded him of Priestess Nomyra. So far, Tanin thought this religion was little different from his own. Why couldn't the gods just tell the people directly what they expected, without all the pageantry of its practitioners?

The robed man rubbed his trimmed beard as he turned in a tight circle, absorbing the energy from the crowd. His straight hair fell below his ears, though it barely rustled in the nighttime breeze. The man raised his arms. The single gesture quieted the audience applause. Light reflected off some sort of finial on the end of the staff. It looked brown in the undependable light but was much too shiny for driftwood.

"My dear friends, Lagaw, God of Man, asked me, His humble prophet, to welcome Prince Tanin Winterlaus of Tarbin into our folds. For He knows that the visiting prince is ready to receive His word." The robed prophet bowed in the direction of the royal box.

Tanin forcibly smoothed away the frown forming on his face, no longer sure the crowd couldn't see him. He didn't appreciate the assumption that he was converting to the bogus religion of a primitive land.

The prophet's dulcet tones carried easily across the massive amphitheater. "Long ago, the corruption of the astropriests drove away belief in the real Gods. The false prophets spoke of light and dark as conscious beings who ruled over us and our destinies. We had no control over our own souls."

The crowd booed and stomped.

"Preposterous!"

The excited voice of the speaker surprised Tanin. He expected something more solemn and intimidating. "Lagaw created us and gifted us with advanced intellect in order to make our own way in His world. He believes in us and knows we will succeed."

Tanin found himself curious about a god who supported his followers instead of tormenting them.

"Not long ago, I was lost and hopeless. I stumbled across the badlands, drunk on my last bottle. I was ready for the sun to rise and the light to cast me out of this world as my family had—justifiably, I admit—cast me out of theirs. I had no future and no faith."

A woman's voice rose from the crowd. "We love you, Prophet Salvo."

The torchlight surrounding the stage reflected off the prophet's teeth as a huge grin cracked his serious expression. "I love you too. All of you. But my love is insignificant compared to the mighty Lagaw's love for you."

As if in a trance, the audience chanted, "Lagaw, God of us all."

Prophet Salvo bent in half, as if he were conversing intimately with an individual instead of a large crowd. "Lagaw knew I needed Him and tried to gain my attention. But I couldn't hear Him through my despair. The voice of my own worthlessness and insecurities shouted above His words of love and forgiveness."

Tanin sat up in his chair. This Salvo guy might be out of his mind, but he sure knew how to work a crowd.

"When I tumbled down a sandy incline, my head hit a rock." The prophet held up his staff and turned in a circle, eliciting awe from his audience.

What Tanin had taken for a dull brown stone reflected the torchlight off its smooth, shiny surface. It was no ordinary rock. It was a huge black opal, bigger than the one on the Tarbin crown.

The prophet continued. "My head cracked and spilled blood onto this buried stone. For a moment I lay there, thanking the light for ending my pain as her daughter glared down on my pathetic soul."

The audience held its breath as one multiheaded beast. They knew what was coming next, and the anticipation pumped through the air. Tanin's skin tingled with the energy of the collective.

Prophet Salvo inhaled as his audience exhaled. "That's when I heard Him for the first time. The voice of the almighty God Lagaw, creator of us all. Even now, my veins warm with the memory, a sense of calm settles on my body. Though at the time, I did not know who spoke to me or how they were able to penetrate my very thoughts with their commands. He told me to get up and hold the stone high. That it would show me the way. I couldn't deny his command. I rose to my knees, blinking the blinding light from my eyes. My blood stained the sand surrounding this stone. The object that had caused such damage, I could now clearly see: a black opal, a jewel as big as an infant's head. As I pulled it from the sand, the sticky residue of my old life flowed along its surface. As I beheld this marvel of divine influence, the black opal drank in my blood. And . . ."

Tanin stood and moved to the edge of the box. He gripped the wooden railing with a ferocity that would snap it in half if he pulled backward.

*It can't be. It's not possible.*

Prophet Salvo pulled a knife from a leather pouch around his neck. He sliced his palm and placed it over the black opal. The audience shuffled in their seats. The prophet yanked his hand free as if the stone wouldn't release him. He held the staff with both hands over his head.

A light, tinted more purple than the pure blue Tanin remembered from the Forging Ceremony, emanated from the gem, blanketing the entire audience in its soft glow. As the light faded, the crowd jumped to their feet and cheered.

Rory took the opportunity to whisper in Tanin's ear. "That's why the Ngaro pirates let us go. The glow of the Holy Black Opal reminded them of their prophet."

Tanin nodded, unable to speak. Maybe there was something to this Lagaw. He could have sent the signal to ward off the attack. After much experimentation, Tanin knew his blood didn't make the Holy Gemstones glow. The entire thing could have been orchestrated by a higher power.

Salvo stamped the staff on the dais three times to quiet the excited people. "The mighty Lagaw used this light to guide my stumbling feet to a cave of wonder hidden in the desert. A copious supply of fresh water quenched my thirst while words of hope carved on every surface filled my soul."

"There, the Gods revealed themselves to me. The Gods of old. The pantheon of love and hope that I had always longed for, that Ngaro, Kani, and Palawa had always longed for. There, Lagaw taught me the true way, and I am here to teach it to you."

The light in the stone faded as the prophet quieted his voice, forcing the crowd into utter silence if they wanted to hear his words. "This is when I discovered the truth, that the power of light and dark is but an illusion. It is a trick of Ydiny, Goddess of Magic and Magical Creatures. The very Goddess who tricked man into using Lagaw's given power of ingenuity to increase exponentially the allotment of magic charged to the planet every thousand years. She purposefully thwarted Lagaw's careful balance between man and magic, between sea and air, between light and dark."

Jeers were tossed down by the crowd. Apparently, Ydiny was not popular among this bunch.

"Ydiny, the enemy of Lagaw, who strives to negate all his teachings and tempt man with uncontrollable power. With the jump into a hierarchy that rewards the sacrifice of fellow man and enlightenment for elves and other cursed creatures. It is time for it to stop." Salvo turned slowly on the stage, appearing to take in the entire crowd to make sure they were paying attention.

Tanin's grip loosened. Although this Salvo character had the same power in his blood as Talia, he at least had the good sense to prioritize man over magic. If this was Lagaw's plan, Tanin could benefit by listening.

"Lagaw asks us to thwart Ydiny's evil plans. Lagaw wants us to thrive and rise above all life on this planet, His creation. He shows us how to manipulate wood and metal to create great machines, such as this lift. The God of Man wishes us to improve our world through our own minds and ingenuity, the very gifts He bestowed upon us when He created us. Lagaw does not wish Ydiny to warp our minds with easy magic and its trickery. Which is why He has brought Prince Tanin to our shores."

Feeling exposed, Tanin took a step back from the railing. He hadn't planned on being part of the ceremony. He just wanted cannon-mounted ships.

"The fortuitous timing is no coincidence. Prince Tanin of Tarbin, the ancient name of the entire southern continent, has come to seek Lagaw's blessing to end Ydiny's tyranny." The prophet pointed at Tanin with his staff. "Do you agree to hear His word? The choice is yours, Prince of Tarbin. Lagaw guides. He does not dictate."

With every face of the crowd turned in his direction, Tanin didn't feel like he had much choice. With a deep breath, he stepped confidently to the edge of the railing and opened his arms toward the prophet. "I will hear what Lagaw has to tell me."

The echo of religious fervor was powerful. "Praise be to Lagaw."

Prophet Salvo bowed deeply before springing up and walking a wide circle around the dais. He seemed to grab each audience member's attention in one swift movement.

"We must staff our expedition to the ancient city in the middle of the Renquist Desert. We must unite to destroy the Machine that warped a gift into a monstrosity. The Recharging must stick within its natural bounds. The Recharging must *not* happen by Ydiny's design."

Lines of light marched up the stairs to each tier of the amphitheater. At first, Tanin thought it was another magical display, ironic considering the prophet just spoke of the evils of magic. On the stairway closest to him, robed people carrying baskets ascended from the ground. Ngaroans tossed coins and jewelry and bags of spices into the woven straw.

Augusta joined Tanin on the railing. "This is how we will finance our crusade to the ancient metropolis of Raqmu. The Machine will fall, and Lagaw will be pleased and bless us for a millennium for our dedication."

Tanin absorbed the conviction in her beautiful face. He had never felt that strongly about anything in his life.

More torches filled the arena floor as a huge choir took to the sand. The voices of its members filled the amphitheater, joined by the crowd in jubilation. Tanin had never seen anything like it. He wished he understood the language of the lyrics. He was pleased to see Hodan jotting them down.

King Juarim handed a medallion with a large diamond mounted in the center to a page. The boy ran through the curtains to place it in one of the offering baskets. Even in the dim light, Tanin could see the eyebrow the king raised as he stared at Tanin.

Tanin gritted his teeth, trying not to show his annoyance at being manipulated. He held out his hand to Rory, who placed a coin purse in his palm before Tanin had to ask. Making sure the coins clanged together, denoting their impressive number, Tanin waved over another page and handed him the entire purse.

"For your cause." He spoke to Augusta, though his words were intended for the king's ears.

One side of her lips turned up slightly. Her twinkling eyes beckoned more from him than a few coins. Tanin swallowed. He had to tone down his charm before he started a war with a kingdom he was trying to forge an alliance with.

# CHAPTER TEN

THE HEART-SHAPED LEAVES of the aspen trees danced in the wind. The rolling sounds of the Ingiris River filled in the background. The Golden Palace, ancient home of the elves, rose above it all.

Lord Thilphiliari grasped the skeletal hand of his tree-interred wife. "I feel them approaching, my love. They are shouting for me. The Holy Gemstones come to reawaken our people."

The elf paced the clearing, seemingly oblivious to the horror of his rotting and long-dead fellow elves. Body parts stuck out at odd angles from the bark of the carefully arranged aspen trees. The decomposing flesh offered no trace of stench for his senses. He'd been surrounded by it for far too long.

Tossing his hair over his shoulder, Thilphiliari refused to look at the streaks of gray that marred its deep brown. The humans had done that too, had tried to steal his youth. He would deal with them, along with all their kind, after the Recharging.

The elf tensed at a cry from a predatory bird high overhead. The smell of wet griffon fell upon the clearing. A bad omen. Who would protect his people while he traveled to the ancient city?

"Mari, Zinni, come to me," Thilphiliari called to his servants while he searched the sky for the bird-lion beasts that had caused so much trouble centuries ago.

When the griffons first arrived, they had made the elf's life easier by driving intruders away from his people's sanctuary. After a few decades, the beasts' numbers had grown until they tried to make nests in the sacred aspen trees that held the sleeping elves. Alone, Thilphiliari hadn't been powerful enough to chase them away. He had been forced to siphon power from a few of his slumbering kin. Initially, the prospect had horrified him. Then the rush of energy had coursed through his veins. That was when he had known he was to be his people's savior, not merely their guardian.

The elf bowed his head in reverence. The sacrifice of a few saved the entire race. They would be celebrated as heroes when the rest of the population returned. Though none would be more highly worshiped than Thilphiliari.

A pair of animate flowers, one dark orange and one bright pink, pushed and pulled their caterpillar-like roots into and out of the ground to approach their master.

"You have served me well, my friends." Thilphiliari bent in half to pet the soft petals of the waist-high plants. His heart swelled as he took in his only companions all these years. "I need you to protect the aspens for a year on your own while I travel with the imbecile humans to ensure the Recharging of the planet."

He placed a hand on the spiny leaf of one and the long, slender leaf of the other. Chanting to help him concentrate his magic and focus his thoughts, he let his deep baritone fill the clearing with a peace that contradicted the enshrouding chaos. The elf's muscles vibrated with power. He sent the energy into the marigold and zinnia, growing them to twice his own height.

Dropping the leaves that now dwarfed his hands, Thilphiliari leaned against his wife's aspen. His breath lay heavy in his chest. "Guard your masters, the last of the elves. But you mustn't attack the bearers of the Holy Gemstones. I need them."

As the giant flower servants scampered into the forest, the elf lord wiggled his fingers, feeling weak after expending so much magic. Casually, as if he weren't about to commit murder, Thilphiliari moved among the aspen. Each tree was identical to the next, except for those with grotesque body parts hanging out of them. The rest held hibernating elves who awaited the Recharging.

The elf lord strolled among the trees, enjoying the spring day. He spoke to his dead wife as if she accompanied him. "I must choose a new face, my dear. The ones who come now are those who came before. I can smell the treachery."

He waved a hand in front of the peeling white bark of an aspen. It became as clear as glass. A young elven male, a generation younger than Thilphiliari stared back. They shared pale, almost translucent skin, but the younger elf's hair was so light, it was almost white. "His chin is a bit pointier than I'd prefer, but his beauty should distract the humans enough that they will not question his identity."

Taking two steps to the right, the elf lord waved his hand once again. The wrinkled forehead, drooping ears, and elongated nose of a much older elf rested snugly in the tree's embrace.

Thilphiliari grimaced. "I'm sure the humans would be fooled by perceived wisdom in an old one, but I could never pretend to care so little for my appearance as to allow time to ravish my face in this way."

The old elf's face disappeared behind aspen bark as Thilphiliari returned to the first specimen. "You will have to do." The elf lord put both hands around the trunk as if he could caress the youthful face deep inside.

Thilphiliari waved a hand as if batting away an annoying fly. "Yes, my dear, I know the fairies won't be so easily fooled. I will absorb his essence, not just imitate his appearance."

The bark returned to its naturally opaque form as the elf lord leaned his forehead against it at the same height as the sleeping youth. The elf sighed deeply. "Please, Anilinaemi, don't get emotional. His sacrifice will be honored by our people until the end of time. The entirety of his family line will be grateful for their existence because of what he has volunteered to give."

Reaching into a pouch on his belt, Thilphiliari retrieved a sapphire no bigger than his thumbnail. "My precious Hailey, you will direct the True Heir to this particular tree and this particular elf. They will never suspect the switch." He pressed the gem into the bark as easily as pushing a knife through warm butter. The facets sparkled with filtered sunlight.

"Now I must recharge. A transformation of this magnitude demands a significant amount of magic." The elf lord journeyed farther into the aspen forest of possible energy sources. He stopped at a tree far enough away from his intended identity to stay hidden.

Once again, he chanted in rhythmic Elvish to focus his magic and thank the sleeping elf for his sacrifice. Thilphiliari pushed his hands through the bark, which bent like silk. Inside, he grasped the warm hands of the hibernating elf. He pulled, gently at first, then with more urgency, as magic flooded into his body. The tickling warmth filled Thilphiliari's throbbing need for power. He moaned as the victim screamed.

The sacrificial elf fought the draining of his life force. He clawed his way from the sleeping chamber, from the place where he was supposed to be safe and protected. His screams echoed through the forest. The other aspens shivered as if they had all felt the cold that enveloped the dying elf. He managed to fight his torso free from the tree, his last attempt to save his own life. Thilphiliari was much stronger, though, and wouldn't relinquish his grip on the weakening elf's hands.

The victim whimpered one last time, then froze in death, his hibernation cocoon now his tomb. His torso squeezed through the white bark, a twisted look of agony on his face, while the rest of him stayed buried inside the trunk.

Thilphiliari released the drooping hands. His entire body tingled as his strengthened magic vibrated through his veins. "I am ready, my dear, to save our people. All will be set right."

# CHAPTER ELEVEN

THE SPRING WEATHER was unseasonably hot for Talia's trip to the northern elven kingdom. With the rest of her exhausted party, she crossed the bridge over the rapids near the waterfall. She wished there was a faster way to travel the vast borders of Tarbin.

She rubbed the dragon charm necklace that hung around her neck. As handy as it would be to use, Ragaropina had been quite angry with Talia for calling her for transportation from Lightndark Lake. The dragon needed to protect her eggs until the Recharging, otherwise there would be no Great Awakening for her young. Ragaropina had told Talia to summon her when they left the desert city of Hajar Ramliun. She would track the True Heir and arrive at Raqmu in plenty of time.

Even Second Emissary to New Tarbin had refused to come along. It was probably for the best since the nadph could only travel at night, needing the Light's Daughter for energy during the day. He did, however, send Philomena along to use her powerful magic, fresh after the mini-charging, to awaken a hibernating elf. Second Emissary had quieted Talia's fears by assuring her that a nadph representative would meet them at Raqmu. They would follow the Renquist

River north from its mouth until they inevitably ran into the ancient city.

Everything would be fine. It had to be. Talia kept telling herself that as she rounded the corner of the Golden Palace and stepped onto the back patio, where she'd killed Lord Thilphiliari. She didn't know how she'd explain to the new representative what had happened.

A shiver ran down her spine as she once again laid eyes on the mutilated elven bodies in what should have been a peaceful glade. "It's worse than I remember."

The party hadn't bothered to knock or try to walk through the building formed of naturally growing, if manipulated, trees and vines. The only surviving elf had been killed by Talia's hand during the Forging Quest. Her actions had been self-defense. She kept telling herself she had had no choice, but it didn't assuage her guilt. Now, no one was left to protect the sleeping elven nation while they awaited the Recharging.

Dew turned the open book in her hand upside down. She gestured toward a back entrance of the palace. "I'm pretty sure the chest we need for the mermaid extraction is in here."

Nomyra shook her robes of the yellow pollen that clung to them, left by the vines growing on the outer walls of the elven stronghold. "I'll go with you." Without waiting for permission, the priestess crossed the patio to the side door.

Talia nodded to Dew, who followed the priestess closely. She still didn't quite trust her.

"By the Light, the horror is never-ending." Nyna placed a hand on the bark of the tree close to where Thilphiliari was buried. The tree that held his wife.

Talia walked to her side, careful to avoid the hastily dug grave that still looked fresh despite the months past. "What's wrong?"

Nyna wiped a tear from her face. "She's dead."

Talia's heart sank into her already churning gut.

Naul joined them. "Dead? But she was fine when we left. The

aspen seemed to be keeping her protected even though she was partially out of the bark."

The elf's face peeked out from the white flakes of the tree. The trunk closed behind her ears as if she were a statue and the aspen had grown around her. Both her hands and one knee protruded a bit farther out.

When Talia had first seen her, her eyes had been closed and a healthy flush had graced her cheeks. Now her skin was mottled by death. Her wide-open eyes were cloudy. The stench of decay emanated from her corpse. Talia couldn't deny the truth. The elf, whose beauty had looked eternal, was most definitely dead.

A deep voice startled Talia. "What is this horrific place? I thought we were to awaken an elf from slumber to aid in the quest. Not visit a grotesque tomb of trees."

Guard Traneck stood so close to Prince Aleck, Talia first thought they were holding hands. Parnim's stance reminded her of Guard Dragick so fiercely, she had to keep telling herself this was a different dwarf guard and she didn't know him.

Reaching up to close the elf's hollow eyes, Talia tried to answer the dwarf the best she could. "Lord Thilphiliari guarded his people alone for centuries. Our best guess is that, in all that time of isolation, he went mad and siphoned the life force of those he was supposed to protect."

Gregor rubbed his bristled chin. "He sacrificed a few to save the whole. I'm not sure he was wrong."

Talia flashed a glare at him. The urge to argue swelled in her chest. The macabre reality of rotting corpses jutting from trees amid a peaceful forest overwhelmed her.

She rubbed her forehead. What would she sacrifice to save her people? She hoped she wouldn't have to answer that question before her quest was complete.

Prince Aleck walked to the edge of the stone patio and stopped at the foot of Thilphiliari's grave. He looked no farther into the clearing. "The flowers are gone."

Naul put a hand on the dwarf's shoulder. "They were probably blown away by the wind."

The dwarven guards stared darkly at Naul, who dropped his hand from their charge and took one step back. Talia shook her head. These new guards hadn't grown with her party the way Dragick and Gallick had. She hoped they wouldn't build a rift between Aleck and her.

Wind from fairy wings tickled Talia's ears as Philomena landed on her shoulder. Ial blushed and turned away. Talia's lips twitched. He was always uncomfortable whenever the wee female landed somewhere. As the fairy flew, she looked like a ball of light, but as soon as her wings stopped their rapid movement, her naked form showed. Talia hadn't met a male fairy. She didn't even know if they existed. Maybe she'd be just as embarrassed by a perfect, naked mini-man.

The fairy tapped her foot until Talia brought Windall up. Along the journey from Lightndark Lake to the Elven Forest, whenever Philomena decided to show up, she taught Talia how to communicate using the ring. It wasn't exactly by words, more by images and emotions. Talia wouldn't consider the process efficient, but it had proved effective so far. She was most relieved when she discovered she didn't have to feed the magic jewelry blood to use it in this manner. She'd also had no sightings or whisperings from the mysterious wizard she saw in the crown. He must be embodied in that ornament only.

The fairy placed her hand on the gem, while the human placed a finger. Talia concentrated on the green of the emerald. She saw Philomena flitting between aspen trees, pointing at one, then another, then another. Then she pointed at Talia.

"I have to choose?" Talia looked at the hundreds of possibilities before her. How would she know if she had chosen wisely? Would any elf do?

Philomena nodded her head in the vision and on Talia's shoulder.

Talia straightened her shoulders, determined to do the best she could. The slight movement caused Philomena to slip across her tunic cloth and lose connection with the ring. The fairy flapped her wings as she tumbled off. She hovered before Talia and crossed her arms.

"I'm sorry," the princess mumbled. "I'm not used to having a fairy on my person. I don't naturally stand as still as your friend, Second Emissary."

Philomena flew to a branch over Talia's head, giving her the distinct impression that she was unlikely to get accustomed to it any time soon.

Nyna's mouth stayed wide open as she watched the fairy with true fascination. "What did she say?"

Ial laughed. Now that he and Nyna spent more time alone together, he seemed to find everything she did amusing. "You want a fairy pet, don't you?"

"No." Nyna kicked some leaves at her feet, not meeting his gaze. "But as a friend, I bet Philomena or one of her sisters could teach me so much more about herbs and what they can do. I'd love to learn."

"Almighty Thoretick, what is that?" Guard Parnim ushered Aleck off the paved patio.

Guard Traneck pulled his sword from the scabbard and stayed a few feet in front of his charge as the dwarves moved away from the Golden Palace. "Stand back, Your Highness. We don't know what the great beast wants."

Talia tensed and looked up. "Griffons. They're probably returning with the absence of the elf lord to protect his people." One more thing to eat at Talia's conscience.

Prince Aleck pushed his guards aside. "Don't be silly. That's no monster. It's just Mari."

An orange flower, taller than the roof of the Golden Palace, scurried onto the pavers on worm-like roots.

"Looks like she's grown up." Naul moved in front of Talia, his hand on the hilt of his sword.

"Are you sure it's her?" Talia asked Aleck. Though the jagged leaves and fluffy flower head looked the same, Mari had only stood to Talia's waist last time.

"Definitely." Aleck shook off Traneck's hand as the guard tried to keep the prince under the protection of the trees. "She has the same kind tilt of her head and the same weepy but still plump leaves."

Nyna cocked her head to study the bloom. "You mean, she looks like any marigold?"

The bloom moved with the same caterpillar movement that the smaller version had used. Though the rhythm of the roots smacking the paver stones sounded much more menacing when the summer flower was as tall as a building.

Aleck waved at the faceless animate plant.

Guard Parnim stood protectively next to his prince. "It can't see you, Your Highness."

Aleck patted his worried guard on the shoulder. "She has no eyes and no ears, but she can see and hear. She responded to us last time."

Naul had one hand on his scabbard. "Where is the pink one?"

A screech came from above.

Naul pushed Talia close to the trunk, out of sight of the open sky.

Ial searched the blue. "Griffon." He pulled his bow and strung it with practiced ease.

The half eagle, half lion brushed the tops of the trees as it flew overhead.

Talia pushed away from Naul. "It's my fault. We have to protect the elves. We can't let the beasts nest in the aspen and destroy the entire race. Otherwise, what are we even trying to do with the whole Recharging and—"

The last griffon the party had come across met his death by a single sword stroke from Tanin's weapons guardian. Aleck had been devastated by the carnage. Talia hadn't felt any better about the loss of such a majestic creature, but she couldn't let the elves die before the Great Awakening.

Gregor held out a large silver charm with a mirror mounted in the middle. "I have the repellant Nomyra gave us. I was afraid I wasn't going to get a chance to use it."

Talia squinted into the bright sky at the hovering beast. "I'm not sure what good it will do unless the griffon lands."

A huge fuchsia flower with bushy leaves rose from the roof of the Golden Palace. Talia swore she heard it roar. With a huge twist of its leaves, a strong breeze blew the griffon back a few feet in the air. The hawklike yell grew in pitch, and the griffon turned tail and flew in the opposite direction.

Gregor put an arm around Talia's shoulders. "Look. They're protected. The elves will be fine until you can awaken them."

Talia leaned into Gregor's warm chest. He knew exactly what to say to calm her panicked breathing.

"By the Light's blessing, you were awesome, Zinni!" Aleck shouted to the protective flower. "We could use one or two guards like her at home."

Traneck and Parnim exchanged a glance that said exactly what they thought of that idea.

Guard Traneck kept his sword out, focused on the giant orange flower poised on the patio. "They wouldn't fit through our passageways."

"Thank Thoretick," Parnim muttered under his breath.

Philomena pinched Talia's nose.

"Hey!" She swatted at the annoying fairy before she realized the foolishness of such a move. With a pat on Gregor's hand, she reluctantly moved away from his warm, earthy smell to study the trees ahead.

"Right. I must choose." Talia rubbed the sting from her nose. "Not that I have any idea how to do that."

She moved into the shadowed forest where the dense upper foliage blocked much of the sun's brilliance. As her eyes adjusted, Ial and Nyna rushed in front of her, anticipating her moves. The forest was oddly devoid of any underbrush, as if a caretaker removed every other plant that tried to make a home here.

Maybe she'd walk with her eyes closed and run into a tree. At that point, she didn't have any better plans. With nothing else to trip her up, it should work.

Arriving at a densely populated area, Talia closed her eyes and turned in place a couple of times. Thankfully, none of her guardians said a word about how silly she must look. A little dizzy but not nauseated, Talia held her arms out in front of her body. She didn't want to compound her awkward walk by ramming her nose into a tree.

Talia quieted the mocking voice in her head. She was supposed to trust her instincts. She could do this.

From the quiet of the sleeping forest, Talia's stomach buzzed, a gentle tugging feeling. A burning sensation, like the first signs of a fever, built behind her eyes. The experience was so similar to what she had felt when she was in the vicinity of the Holy Gemstones. Thankfully, the feeling had faded once they were mounted on the Key. She was relatively sure this feeling was not from them. Talia decided to focus on the intensity, moving in whatever direction pulled at her the strongest.

A few steps forward and her hands hit the peeling bark of an aspen. She opened her eyes, expecting some sort of revelation. Nothing changed. Windall hummed slightly, a light in its depths blinking feebly. Somehow, she knew this was not the right tree.

Concentrating on Windall and the persistent pressure behind her eyes, Talia moved deeper into the woods. She moved to her right a few steps, then a tight left around a copse of trees. Strands of her light hair flew around her face as Philomena hovered over her head. The royal guardians followed silently, ultra-aware for any impending threats. Even talkative Aleck kept quiet.

Talia blocked them from her mind and thought of nothing but the insistent tugging. She was trying to walk around another trunk when her entire body vibrated. Her ring flashed a bright green. Running her finger down the bark, a tingle of magic, unlike anything she had felt with the other trees, flooded her system. It wasn't as intense as the mini-charging, but it was certainly strong. She didn't know how she had missed this the first time they traveled through the elven kingdom. Something had changed in her.

Philomena flew down to Talia's eye level. Talia nodded at the fairy. "This is the one. I can feel it."

The fairy motioned for her to stand back. Her companions moved with her. Philomena was the only one powerful enough to awaken the elf slumbering inside. Everyone trusted that if she said to move back, they should get out of the way.

Philomena's greenish hair flew back from her head as spikes of magic sparked from her fingers. Talia flung an arm over her face to block the painful flare. She couldn't believe such power came from such a tiny being.

Pain pierced Talia's hand. The silver leaf band of Windall glowed a deep red as though it were melting. She burned the fingers of her other hand as she pulled the jewelry off and dropped it, sizzling, onto the leafy ground. The agony of her injured finger made her think she'd pulled it off with the ring.

Ial pushed Talia away as the leaf pile burst into flame. Gregor stomped on the sudden fire.

Talia clutched her hand to her chest as the white glowing aspen tree drew her attention. The bark opened like a curtain parted in the middle. As if Light herself slept within, pure brilliance stepped from the trunk.

Talia might hold the title of Bright One, but if anyone deserved such a moniker, it should be whoever stepped out.

# CHAPTER TWELVE

On the patio of the Golden Palace, Talia sat in a woven chair, unable to look away. The only elf she'd ever met was Lord Thilphil-iari, tall and emaciated with long brown hair and pale skin. This much younger elf carried himself the same way, but he looked quite different. He was proud, maybe touching on arrogant, but quieter in tone. Sinewy muscles rippled under his loose-fitting sleep wear. His only words so far had been his name, Rodianiari of the House of the Sparrow, and his insistence on immediate sustenance.

As Talia introduced her party, Rodianiari's natural good looks made Talia's toes curl. His blond hair flowed over his shoulders without a single knot or crinkle. If Talia took a quick nap, her waves would stick out at ridiculous angles with painful knots. His pale skin spoke of centuries buried away from the Light. His slightly pointy nose and chin mirrored his ears.

"Ow!" Talia pulled her hand from Nyna's mending. The burn from the ring encompassed her entire middle finger, where a blister had already formed.

Her medicinal guardian looked intrigued by the challenge, not sympathetic. "I'm sorry, Talia. I know it hurts, but if you can hold still long enough, this ointment will soothe the swelling."

Talia tried to hold still. Since she already had all the Holy Gemstones, she didn't have to prick her finger every time someone demanded proof. Talia had hoped that meant she wouldn't have sore fingers the entire journey. Apparently, it was her destiny. Maybe she should wear her riding gloves all the time.

Ial tied a string around the band of the ring. "You can wear it around your neck now." He slipped the necklace over Talia's head.

Gregor sidled close. "Great idea. Now her tunic will catch fire instead of a few leaves."

Talia's face scrunched as she considered his words. "I wore the emerald for a month without anything more than a gentle glow here and there. Maybe Philomena used some of its magic when she awoke Rodianiari."

The young elf put down his water glass. Every other eye on the patio turned to him. "It was a side effect."

He stood from the table that Mari and Zinni had set up for the guests. "I was not supposed to awaken alone. The entirety of my—" Rodianiari hesitated.

Talia saw something familiar in his whiteless eyes but couldn't place it.

"The elven nation was supposed to rejoin the Light altogether. I believe the aspen fought my solo awakening and drove off any foreign magic sources, afraid I was under attack."

"Why didn't it attack, Philomena?" Aleck leaned forward. His eyes glowed with curiosity. "She is a foreign source of magic, right?"

Rodianiari's eyes turned cold as he focused on the much shorter dwarf. Talia remembered the same hatred in Thilphiliari, who hadn't even allowed the dwarves inside the Golden Palace. She wondered if such racism was engrained in his species.

As a Krimmel Dwarf, Prince Aleck didn't seem to share the same prejudice. She knew the Eckerd Dwarves spoke disrespectfully about the elves. It had never bothered her before. Then again, she had thought they were extinct. How could a few off-color jokes hurt a race that no longer existed? Lots of things were going to have to change after the Great Awakening.

Nomyra and Dew pushed through the back door onto the patio. They struggled with a large shiny wooden chest that had symbols carved on all sides.

Dew huffed as the they set the chest down by Talia. "Okay. We should be set for the next leg of our journey."

Nomyra tugged her hands inside her sleeves and focused on the new addition to their party.

Talia made the introductions, indicating each person with her uninjured hand. "Dew of the Cultural School and Priestess Nomyra Highwind, meet Rodianiari of the House of the Sparrow."

The elf ignored Dew but bowed deeply before the priestess. "It is a pleasure to meet an Interpreter of the Stars."

Nomyra straightened, affecting a more regal pose. Bowing her head with a flip of her hand, the priestess looked the very picture of elegance. "I am honored to meet the elf representative during this crucial Recharging. Everything will be set right soon."

Rodianiari's lips twitched. "Yes, it's time for a reset."

Dew touched Talia's shoulder. Her cultural guardian sensed the same thing Talia did. Something was off with both of them.

The elf and the priestess both tensed when Ial caressed the chest from the palace.

"Driftwood." The husbandry guardian's eyes sparkled, and his legs bounced with excitement.

"What's driftwood?" Aleck asked.

The elf spoke to Ial, refusing to address the dwarf. "It is bits of branches and other such plant life that is tossed about by the sea until it either drowns in the abuse or transforms into perfection."

Ial continued to run his hands over the surface. "We used to collect it from the shore and carve statues of all sorts of sea life. My father used to say that a creature of the sea would guard a piece of driftwood, imbuing the material with the animal's essence. When it reached shore, you only had to listen carefully to discover what companion had bonded with the piece."

Guard Parnim scratched his beard. "I didn't know that human could string so many words together."

The normally quiet husbandry guardian winked at the dwarf.

Rodianiari mirrored Nomyra's annoyed expression, until he saw Talia studying him. His face softened. "That is a romantic sentiment, Eel."

"*Ee*-all," Nyna corrected. She pushed back the husbandry guardian's bangs. Talia smiled. She was getting used to the Nyna–Ial relationship.

"My apologies, Guardian Ial. I meant no disrespect." Rodianiari touched the chest, and the engraved symbols moved.

Talia leaned in for a better look. The colors swirled together, forming the image of a palace constructed from humongous bones and decorated with seashells. The vegetation looked like long swaying grass, cultivated on either side of the grand entrance.

Talia pointed above the palace at the large animals flapping above it, thin tails swishing behind them. "What are those strange-looking birds?"

Ial shook his head. "Not birds. Those are Manta Rays. This must be under the ocean."

"Mermaids. Just like the book said." Dew pushed in close beside Talia to get a better view. "A whole race of people that live under the ocean."

Aleck hopped up on a chair, giving him a slight height advantage to see over Dew's head. "Are they asleep like the elves? If so, will Philomena wake one up?"

Nomyra raised an eyebrow. Talia crossed her arms, frustrated with the woman's annoyance. It must be exhausting to have all the answers all the time. Maybe the priestess could share more with the Bright One so Talia could complete the Recharging.

"They are indeed sleeping. They do not have as long a lifespan as the elves, so they won't have a representative guarding their palace. And fairies are not known for their fondness of water."

Rodianiari scoffed. "That's why the dirty little things always stink. And why they abandoned us for the shelter of the nadph. We demanded a certain level of cleanliness in our servants."

Nyna looked shocked. "Fairies weren't always companions to the nadph?"

Rodianiari set down his mug a bit violently. "Of course not. My people have been around millennia longer than the walking twigs. When Ydiny granted the nadph sentience, the fairies left by the flock." He cocked his head. "And good riddance."

Talia crossed her arms. This was going to be a long trip with this much hatred for one another blended into one party. She wasn't sure how she would keep them from killing each other before they got near the dome.

She tried to smooth things over. "Maybe the fairies left because you considered them servants. The nadph treat them like partners."

Rodianiari blinked slowly. When his whiteless eyes found Talia, he smiled. "That could very well be true. My people might have to reconsider our treatment of lesser beings."

Talia wasn't sure that counted as a concession of wrongdoing.

As if his rude comments had summoned Philomena, the feisty fairy swooped into the middle of the crowd. Though still pale from the exertion of awakening Rodianiari, her nap seemed to have revived her.

She perched on Talia's palm. With a jerk backward, Philomena shook her foot, trying to get the sticky ointment off.

Talia bit her lip to prevent a laugh from escaping at Philomena's cross expression. "I'm sorry. Windall burned me for some reason."

Philomena flew into Talia's tunic and pulled out the ring. She motioned for Talia to touch the surface. Apparently, she had something to say.

As they both touched the emerald, Talia watched a scene unfold in her mind. In the vision, Philomena flew around Rodianiari and shook her head in disapproval. The elf's skin changed color from pale to tan. His hair went black, then streaked with white, then turned back to blond. Lines around his eyes appeared then disappeared. His chin smoothed out, then sharpened to its current angle. It was like Philomena couldn't see him clearly.

Talia blinked as the clearing came back into focus. She tucked the ring back under her tunic. She had no idea what the fairy was trying to show her by changing the appearance of the elf representative. Philomena hovered just far enough from Talia's nose that she didn't have to cross her eyes to see the fairy. Her tiny fingers opened her bright eyes as wide as they would go as she nodded her head back toward Rodianiari.

Talia at least understood there was a warning in the fairy's visual. "I'll be careful."

Philomena must have been satisfied with that response, for she picked up her ball-of-light speed and disappeared around the Golden Palace, heading south.

Naul rubbed his head. "Is she leaving?"

Nomyra nodded. "Her work is done. She will report to the nadph swamp and ensure the arrival of their representative."

Gregor cleared his throat. "So how are we going to wake up a mermaid?"

The priestess opened the lid of the chest. Talia sucked in a deep breath as the now-familiar tingling sensation flowed through her muscles. Inside the box lay a sapphire, three times the size of the one on the crown. Velvet lining hugged the deep blue facets, ensuring its safe transportation.

"It's full of magic," Talia whispered.

Nomyra slammed the lid shut. "Yes, Bright One, it is. Enough to awaken one mermaid."

Naul rubbed his bald head. "I have a question. How are we supposed to get to the slumbering mermaids without drowning?"

Dew hugged the book to her chest. "There's supposed to be something in the chest to aid us, but we couldn't find anything hidden in the lining besides this huge sapphire. That's what took us so long. We were searching to see if there was another chest."

"There is a way." Ial wrapped some cured meat in a piece of cloth and stuffed it in his bag. "Mantas."

Nomyra held up her glass of wine in salute. "That should do the trick."

Naul took a large bite of apple, then stuffed the rest of the fruit into his bag. "I guess we should get ready for the road, then?"

"Are we heading to North Port?" Gregor asked, sniffing some dried tea leaves.

"Thurrelrun," Dew and Nomyra said simultaneously.

Nyna took the tea from Gregor to wrap it properly for travel. "Isn't that your hometown, Ial?"

The husbandry guardian nodded, a light dancing in his eyes.

"Hmm . . ." Gregor scratched his beard. "A town of fishermen and Manta Ray trainers. I don't think there's any other industry there."

"And tales of mermaids," Ial added.

"I guess that means you're in for a family reunion, my friend." Talia studied Ial's face, searching for clues. She remembered the turmoil caused by Dew's trip home last year. She wondered what awaited them in the coastal town.

The most Talia got was a shrug from the contemplative guardian. She helped the party pack rations for the trip to the coast. What was an adventure without a few surprises?

# CHAPTER THIRTEEN

THE SCORCHING HEAT of the desert boiled beads of sweat from Tanin's skin. He wiped his forehead for what had to be the hundredth time in as many steps. He had agreed to travel into the desert with Prophet Salvo, Meerin, and Augusta. He probably would have followed Augusta's tantalizing hips anywhere she led.

But that wasn't his only motivation. He had sensed a truth in Salvo's words, a missing part of his life, and he hungered for answers.

The prophet marched ahead of the party, his staff acting as a walking stick as his other hand held his robes above the ground.

Orui sneezed. "How much farther?"

Rory smacked the medicinal guardian with the hilt of his sword. His confident stride told Tanin more than any words could that Rory felt much better with his dual swords in hand. He'd refused to allow Tanin into the wilds without the guardians properly armed. Not that he could have stopped Tanin if he'd decided to order them to go anyway. But while Tanin was curious about this prophet and his gods, he wasn't stupid.

Kettlor uncorked a bladder of water. "I don't see why we had to leave the horses and the rest of the supplies on the other side of the dune."

Prophet Salvo didn't slow his focused pace through the sandy terrain. Without any landmarks, he seemed to know exactly where he was going. "The entrance is a secret. Only those Lagaw Himself invites can see what it contains."

That part bothered Tanin. "So Lagaw allowed you and two princesses to find its entrance, but not the king of Ngaro?"

Meerin laughed. "Can you imagine the future king of our combined kingdoms making this journey?"

Tanin envisioned Juarim's meaty legs sinking deep into the sand, only stopping at his bulbous belly. He barely contained a snort. "Maybe not."

Augusta lowered the veil that protected her face from kicked-up sand. "Our future husband has other duties that demand his time. Meerin and I are both betrothed to the king and are sworn acolytes to the Gods."

Tanin couldn't imagine that was a good idea. "What happens if Lagaw demands something contrary to what your husband demands?"

Augusta raised an eyebrow at Tanin. "*That* is an impossibility."

With a slam of his staff against something solid beneath the sand, Prophet Salvo drew Tanin's attention. "We are here."

A huge mound of reddish silt rose above the meandering terrain. It looked like every other rounded hill Tanin had passed since they entered the desert hours ago. His feet slowly sunk deeper into the shifting ground. Maybe the prophet saw something he didn't. Tanin moved forward to stand beside him. The support of solid ground balanced his unease.

Hodan jumped up and down beside Tanin. "There's something underneath."

Meerin shushed him with a wave of her hand. She pulled out a thin knife as Augusta presented Salvo's flattened hand. The prophet closed his eyes. His lips moved in what Tanin could only describe as silent prayer. Meerin sliced a new cut through other scars on the prophet's palm. Augusta tipped Salvo's bleeding hand over the Black Opal on the staff. Each drop was absorbed into the stone, much as Talia's had been by the Holy Gemstones.

Tanin swallowed his jealousy as the gem flashed to life. The prophet waved the active stone over the shifting sand. A glow answered the staff from beneath the thin layer. The scraping of rock on rock accompanied a cascade of sand into a hole that was opening in the ground. Somehow, the rest of the desert didn't drain into the hole as a set of rough-hewn steps appeared.

Meerin and Augusta chanted together. "Praise be to Lagaw, God of us all."

Salvo's eyes twinkled with what Tanin hoped was wonder, rather than madness. "You will understand when you see His word." His still bleeding hand gripped a cloth Augusta pressed against the wound.

Fine particles tickled the back of Tanin's throat as he climbed down the stairs. He stopped and coughed, which also gave him time for his eyes to adjust to the darker cave. An odd blue light seemed to emanate from the ceiling as from an eerie underground moon.

Tanin pulled a cloth from inside his tunic to wipe gritty sweat from his face. "I thought Lagaw forbid the use of magic?" He pointed to the unnatural lighting.

Salvo shook his head as he waited in front of a smooth limestone wall. "That's not it at all. Magic is natural. Lagaw aligned the planets Himself to charge our precious world with the power."

The stone beneath Tanin's feet was too even to be naturally formed. When Salvo had said Lagaw led him to a cave, Tanin had pictured hollowed-out earth with unpredictable twists and turns. This underground feature had to be manmade. It reminded Tanin of the chiseled walls in the Eckerd Kingdom. The most sacred buildings of the dwarves were carved out of granite inside the mountains.

These walls, however, weren't simply structural. Tanin turned in a tight circle to view the entire enclosure, which was larger than his wing of the castle at home. Intricate carvings covered every surface. Pictographs of animals, crops, and people decorated some areas, while symbols that might have been letters of another language lined others. On a few walls, frames dug around reliefs highlighted sketches of intricate machines.

Tanin could only guess what they were for. "What is this place?"

Salvo held his staff with both hands, leaning on it casually. "This is the Cave of Knowledge, created by Lagaw's prophets of old. He brought me here to prepare for the Recharging, so that when the time came, His new acolytes"—he indicated Augusta and Meerin—"and I would be ready to fulfill His wishes and end the tyranny of Ydiny and the magical races."

Meerin tapped a portion of the wall that displayed an intricate sketch of some sort of apparatus. "This Machine, engineered by rogue followers of Lagaw, is the problem. It multiplied the charge from the conjunction."

With a shake of her skirts in a perfect swirl, Augusta took over the lesson. "The extra magical energy created whole civilizations of elves and dragons, as well as new races of mermaids and nadph. Ydiny's followers thrived at the expense of Lagaw's favorites, humans."

Prophet Salvo pointed to symbols high up on the wall. "Grand Wizard Maitliin saw the error of his people and sabotaged the Machine a millennium ago, ensuring only the natural Lagaw-designed Recharging. But the followers of Ydiny stopped him before he could annihilate the threat."

Meerin tossed her sand-laden robes aside. "Which is where we come in."

With a look of ecstasy, Salvo reached toward the ceiling. "Lagaw's message on these walls told me what my purpose was. I, as the Bright One, am to lead the True Heir to Raqmu in the Renquist Desert to destroy the Machine before it can be used by His enemies again."

Tutor Grayson traced the symbols with a finger. "These reliefs. They're in Veni, the ancient language of the first people. My friends and I learned it in school to exchange secret messages with one another." He squinted at Prophet Salvo. "But it's a dead language. No one has spoken it for centuries."

Salvo smiled sweetly. "Maybe no one has spoken it on your side of the world, but here, the desert people have long memories. They still speak the language, though I had difficulty finding anyone who could read it. Lagaw gifted our very own Augusta with an innate skill for languages. She found artifacts in Palawa's collections that contained multiple translations, including Veni, on each item. She used those to interpret the walls."

Tanin wiped his lips to hide his surprise. The beauty had more useful tools to aid her king than just a pretty face. King Juarim was a lucky man.

"Hodan." Tutor Grayson motioned the boy to his side. "Copy as much as you can. It seems a long-dead language has been reincarnated. We'll begin your lessons today."

"No." The sharp crack of Salvo's staff against the floor accompanied his command. "Nothing viewed in these sacred rooms is to be shared with the outside. Lagaw, and Lagaw alone, decides who sees His wisdom."

His eyes wide with embarrassment, Hodan tucked his notebook back into his jacket pocket. Tutor Grayson crossed his arms but did not offer an argument.

Augusta placed a calming hand on Salvo's shoulder as she addressed Tanin. "We cannot risk the followers of Ydiny discovering these secrets. It does no good to destroy one Machine if Her followers simply build another."

Cracking her knuckles, Meerin grabbed a lever the size of a tree branch and pulled. A huge slab of limestone crawled up into the ceiling. Tanin marveled at the strength of such a petite woman.

Prophet Salvo placed his staff under the slab as a prop. It didn't seem sturdy enough to hold such weight, but the wood stayed firm under the strain. "Come, Prince Tanin. I have something more to show you."

Meerin skipped ahead as the group entered another large cave lit with the same blue glow.

The prophet laughed at her enthusiasm. "Lagaw, in His wisdom, gave Princess Meerin a gift as well. She can bring to life any schematic of the old apparatuses. The mechanisms speak to her, much as the translations speak to Augusta."

Tanin bumped into Rory's outstretched arm. "What are you doing?" He pushed his guardian aside.

His anger drained as he beheld a huge tangle of gears and piping in the middle of the branched cave. The smell of burnt oil, as if a cook had fried the best part of dinner, hung in the air.

Meerin leaned against a panel with color-coded levers and dials. "This is the Machine. The designer was a genius. If only he had used his Lagaw gifts in His service instead of against Him."

"This is the Machine?" Tanin encircled the contraption, Rory close by his side as if the inanimate object posed a threat. "I thought it'd be bigger."

Meerin laughed. "This is not *the* Machine. It's a model. The actual thing we must destroy is in an ancient city in the middle of the Renquist Desert on your continent."

Salvo climbed a ladder to a raised platform in front of a different control panel. "It was but a lump of metal and broken bits when I came across it. Our Meerin was able to put it back together based on the writings out there." He pointed to the room they'd just left.

Orui scratched his chin. "Why would we want to know how to put it together if we need to destroy it?"

"Ah . . ." Salvo leaned over the railing of the raised platform, as comfortable as if he were back on the stage. "That's the part Lagaw had to show us."

Meerin flipped a few switches, and the gears trembled with a whine that swiftly intensified into a rumble. "You see, we will destroy the Machine by focusing the magical energy into its parts instead of allowing the influx to flow into the core of the planet."

The soft drag of Augusta's skirts on the ground accompanied her.

"For this, we need the True Heir of Tarbin to start the Recharging, along with the Bright One."

Salvo motioned Tanin up to the platform. "Come. You need to see this."

Tanin's mind raced as he climbed the rungs behind Rory. He had a role to play in this mysterious event that had seemed to only involve his sister. High Priest Seamus had declared him the True Heir of Tarbin. Did that mean this was his destiny?

"Once every millennium, when the planets align, the True Heir and the Bright One unite." Salvo removed a metal plate on the control panel, exposing a round hole with five slots. Gears turned one way, then the other, on each side of the opening. "The Key, the crown of Tarbin with all five Holy Gemstones, fits into this slot and must be placed there by the True Heir." He held up his scarred palm. "While the Bright One donates his blood."

Now Tanin understood the displays of light. "You are the Bright One."

Tears of joy dripped from the corners of Salvo's eyes. "When the pre-Recharging filled the sky with magic, my soul shone through my skin and joy filled every nerve. That's when I knew my full role and that you, the True Heir, would find me."

Orui coughed to gain Tanin's attention. He rubbed his head with both hands like he was turning a hat he didn't wear.

Tanin realized what he was trying to say. "By the Dark . . ." He'd have to learn to curse again. He didn't want to offend the prophet.

"I might have a slight problem." Tanin looked away to avoid Salvo's disappointed accusation. "The Tarbin crown, or the Key as you describe it, is not currently in my possession."

Meerin gasped from the ground below. "May Lagaw protect us."

"But I know where it is and how to get it back." Tanin rolled his shoulders and squinted at the surrounding stone like he could see his treacherous sister from a continent and an ocean away. He turned, his face solid with determination. "You're right, Prophet Salvo.

Lagaw must have sent me here, for you need the crown and I need weapons to get it back."

Prophet Salvo folded his arms into his sleeves. "King Juarim will do whatever it takes to ensure Lagaw's commands are fulfilled. Tell me what you need."

Rory squeezed Tanin's shoulders. Tanin exchanged a look of triumph with his weapons guardian. Not only would he get the technology he'd come for, Tanin would return home with a God-given mission to save the planet from magic.

Talia had chosen the wrong side, and Tanin would make sure their father saw how dangerous his precious little girl really was.

# CHAPTER FOURTEEN

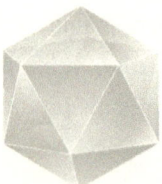

THE COOL OCEAN breeze bit through the early summer heat. Talia could hear the waves crashing against the shore, but she couldn't see the ocean beyond the houses built on stilts that made up most of the town of Thurrelrun.

"Well, these are familiar." Dew moved around a set of stairs that stuck into the street from a home sitting up on thick pillars.

Just like here, the cultural guardian's hometown of Mahanagara in the Krimmel Mountain Range was built on massive wooden logs. The mountain town did it to protect the properties from snowmelt flooding each spring. Talia wasn't sure why they'd need such structures in this town. Tarbinulus was a port city, and those houses weren't elevated.

"The ocean is yards away. Surely high tide doesn't come up this far." Talia tried to reason out why the village would work so hard to build up this high.

Ial's smile stretched from ear to ear. "Summer storms bring huge waves. My father used to say that the warm water gets angry. When the heat of the sun is at its peak, the water attacks everything around it, like a toddler having a temper tantrum."

Talia reflected his contagious smile. She was relieved to have the potential for a happy family reunion. Though Ial only talked of his father. She wondered if he had had any other family before he became a guardian.

Naul jumped down from the wagon he'd been driving. "You mean the summertime, like right now? Are we going to have to go out to sea in the midst of some sort of storm season?"

Gregor patted the big man on the shoulder on his way to the back of the wagon to help Nomyra and Rodianiari down. "Don't worry, Naul. We'll be *under* the water, not on top."

Naul wiped sweat from his shiny head. "I feel so much better now. Thanks."

Ial held the horses at the opening of the main road. "My father's place is close to shore, but it's going to be tough to get everything down there."

A short, bulky man with his hair tied high on his head swung over the railing of the closest building. Talia instinctively grabbed the crown swinging from her belt.

The man studied the group. "You're a bit early for beach visitors. Do you have a reservation?"

Talia cleared her throat, gaining the man's attention. "I am Talia Highwind." She swallowed hard, still finding it difficult to use her new name. Though it did make it easier to hide who she was in this part of the world. "We're here to hire a group of Manta Rays for deep-sea fishing."

Ial had thought of the clever ruse. Talia hoped she sounded believable.

The man, who hadn't given his name, gripped his belt tighter as his body tensed. "Braiden," he called.

A young man, more bone than flesh, hung over the railing of the nearest house. "What?"

"Don't 'what' me. Do your job. Check the books for our next deep-sea trip."

"Lieutenant, I haven't split the fees for this week yet. We can't just let . . ." Braiden's mouth went slack as his gaze fell on Talia. "I'll see what I can do."

No sooner had his head disappeared into the building than two more men jumped out the back and took off at a run toward the shore.

Nyna planted her staff on the ground beside Talia. "What's going on?"

The lieutenant jumped at the aggressive movement. He bowed to Talia. "I'm sure Braiden can find someone available to host a tour."

Prince Aleck ripped a piece of paper from a pillar. "Maybe this has something to do with our unfriendly welcome?"

Dew took the paper from him. "Princess Talia Winterlaus has been abducted by enemies of Tarbin. If seen, please contact the royal guard. Two hundred fifty gold pieces for any information that leads to our princess's freedom."

Aleck rubbed his bearded chin. "I'm not an enemy of Tarbin."

Talia's face flushed in anger. "By the Light, why can't King Roland just let me be?" She turned to the lieutenant. "Please call back your messengers. I have not been abducted. I'm on a vital mission."

Guard Parnim whispered loud enough for Talia to make out. "We should not be involved in the affairs of a foreign government, my Prince. We don't even have trade agreements signed yet."

Guard Traneck tugged on his beard. "We should go home now, before a war starts and we have to choose sides in a conflict we're ill-prepared for."

Aleck yanked his arm back. "I am your prince, and you will do as I command. Or you can go back to your families and *pretend* our people can remain separate from everything else happening in the world. Our complacency does not serve us well. I'm needed to open the shield protecting the Machine. I won't allow the magical peoples around the world to perish because I was scared of a vengeful king."

Onlookers were gathering on balconies all the way down the road on both sides. More than one pointed. The whispers were so loud, they almost drowned out the ocean waves. A group of armed guards jogged down the main road.

Talia paced in front of the party. Should they hop back on their horses and canter the other way? The sea had a wide shore. They could enter from any point, right? The Husbandry School was only twenty miles or so down the coast. Maybe the master there would understand the importance of the Recharging?

"Ial? My son, is that you?" A stout old man, no taller than the husbandry guardian, approached the party. A dozen or so servants rushed behind to keep up.

Ial released the leather strap around his mare's nose and fell into the man's arms. "Papa!"

The old man gave him a giant squeeze, then ushered his servants forward to tend to the horses and cart. "They will ensure that everything is taken care of while you're visiting our modest town."

Nomyra grabbed the chest from the wagon as the rest of the companions retrieved their weapons and a few choice belongings.

Talia twisted Windall on its chain around her neck. The guards were only a few blocks away.

She held her hand out to the old man. "It's wonderful to meet the father of one of my guardians. I'm Talia. Do you mind if we walk as you two catch up?"

"I am Huin Pferd. Welcome to Thurrelrun." The old man kept one arm around the shoulders of his son as he shook Talia's hand vigorously.

The lieutenant grabbed the old man's shoulder and backed him away from the rest of the party. Talia shook her head at Ial as he reached for the hilt of his sword.

Huin patted the lieutenant's hand. "Torent, what kind of greeting is this for a guardian of Tarbin and his charge?"

Torent scratched his neck. "Look, Huin. Having a guardian for a son has brought you fortune, and many in this town still honor your sacrifice. But Ial failed to protect the princess. Your time at the top of the food chain has ended."

The old man's face grew dark. He jabbed a finger into Torent's chest, forcing the lieutenant backward. "You do not get to talk about my son that way. Does the princess appear to be compromised in any way?"

Talia curtsied in her most ladylike manner, all the while wanting to punch the lieutenant in the face and get out of there.

"Well, no, but she didn't even introduce herself as the princess. She's obviously been brainwashed or something."

Huin poked Torent one more time for good measure. "May the God of the Sea break that stubborn paranoia of yours. I'm taking my son and the rest of his party to the big house. You'll know where to find us when the royal guards get here."

Torent sighed in obvious relief. "That sounds reasonable, Huin." He waved his men to the back of the party. "But I'm sending them for extra security." He leaned toward Talia. "Unless, Princess, you'd like to come with me. I can ensure your safety." He gave Aleck a pointed glare.

Talia had had enough. "I am no longer a princess of Tarbin. I am Talia Highwind, True Heir to Raqmu and Bright One of the Recharging." She ignored the lieutenant's shocked expression as she turned from side to side, wondering which direction to take. Storming off had a lackluster effect when she didn't know which way to go.

Huin took her elbow and glided her under one of the houses. "This way, my dear. You must be famished. My cook can prepare you the best stuffed halibut you've ever eaten. You're in for a treat." He grabbed Ial with his other hand. "And you have to tell me about your adventures. I thought I'd never see you again. I can't wait to catch up."

Huin Pferd kept up the constant banter all the way from the crowded street to a large house built on a natural bluff overlooking the sea. Talia couldn't believe the father of her quietest companion could so easily chatter on for so long.

Another servant opened the door before Huin had to slow his pace to enter. The old man ushered everyone inside. As the first guard lifted a foot to cross the threshold, Huin slammed the door shut. He yelled through the wood, "You can wait outside. This is family business."

The guards stomped on the porch, but they didn't try to enter. Apparently, the old man still held some pull in Thurrelrun.

"Thank you, Mr. Pferd."

He patted Talia's hand. "Please, call me Huin."

His rushed speed through the house made Talia jog to keep up. "Huin, I'm grateful that you saved us from immediate arrest, but we really need to get our hands on some Manta Rays."

Just ahead, the servant that had opened the front door dragged a carpet out of their path.

"I believe you." Huin stopped in the middle of the room and waved at Naul. "Come, big guy, help me lift this thing. I left my muscles with your horses, and I can't budge this salt-blasted thing on my own."

Naul accepted the handle Huin had pulled from between the floorboards. His muscles strained as he lifted a trapdoor.

Huin clapped him on the shoulder. "Well done, lad. Now you go down last so you can close it again." He nodded Ial toward the ladder leading down to a dark chamber below. "You first, my boy. There are torches on the wall, with strikers."

Ial slid down the ladder as if he were on a ship. Nyna followed. Talia took one rung at a time. She adjusted the crown, which had shifted to the front of her belt and bounced painfully against her knees. She had no idea what was going on and felt foolish for following a person she had never met. Her trust in Ial kept her moving forward.

Ial lit the first torch and handed it to Nyna.

Talia scratched her chin. The rough-hewn chamber had shelves of wine and baskets of root vegetables. The sound of crashing waves was amplified by the stone walls, sounding like they were trying to get in.

Huin's feet slapped the ground just as Naul slammed the trapdoor shut. A shuffling upstairs told Talia the servant was re-covering the entrance with the rug.

Huin clapped his hands. "Much better. Now you said something about Manta Rays?"

With his nose almost plastered against one of the walls, Rodianiari stood completely still. "I can hear it."

Priestess Nomyra set the chest by her feet and inspected the wall. "I didn't think any more of these gateways existed."

Rodianiari held his hands up and smiled an eerie expression. "I have not seen one of these in centuries. I also believed them to all be closed."

"What to be closed?" Dew pushed against the solid wall with one fist.

Nomyra wrinkled her noise at the cultural guardian. "A lifetime of experience and research cannot be replaced with a couple books."

"Shall we?" Rodianiari held his hand up for the priestess.

She adjusted her Krag ring, then placed her hand on his palm. The elf shivered. He closed his fingers, and the two walked straight through the solid wall.

Gregor squeezed Talia's hand. "By the Light, they just walked through a wall."

Aleck leaped in excitement. "My turn." He ran after the priestess and elf.

Huin held up his hand in protest. "Wait, you need—"

Aleck's head whacked into the cliff and bounced off. Talia leaped forward and caught him before he could dash himself on the rocks at his feet. His guards fell to their knees at his side as a nasty gash on his forehead slickened with blood.

Yanking on his beard, Guard Traneck turned the prince's chin to face him. "What more proof do you need that we don't belong here?"

"Don't let them get to you." Gregor helped Aleck to his feet while Nyna pressed a cloth to the dwarf's head. "Women love scars. You won't be able to beat those dwarf gals off you."

Guard Parnim scowled at Gregor. "We don't beat our women."

Gregor blanched. "I don't mean actually beat . . . never mind."

Aleck took the cloth from Nyna and tried to stand up straight. He tilted to one side, forcing Guard Parnim to grab his elbow.

Talia felt the wall again. It was solid. How did the others get through? She rubbed the damp skin of her forehead, exhausted from the day and not in the mood for puzzles.

"Look, Prince Aleck is bleeding. We need to get him somewhere he can lay down."

Huin shook his head. "The tall couple made it through instinctively. How was I to know the rest of you didn't understand?"

Dew stood on one leg, deep in concentration. "Maybe the elf sensed whatever magic must be in play?"

Huin smacked his knee. "A what now? I thought they were extinct."

"Kind of like mermaids?" Ial exchanged a knowing look with his father.

"Ah . . . I see your point." Huin pushed the party back from the opening. "You have to step on a precise alignment of stones to make the wall permeable."

The old man exaggerated his steps as he hopped from stone to stone in a specific pattern. Talia didn't remember Nomyra and Rodianiari using such exaggerated motions.

Naul shook his head in disgust. "By ever-cursed Darkness, I'll never make it through. My stumbling feet betray me again."

Gregor scoffed at the weapons guardian. "I saw you dancing with that girl in the last town. Just imagine her hips in your hands."

Nyna easily hopped across the correct stones, Ial on her heels. The room got darker as more torches disappeared to the other side.

Parnim, then Aleck, then Traneck, cursing the entire time, walked through.

Huin peeked back through the wall. "You can walk through if you go with someone who is hitting the proper stones, big guy."

Dew squeezed Naul's hand. "Let me be your grace. This way."

She hit the proper stones with pointed toe and leaped through the magic wall, her confidence contagious. Still holding her hand, Naul rushed through with a war cry.

Talia soaked up the quiet for a minute. She took a step forward but was stopped by Gregor's hand on her elbow.

His roguish smile melted her heart. "You know, we could take just a few minutes for ourselves. This might be the only time we're alone for a while."

Talia lifted the torch up and out of the way as he wrapped his arms around her waist. Her heart beat so loud, it surely echoed against the stone walls. Talia's mind swirled with the possibility. She wasn't a princess anymore. She could be with whomever she wanted, right?

Gregor pulled her close with a desperate heat.

Pain stabbed Talia's thigh. At the same time, Gregor cried out in shock. Jumping apart, they looked down to see what had bitten them.

The Tarbin crown swung from Talia's waist like an omen. Talia sighed. She didn't know why she even tried. The True Heir didn't have time for personal relationships. The Bright One had a destiny to fulfill. Love was for ordinary people. As Gregor rubbed the taut muscles under his leggings where the Key had almost impaled him, Talia wished she could be ordinary.

Talia shoved the torch into Gregor's hand. "I'll see you on the other side."

# CHAPTER FIFTEEN

COLD SPLASHED her foot before she realized she had made it through. Aleck was trying to help Naul up from the slippery ground. Talia laughed at the ludicrous scene of the petite dwarf assisting the giant human to his feet.

Gregor touched her shoulder, his wrinkled brow asking if she was all right. Talia couldn't talk, but she motioned to the mess in front of her.

Water pooled away from Rodianiari as though it was repelled by him somehow. "Not that it isn't fun to camp out in a dank cave when traveling across the world, but may I ask why we had to hide in the dark like dwar—"

Parnim and Traneck cracked their knuckles in unison.

The elf didn't blanch at the threat, but he did sigh and choose to take a different approach. "Like rats, instead of heading straight for our destination?"

Talia was grateful she didn't need to break up any extra dwarf–elf incivility. As she had just learned, being with her put everyone else in danger. She didn't need internal bickering to complicate the conditions further.

Nomyra patted Rodianiari's arm. "Apparently, King Roland wants his daughter back."

Talia marveled at the odd relationship between the elf and the priestess. She supposed it was only natural for the two most conceited, self-righteous members to find something in common. Nevertheless, the alignment gave Talia the creeps.

Dew crossed her arms. "To face trial for treason, maybe."

Talia shifted the Key across her waist. "More likely, Tanin wants the crown back and convinced Fath—the king to offer a reward for my return."

Huin shook his head. "Actually, King Roland believes you've been magicked by Priestess Nomyra to take his kingdom from Tanin and rule it with all sorts of oddities beside you."

"Oddities!" Rodianiari grew two inches as he rose on his toes. His arms curved out, and his face reddened.

Talia expected to see his hair stand straight out like a cat's. "King Roland is not the most understanding man. But he can't stop the Recharging or the Great Awakening. Right now, we just have to keep going." Talia's feet squished in her sodden shoes. "Thank you for saving us from a brawl in the streets, Huin, but where exactly *have* you taken us?"

The stout man moved with ease along the slippery, uneven floor. "It's quite a tale. We need to move away from the entrance. Though they can't see us and can't pass through unless they know the trick, they can still hear us. Last thing we need is someone stumbling through on accident and the entire village discovering my cave."

The sound of Aleck's excited squeaks filled the tunnels ahead. The echo made the words indecipherable. Uncertain whether he had found something fun or deadly, Talia jogged ahead, one hand on her sword, with Dew keeping pace beside her.

The passageway opened into a large cave, much like in the Krimmel Kingdom, except this cave smelled like brine and dead fish and the ceiling was studded with stalactites. Light danced among the spikes like a family of fairies playing hide-and-seek. A huge pool of water rocked back and forth in the center of the cavern.

Aleck's squeal drew Talia's attention from the sparkling water. "Where is the light coming from? I see no mirrors or holes for the sun."

Huin waved his hand at the shimmering pool. "We're not that far from the surface. The Light travels on the water to come play in the cave. She comes and goes with the tide. When Darkness comes, she returns to the sky to give us Her messages."

Rodianiari picked at his fingernails. For an elf who had spent the last thousand years sleeping in a tree, he certainly didn't like getting dirty. "Is that what you truly believe?" he asked the old man, but Talia felt the question was directed at her.

"I have seen nothing to sway me from my belief." Huin didn't seem upset by the elf's tone. He turned to his son. "Now, come to me, boy. I thought to never see you again."

Ial grasped his father in a tight hug. Talia thought she saw a tear on the husbandry guardian's cheek. "You don't have to be alone anymore, Papa. My circumstances have changed." He glanced at Talia and away. "I will always serve the True Heir, but we have been released from our pledges, which means we can visit, and have families." He reached his hand out to Nyna, who squeezed his fingers. "Let me introduce you to my friends." He started with Talia and worked his way around the guardians, saving Nyna for last.

Nyna managed to tuck herself under his arm, even though she was taller. He pulled her close, love shining in his eyes.

Talia chanced a quick glance at Gregor, who stared unflinchingly at her. Immediately regretting the decision, she looked toward the water instead.

Traneck held the back of Aleck's belt as the prince leaned precariously over the edge.

Aleck cocked his head. "By Thoretick's beard, the lizard down there is tiny. How are you ever going to keep your cave protected?" He seamlessly stood and shook his guard off.

Offering a proper hand to Huin, Aleck introduced himself. "I'm Prince Aleck Stoneworth of the Krimmel Dwarves, and these are my guards, Parnim and Traneck."

Huin shook the dwarf's hand without hesitation. "It's a pleasure to meet you, Prince Aleck." He rustled his son with a jovial elbow. "You know, your great-grandfather was a dwarf."

"I knew it." Naul snapped his fingers. The quick movement made him slip on a rock, but he caught his balance by hugging a stalagmite.

"You are all very safe here. There is no way in or out except by the magical passage or through this pool, which no human could traverse without drowning, even in low tide." Huin laughed, the outburst an obnoxious echo in the closed chamber. "They think I'm consorting with mermaids. I only wish I were."

Suddenly melancholy, Huin approached the water's edge. The Light gained an orange undertone as sunset approached.

Ial's father stared into the rocking water. "This is where she brought me. After . . ." He squeezed his son's shoulder. "Well, you know.

"One night, when I was feeling particularly down, I discovered something by accident." Huin pulled the lid from a large barrel. The overwhelming stench of dead fish rushed into the closed chamber.

Parnim held his thin beard over his nose. "Put it back."

Talia gagged in a very unroyal manner. "What is that?"

"Food." Ial stuck his hand into the disgusting bucket, without a wince, and tossed a handful into the darkening water.

Talia took an unconscious step back as she heard a splash. Dew and Naul moved closer to Talia. The weapons guardian's green face did not give her much confidence in his ability to protect her at the moment.

Huin threw in another large handful, resulting in more splashing and an odd flap against the stone at the edge of the pool. Ial bent down and stuck his hand into the water.

If he wasn't frightened, she certainly shouldn't be. Talia grabbed the torch from Dew and weaved through the stalagmites to stand beside Ial. Her stomach twisted as the water writhed with flaps of flesh. Then she remembered night swims at the Husbandry School during her two years of study there.

"Trained Manta Rays."

Dew crouched down as well and imitated Ial's cautious petting. "I've never seen one in real life. I thought they'd be bigger."

Naul shook his head as he stayed back from the water. "I'm not sure they'd be big enough to hold me."

"You'd be surprised what these fish can carry in the water. I've tied three up to a large sailing boat, and they were able to tow it back to dock." Huin plopped the lid back on the rotting fish barrel. "These beauties came to visit me after I had dumped my uneaten dinner in the saltwater for a week. Must have smelled the rotting food. After training these babies my whole life, the great Manta Ray can still surprise me."

He rinsed his hands in the water. The largest Manta Ray Talia had ever seen brushed his hands and flapped. It reminded Talia of her father's hunting dogs. They were always pleased to see him.

"I didn't realize they could be so affectionate." Talia rubbed the underside of one. There were so many rolling on top of each other, she couldn't tell where one ended and the next began.

"They communicate differently, but they're definitely as intelligent as horses." Ial sat on the edge with his legs in the water, completely unafraid of the beasts.

Gregor looked over his shoulder. "What about the spike on their tail? I've heard that thing can be a doozy."

"We break them off when they're very little." Huin's voice echoed from the back of the cave. "Though some of those boys might be wild. You should probably be careful."

Naul tugged on Talia's elbow to get her to move back. She obliged him, though it annoyed her. Why did her guardians earn freedom, but she still had to be protected all the time?

"That's quite enough." Rodianiari snapped his fingers, and the Manta Rays settled down. "The noise is absolutely uncalled for."

Huin dragged over large flexible tubing. "That's quite a thing you can do. Maybe you'd be interested in helping me train."

The elf's face clearly said that was never going to happen.

The old man dropped the load next to the barrel. "So, are we ready?"

Gregor moved one with his foot. "What are those?"

"Breathing tubes." Ial showed the lordling the jagged end. "This part anchors in the swim bladder, where the Manta Rays store air. You breathe from the other end." He put his mouth on the straw-like part.

Aleck took a huge breath through one. "Why do the fish have pockets of air? Seems pointless."

Nomyra looked impatient with the dwarf's constant questions. "The Light gives us means to traverse our entire planet. We never know where we'll need to go to ensure the Dark does not consume us."

Huin shrugged. "Maybe. Or maybe Vinta Himself offered a gift of His own."

Nomyra rolled her eyes. Talia hid her own surprise. She wasn't sure how Huin could believe in both the old gods and the Light.

"How do we hold on without swirling off into the abyss?" Naul looked more frightened of this next step than he had when the dragon awoke.

Ial's father dropped lengths of rope tied to a flat piece of padded netting. "The reverse saddle. The part you would think you'd sit on goes under the belly of the Manta. Then you ride standing up, using the ropes to balance and fight the current."

Grabbing a reverse saddle and a tube, Aleck marched to the water. "I'm ready."

Parnim tried to hold Aleck back. "But, my Prince, even if these creatures are completely full of breathable air, they couldn't carry enough to get us to the mermaid stronghold, awaken a representative, and return without running out of fresh air."

Traneck nodded. "Think of the cave-in the year of the floods. The city of Hinterel was blocked behind a wall of rock. Half the citizens suffocated before we could breach it and provide a flow of fresh air."

"He's got a point," Naul agreed.

Nomyra stood in a huff. "Has your cultural guardian done none of her research?"

Dew's hands curled into fists at her side. "Of course I have. But it's not like I've been hiding in my private chambers memorizing everything about the Recharging and the races involved."

Talia came to her defense. "Since you engineered the entire thing, even my conception, you'd think you would have taught us what we needed to know so far. Don't attack my friends because of your inadequacy."

Nomyra raised an eyebrow as she turned to the elf. "Such a temper tantrum."

Rodianiari released a mirthless laugh. Talia found the sound familiar but brushed it off as her anger grew.

Ial broke the tension. "Mermaids breathe like we do. Their underwater structures are airtight and full of many plants that keep the air fresh. We'll be fine."

"That's my boy." Huin tapped along the water's edge with the heel of his boot. Every time his heel hit, a Manta Ray jumped from the water to lay mostly on the rock, giving Ial easy access to strap them into the reverse saddles.

Huin crossed his arms. "The real question is how do we know where to go? There's a lot of water to cover out there and no landmarks to guide us."

Dew smiled and reached for the chest. "As long as it works like it says in the tome . . ."

Nomyra bent to grab the other handle. They placed the whole chest in the water. The driftwood surface glowed an iridescent green, which spread through the water like a dye. They released the chest, and it started to sink. The chest traveled through the waterway to the ocean outside as if something called to it, leaving a trail of green glowing light behind.

Dew clapped her hands. "The chest was used to summon guests to the mermaid's North Sea Palace."

Talia jumped up and took the reins of a Manta. "Let's go before we lose it."

# CHAPTER SIXTEEN

A PALACE MADE ENTIRELY of seashells loomed in the depths of the ocean, lit only by the glowing chest sitting at the front gate. As the ocean grew dark, the group had followed the relic through the murky water until they hit the calm of the deep.

Talia's lungs felt tight as she almost forgot to breathe. She took her turn at the air bladder straw, then handed it to Nyna, who balanced beside her. Talia was determined not to do anything foolish this time and injure the medicinal guardian. More than once, though, they both almost got knocked off when Nyna reached to grab a sample of a plant. With air in such short supply, Talia was unable to yell at Nyna for her innate curiosity, so she settled with throwing her meaningful looks instead.

Now that the party hovered in front of such an astounding sight, Talia realized how stale the air had gotten. They didn't have much time to waste. However, Talia couldn't see a door to enter the palace.

A huge window made up at least half the structure in the front. The view must have been stunning during the day, with all sorts of sea life swimming by. Right now, the view was in shadow except for the glowing chest, which floated just off the sandy bottom where a grand entrance should have been.

Nomyra released her Manta Ray and swam to the chest. Rodianiari, who had become her shadow, followed behind her.

The oppressive darkness, along with the weight of the water pushing on Talia's chest as she held her breath, built panic in Talia. She squeezed the rope with all her strength to fight the urge to let go and swim to the surface. If she got lost in the darkness, would she even know which way was up? It was so hard to tell how far down they were; she didn't know if she could hold her breath long enough to reach the surface. For a moment, Talia feared the Darkness had tricked her into this part of the journey so she would drown in His embrace and the Recharging would never happen.

A pounding sound drew Talia's attention before a full-on panic attack could take over. Nomyra was slamming a piece of coral against a large conch shell. When Talia caught her eye, the priestess pointed to the huge conch shell, then swam under it.

That must be the way in.

Taking her turn at the breathing tube, Talia felt the fresh air calm her heartbeat. She directed her Manta Ray into a tight circle slightly above the rest of her party, to make sure everyone was paying attention. Then she kicked off her mount and swam for the Light, away from the Dark.

She quickly found that determining which way was up wouldn't be much of a problem. She had to push with all her strength to go down. Her ears throbbed, and her lungs burned, but there was no going back now. She grasped the conch and ducked under the seashell.

Panic gripped her as the light from the glowing chest made everything in the tunnel pitch black. She didn't know where to go.

Her lungs begged her to breathe in. She pushed some air out to lessen the pain. The bubbles flowed along the ceiling of the tunnel. A few feet down, they swooshed up and disappeared. Talia kicked off the sandy bottom, following her expelled air and trying not to think about how badly her chest burned.

Her head popped up into a dimly lit chamber. She sucked in so much air, she thought her lungs would burst. Her eyes sparkled as Rodianiari hauled her onto the smooth, slick floor. The elf was much stronger than his wiry limbs suggested.

She didn't take time to be thankful but dropped onto her stomach and hauled Nyna up. One after another, she and Rodianiari pulled up the party.

Talia took a quick head count. She was missing some. "Where are the dwarves?"

Gregor scraped the saltwater off his arms the best he could. "Parnim let go of our Manta after I did. He was right behind me." He dropped to the floor to look through the tunnel.

All Talia could see was the green light from the still-glowing chest. No dwarf-shaped shadows swam toward the air.

Nyna plastered her face against one of the convex windows. "They're out here. Something is snapping at them. The Mantas are swimming erratically."

"I'll go get them." Ial took a deep breath and exhaled. Then took a few quick in-and-out breaths.

Huin followed suit. "I can help."

Gregor peered over Nyna's head. "It looks like crabs. Giant ones."

A high-pitched voice seemed to fly into the entryway, growing louder as it came. "I got 'em. I got 'em. I got 'em."

Talia scraped her fingernails on the stone as she suddenly slipped backward. She kicked at the hands gripping her feet, until she realized it was Naul pulling her out of the way. A skinny figure with bright pink hair dove off the railing and into the water with barely a splash. Her strange appearance didn't stop Ial and Huin from jumping in right after her. Talia stood with Naul's help and ran to Nyna at the window.

"Who was that?" Talia pressed her face against the glass. The convex shape provided an excellent view of the front of the palace.

Aleck clung to his Manta as it rose too quickly in a water column. A crab as big as a horse bounced off the seafloor and snapped at the tip of the Manta's tail. Traneck tumbled off the bucking winged fish.

"Please, not again," Dew whispered.

A tear fell from Talia's eye. They couldn't lose the dwarf guards again. The whole race would have been better off if Talia had never involved them in her lunatic quests. "I can't just stand here."

As she turned to dive back through the tunnel, Nyna grabbed her arm. "No, wait. Look!"

The skinny figure burst out of the tunnel. Her skin shimmered with pearlescent scales. Her legs molded together to form one muscular fin. Just before the crab could snap Traneck in half, the mermaid smacked her tail against a large shell embedded in the ground. The giant crustacean pulled its claws in and crept toward her like a reprimanded guard dog. She pointed beyond the palace, and the monstrous crab scurried out of Talia's view.

Aleck's Manta didn't calm down with the crustacean's absence. The mermaid swam up after it. She sandwiched one of the Manta's wings between her arms. With a twist, she flipped the entire panicked fish upside down, holding it steady until it stopped struggling. Aleck hung on the back, caught in the straps of the reverse saddle. Talia had no idea what the mermaid said, but Aleck nodded and took a long breath from the bladder tube.

Once Aleck was untangled from the twisted reverse saddle, the mermaid flapped her tail strongly enough to send the floating seaweed into a flurry.

Dew whooped. "Go Ial and Huin!"

Huin had grabbed the unconscious dwarf from the seafloor while Ial wrestled Traneck to the tunnel. The humans headed toward fresh air as quickly as they could.

The mermaid rushed past them as if they were standing still, carrying Aleck. After plopping him onto the floor, she flipped in a circle, her powerful tail splashing saltwater over the already damp floor, and dove back out.

The half human, half fish rushed back into view and scooped up Parnim and Huin.

It would have taken Talia the same amount of time to walk to the tunnel exit as it did for the mermaid to swim twice that distance dragging two full-grown people with her.

"Two more," the mermaid said before she disappeared into the tunnel again.

Nyna slid to a halt beside the unconscious guard. "Come on, Parnim. Breathe." She turned him on his side and smacked his back as hard as she could. Water poured from his mouth.

Talia brushed a tear away. "This Dark-cursed Recharging better be worth it."

Returning through the tunnel, the mermaid slid Traneck over the floor. With a rounded leap, she dove back under the water.

Traneck coughed and took in a ragged breath. "Prince Aleck."

"I'm here." The prince crawled to Parnim's side as Nyna tried to resuscitate him.

"Come on, you stubborn dwarf!" Nyna shouted. "It's just breathing. You've been doing it your whole life." She grabbed her side for a bag that wasn't there. It had been left in the cave. There hadn't seemed to be a reason to bring a bag that would just get flooded on an underwater journey. She pulled at her drenched hair. "I need my smelling salts."

Gregor turned in a circle. "Where's Ial?"

Terror etched across Nyna's face. Talia's blood ran cold.

Before either could panic, Ial's head popped through the opening. "I could use a hand here."

Gregor reached down and helped him pull the chest to the surface, while Naul grabbed Ial's wrist.

Rodianiari stepped back toward the stairway, covering his nose. "What is that smell?"

Ial yanked a piece of seaweed off his ankle. "I think it's this. The chest got tangled as I dragged it through the tunnel."

Dew stopped him before he could drop the stinky weed into the water. "Wait." Dew took the oily vine to Nyna. "Will this work?"

"It can't hurt." Nyna snapped a fresh leaf in half.

The oozing plasma inside dripped onto the stone by Parnim's nose. Talia resisted the urge to cover her own face. The smell was so rotten, she could taste it.

With sudden strength, Parnim pushed back from Nyna and rolled over. He spit up more water and breathed in short, painful puffs of air.

Aleck knelt beside him. "Welcome back to the Light, my friend."

"Where did the mermaid go?" Nomyra stood beside the chest like she wanted to pick it up. Talia wondered why she hesitated.

"Here I am." The mermaid held her body up above the water with the strong movement of her tail. Her scales shimmered in the green light of the still-glowing chest. Sitting down gracefully on the edge, she splashed her fin casually in the water. "Hello, and welcome to my home. I'm sorry about the crabs. They're on guard duty, and you're obviously not merpeople."

She pulled her tail out of the water and flapped it once against the stone. The solid fin separated into two pieces. The scales morphed into a shimmery skirt and matching top with long sleeves. She rose to her feet and set the chest on a pedestal where the front door should have been.

Talia took a moment to anchor herself in her foreign surroundings as she'd been taught as a member of the royal court. The staircase, with the smooth banister the mermaid had slid down, twisted up from the entryway, which was wide enough for an entourage of guests. Woven around each rail, a bright green plant with oval leaves hung over the sides. The steps themselves were made from small seashells fused with some sort of white binding. The entryway was made of the same material but polished to a much smoother finish. If it hadn't been the middle of the night, the windows all around the room would have permitted a generous amount of sunlight to penetrate the palace. She wondered where the stairs led.

"I am Talia Winterlaus," she said, hoping the native would reciprocate.

Nomyra cleared her throat.

Talia blanched. "They call me the True Heir and the Bright One. We've come to awaken a mermaid representative to participate in the Recharging, but I see you've already awoken."

The mermaid opened the chest. The glow ceased, throwing the large entryway into momentary darkness.

Bit by bit, tiny beacons of soft blue light popped up around the ceiling and walls. Nyna poked at one of the water-filled jars, causing a glowing jellyfish to swish from one side to the other. The living lanterns were spread across the large welcoming room. As her eyes adjusted, Talia realized the softer light gave the place a more romantic feel.

Huin stepped forward, almost touching the mermaid. "You're the one. You're the one who saved me."

The young magical took the old man's face in her hands. "The Stars commanded me to save the father, for he would be needed to bring back my people."

Huin put his hands over her much-paler ones. "The father?"

She looked around him at Ial. The husbandry guardian took a step back.

"But that was just a dream. Mermaids aren't . . ." Ial looked at his father, then the mermaid, then Talia.

"Real?" Dew finished his sentence.

The mermaid made a high-pitched squeaky noise that could have been interpreted as giggling.

"I don't know why you didn't use the rings." The mermaid pulled down the lining in the top of the chest, exposing a dozen stone rings embedded in the wood. "These will help you breathe on your way home." She plucked them out, one by one, and piled them into Talia's hands. "Oh, and I'm Jura. It's very nice to meet you. I would love to chat, but not until after the Great Awakening. I'm sure you understand."

Jura pulled the huge sapphire from the protective felt and marched up the stairs.

# CHAPTER SEVENTEEN

"WHAT JUST HAPPENED?" Talia spun on her heels with the cold rings in her grasp. She didn't have anywhere to put them.

Nomyra took one and held it up to the dim light from the jellyfish. "Huh. I didn't know those were in there."

Rodianiari was cleaning his fingernails again. Talia wondered how they seemed to get so dirty all the time. "I didn't either."

Talia didn't believe him.

Dew studied another one. "I wish I had the tome with me to search for them. I'm not sure how I missed that part, but of course, our ancestors would have considered the inability of mundanes to reach this far below the surface."

"What do they do?" Gregor almost took the one from Nomyra, but her stern glare caused him to redirect his hand to Talia's stash. He slipped one on his finger.

"Don't—"

Nomyra's warning came too late, but nothing happened. Gregor shrugged.

As he stepped away, staring at the ring, his face turned red. He threw a hand to his throat, and his eyes bulged out. Nomyra pushed him into the water.

"Why would you . . . ?" Talia slid to the edge of the water but couldn't figure out how to jump in and rescue Gregor with her hands full of stone rings.

Under the surface, he waved up at her nonchalantly. He took a dramatic breath of water into his lungs and smacked his chest like he had just won a game of Five Ball.

Was he breathing? He certainly didn't look distressed.

Talia motioned Naul over and dropped all but one ring into his hand. He tucked them into a pocket of his tunic as she slipped the remaining ring onto her much-smaller finger. As soon as it passed her last knuckle, it shrank to fit snuggly. She shook her hand. It didn't budge. A tightness in her chest reminded Talia that she should probably dive into the water.

"Talia, we don't know how long this effect lasts. What if—"

Dew's voice disappeared as Talia's ears filled with sea water.

At first, she held her breath, instinct making her unsure of her next move. Gregor tugged on her elbow and swam a circle around her. His teasing annoyed her. Gregor wasn't going to win this battle. With a look at the small surface hole, she knew her guardians were right there if she needed help. She closed her eyes and took a deep breath of water.

A chill filled her insides. Usually, sharp pain stabbed her head when water penetrated her nose on a clumsy dive. This time, as the saltwater filled her lungs and nose, the uncomfortable tightness morphed into a loving embrace. She laughed, the sound foreign but not unpleasant.

A vibration, both dull and sharp, reverberated from the floor above. Talia squinted up through the opening as she treaded water a few feet below. Nomyra's impatient face pierced the shadows. Talia felt like a chastised schoolgirl, but she also knew the priestess was right. She didn't have time to play around. She had to find out what the mermaid, Jura, meant when she said she wasn't going.

She grabbed Gregor's hand to pull him up with her, and he swirled to her and into a tight embrace, like a fancy move at a formal ball. Shocked by his closeness, Talia felt her cheeks flush as her nose brushed his. The twinkle in his eyes reminded her of everything she adored. She wanted nothing more than to press her lips to his and swim away into the currents. Away from her duties and titles and prophecies. Though her body floated weightlessly, her mind was still bogged down with heavy responsibilities.

She pushed off toward the entryway. The shock of cold air on her face woke her from her momentary fantasy. She didn't have time for herself, but it would come.

"Hold your breath." Nomyra's voice still sounded as though it were filtered through water.

Ial and Dew each took a hand and pulled Talia to the surface. She felt like a fish flopping on the shore. The air no longer welcomed her in its embrace. She was shocked by how quickly her body had adjusted to the new environment. Gregor landed right beside her.

Aleck bent to look Talia in the face. "Interesting. You could breathe the water, couldn't you? We really could have used those earlier. I wonder if they work in fresh water. Can we borrow them to explore the underwater sections of our kingdom? We'll give them back."

"My Prince." Guard Traneck guided him back as Talia turned blue.

Dew looked cross and anxious at the same time. "Take the ring off."

Talia yanked the ring from her finger, but she still couldn't breathe.

"Cough!" Nyna yelled, smacking Talia on the back.

Naul repeated the motion on Gregor.

Talia pushed her chest with all her might, her free hand wrapped around her gut with the effort. Water poured from her lungs as if she were vomiting seawater, but there was no bile flavor. She stuttered a few more coughs as she realized how cold she was.

She tried to stand. A sudden light-headedness overtook her. Aleck held her steady as she teetered on the slick floor. She smiled down at him, feeling a bit drunk.

Gregor winked at her, making her blush. "By the Stars above, we need to do that again."

Naul shook the rings in his palms. "So, everyone take a ring and we go home?"

Nomyra crossed her arms, her eyes narrowed to slits. "We must have a mermaid first."

Talia squeezed water from her hair and stared up the steps Jura had taken. "Well, let's go talk her into coming with us. She obviously doesn't know about the extra barrier to Raqmu. Otherwise, why would she refuse to come with?"

As she climbed the stairs, seashells sticking up from each step bit into Talia's feet. At least it wasn't slippery.

Naul cursed behind her. "Stupid sharp pieces."

Nomyra jogged to catch up with Talia. "If she wishes to stay, we can awaken another, but we'll need the sapphire she stole."

Talia had the distinct impression that Nomyra was more worried about the sapphire than the mermaid.

At the top of the stairs, Talia froze. Nyna bumped into her, forcing her to slide a few feet farther into what should have been a glamorous ballroom. Stunning chandeliers hung every few feet, crowded with candles all ablaze. The light was almost stifling compared to the dull glow of the lower levels. A reflective material lined the walls like the inside of oyster shells. Though if that was what had been used, they must have consumed billions of them to get enough material to cover those surfaces.

The same convex windows from the entryway were set into the walls from floor to ceiling, building a kind of pearl-necklace pattern. When the Light's Daughter pierced the Dark, the ballroom must have sparkled like a Star sitting under the sea. Deep red foliage surrounded each window. The air in the room was easy to breathe, if a bit stale, as though a window needed to be opened after a long winter.

Piled against the walls were stacks of chairs and round tables. Armoires protected wine glasses of all shapes, along with plates and boxes of silverware. The smooth floor must have held hundreds of dancing dignitaries in its time. Talia hoped she'd get to see it all decked out someday.

The far side of the room was shadowed in complete darkness. A shuffling alerted Talia to someone, or something, moving on that side. Huin rushed past her and disappeared, quickly followed by the dwarves. Naul, Gregor, and Dew stayed close by her side, while Nyna and Ial spread out to check the far walls. Two stoic statues, Nomyra and Rodianiari followed behind them, arms clasped out front.

The Key hummed softly as Talia reached the far end of the ballroom. The dark area produced an eerie vibe. Temporarily blind, she knew the crown's reaction, as well as the tingling in her gut, meant the sapphire was here. Talia guessed the mermaid must be close.

"Jura? Can we speak for a mo—ment?" Talia choked on the last word as she took in a huge gap in the structure over her head.

Ial and Nyna rushed to her side.

She knew why this side of the ballroom was thrust into darkness. The chandeliers lay on the floor in pieces. An entire wall of windows had been crushed. The ceiling gaped open as though a sea monster had taken a giant bite. The thought of the hundreds of gallons of water over her head made Talia want to run. She didn't know why the whole place wasn't flooded.

Nomyra picked up a piece of crystal from one of the fallen chandeliers and threw it at the far wall. A shimmer sparked from the point of impact and scattered along the surface, before dissipating at the solid wall.

"An emergency system produces a magical barrier to keep water out of the living areas in case of a breach. After hundreds of years, it's still working." The priestess pursed her lips in appreciation.

"Not for long." Jura leaned against a jagged pillar that should have been between two windows. Instead, it jutted out into nothingness. She splashed the water at her feet.

Rodianiari stared down from the lip of the invisible shield. "Were the sleeping quarters not through a corridor on this side?"

Talia squinted at the elf having such intimate knowledge. How would he know where the sleeping quarters were?

Jura dropped to the floor with a splash. With the huge sapphire cradled in her lap, she threw her upper body over its smooth surface. Her pink hair cascaded over the sapphire. Jura's cries echoed behind Talia but faded to silence above the damage. The effect was eerie.

"Groundquake." Jura couldn't get out another word.

Almost afraid to look, Talia walked through the ankle-deep water to the spot where there must have been a corridor. She shaded her eyes, blocking the ambient light so she could see below. What looked like beds of corral sprawled across the seafloor, though white instead of the bright colors she remembered from her training excursions with the Manta Rays. Otherwise, it all looked normal.

Aleck pressed between Talia and Naul to see. "That building looks like it could still be in good condition. We could use the rings to go have a look."

Talia stared where the dwarf pointed. He was right. She could just make out another large building surrounded by branches that led farther into the darkness. She'd never wished for daytime travel so much in her life. She couldn't see enough.

Then she realized that what she had mistaken for coral was actually a bridge that would have connected this ballroom to the other central building ahead. She still didn't understand, though, why Jura was so upset.

Talia knelt beside her. "We'll fix everything. But we need you to come with us. There's an extra barrier—I'm guessing similar to this one—that blocks the entrance to Raqmu. We need a sample of blood from each sentient race, mundane and magical, to open it. Without them, without you, we won't be able to Recharge our world with the magic needed to awaken your people."

Rodianiari put a hand on Jura's shoulder. Talia hadn't seen him show any affection. The effect was immediate. Jura quieted, though she didn't lift her head or say anything.

"The slumbering chambers are under the collapsed bridge." He looked down at Jura, his dark eyes somehow expressing kindness. "You should have been sleeping with them. How did you escape?"

Talia recalled Rodianiari's reaction when he saw his mutilated kin in the elven aspen forest. If Jura had witnessed the same kind of event, he would understand what she felt better than any of the humans or dwarves.

As though a string pulled her from above, Jura stood in one fluid movement, the sapphire cradled in her grasp. "Well, I'm not leaving them. I can't let the ocean finish what it started."

Jura swirled, her fuchsia hair sizzling against the water barrier. "The seafloor shook with a ferocity I'd never experienced before. Our beds cracked. We had no time to prepare for the onslaught of the saltwater. We don't breathe water, you know."

Talia folded her arms over her stomach. "We know, Jura. I'm so sorry."

"Couldn't be helped." She turned deep purple eyes to Talia. "My father was crushed by a stone. My little brother drowned. The current was strong. So strong, I couldn't keep hold of my mother or my aunt. We swirled in the water as we struggled to reach the palace. It pushed me up and up, but not fast enough to relieve the pain of no air."

Jura turned in tight circles as if reliving the nightmare. Ial grabbed her shoulders, steadying her awkward movement.

"It was you," he said.

"And it was you," she mirrored.

Tears fell from the mermaid's eyes. "I thought I would not live to see the Recharging. I almost didn't want to if my family was gone.

But you were there on a great Manta Ray, like Vinta himself, saving me from the waves."

"I was only fourteen when I brought you to the shore at the Husbandry School. I couldn't believe what I'd found." He pushed her hair out of her face and wiped her cheeks with his hands. "By the time I returned to the beach with help, you were gone. They made fun of me for years after that. Thought I made up the whole thing to distract from the fact that I was out on a Manta Ray before my training day."

"I had to return home and save who I could." Jura broke from his grasp and pointed to a long pipe connecting the ballroom to the remaining sleeping chambers. "This shield is the only thing keeping the survivors from drowning." Strewn across the broken wall were gems that must have been worth a fortune. Jura kicked them aside like so much garbage. "When I had used all the emergency power we had, I thought that was it. That we'd never make it to the Recharging. Then you brought me the sapphire. I must stay."

Huin blinked. "But why did you save me?"

"Two years after the Manta rider saved me, a storm crushed a vessel on the surface overhead." Jura spoke to Huin as if everyone else had left. "I smelled my rescuer on you and knew I had to fulfill my debt. The boy who had saved me deserved to have his father returned to him."

Huin breathed in reverence. "I knew I had not imagined you."

Nomyra tapped her foot impatiently as she always did when someone didn't do as she expected. "Fine. Stay here. The Bright One can easily choose another, but we require the power in that gem."

"But then they will all die." Jura spun with such ferocity, sparks flew from the gem and hit the puddle by Nomyra's feet.

Nomyra screamed as her hair fluffed out like a scared cat's.

Huin held up a hand. "I can stay."

"No, Papa," Ial said.

Nyna put her hand on Ial's shoulder.

"I wouldn't be alive if it wasn't for this lovely lady." Huin held out a hand to Naul. "With one of those water-breathing rings and some guidance on how to work the magic, I'm sure I can keep them safe."

Jura tilted her head. "But it is my duty."

Talia knew a bit about heavy burdens. She knew what words to use. "It is your responsibility to make sure the Recharging occurs and all your people can awaken to swim the seas again. I'm the Bright One, and I choose you. That is your duty."

The mermaid's eyes sparkled with tears once again. Her arms shook as she folded the sapphire against Huin's chest. "You will need this if the structure starts to fail. Put one hand on its surface and the other hand here." She moved his wrinkled fingers to the edge of the shield.

Huin giggled with unfettered glee. "It tickles."

"Now, wish the magic into the shield." Jura nodded her head like it was the easiest thing in the world.

Nomyra spoke up but didn't come any closer, just in case the mermaid attacked again. "It doesn't work that easily for humans, Jura. We are not made of magic."

Huin's face sagged. "I can't help, then?"

"Yes, you can. Do as the mermaid commands." Rodianiari waved away Nomyra's concerns. He came to stand beside the two and put his hand on top of Huin's.

The old man closed his eyes. A ripple cascaded along the shield as it had when Nomyra threw the crystal.

"Beautiful." Aleck turned in a circle as the ripple passed over his head. "Can I try?"

"No." Rodianiari snatched his hand from Huin's and crossed his arms.

Parnim and Traneck stepped in front of the prince. Talia sighed. After the Recharging, she was going to have to find a way to make the elves and dwarves get along. Not be friends necessarily, but at least not constantly want to kill each other. She was sure Aleck would be easy to convince, but judging by the actions of his guards, the rest of his people might be a challenge. And the elves. She'd only met two, and they both loathed anything to do with the dwarves.

However, one problem at a time.

"Jura, are you willing to join us?" Talia offered her most welcoming smile.

Dew's grimace and subtle headshake made Talia tone it down some.

Jura kissed Huin's forehead. "Now let me tell you how to handle the guard crabs."

# CHAPTER EIGHTEEN

The waves at the edge of Tarbinulus Harbor rocked the ship gently as Tanin leaned over the railing. He couldn't stop staring at the doors the cannons would thrust through when they were armed to fire. He thought about having the crew open them and place all the new weaponry in view so his kingdom could appreciate how their heir would defend them.

Rory stood beside him, silent as usual. Tanin enjoyed the weapons guardian's serenity, but he really wanted to talk strategy. He followed his stoic guardian's gaze to the quarterdeck where Orui trained with Hodan.

The boy held his own against the older guardian, but he still lacked practical experience. More accustomed to his staff than the hand-to-hand combat of the cultural guardian, Orui had picked up a few tricks for combining the two skills. He punched right without vigor. When Hodan raised his hands to block the thrust and counter, Orui dropped and kicked the youth's legs out from under him. Hodan fell straight back, smacking his head on the wooden deck.

"No, no, no." Tutor Grayson gave Hodan an arm up. He

inspected the back of his student's head without pausing in his reprimand. "You have to watch every muscle and every facial expression."

Rory called over from his vantage point. "And you need to roll when you fall, especially when you're not trying to hold onto a weapon. You have to minimize your injuries while maximizing your opponent's."

Hodan was still breathing heavily as he bowed in acknowledgment. His eyes narrowed as he regained his battle stance. "Again."

Orui laughed. "Again, then."

Salt-encrusted hinges creaked as Salvo pushed up the hatch from the lower decks. Rory tensed, though he knew everyone on board. Tanin rubbed his forehead. He needed to get his man drunk. Too bad Salvo wouldn't allow alcohol on board. Tanin was so taken by his teachings, though, he didn't argue the point.

Prophet Salvo pulled his hood over his head to protect against the bright light as he stepped onto the deck.

Meerin and Augusta, seemingly attached to the prophet like the guardians were to Tanin, came immediately after. With their begging, King Juarim had agreed to allow his future queens to accompany the mission. Tanin had been shocked. He never would have allowed his fiancée to travel across the ocean with any man, prophet or not. As Augusta leaned in to whisper in Salvo's ear, Tanin wondered, not for the first time, what exactly the relationship was between the two women and the man who said he spoke for Lagaw.

Pale from lack of sleep, Princess Augusta was no less gorgeous than when Tanin had first laid eyes on her. He hadn't made a move to invite her to his cabin. He didn't want to ruin the relationship with the Ngaro king at this early stage of their partnership. Maybe after he had thwarted the Recharging and established man as the superior race, he could broach the subject of a reward in the form of a princess. The king didn't really need two, did he?

He'd have to be specific in his request. Though cute in her own way, Meerin wasn't for Tanin. Too energetic. The engineer princess had loved the trip so far. A short stop at North Port to show off his new vessel had left Meerin fascinated with what she called a primitive port. Tanin had offered her a position in case she wanted to update the mechanisms for loading and unloading the cargo. Their countries were about to be partners in trade, after all. With their knowledge of machines and Tarbin's international trade relationships, the two countries could take over the known world.

As long as Tanin didn't blow it up by seducing Augusta.

Even with the quenching breeze, the heat of the summer air stifled Tanin's enthusiasm for activity. He needed a bath in a cold spring, and not just because of the weather, as Augusta swept up beside him.

"That is your home?" Princess Augusta motioned to the jutting buildings of the skyline.

Tanin ignored the heat as he leaned in close to Augusta and pointed out the sights. "That is Tarbinulus, the gleaming capital of the developed world. I will rule my kingdom from the huge castle at the top of the hill overlooking the bay."

Meerin's loud voice assaulted Tanin's ear. "Those structures are quite impressive. But where are all the ships?"

Tanin straightened, taking note of the lack of activity in his usually bustling port. Generally, the entrance to the bay was crowded with trading ships, ambassador yachts, and fishing rigs.

"Where *are* the ships?" Tanin asked.

The captain of the Ngaro vessel shouted for a sailor to climb to the crow's nest. Kettlor followed the nimble man up the mainmast. As they sailed into the bay, Tanin spotted flotsam in the water, much more than was normal for the busy port. He gestured to Rory. The weapons guardian took out a spyglass and scanned the land bordering the bay.

He frowned and handed the glass to Tanin, who picked out a few vessels hugging the shore. None of them were moving. On the north side of the bay, a trading ship lay in ruins, the waves washing the inside of the hull. A few of the crew stood on the shore. They were jumping up and down and shouting at the arriving vessel.

"Maybe we should turn around," Rory suggested.

Orui squinted at the shores. "What's going on?"

"Copper in the flame!" Kettlor yelled from the crow's nest. "Hard stop. Hard stop."

Tanin focused the spyglass on the center of the port, where the signal fire flashed green—once, twice, then once again. "Foreign invader. We're not stopping. It's my port, and no invader's going to stop me from docking." He shouted to the captain. "Arm the cannons."

Salvo placed a hand on Tanin's shoulder before he could search the bay for the culprit. The prophet held his eyes closed as he spoke. "It's not the kind of invader you picture, Prince Tanin. This one lurks beneath the water."

Meerin scanned the waters. "The minor influx of magic a few months ago could have awakened denizens of the deep."

Augusta covered her mouth, her eyes wide. "Ydiny fights back."

Orui rubbed the scar on his arm from the battle with the giant squid last year. "It better not have tentacles."

"Kettlor!" Tanin yelled up to his husbandry guardian. "We're looking for a creature below the water. Look down, not out."

Even from this distance, Tanin saw Kettlor's face blanch. Taking out his bow and loosening his arrows for easy retrieval, he elbowed the sailor next to him, urging him to scan the water instead of the shore.

Tanin sprinted to the quarterdeck and pushed the Ngaro navigator from his post. Tanin knew his home waters intimately. It would be quicker for him to do this himself.

Rory commanded Hodan and the tutor to stay by Tanin's side, while he and Orui slid belowdecks to check out the cannons.

Tanin smiled. He hoped his father was watching from the castle walls. Tanin had left to get cannon technology, and he returned with an entire armed ship. Now, he just had to get it to the dock in one piece.

Prophet Salvo joined Tanin by the wheel. "I will pray for Lagaw to lead us safely to port and for Vinta to lend us a hand."

He reached out for Meerin and Augusta. Both women clasped his hands and then each other's, bowing their heads. Tanin put the navigator's hands exactly where he wanted them on the wheel. It was time to test the old god's allegiance. He could feel Lagaw's approval as he joined the prayer circle between the women.

The prophet nodded his approval. Salvo held his head up to the cloudy sky. "Oh, Great One, God of Man, Lagaw the All-Knowing, please protect us as we bring glorious word of You to the kingdom of Tarbin. Please honor us with Your blessing as Your newest follower, Prince Tanin Winterlaus, the True Heir, returns home to tell his people of Your love and Your desire for our victory over all other beings. Vinta, God of the Sea, please aid in Your revival by allowing us victory over Ydiny's beast, who blocks the entrance to the port. May our survival serve as proof that the Gods wish us to spread word of Their return. Praise be to Lagaw."

"Praise be to Lagaw." Tanin was growing accustomed to the phrasing. The words brought him peace as he realized someone was finally on his side. Someone no less than the God of all men.

Tanin kissed the hand of each princess before releasing them. "Let us show King Roland the strength of Lagaw."

Orui returned to the upper deck, clutching his staff. "Everything's ready below, my Prince."

Kettlor shouted from the crow's nest, "Sea serpent forward."

The captain commanded the crew to trim the sails to slow the ship's acceleration. They had to flank the beast if they were to attack with the cannons. Meanwhile, he readied the crew with the more typical weapons used against sea beasts. "Prepare the harpoons."

The burliest of the sailors, their feet bare to maintain their footing on a slick deck, grabbed the long spears tipped with barbed points.

Tanin gestured to the wheel man. "Orui, help him please."

Orui put a hand on the Ngaroan's shoulder. "Mind the shoal on the northern side of the bay. I only see one floating pot. Most of the rocks should be low enough under high tide that we'll be safe, but just in case, let's not get too close."

Tanin jumped off the quarterdeck to snag a harpoon from one of the hunting sailors. As a boatswain tied a heavy rope to the looped end, Tanin tested the balance. Though much lighter than the hook blade they'd used to kill the giant squid last year, the weapon was still heavier than his sword. He hoisted it over his shoulder, following the example of the more experienced wielders.

The men nodded at Tanin, respect in their eyes. He patted the bare shoulder of the closest sailor. He appreciated their admiration and hoped the men spread the tale far and wide of the warrior prince who defended Tarbinulus Harbor from a magical invader. Tutor Grayson could write an epic poem detailing the adventure.

Tanin squinted across the murky water, searching for the sea beast. "Kettlor, I don't see anything."

The husbandry guardian pointed to a rocky island on the southern side of the bay. "It faded below the surface, but the barkers on Sea Lion Island are climbing over each other in a panic to get out of the water."

A pair of flippers, larger than those of any whale Tanin had ever seen, flopped out of the water and smacked the surface. The resulting wave swept sea lions from their tentative hold on the edge of the rocky shore.

"It's not a sea serpent, not with those fins." Hodan gripped the railing next to Tanin. The cultural guardian's flushed face showed a mix of excitement and fear. The boy hadn't seen battle yet.

Today was the day.

"Thank the L—Lagaw for some good news." Orui wiped sweat from his face as he kept the helm steady.

One of the sea lions leaped out of the water. Right behind him, a mouth full of jagged teeth, attached to a neck as long as the mainmast and twice as thick, snapped at the wailing animal.

"What is that?" Tanin's arm hung, the harpoon heavy, as the unknown beast attacked the pack of sea lions.

Another head burst from the surface, shaking a flailing kill. A third head came from below and grabbed the tail of the sea lion. The two beasts pulled at the animal until it split in two.

Hodan walked backward to the railing of the stairs to the quarter-deck. "There's three of them."

Tanin shouted at the captain, "Bring the ship around the island. If we can attack while they're occupied with eating, we could kill the lot before getting close enough to use these."

The Ngaroan nodded and shouted at his men to adjust the sails to maneuver the ship at an angle to the feeding frenzy, creating the best chance for a full cannon assault. Tanin had to give credit to the Ngaroan and the sailors on board. None of them showed a stitch of rebellion. The two countries would get along just fine as they enforced Lagaw's Law throughout the world.

From below, a cabin boy rushed to Tanin's side. "Your Most Royalship, I have a message from Guardian Rory."

Tanin's lips twitched as he dropped the heavy harpoon to his side. Everything sounded funny from the boy, whose accent slurred words together in odd ways. "Prince Tanin or Your Majesty is fine, Yogm. What is it?"

Yogm bowed deeply, his voice bouncing up from the deck. "Guardian Rory says we should attack now. Get in as much damage as possible before they turn their wrath on us." He looked up without moving his head. "The Trickster God Ydiny creates fierce beasts with the hunger to defeat all that is Lagaw."

The tail of one of the beasts swiped the shore, sending sea lions flying into the water. Tanin didn't want to end up like the easy prey. He squeezed Yogm's shoulder. "Tell Rory to arm the cannons and light the slow matches. We fire as soon as we're in range."

"But, Your Majesty . . . ?" The captain stopped in the middle of ordering his men and raised his hand, like a child in class waiting to be acknowledged.

"Yes, Captain?" Tanin crossed his arms and raised an eyebrow. Technically, it was his ship, but the captain was a foreigner and had no right to brandish weapons in Tarbinulus Harbor.

The older man cleared his throat, considering his words. "As commander of this vessel, I will go belowdecks to make sure your man knows how to properly work the cannons. We haven't had enough training time on aiming and recoil."

Tanin loosened his arms. Good. The captain knew his place. "Of course. We appreciate your expertise in our first battle."

In a practice run off a deserted island in the middle of the warm Ngaro Sea, the crew had shown Tanin and his men the basics. This would be the first real test.

Orui jumped down from the quarterdeck and landed beside Tanin. "The navigator knows how to swing the ship better than I do. I warned him about the shoal and the shifting sand closer to port. If we survive this, we can worry about that later."

"I agree." Tanin hefted the harpoon from the edge of the railing. He moved Hodan back. "Remember how far the ship tilted when the cannons fired? We should probably find something to hold on to."

The three monsters whipped about, snagging and fighting over prey as if there were a shortage.

Hodan wrapped cloth around his blade handle, which would give him a better hold when the saltwater inundated the deck. "They certainly stay close together. I don't know why at least one doesn't swim to the other side of the island and get the sea lions escaping that way."

Orui slapped the cultural guardian on the shoulder. "Don't complain, squirt. It makes the morons a bigger, easier target."

Grayson's eyes narrowed. "I agree with, Hodan. We're missing something."

Tanin gripped a rope fastener with one hand as the ship slowed at a perfect angle for full cannon fire. "No time to worry about it now."

The splashing of the huge flippers aerosolized a torrent of water.

It felt like it was raining. The crunch of sea mammal bones invigo-rated Tanin. Being close enough to hear that detail meant the cannons would tear through the beasts.

"Fire!" Rory's voice carried through the wood moments before the multiple, almost simultaneous explosions.

# CHAPTER NINETEEN

For a few moments, Tanin couldn't hear anything. His nose filled with the burn of gunpowder. His eyes watered as smoke swelled from below. He rushed to the railing, joining the other sailors with their harpoons, ready to stab anything that moved in the water.

A slick head the size of a canoe, with triangular shark teeth, broke through the smoke and dove for Tanin's head. His heart thumped against his chest as he ducked. The harpoon in his hand jabbed into the deck. Sizzling liquid dripped from the beast, and Tanin was sure the thing was drooling, drenching his hair.

Before he could react, Tanin was enveloped in a warm embrace. At first, Tanin feared it was a tentacle, ready to plunge him into the deep. He fought off the attacker, until he realized they were rolling away from the sea.

They stopped as a harpoon-armed sailor rushed by. Hodan released Tanin and offered him a hand to gain his feet.

Tanin smiled at his new guardian. "You did well."

Orui slid to his side. "You're bleeding."

The wet locks of his hair were coated in blood, not saliva. Tanin laughed as adrenaline energized his muscles. "It's not mine." He snagged a harpoon from a slack-jawed sailor and jumped back into the fray.

The ship rolled to the side. Blood slickened the deck much more effectively than saltwater. Tanin slid toward the sea creature as another head popped out of the water. It slithered through the air on its snakelike neck.

Tanin shivered with adrenaline and fear. Snakes creeped him out. He needed an ax, not a harpoon. He threw the weapon like he would a javelin. The jagged end pierced the lower jaw of the second beast.

Both animals roared as the crew cheered and rallied to increase their attack. A few of the sailors grabbed the harpoon's attached rope and tightened it around the belaying pin on the railing. They'd managed to bring the head close enough to the deck to chop it off when Kettlor yelled a warning from the crow's nest.

"Watch the third beast's head!"

The ship tilted to port as it banked around the gathered sea monsters. The third, and hopefully final, beast wove under the middle head to snap at the men tying down its brother. The ship cleared the smoke from the cannons as the newcomer tore the harpoon rope to shreds, freeing its mate. All three beasts simultaneously bashed into the ship, sending it reeling to starboard.

Tanin slipped across the deck and slammed his arm into the foremast. He grabbed a belaying pin with his other hand before he could tumble farther. Two sailors found no strong hold and splashed into the bay. The ship teetered the opposite way as it tried to right itself.

A woman's scream echoed from the quarterdeck. Augusta clawed at the boards, trying to find a handhold. An arrow sunk into her dress at the waist, embedding itself deep into the wood. She came to an abrupt halt and swung around, with the arrow as a pivot point. As her dress ripped, she frantically clung to the shaft.

Tanin tossed Kettlor a well-done gesture. What a waste it would have been to lose such a beauty to the deep.

Metal scraped on metal beneath the deck. Tanin hoped the erratic rocking wouldn't jar the cannons off their tracks.

Orui slid past Tanin, who was unable to grab him. The medicinal guardian managed to snag a rolling harpoon. He swung it like his staff, jamming the end into a hole in a plank. He used the momentum to swing around and grab the hinges of the hatch.

The ship continued to shudder sideways, but less dramatically. Tanin rushed to Orui's side and slung his head belowdecks. Yogm leaned over the prone captain, weeping.

Tanin cursed the loss of the captain, but there was no time to mourn. He whistled to get Rory's attention through the chaos of positioning the huge iron weapons. "Are the cannons ready for another volley? I don't know how much more abuse the ship can take."

"Almost, my Prince." Rory pushed a sailor with a torch away from the gunpowder keg. "I can't see down here."

Tanin peeked over the railings to see which side the beasts would dominate. "They're still off the port for now. Hodan!"

The boy jumped to his prince's side. Tanin didn't see the tutor, but he didn't have time to worry about his absence. "Stay here and convey the monsters' positions to Rory. So far, they've stuck together, but if they hunt like most pack animals, that won't last."

"Yes, my Prince." Hodan knelt next to the hatch and braced himself against the rocking of the ship.

Tanin rose to his feet. "They're hurt. We're going in for a second attack."

Orui repositioned the harpoon between two joist and motioned for Tanin to steady himself with it. Pain surprised Tanin as he lifted the arm he had slammed into the mast. He took a deep breath and gripped the harpoon with his good hand. With his legs spread apart for balance, he pulled his sword from its scabbard. He couldn't stand there unarmed.

"Ready!" Rory commanded from below.

Tanin's body tensed as he awaited the next volley.

One of the injured monsters shook its head, trying to dislodge the harpoon from its jaw. The other two beasts worried over the injury. One pushed the weapon the rest of the way through the jaw, while the second beast tenderly gripped it from the top and tossed it aside.

"Did you see that?" Tanin couldn't understand the careful tending of a fellow predator. "Why would it want to save the other? Are they not in competition?"

"It's more than that." The medicinal guardian rolled his shoulders. "If one had pulled out the harpoon the way it went in, they'd probably have torn its jaw off. They didn't just help each other."

"They did it intelligently." Grayson squeezed the sleeve of his sopping-wet clothes. His knees bent and swayed with the ship, while his feet stayed glued to the deck. "There's something else odd that I can't put my finger on."

The three comrades in the form of sea monsters dove under the water.

"Tell Rory to wait." Tanin ordered Hodan, who conveyed the message. "Where'd they go?"

A slam against the keel deep underwater answered his question. The masts shook in an unsettling manner.

Kettlor pointed to the other side of the boat. "They're surfacing on the starboard side."

Hodan shouted to Rory to switch sides. Tanin shouted at the navigator to turn the boat. They had to be flush with as many of the beasts as possible for maximum damage. Tanin pushed Orui aside so he could see that way. His injured arm throbbed. He wasn't sure how he would attack and balance himself at the same time.

"Ready!" Rory shouted again, his voice floating up from the hatch.

Tanin motioned to Hodan to look up. "Kettlor, give the fire command. The boy will relay it."

The husbandry guardian nodded as he reached for another arrow.

Squinting into the sunlight, Tanin couldn't make out any details. Three large bubbles burst through the water's surface in a perfect straight line. The beasts had planned a coordinated attack. They jumped out of the water, they're snakelike necks forming a huge arc, like a mutated pod of dolphins.

"By the Darkness." Grayson moved to his student's side and held the hatch.

Tanin's mouth fell open. All three necks were attached to one huge body. As the humongous beast cleared the water, his bulk blocked out the sun and much of the shoreline behind him. It wasn't three individual beasts; it was one massive monster. Its flippers swung through the air as though it could fly.

"Fire now." Tanin's hand turned white from his tight grip. "Fire now."

"No, wait." Tutor Grayson put his hand on Hodan's head. The boy looked between his tutor and his prince; his wide eyes begged them to make a decision.

Tanin's fear morphed to anger at the disobedience of his servant. "I give the orders. That thing is going to bounce on the ship and tear it to pieces. We attack now."

"That would explain the wrecked ships and the debris covering our port," Orui agreed. "Very effective method for sinking a ship."

Meerin ran into Grayson and bent in half to catch her breath. "He's right. Wait. It's too far away for the cannons to really injure it. Let the Ydiny-cursed thing breach one more time. That's when we'll fire."

Tanin gripped his steady harpoon. Meerin knew these weapons better than anyone. He chose to trust her. "On Meerin's orders."

The sea monster dove into the water, producing a wave large enough to set the ship rocking again. Tanin didn't think his body could get any tenser without snapping. He hated standing here and waiting. He'd rather swim to the beast and punch it in the jaw. One of the jaws, anyway.

As soon as the three heads burst through the water a second time, it roared so fiercely, the sails shifted.

Meerin shouted, "Now!"

Rory echoed Hodan's "Fire!" so quickly, they almost spoke with one voice.

The sea monster reached the pinnacle of its arc. The crack of the cannons vibrated the deck, forcing the ship to port. The cannons blasted into the body of the beast, flinging the sea creature backward. Its graceful arc transformed into a clumsy somersault and a violent flop. The splash turned purple as it blended with a large quantity of blood.

The crew cheered. The sailors on the closest shore echoed the crew's joyous shouts.

With Meerin close behind, Tanin sprinted to the quarterdeck to get a better view. Salvo helped Augusta free her dress from the arrow. The beauty shook with fear, and tears ran down her face.

Meerin winked at Tanin. "You want a head, don't you, True Heir?"

He didn't try to hide his pleasure at her correct guess. "All three would be better."

The quartermaster overheard his comment and armed sailors with harpoons to drag the body closer to the deck. Meerin shouted commands to the crew to check the ship for damage. His face covered in black ash, Rory appeared from the lower deck.

Tanin shifted the sword in his hand. He didn't know how much strength he could maintain with his injured arm, but nothing would stop him from earning his trophy.

Hodan leaned over the side as the mutilated beast bumped against the hull. "It's almost sad."

Tanin frowned at his weakness. "It's only a beast. This is a victory for Tarbin." He pointed to the cheering men on the shore. "They will sing of their prince's prowess as he freed Tarbinulus Harbor from a rampaging monster. That is what it means to rule."

Salvo came down the quarterdeck steps, his hands tucked into his robe sleeves. "We have given a victory to Lagaw over His would-be usurpers. He will reward us and watch over you, Prince Tanin."

The sailors heaved one huge neck onto the deck, the one with the pierced jaw. Tanin gripped his sword with both hands and yelled a battle cry to carry across the water. "To the great God, Lagaw, I offer this sacrifice."

He swung down so quickly, the sailors immediately next to the neck jumped out of the way. A few more hacks severed the head.

Sailors shouted and dashed away from the railing as another head fell onto the deck, its jaws snapping. Tanin bounced backward as spittle from the beast's mouth soaked his leggings. The third head popped up on the other side of the deck.

"It's acting weird for a dead beast." Orui used his harpoon as a staff and smacked the drooling head in the jaw, then smartly on the nose.

The sea monster cried as its third head reached across the deck, teeth soaked in its own blood. Kettlor shot an arrow through one eye. The head fell to the deck with a crashing thud. Rory stepped forward and severed the head with one swift swing.

Focused on the last head moving, Orui twirled his harpoon to point the tip down. He jumped, adding momentum to his final jab through the snout, nailing the last bit of movement to the deck. The entire ship shook with the final death throes of the massive sea beast.

Tanin leaned on his sword with his good arm. Lagaw really was looking out for him. He raised his head to the sky and shouted, "Praise be to Lagaw!"

# CHAPTER TWENTY

BABLA VILLAGE WAS EXACTLY as Talia remembered it. For some reason, that disturbed her as she crossed into the dwarf side of town. So much had changed for her, she expected everything else in the world to be different as well.

Touching the crown at her side to make sure it was still there brought her some comfort. She'd almost had to wrestle Nomyra to get it back. Talia glanced over her shoulder. Rodianiari and Nomyra had run off again. She didn't like how close those two had grown. It made Talia feel off-kilter, as if she were still out of the loop.

She could understand Rodianiari's reluctance to appear. She wasn't sure how these dwarves, outcasts themselves, would take to their long-lost enemy showing up at their door. But Talia had no clue why Nomyra continued to disappear. Her separation became more and more pronounced the closer they got to the end goal.

Talia's group took up an entire row of log seating at the outdoor stage. She'd chosen to give them a break after their mad dash across Tarbin territory. They couldn't risk staying in any one spot long enough to be captured. Babla Village was independent. King Roland wouldn't be able to send his guards there. Money could persuade anyone, though, so they weren't going to stay long.

Jura kicked her legs up and down as if they were still one big fin. "By the curly tail of a seahorse."

Talia leaned over Ial to address Jura. "Have you never seen a show before?"

Jura vibrated with excitement as she shook her head. The entire trip across Tarbin had been like that. One thing after another brought sheer delight to the mermaid. The first time she swam in fresh water as they crossed Lightndark Lake. The first time she tasted a land animal—Jura didn't like the deer, too tough.

After weeks on the road, Jura still enjoyed exploring new experiences.

A hodgepodge of instruments warmed up near the stage. Jura jumped up on her tiptoes, one hand on her straw hat. That was the biggest change to her appearance. Not only did Jura's pink hair get funny looks and questions Talia wasn't prepared to answer, but the glaring sun wreaked havoc on her skin. Accustomed to layers of water between her and the Light's Daughter, the first day of hiking through the plains had turned her slightly pink skin a deep bright red.

Nyna had done the best she could to keep the pain under control and the peeling to a minimum. But the beauty had looked more beast for the first leg of their journey. Ial had found her a large-brimmed hat in one of the small villages the party passed through. The villager had gouged them with the price of the plain straw hat, but Talia had been willing to pay the extra amount as more of a bribe to keep quiet about seeing her than anything else.

Ial quietly took Jura's hand and put her hat in her lap. The dwarves standing behind the party had a hard enough time seeing over the seated humans as it was.

Talia's amusement turned to concern as Nyna crossed her arms. The medicinal guardian's crossed legs bounced much like Jura's, though Talia suspected agitation over excitement. Ial was giving Jura a lot of attention. Of course he was. She was the mermaid who had saved his father's life. The mermaid he had saved when he was a boy. She now understood why guardians weren't supposed to fraternize. Talia would have to talk to Nyna. Not that she had any idea how to settle a lovers' quarrel.

Gregor sat on the opposite side of the party from Talia. She'd refused to show him any affection on the journey. She needed to focus on the end goal instead of indulging her whims. She rubbed her knees as her muscles vibrated, eager to keep going.

Prince Aleck sat in front of Talia, his guards plastered to his side. Those two dwarves really needed to lighten up. Talia considered having Naul take them to a tavern tonight. Though she understood their discomfort. They were meeting their cousins for the first time and, against Aleck's wishes, had decided not to tell anyone who they were. Convincing Traneck and Parnim to leave their pikes behind and only carry smallish knives had been a complete struggle all on its own.

Gregor poked Naul in the gut with his elbow. "Community theater? From the dwarf who forced us to carry landscaping stone up the slope of death if we forgot to turn in a homework assignment? Are we *sure* this is Master Overstone?"

"It's not. He's Old Stoney now." Naul's guffaw carried through the crowd, causing the children on the ground by the stage to laugh even though they didn't know why. The cascade of laughter through the outdoor facility cued the orchestra.

With all the children present, human and dwarf, Talia hoped that the show was a comedy. She needed to catch some of the cheer the audience already exuded. The anxiety that tormented her had no purpose, and she was tired of bearing it. Everything was fine.

The party had decided to stop in Babla Village before heading over the mountains to the Renquist Desert. They had encountered very little trouble in the couple of months it took to get this far. Talia had made sure they stayed off the main thoroughfares. Gregor had used his swift tongue to get the most favorable deals when resupplying. The trip had been pretty tame except for whispers speaking of the old gods. Talia wondered how ancient myths were surfacing just as the Recharging was about to occur, verifying the strength of Light and Dark.

She didn't know why she felt such apprehension. She was almost to the finish line. Even Nomyra seemed confident in their progress when she was normally angry and impatient. Maybe it was the fact that Talia knew there was something the priestess wasn't sharing.

The curtain dropped on stage, revealing a set of bright colors and impossible shapes. Definitely a comedy.

TALIA SAT by the fireplace in the crowded tavern. She had had no idea actors liked to party this much. After a full performance of *The Known and the Suspected* with many musical numbers in completely odd places, the players *still* wanted to sing. Talia stifled a yawn. She wasn't built for this all-night revelry.

Aleck, on the other hand, danced on the table with the star of the performance, Iona Skyborne, a dwarf with a Light-blessed voice. His guards sat between two musicians, who somehow still had skin on their fingers after strumming their strings for hours. The guards looked just as done with the party as Talia was.

Gregor and Naul had a couple of townswomen in a dark corner. She couldn't hear anything they were saying, but their body language shouted. Talia shifted her legs to expose the other side of her body to the heat of the fire. She had no right to be jealous of Gregor. She had rebuffed his attentions repeatedly. But a little twinge in her gut refused to settle as his curly head bent down and he whispered in the stranger's ear.

"Princess." The director and star of the show plopped down next to her on the hearth, a welcome distraction.

"Master—"

"Old Stoney." The exiled dwarf shoved a beer into her hand before she could protest.

"Old Stoney. But then you must call me Talia, especially since I'm no longer a princess." She took a small sip of the bitter ale so as not to be rude. Truth be told, she'd be on her butt all morning tomorrow if she drank much more. "I loved the show."

"Of course you did. Who wouldn't? It's a classic tale of valiant dwarves and their human companions." Old Stoney took a much larger gulp from his mug.

"Though I wasn't sure of the importance of the green—I think he was a . . . donkey?"

Old Stoney smoothed down his beard with a chuckle. "That's Arnie. He's been Dark-cursed, which makes him a bit slow. But we all love him." He tilted his head to Aleck bouncing on the table. "He's a Krimmel, isn't he?"

Talia should have known the old dwarf would figure it out. "We decided, against Aleck's wishes, to keep his origin secret. We weren't sure what the response would be."

"Probably for the best." Old Stoney drained his mug. "Keep it that way over the mountains."

Talia set her full mug next to his empty one. "It was tough to get Aleck to agree to this much secrecy. He's set up trade deals with almost every city we've spent a meal in."

"There's rumors of a new religion sweeping the region." Old Stoney yanked on his beard a bit fiercely. "An old religion renamed, really."

Talia squinted into the crowd. "We've heard talk of old gods returning, as if gods come and go like the seasons. The Dark and Light are always here."

"The argument is, the Dark and Light are not gods. They were created by gods with other intentions. Have you heard Aleck or his people speak of Thoretick?"

Talia turned her mug in circles, the scratching on the hearthstone focused her memories. "Sometimes. And Jura has talked about the god of the sea."

"Has she?" He stared at Talia's down-turned head.

She could almost feel the tendrils of his thoughts trying to dig out more details. Talia wasn't sure why she didn't just tell him that Jura was a mermaid. Maybe later in private quarters.

Old Stoney cleared his throat. "The point is, someone is preaching about the old gods, putting Lagaw, the god of man, above all others, including Thoretick, the god of the dwarves, and Ydiny, the god of magic."

"There's a god of magic?" Talia looked up, annoyed by the noise of the crowd that made it difficult to concentrate on his words.

"According to the old teachings, there is." Old Stoney stood and stretched his back. "The old gods built the city of Raqmu in the middle of the Renquist Plains—"

"You mean the Renquist Desert?" Talia interrupted.

Old Stoney's face wrinkled in amusement. "It wasn't always a desert. After the Sundering a millennium ago, the entire landmass around the central city died and has never recovered."

Talia motioned for her cultural guardian to join them. "Dew noticed how off the maps were in the book you gave us. That disaster could explain why."

Dew swayed a bit on her feet from her partying, but her mind was sharp and focused. "Hey, Talia. Are you ready to go?"

"Not quite yet. Master—Old Stoney says the Renquist Desert used to be grasslands."

Dew was short enough, the dwarf barely had to lift his head to meet her eyes. "The map in that book should be accurate, landmass-wise. Those probably haven't changed much, but the cities will be all wrong."

Dew patted her side, then looked annoyed that she didn't have the reference on her. "There was a river running through the center on the map. But there's no river running through the Renquist Desert."

Old Stoney swayed in time with Dew. "The water has gone underground. I believe that's why the area has never recovered from the Sundering. Life is tough without water, for both plants and people."

The cultural guardian cocked a hip. "Then I'm not sure how we're going to find the city."

"The mermaid will be able to sense the water."

Talia sucked in a surprised breath. A hot blast of ashy smoke from the fire burned her throat. She bent in half, coughing.

Dew patted her on the back.

"I'm fine." Talia waved her off to focus on Old Stoney. "How did you know?"

"She moves as if she's underwater, and you said she spoke of the sea god. And that pink hair." Old Stoney's beard had to be attached with extra-strength adhesive, for he tugged at it again and it didn't fall out. "What I'd like to know is *why* you have a mermaid."

Talia dropped her voice to a whisper. "We learned of a dome that protects the city. For it to open, we need a sample of blood from all the races."

"Darkening swine, what is it with you humans and blood?" Old Stoney rubbed his hands on his pants, cleansing them of imagined contamination. "When are you heading out?"

"We planned to stay for a week." Talia flinched as Naul and Gregor escorted their dates out the door. "We need some rest from our constant movement."

Dew added, "We need to resupply too. The next known stop isn't until Hajar Ramliun, on the south side of the range."

"There are a few settlements here and there. Most of them are ours." Old Stoney lifted his mug and tried to get another swig from the bottom. "Which means you should probably have the female guard shave. You wouldn't want anyone else to guess they weren't Eckerd Dwarves."

Talia blinked at the Krimmel guards. "The female?"

"I believe you introduced her as Parnim?"

Dew sat heavily on the hearth, knocking beer out of Talia's mug. "But Eckerd females don't grow beards. How?"

Old Stoney rescued Talia's mostly full mug. "All dwarves grow facial hair." He took a double swallow and burped. "Extended exposure to humans influenced us. To appear more human, our women shave on a regular basis."

"Huh." Talia couldn't come up with anything more intelligent to say. She'd have to bring it up with Aleck and see what he thought. Talia was not about to demand another culture conform to her own.

It just couldn't be easy, could it?

# CHAPTER TWENTY-ONE

P̲ʀᴀɪꜱᴇ ʙᴇ ᴛᴏ L̲ᴀɢᴀᴡ," Tanin repeated with the small human community as Prophet Salvo finished his sermon.

He had watched the prophet preach multiple times in Tarbinulus, and then in every gathering of humans he could reach, from the Tarbin capital to the smallest village in the countryside. Every time, it was the same. The humans would listen, mesmerized by the talented speaker. By the end of his almost-identical sermons, just modified enough to appeal to his current audience, the people would jump up and praise Lagaw with one united voice.

Tanin had to admire the power Salvo had over the minds of the common man. Obviously, the Light and Dark didn't offer the message the people needed. He watched group after group convert like starving men, starting with King Roland himself. Tanin's father had agreed to finance the journey to Raqmu, to ensure the victory of Lagaw and His followers.

The astropriests in larger towns tried to counter Salvo and reinstate control. The Light had done nothing but make the priests rich. Tarbin wanted another answer. Plus, the glowing display of the Black

Opal that served as the climax of each sermon helped sway even some priests.

Having Tarbin's prince and heir apparent sit beside the prophet bolstered his influence. Normally, Tanin would stay with the wealthiest member of each settlement, which tended to be the priests in the smaller towns. This time, at the prophet's suggestion, Tanin and his companions slept under their tents just outside the property's borders. At each stop, a flock of townspeople and farmers came out to see their prince. That's when Salvo would speak and feed the people. Tanin had watched him convert entire towns at a time.

Tanin took careful note of the noblemen who left their keeps to swear fidelity to Lagaw. They would be the foundation for his new Tarbin, a kingdom reborn.

Tanin looked forward to this new order. Without his sister to challenge his every move, Tanin found his mind was more peaceful. He praised the soft blue mountain sky, sending his thanks to the ears of the great Lagaw for showing him the way.

He turned to the prophet. "We should arrive at the Stonemason School by lunchtime."

Salvo tucked his arms into his robes. His body physically shook from the chilly mountain air. "I have to confess, I would welcome a respite from this biting wind."

Tanin nodded. "Rory and Hodan should have already made it and will have our quarters prepared."

Orui removed his cloak and put it around the shoulders of the thinner man. "This is only the beginning of autumn. You're going to freeze when the snow falls for winter."

Meerin dropped her arms and the blanket she had brought for the prophet. She cocked her head at Orui as she wrapped the blanket around her own shoulders. "I've never seen snow before."

Kettlor handed Tanin the reins to his horse. "If we're lucky, we'll be well on the other side of the mountain range before we have to deal with that complication."

Augusta swept up next to Tanin, already mounted on a gray

mare. She claimed to have never ridden a horse before this trip. "I have wondered. Why is it called the Stonemason School if you learned to fight there? Seems to me, battle is about tearing down, not building up." She continued along the path as Kettlor gave Tanin a leg up.

She might have been new to riding, but she'd taken to it quickly. Tanin admired the way her body moved with the horse's gait. It made him think of other activities. "The dwarves run the school. They have for centuries."

Orui snickered immediately behind Tanin. "Millennia, if you ask a dwarf."

With a slash of his hand, Tanin motioned for Orui to stay out of the conversation. Squeezing his steed into a trot, Tanin pulled even with Augusta. He wanted some one-on-one time with the beauty. "The Eckerd . . ."

"Eckerd?" Augusta held her reins in one hand to free her other so she could straighten her skirts modestly over her lap.

Tanin resisted the urge to lean over and help. "The dwarves who live in these mountains call themselves the Eckerd. They have cousins who live in the western mountain range, called the Krimmel, but they don't talk to each other. An ancient war split them into two kingdoms."

"Much as the human kingdom was split."

"Maybe." Tanin squinted as the tree-lined path opened into a large valley. The sun soaked his face, reminding him of how cold he was.

"By Lagaw on high." Augusta sat back and pulled on the reins.

Her mare pranced in place, uncertain of what her rider wanted. The black-streaked granite of the mountain reflected sunlight from specks of quartz. The grand carved gate of the Eckerd Kingdom never failed to impress. An oval-shaped hole, large enough to fit the cannoned ship if it could sail through the air, gaped beneath a massive carving of Thoretick wielding his hammer in one hand and his sword in the other. Tanin routinely volunteered to lead dignitaries to this location just to watch their reaction.

Tanin spurred his horse forward, giving the mare someone to follow. "Stunning, isn't it?"

Augusta's caramel skin flushed, her open mouth refusing to form words. Tanin didn't think it was possible for her to look any more beautiful.

"The surface is buffed every summer to remove any damage from the winter cold and spring storms. Each carving is touched up and repaired, if necessary." Tanin had spent one summer working on the side of the mountain as part of his schooling. He remembered raw hands and stone dust in every pore. At the time, he had refused to excuse himself from the work, though he could have as a royal student with special privileges. But his sister had bragged about working her fingers to the bone the summer before, and Tanin couldn't have let her outshine him. Thinking back, it hadn't been the worst bit of work he'd ever had to do. At least Gregor had been strung to the side of the mountain with him.

Tanin shook his head. He couldn't think of that traitor now. Whatever friendship they'd had, had died when Gregor chose Talia over him. Tanin had ensured that Gregor lost his title and any inheritance to his younger brother by threatening Lord Rivenwood with the loss of his entire estate if he didn't comply.

Meerin rode ahead of the group. "That is the most stunning thing I have seen since the Gods-blessed desert. That's Thoretick, isn't it, Prophet Salvo?"

Pushing through the last of the evergreen bushes, the cart came into view. Salvo sat beside Kettlor, who urged the nervous horses forward.

The prophet blinked at the carving. "Yes. Thoretick, God of the Dwarves. It is right that he should bless their mountain." His long hair whipped in a cross breeze. "Lagaw and Thoretick have like minds. Dwarves and humans should follow the lead of their Gods."

Unwilling to lose his momentum, Kettlor forced the single

mounts to the gravel side of the path. "I, for one, welcome a respite from the cold. Shall we?"

The wagon rumbled along the stone path, which was crowded with stalled horses and riders. Tanin coughed as dust was thrown into the air by its wheels. He kicked his steed to get ahead of the wagon, Orui close behind.

Augusta pulled even with Tanin as the horses slowed to a walk. "You didn't finish your explanation. How can a school both build and destroy?"

Tanin's blood pumped. He liked that she had started the conversation this time. Maybe he could trade Talia to King Juarim for Augusta. "First of all, weapons aren't meant for destruction. They're meant to build a kingdom by protecting its citizens."

She acknowledged his point with a slight nod.

"Plus, the building blocks of both, stone and metal, are found within the ground where the dwarves prefer to live. It's a natural fit for them to be experts in both."

Augusta offered no counter argument. Tanin straightened in his saddle. She really would make a perfect queen someday.

THE DARK CAVE felt warmer than the surface above without the constant wind. Yet there was still something cold about the lack of greenery and sunlight.

Grand Master Milton Ironsmith clasped Tanin's arm below his elbow. "Prince Tanin Winterlaus, welcome back. Have you finally decided to abandon your crown and join our ranks?"

The old dwarf wore the same clothes Tanin remembered, a thick red wool undershirt with mushroom-brown overalls and heavy leather boots. A quick glance would lead a visitor to believe he worked beside the men in the mines, until they saw his clean fingernails and meticulously groomed beard. The grand master hadn't seen the inside of a mine or the working end of a forge for decades.

As chancellor of the Stonemason School, he chose to dress as if he did.

Tanin laughed with the grand master. "Not yet." He gestured to Prophet Salvo. "I *have* brought an important dignitary with me who is in need of your knowledge. I assume Rory filled you in."

"He did. He did indeed." Concern crossed the dwarf's face, quickly replaced with jovial welcome.

Tanin was prepared to battle to get the influential dwarf on their side. "Grand Master Milton Ironsmith, I'd like you to meet Prophet Salvo of Ngaro."

Salvo flinched at Ironsmith's tight grip on his arm. "Working the ground has made you strong, Master."

"And studying the ancient scripts has made me smart." The twinkle in Ironsmith's eye felt more like a threat than an expression of joy.

Tanin flinched. It was going to be an uphill battle. The master of the Stonemason School was a much harder mark than the uneducated villagers Salvo had converted.

Salvo sized up Ironsmith with his full focus. "Lagaw and Thoretick are united in a single cause. Augusta?"

The princess dug through her bag and handed Ironsmith one of her books.

Salvo introduced her. "This is Princess Augusta Maywin of Palawa. She is Keeper of the Written Word."

"It is an honor to make your acquaintance, Grand Master." Curtsying with a courtly flourish, Augusta pointed to a ribbon in the book. "I have marked for your convenience the passage where our Lords, Lagaw and Thoretick, united against Ydiny, forcing the Goddess of Magic to keep her unnatural creations under control and out of the lives of men and dwarves."

Meerin joined the conversation with gusto, per usual. "To help us combat the threat, Thoretick granted dwarves the gift of stone and metal manipulation as Lagaw gave man the gift of machinery and ingenuity."

Salvo jumped in. "And this is Princess Meerin Cragforth of Kani, Keeper of the Vision."

Ironsmith's face lightened as he shook arms with Meerin. The old dwarf held the book to his chest as he took in the strangers. With a deep breath, Ironsmith found his smile. "Welcome to the Eckerd Kingdom and the Stonemason School. We have arranged a tour of the mines. Any other requests can be made at our feast tonight with the king." He tapped the book absentmindedly. "You've given me much to think about."

Tanin marveled at Salvo's gift for opening people's minds so quickly.

"Meanwhile, quarters have been set up for you to refresh yourselves after your long travel." Ironsmith gestured to two assistants dressed in wool frocks and heavy boots. "Kilo and Ton will show you the way. If you have any other needs, they will see to them as well."

"Will we see you for the tour, Master Ironsmith?" Tanin asked.

"Maybe, Prince Tanin." He looked at Prophet Salvo. "I have some reading to do."

# CHAPTER TWENTY-TWO

THE KING'S feast chamber smelled like a gift from the Gods. Tanin had always thought it strange that the dwarves put all the food on the table at once, from the roasted elk to the soup to the cherry tarts. This time, he appreciated the variety.

Tanin stuffed a whole spoonful of sweet potatoes into his mouth. His palate rejoiced over the change in food. The months on the sea and on the road had left him desiring fresh vegetables. His younger self would cringe.

Salvo wiped his fingers on a plaid napkin. "You have an impressive mining operation, King Igneous."

The king of the Eckerd Dwarves sat in the middle of the table, literally. The round table in his private entertaining quarters had a hole in the center, where the king sat in a pivoting chair. The copper-colored upholstery contrasted with the simple white-gold crown that hung from the tall back of the chair. This allowed the king to turn and speak with any guest he chose while hiding the conversation from anyone behind him, should he desire a bit of clandestine talk.

Meerin talked through a mouthful of baked apple. "At home, we have to sift, scrounge, and dig randomly in the hope of finding a few pounds of iron. You are lucky to have so much raw material to work with."

Augusta put a hand on Meerin's shoulder. The younger princess clamped her mouth shut and chewed a bit more quietly.

"What my future sister is trying to say is that your valuable resources will do wonders for promoting the wishes of both Lagaw and Thoretick." Augusta's elegant translation earned a nod from King Igneous.

The cushioned ceiling and walls of the stone chamber muffled the sounds of conversation to the extent that if the king spoke to you directly, he could be relatively certain the guest behind him didn't get the full content. Tanin admired the clever design of camaraderie combined with privacy. Maybe he could get one of these installed in Tarbinulus Castle.

The downside for a guest? It prevented him from addressing the king until the monarch chose to turn in his direction. Tanin's foot tapped. He liked that power as well. He'd send a sketch and message home to Father before leaving for the desert. He wasn't sure what the line of communication would be like once they entered the land of the primitives. It was rather ironic that the future of technology for all humans resided in the land held by the most backward people of the entire continent.

"Thank you. I am sure we can work out a mutually beneficial trade agreement." King Igneous took a long quaff of his wine, his eyes never leaving Prophet Salvo. He set down his glass and took another moment, lost in his thoughts.

Tanin wanted to spout words to end the uncomfortable silence. Even though he had attended school in King Igneous's homeland, Tanin hadn't had many opportunities to eat with the king himself. He'd never warranted a dinner in the private quarters. He didn't know if Igneous was always like this or if the presence of the prophet had put him on edge. Tanin didn't much care. He just wanted the information they needed, then they'd be off.

Tanin sighed in relief as the king broke the silence. "Why have you come to my kingdom?"

Tanin drew the king's attention. "Direct. Good." Igneous's intense dark eyes made Tanin fidget under his gaze. He cleared his throat. "We're here for a map."

Salvo seemed unsatisfied with the prince's answer. "We need help defeating Ydiny's followers. The Goddess intends to magnify the Recharging through the blasphemous use of Lagaw's gifts."

Tanin swallowed as the king's stare never left him. "We must destroy the Machine before magic dominates the world once more." Saying it out loud sounded so ridiculous, Tanin was ready to kick himself out of the honored chamber. How did he fall for such nonsense?

His long black beard, streaked with white, not gray, trailed behind him as King Igneous swiveled his seat to face Grand Master Ironsmith. Tanin had almost forgotten the grand master was in the chamber. The dominating seat in the center of the table worked better than Tanin had imagined.

Prophet Salvo nibbled a bit of cherry tart. "Lagaw will lead them to the right decision."

Tanin envied his complete faith.

Meerin stretched in an attempt to see around the chair. "Those astropriests don't look thrilled."

Augusta delicately sliced through a honey-glazed carrot. "Yet Thoretick remains carved into their entrance. They hold onto the old ways. King Igneous will help us."

As if summoned, Igneous turned around. For a moment, when the back of the chair stood perpendicular to Tanin, he could hear the astropriests begging for a reconsideration. Ironsmith sat with arms crossed, giving away nothing.

"I hear rumors of our cousins, the Krimmel, opening their sealed kingdom." That same intense stare dared Tanin to lie. "Is that true?"

Tanin straightened his back. This ruler of an enclosed kingdom, which had nothing if not for trade with Tarbin, was not going to intimidate the heir apparent of a much-mightier kingdom.

He shrugged. "We don't know for sure."

The king's eyes narrowed.

Tanin pushed his plate away. "I've met a dwarf claiming to be a Krimmel. Prince Aleck Stoneworth, he calls himself. Whether the kingdom has been opened or one dwarf escaped, I don't know." He leaned forward. "But I am here making this request of you because you are *my* ally. I have no obligation to any other dwarves, past or present."

Igneous smoothed down his slicked mustache. He nodded once, then turned to talk with his advisers once again.

Tanin exchanged a look with Rory on his right. "He must have heard of Aleck traveling with Talia. She must be dealt with before her defiance threatens everything we've built."

Rory shifted in his seat, obviously uncomfortable with the political wrangling. Maybe Tanin should have brought Orui. He seemed to jump on board with any sort of intrigue.

The back of the swivel chair scraped the inside of table. The king stopped in front of Tanin's party so they could all hear him. "I have been informed that a rebel dwarf master of the school stole an entire collection of books from our great library. I cannot give you what you ask."

Meerin groaned and tossed her napkin onto her plate. "Now what?"

Steepling his fingers against his chest, Salvo stared off into space.

The king absorbed all the reactions without giving away any of his own emotions. King Roland would have been drinking heavily and carrying on about how untrustworthy his people were. He would have grumbled that he would get to the bottom of the disaster and would do whatever he could to find a mutually beneficial solution. Tanin didn't know what to do with the silence.

Tapping on the back of Igneous's chair caused the king to change his audience once more.

A hand touched Tanin's. Augusta winked at him. "The prophet is praying. Lagaw will offer a solution."

Tanin's heart beat faster. Between the stress of this dinner and the touch of a beautiful woman, Tanin didn't know which had a larger effect. He squeezed her fingers. Augusta wasn't the first woman he'd been attracted to, but it had never run deeper than that. Was he obsessed with her because she was forbidden or because of her innate charm? He determined to bed her to end the beguilement. He couldn't take the constant temptation interrupting his every thought any longer.

Prophet Salvo plopped his hands onto the table as a look of complete peace relaxed his face.

King Igneous faced his guests once more. "I have decided to allow you into the ancient records hall. If your god Lagaw and our god Thoretick wish to work together, they will give us a sign and show you the way."

"Agreed." Salvo stood and grabbed his staff. "Shall we depart?"

Igneous stared at the eager prophet as he casually took another sip of wine and nodded.

THE DINNER PARTY entered through the towering doors of the library. Tanin didn't understand why such a diminutive populace demanded such impractical giant doors.

Most of the rooms they'd been in so far had been converted from natural chambers in the rock. The records room was something wholly different.

Huge beams stabilized the arched stone ceiling, allowing for a room that felt as tall as the mountain itself. Attached three rows high, torches too large to carry adorned two sides of each pillar. The massive amount of light still left every corner shadowed. The heat from the flames barely cut through the chill. The records room was simply too big to be lit or warmed with such contained fire. Yet any more torches would threaten the safety of the bookshelves.

The group followed the king and his priests down the steps onto the main floor. The astropriests looked wholly unhappy with the situation, but their smug expressions told Tanin that they didn't think any sort of miracle would occur. They walked with confidence, secure in their positions.

Tanin looked over his shoulder at Prophet Salvo, flanked by his disciples. His walk mirrored the confidence of the old dwarf priests. Tanin crossed his arms as they descended to the bookshelf-lined paths. It was true Lagaw had provided Tanin with the means to defeat the sea monster, but he didn't know how the god could replace a missing book. He'd entered a maze, both physically and mentally, and he wasn't sure he liked the feeling.

When he was a student here, Tanin had had to make formal requests for specific books from lists held in each master craftsman's office. Gregor had been the only student during Tanin's two years allowed into the records room. That fact still angered Tanin.

The bookshelf corridor dumped them into a grouping of rectangular tables. A large circle of bookshelves, flat sides facing inward, bordered the area like carefully planted trees around a clearing. A couple of dwarves looked up from their studies at the curious interruption, but most remained hunkered down, lost in concentration.

King Igneous moved to the center and opened his arms wide. "Where does Lagaw tell you to go?"

To his credit, Prophet Salvo didn't pause before choosing a path to the left. His staff clicked against the stone floor in a quick rhythm. Tanin had to lengthen his stride to keep up with the focused and determined prophet. The dwarves jogged along behind. The astropriests slowed to a walk as the group flowed around a roadblock of books and then turned immediately back to the left wall. King Igneous didn't miss a step. He wasn't even breathing hard, as far as Tanin could tell.

The next turn dead-ended at a perfectly vertical wall. Small holes bored into the granite held countless scrolls. Each layer of paper was separated from the others by a metal railing. Two ladders, one that ended halfway up the wall and one that reached from the floor to the top of the collection, rolled along metal tracks.

Prophet Salvo gestured at the documents. "May Princess Augusta peruse your impressive collection of ancient scrolls? She is an expert in many languages and has a knack for finding the information we need."

Augusta acknowledged his compliment with a blush. "The great Lagaw guides my hand."

It was a miracle the king had any hair left on his upper lip as he stroked his mustache again. He reached forward and rang a bell attached to the shorter ladder.

A dwarf wrapped in a scarf to fight off the chill hustled around a corner carrying an enclosed oil lamp. He bowed, the light bobbing in his hand as he caught his breath. "I am Scroll Keeper Hardin. How may I be of service, my King?"

"Please help this young human find the scrolls she desires." Igneous squinted at the scholar. "None are off limits, though no copies shall be made."

"Of course, my King." Hardin turned to Augusta.

Grand Master Ironsmith motioned for two of the astropriests to stay behind. Tanin repeated the action with Tutor Grayson and Hodan. He wanted to stay informed.

Prophet Salvo had already moved away, and Tanin hurried after him. The prophet skirted along the outside of the book maze, one hand trailing the rugged rock on the unfinished part of the wall.

Tanin thought he stopped at the south wall, though his sense of direction had gone blind from being underground and switching direction with every bookcase.

Chatting eagerly with Meerin, Prophet Salvo pointed to oil lamps on the smooth wall. "We need to get these lit. Lagaw has led me here."

The mechanically inclined princess studied the series of ropes and pulleys attached to the lamps, though Tanin couldn't imagine their purpose. Rory left Tanin's side to analyze the problem with Meerin.

Kettlor took his place. "This wall looks odd. Can you see the dimension that stands out from the polished surface? I can't tell if it's carved or plastered out."

Tanin squinted through the darkness. He picked out some oddities but couldn't discern what they meant. He had to speed this along. With his hands held behind his back, he sauntered over to King Igneous. "Are there any helpful dwarves whose duty it is to light these handy lamps for us?"

The king blinked twice, then turned to Tanin. "If your god wishes to see the creation guided by ours, He will show his prophet the way."

Squeezing his hands until they ached, Tanin resisted the urge to throttle the king. How could he rule a kingdom so passively? The security of his granite fortress gave him a false sense of immunity. After Tanin brought the astropriests to their knees, he'd teach the Eckerd a thing or two about authority.

Tanin rocked back and forth on his heels. The picture of his father doing the same move caused him to stop. He wasn't going to become his father. No little girl would control his decisions or weaken his resolve. He unfolded his hands and leaned casually against one of the bookcases as Meerin and Rory attacked the problem.

Salvo joined the prince. "It's a map. Augusta uncovered talk of such a piece carved into the side of a mountain. When I saw Thoretick at the entrance, I knew it would be here. Then King Igneous said works had been stolen from a large records room. What's more important than the layout of your entire creation?"

Tanin looked up at the clicking of a chain. Was the ceiling opening? The noise bounced off the stone walls, only slightly muffled by the stacks of books. A few dwarves peeked their heads around the nearest bookshelves.

Rory called Orui to his side. Tanin couldn't hear anything they said over the cacophony of metal on metal. Orui pulled his fire starter from his bag and handed it to the weapons guardian. The noise stopped as abruptly as it had started. Rory struck the steel on flint. Tiny sparks flashed to life, then faded until the wick in the oil caught. Tanin averted his eyes as the flame pierced the darkness. Meerin enlisted one of the curious dwarves by handing him the end loop of a chain. Very unprincess-like, she wiped filthy hands on her tunic as she nodded at the dwarf to pull.

Grating filled the room again. Meerin moved down the line to the next chain and pulled on the dust-covered metal. She hung from the stubborn chain, pushing against the wall to get it to move. Grand Master Ironsmith rushed to her side and added his strength to hers. The strain of two chains moving at once shook the wall. Dust that had to be older than Tanin dropped from the surface in chunks—no gentle swaying in the air like cleaning day in the castle. The smell of mold strengthened until Tanin had to cover his nose with his shirtsleeve.

Rory lit the lantern attached to the new chain as Meerin moved along the line to the next pulley system. Dwarves poured from the inner sanctum to the wall as if the grating noise had called to them. Tanin looked up at a flash to his left, about ten feet up. A wax candle flared to life with a sputter as a layer of grime burned off and the wick caught fire. Around the spotlight, layers of granite were cut away, forming an inverse map of a huge continent. A form Tanin had never seen before.

As the chain continued up, his eyes followed the lantern like a beacon. The next candle flashed to life simultaneously with the lowest one next to Ironsmith.

"It *is* a map," Tanin muttered as he moved to the center of the piece. He marveled as each new section was revealed by an old, neglected candle.

Prophet Salvo clapped his hands together, his eyes tearing up. The gathered dwarves mumbled as the map grew, as if the light had brought it to life. More than one covered their ears against the scraping noise. Kettlor sneezed next to Tanin. The mold-filled air paled in comparison to the vast world map. Tanin had never seen anything so complete. Many of the islands and continents depicted on the map were completely foreign to him. Were they real?

King Igneous climbed up one of the bookcases, ignoring the pleas of his guards to be cautious. He sat on the edge of the very top, his feet dangling over empty air. Tanin followed his example, mounting the tall bookcase closest to what he thought was the center. Kettlor balanced on the side, beside his prince.

One chain after another grew quiet as all five candles on each route were lit. The silence was almost more disturbing than the roaring of the mechanisms. Lagaw whispered through the cavern. Tanin could hear Him.

*This is what you were meant to see. Take note.*

Directly in the middle was the Renquist continent. The Eckerd Mountain Range Tanin sat in was a deep indention in a large cavernous hole carved in the shape of what he recognized as the Eckerd chain of mountains. His attention flickered to small fires inside a couple of holes, where the starter lanterns had caught the compact dust on fire. It looked like the life-sized war map of a world foreign to Tanin, though the typical rectangle was more of a flattened sphere, with the middle much wider than either the top or the bottom.

Meerin moved along the map, yanking on each chain to make sure it stayed in place. As she passed Prophet Salvo, he swept her off her feet in a swirl of a hug.

"Praise be to Lagaw! He has shown us the way. We will be victorious." Salvo pointed to a large city sticking out from the flat background of a desert. The structure looked odd in a map where all elevation was carved into the rock instead of standing out from it.

Tanin called down, his voice sounding empty in the quiet chamber. "Why is that city different from the rest? Should it not be carved in like the others?"

Salvo bubbled with religious fervor. "No. It is perfect. The ancient holy city of Raqmu lies beneath the surface. The desert came, and Lagaw lead the people to protect His holy city from the biting sands. It's still there, and He has shown us the way."

Tanin felt the same enthusiasm, but he wanted a bit more control. He motioned to Rory with a flattened hand and mimed a pen and paper. The weapons guardian nodded and tapped Meerin on the shoulder. The two eagerly pulled out paper and charcoal to sketch the map. Tanin wondered if he should send Orui to help. He didn't need the two engineers to measure everything so carefully that they wouldn't get the map complete.

Instead, he leaned toward Kettlor. "Make sure a message gets to King Roland to send a delegation to reproduce the map. As we reclaim ancient Tarbin lands, it would be nice to know the terrain first."

The husbandry guardian nodded.

On the adjacent bookcase, King Igneous stared at the wall, his hand planted over his mouth.

Tanin rubbed dust debris from his eyes. "You didn't know this was here, did you?"

Igneous didn't move for another full minute. Tanin tapped his knees impatiently. Council meetings must take an eternity with this dwarf in charge.

"We had wondered about the chains and saw some of the holes as flaws in the granite. But we didn't know we possessed such a blessed treasure." The king took a too-long pause again. "Thoretick and the Light who guides us on this path have approved of your mission. I will aid you however I am able."

Tanin smiled. "We humbly accept."

# CHAPTER TWENTY-THREE

EVERYONE IN TALIA'S group carried backpacks with their personal gear and a share of the party's supplies. Though wide enough for two people to walk along without too much hazard of falling, the path through the Eckerd Mountain Range was too twisty for a cart.

Talia hadn't realized this route was so much tighter than the normal road she had taken from Tarbinulus to the Eckerd capital. They'd just have to pare down their supplies. They shouldn't have to carry water, and the mountain had pretty healthy hunting except above the tree line. Talia knew they'd be fine, just inconvenienced. She was much more worried about the desert trek.

When the party reached a large curved valley at the center of the range, Talia picked up the pace as much as she could. Her companions didn't thank her for the effort. Time was streaming through her fingers. The thought of being late and missing the Recharging motivated her to ignore her exhaustion and continue.

Since it was more difficult to breathe this close to the Light's Daughter, Talia sighed when the pass opened up to a flat plain. She could use a break from climbing steep inclines for a few days.

The landmass itself had oddly placed boulders scattered across the plain, as if one god were constructing a mountain and another god were knocking the building blocks all over the floor. A tiny stream of ice-cold water ran through the middle of the valley. The water tasted fresh. Talia dumped out her water bladder and refilled it with the snowmelt, the last trickle before winter froze the whole valley again. She sat beside the stream and let the cool liquid soothe her dry throat.

Gregor slipped his backpack off his shoulders and leaned against one of the boulders. "The chilly air is invigorating, but I wouldn't want to be wading through feet of snow."

Naul nodded his agreement as he dropped down beside the same boulder and untied his boot laces. The trail the companions were following through the Eckerd Mountain Range was relatively safe, but the weapons guardian still managed to injure himself.

Aleck plopped down next to Talia. He wasn't even breathing heavily. Climbing steep rock was nothing new to the cave-dwelling Krimmel. "This is so much safer than the pitch-black hiking of my youth. You never knew where the edge to a drop was. Here, the Light's Daughter protects your feet."

The weapons guardian guffawed as he loosened the laces of his boot. "Easy for you to say. She didn't warn me of the loose gravel that twisted my ankle."

Dew raised her arms to welcome the Light into her cold body. "Or the tree branch that snapped you in the nose."

Nyna retrieved a salve from her bag and knelt by Naul. "Or the mountain goat that used your shoulders to move from one cliff to the next."

Sighing at her touch on his ankle, Naul rubbed his shoulder. "That goat had tiny hooves. It felt like knife points digging into me."

Talia tapped her companion on the thigh. "Apparently, the mountains don't like you any more than the Royal Forest." The thought of home brought a bit of sadness with it, though she had no place there anymore. The once princess observed her loyal companions, her friends. Their destiny was attached to hers. She hoped she could make something of Raqmu.

Rodianiari slumped, as if every moment of exertion had caught up with him in one fell swoop.

Talia stood, wanting to give him some sort of comfort, but not knowing where to start. "Why don't we make camp for the night? It's a bit early, but not ridiculously so."

Dew shook out her coat. "It would be nice to get at least somewhat clean."

Gregor squeezed her shoulder. "Why do you always want to bathe when the only available water is icy cold?"

The cultural guardian pushed him away playfully. "This from the man in constant need of a cold dip."

Naul laughed, then grabbed his ribs. "Don't make me laugh. It hurts. But she's not wrong."

Off to Talia's right, Rodianiari dropped his bag and headed toward the huge ice wall in the distance. She grabbed Aleck's attention. "There he goes again."

Aleck moved to the other side of the boulder to watch the elf go. "I wonder why he disappears every few days?"

She shrugged. "Maybe he just needs some time alone?"

Talia jumped as Parnim dropped firewood near her feet. The dwarf pulled her scarf from her almost clean-shaven face. She had complied with Talia's request but had passive-aggressively punished her for it ever since. "Do you want me to follow him, my Prince?"

Aleck considered for a minute. "No, he hasn't done anything harmful. He's given us no reason to mistrust him."

Talia could think of a few incidents that were strange, but she might have been reading too much into them. Her only experience with an elf was Thilphiliari, who had gone mad after centuries of being alone. She had to block that memory in order to give this elf a fair shake.

"This has to be more difficult for him. Like the nadph, the survival of his people depends on this Recharging."

Aleck nodded to the cheerful Jura, who proudly showed off the knot Ial had taught her for lashing the tent to a ground stake. "She doesn't seem too worried."

Talia smiled. "She's young. You know, she reminds me of you when we first met."

Aleck's face darkened. He tugged on his beard, worry instantly aging him. "Let's see if we can keep her that way." He squeezed Talia's elbow and moved to help Jura and Ial with the tents.

Gregor moved next to Talia. "Are you all right?"

She turned to Ial before she could get locked in Gregor's caring gaze. "Hey, Ial, I think I saw some small deer. What do you say to a little hunt?"

Naul hopped up on one foot. "Yes. Fresh meat is just what my aching body ordered."

Nyna laughed at the weapons guardian. "You are not going hunting. Any prey would hear you coming well before you got in arrow range."

"Fine. I'll hobble along and gather enough wood to make a blazing fire for a fine roast." Naul slipped his boot back on without tying the laces.

Talia strung her bow and grabbed her quiver. With Ial at her side, she set off as quietly as she could over the gravel ground. Rodianiari was little more than a shadow in the distance. She understood his need to leave the party for a bit of solitude. Hunting with Ial was about as peaceful as it got for Talia.

A tiny horned head popped up over some scrub in the south. She gestured to the small group. Ial nodded and followed silently behind. Fresh meat would cheer the whole party. Talia focused on this immediate goal, blocking out the big picture for one evening. All the worry would return in the morning. For now, she focused on the hunt.

# CHAPTER TWENTY-FOUR

THILPHILIARI KEPT HIS HEAD DOWN, scanning the rocky ground for any hazards. His hair flashed dark streaks that had nothing to do with shadows. He had to get away from the group before they recognized the supposedly deceased elf beneath the magic film of Rodianiari.

He needed to recharge. He had needed to recharge for a couple of days now but hadn't felt any sources nearby. Within the disgusting dwarf realm, Thilphiliari had found a few pockets of magic, but nothing transportable. He absorbed as much as he could from each source, but the trying time in the dry mountain air was getting to him.

It was the sacrifice he made for his people. After this torment, he would return to his waterfall and his palace and awaken the elves. The high council would be grateful and insist he wear the crown of all elfdom for his loyalty and sacrifice.

Scanning the valley for the source of magic he could sense, Thilphiliari picked out a few twisted bushes. The evergreen needles formed a dome as if they grew over a glacier rock, but he knew the structure wasn't natural. It was an ancient elf hut. At one point, this valley had been speckled with thousands of these manipulated-nature homes, one elf family in each. During the post-cataclysm wars, the dwarves had slaughtered the peaceful elves and driven them from their ancestral homes.

He stole a glance over his shoulder. No one seemed to be looking his way. The humans and dwarves were morons. Thilphiliari couldn't imagine what god had seen fit to create them in the first place. Elves and dragons had roamed the world first. What need had the planet for parasites when the ideal cultures had already been developed by the dragons and elves? How useless was a people without magic?

Slipping underneath a bush canopy, he ran his fingers along the woven interior. The evergreen thrived, after all these centuries. That would be the elves too. His people would clear the forest of all the griffons, then move to the hills and reclaim what was once theirs.

Thilphiliari lifted the lid of a rotting chest. The neglected wood broke into pieces in his hands. If the box hadn't been propped up off the ground on smooth glacier rock, the bottom would have rotted out. He hovered his hand over its unidentifiable contents, reluctant to touch anything. He felt no magical item inside. His lip curled in disappointment.

Kicking the chest from its perch, Thilphiliari sat crossed-legged on the ground. He closed his eyes and smoothed his long hair around his shoulders. The thought of the gods haunted his mind. As the unlikely group of companions traveled across the plains, he had listened intently to the story. A prophet roamed the land, spreading word of the ancients' return. The humans spoke of Lagaw as if he were the great leader. Of course they would think that, but they were wrong. Ydiny, Goddess of Magic, Creator of the Elves, was older and more powerful than any in the pantheon.

When the Recharging failed, the elves thought Ydiny had abandoned them. She had left them to Lagaw's mercy, of which he had none. The dwarves and humans had teamed up and driven the elves back. They had relegated the magical race to one small forest. Thilphiliari remembered the torment of the council as they tried to decide how to save their people from a millennium of weakened magic. Instead of sacrificing their lives as the dragons chose, they decided to wrap themselves in aspen and pray for Ydiny's returned love at the next Recharging.

Thilphiliari steadied his breath and centered his mind. "Ydiny, great Goddess of my people, show me the way. Lead us to our salvation. I see now that You did not abandon us. Lagaw betrayed You. Allow me the power to seek Your revenge and capture Your blessing."

The tingle of a massive source of magic pulled at the edge of his senses. Not here, but close. The mini-charging had awakened something. He reached out with his consciousness. In a mountain cave, just ahead. Thilphiliari jumped to his feet and pushed aside a branch as though it were the flap of a tent.

The angle of the sun flashed on speckled granite. A jagged opening, large enough to fit a city, seemed to swallow the brightness.

"Thank You, Ydiny, wise Goddess. I will not fail You."

Full of faith and hope, Thilphiliari jogged with renewed energy to the mountainside a couple hundred yards away. At the edge of the vertical slit, he peered inside but couldn't see anything. The magic, however, hummed through his body and tingled his senses. He pulled his bag off his shoulders and flipped the flap open. This source was too large to absorb all at once. He needed to seed the gems he carried. With the bag in hand, he hugged the wall of the cave as his eyes adjusted to the pitch black.

As he moved around a stalagmite, his foot slipped on dried leaves piled on the floor. A wind of warm air blew Thilphiliari's hair, the tips crackling against the rock behind him. He froze. The wind hit him again. The stench of rotten milk filled the room like mist off an ocean of dead fish. Either an entire herd of nursing cows was rotting in this cave or . . .

"Giants." The word slipped from Thilphiliari before he could silence it.

The meager light from the autumn sky reflected off a sleeping baby. Thilphiliari covered his nose with one hand as he studied the grotesque creature, which was taller than an aspen and as wide as his waterfall. He hated giants, even if they lay harmlessly in a rough blanket. They were nasty things without manners and with only the most basic brain activity. He admitted he'd hoped this species wouldn't return with the Recharging, but Ydiny knew best. Brand-new magic, fresh from Ydiny herself, flourished in the small beast. And it was just what he needed to finish his journey to Raqmu.

Setting out his jewelry in a line beside the sleeping giant, Thilphiliari rolled up his sleeves. He placed one hand on the baby's crusty forehead and whispered words of calming magic to place it into a deeper slumber. He couldn't have the little brat waking up and disturbing the stones or, worse, alerting its parents. He didn't want to waste any newly acquired magic on annoying adult giants. And he didn't have enough storage to sap all their power.

Plus, the last thing he needed was meddling from the other party members. As slow as Talia and her guardians were, not even those morons would miss a giant storming through the valley.

Thilphiliari took a deep breath. His limbs ached from weakness, the sleeping spell having taken the last bit of spare power he'd had. He fought the overwhelming drowsiness that threatened to collapse his knees onto the nested floor. Blocking the sight of grotesque warts on a bald head, he leaned in and whispered a prayer to Ydiny.

A flood of warmth flowed into the gem and through Thilphiliari's arm into his chest. Euphoria set in as the tingling filled his body and blocked out all other senses. When his body brimmed at full strength, he placed his other hand over his ring. The sapphire lit the cave with an iridescent glow as if the stone were just as happy to be full again.

Taking a deep breath, he wrapped his free hand around a palm-sized diamond he normally kept under his belt. Energy flowed through him and into the stone. He relished the fresh magic, which was much richer than the thousand-year-old variety he had siphoned from the sacrifices in the aspen forest. The thought of a million times that amount sheltering in a huge underground grotto, available for his use alone, motivated him to refocus on his mission.

As each jewelry-mounted gem filled, its light added to the one before. Thilphiliari moved down his line of batteries. These life rafts would keep him strong. As the elf approached the end of the line, the baby giant's breathing slowed and its body cooled. Every fiber of Thilphiliari's being vibrated with renewed energy. The cave's drop in temperature didn't register.

Once he had filled the last stone, a rather dull agate that was good for little else than storing magic, the inner glow faded from each piece like a mini-sunset. The cave dropped into blackness again. Thilphiliari picked up each battery with the tenderness of a father with his newborn child.

With each piece back on his body and the extra gems in a protected bag hidden in his robes, Thilphiliari tilted his head to examine the comatose baby. Its skin looked grayer than it had initially, but its chest still rose with shallow breath. It didn't look healthy, but it had fared better than the elves who had sacrificed their lives. Thilphiliari thought of his wife, drained of her life force to ensure Thilphiliari could fulfil his destiny to save his people.

Suddenly angry that the monstrosity had lived while so many of his kind had died, Thilphiliari thrust his sapphire ring into the side of the giant. Pain gripped his senses as magic poured into his cells. He siphoned every bit of power he could from the squirming infant. Strands of energy burned through his arms. Flames shot from his toes and scorched the rough-hewn, tent-sized blanket. His nerves screamed in agony until screams flew from his mouth.

The cave shook, shedding layers of dust from the stalactites to cover everything below. The baby wailed as the sleeping spell was broken by the deadly draining of its life force. Thilphiliari's scream morphed into laughter. He saw the pain as his sacrifice to his people, his fulfillment of his duty to protect them from those who wished to destroy them.

The sapphire blinked, almost faster than his brain could register. Each time the light returned, it was brighter, until the gold of the ring liquefied around his finger. Thilphiliari yanked his hand from the giant. The intensity of the pain was worse than when he'd been impaled by the treacherous human.

As the agony faded to no sensation at all, he was sure his finger had been severed. Lifting his hand to his face, relief calmed his fear. His finger was still there. His chest heaved as he adjusted to the steady flow, instead of the intense rush, of magic through his veins. The sapphire still blinked, though it was much slower and fainter. The gold of the band, however, had melded with his skin as an extension of his own flesh.

"As it should be." Thilphiliari blew on the ring with easy confidence. As if he had put on the glove of a perfect hand, magic shimmered over his skin, reinstating his Rodianiari disguise.

The giant lay still. Dead. One less monster his people would have to destroy before reclaiming their ancient lands.

The last bit of light faded from the cave as Thilphiliari found his way to the exit. The sun hid behind the mountain peaks. Much time had passed. He hefted the gem-laden bag with his good hand. He'd better return to camp before the murderess sent someone to find him. He desired no conflict. He rubbed his new finger with his thumb.

Not yet.

# CHAPTER TWENTY-FIVE

TALIA PUSHED around the coals of the fire. The sky behind the mountains announced the coming dawn with a glowing orange line. She yawned, her eyes heavy with exhaustion. Turning to grab another piece of mesquite bark to throw on the fire, Talia cursed her lack of a regular schedule. She could collapse in her blanket and easily fall asleep now that the morning approached. A couple of hours ago, she hadn't been able to shut her mind off long enough to join the peace shared by her companions.

Naul handed her a mug of warm tea. "Looks like you need this more than me."

Talia held the mug in both hands. The comforting warmth freed her skin from the biting chill of the mountain air. "I don't know why I couldn't sleep."

After pouring hot water over tea leaves for himself, Naul sat across from Talia. "You just wanted to keep me company."

She smiled at the weapons guardian. "Yep. That was it."

Steam chased the cold from her face as she breathed in the refreshing herbal fragrance. A deep grumbling vibrated through the mountain valley.

Naul stood. "Thunder?"

Talia looked up. "No clouds."

Aleck rubbed his eyes as he stumbled next to Talia. "Sometimes, a storm from far away can rumble through a great deal of rock to bounce around in a valley."

Talia scooted over to make room for Aleck to plop down. "For a cave dweller, you know a lot about the above-ground happenings of mountain ranges."

Accepting a cup of tea from Naul, Aleck pulled a bladder of beet juice from his bag. "We spent many nights above the protective ceiling to hunt deer and other delectable meat."

She cringed as he dumped some of the bright red liquid into his tea. "I don't know how you drink that."

"I don't know how you drink the bitter herbs. It needs the sweet of the beets for balance." Aleck took a loud slurp of appreciation.

Another rumble, louder this time, vibrated along the ground. Talia put down her mug and stood up to get a better vantage of the sky. It was crystal clear.

Ial, Nyna, and Jura joined the fire circle.

The legged mermaid bounced slightly as she walked. She was never grouchy in the morning.

Nyna shivered, her arms clutched across her chest. "Was that an avalanche?"

Ial rubbed her arms to add warmth. She leaned into him.

Talia nodded toward Aleck. "He thinks it's thunder in the distance."

Jura crouched and closed her eyes. "It comes from the ground, not the air."

Traneck stuffed Aleck's bedding into the prince's bag. "The elf kicked us awake."

Parnim rested the guards' bags next to Aleck's. "He's lucky we didn't stab his feet." She scratched her shaved face, obviously not accustomed to the lack of beard.

Talia waited for the punchline, then realized the guards weren't kidding. "Rodianiari is awake and packed and forcing everyone else up?"

Naul shook his head. "Impossible. Two days ago, I threatened to throw him over my shoulder if he didn't hurry up and get his bag packed."

Talia's mug clicked against the stone as a third rumble shook the ground. A growing sense of urgency teased the back of Talia's mind. "Something's not right."

She studied the glacier. Maybe it was cracking. It was too dark to make out any details beyond a glint of reflected orange, like a heart-beat deep inside. The Light's Daughter needed to illuminate the Dark before Talia could make anything out.

Rodianiari rushed through the camp and tossed Talia's bag at her. She caught it before it hit her in the head. "What's the rush?"

The elf cleared his throat and stood ramrod straight. His lips tightened and loosened multiple times as if he were considering his answer carefully. "My ancestors lived in this valley before the," he cracked his shoulders, "dwarves drove them out."

Talia wondered what he had been about to call them. "And the valley is angry?"

Rodianiari shook his head, his long hair flying around his shoulders. "No." He bent over and tore the blanket from Nomyra's spot.

Talia called out, "Priestess?"

Nomyra swept in from outside the camp, her face covered in sweat. Talia had never seen her so disheveled.

"Were you running?" It was all she could come up with. "In the dark?"

Dew stood in front of Talia as if sensing danger. "What's that rumbling?"

"Thun—"

Talia was interrupted by the priestess's labored response.

"Giant. We have to go. Now." Nomyra held the bag with the crown against her chest as though she were protecting a baby.

Anger rushed through Talia. She yanked the crown from

Nomyra and secured it to her belt. "What are you doing with the Key?"

Nomyra's breathing stopped as her wide eyes met Talia's. Her head shook back and forth gently as if searching for an acceptable answer.

Talia would deal with her later. First, they had to pack up camp and leave the valley before the sun gave them away. "Let's move it."

Dew shoved everything in her bag without the careful folding and packing she normally practiced. "A giant? Elves, then mermaids, then giants?" She paused and stared at Talia. "Do we know what we're doing?"

"Nope. But it's too late now." Talia dumped her tea on the fire and tied the mug to her pack.

Gregor waved his hands to disperse the ash that burst in his face. "Whoa. Careful there. What's the hurry?"

Dew dropped Gregor's bag at his feet and handed him his sword belt. "It looks like we decided to camp in a giant-infested valley."

Colored drained from his face. "That wasn't thunder or an avalanche?"

Nyna dropped her arms. "Giant footsteps."

Adrenaline pumped through Talia's system. She was awake now. She grabbed the water bucket beside the fire and dumped the whole thing on the flames. "No time to lose. Let's go."

The whole area flashed dark until Talia's eyes adjusted to the meager light of the morning sun.

Jura climbed a boulder close to the modest stream. "I want to see the giant."

Ial slipped his bag onto his back and strung his bow, the cold wood giving him a bit of trouble. "I thought giants were extinct," he muttered through clenched teeth.

Aleck got a leg up from Traneck to sit beside Jura. "We thought the same thing about mermaids."

Talia gestured at Rodianiari. "And elves."

Nomyra paced around the stone, impatient to get going. "The

small alignment likely awakened random magicals. We might even run into something we've never seen before."

Rodianiari crossed the stream by jumping across a few rocks as easily as a prancing deer fleeing from a hunter. "Forward. We must go forward."

The priestess followed, choosing to walk through the water rather than risk a fall on the slippery surface.

Nyna helped Talia get her heavy gear situated on her back. As she turned to repay the favor, a shattered cry shook the gravel at their feet.

In the dim light, Talia thought she saw a large form cross in front of the glacier. If what she glimpsed was actually the giant, it was huge, taller than the highest tower of Tarbinulus Castle.

Aleck's guards dragged the prince and the mermaid off the rock. They pushed them toward the elf and priestess. Neither offered any objections.

Dew stretched as Nyna swung her staff. Both helped Talia pack up the last tent.

Talia surveyed the area to make sure they weren't leaving anything vital behind. "I don't know what upset the giant, but I have a feeling we don't want to get in the middle of it."

Gregor walked beside her as they headed to the east. Sunlight filled the sky before them, shadowing the eastern mountainside. Talia had seen the pass they needed to get to yesterday, but right now it was invisible. She thought they were going in basically the correct direction. This route was taken so rarely, there was no path to lead the way. There was a reason the dwarves traded up north instead of traveling to the south. It was too treacherous. But Talia couldn't risk getting caught on the Tarbin side of the mountain.

The occasional rumble morphed into a jagged, regular cadence. The ground bounced, shifting the loose gravel and soggy peat moss beneath her feet. Talia navigated her footing the best she could. Naul tripped over a piece of wood that spiraled in front of his step. Aleck held up his arms to catch him until Traneck shoved him out of the way. Naul hit hard, but his cursing told Talia he was fine.

In the lead of the party, Rodianiari didn't slow. "Come, come. We must keep moving." He was completely unhindered by the movement of the ground.

Dew fell against Talia's arm as the cultural guardian's ankle twisted on a rock. Talia balanced Dew as she hopped a couple of times.

Tenderly putting pressure on the injury, Dew released Talia. "I can still walk."

Adjusting the strap of her shoulder bag where it was tucked under her full pack, Nyna shivered. "This doesn't feel right. We can hear something big, but we have no idea where it is. What if we're running right toward it?"

The elf answered before Talia could form a response. "Definitely not. It's coming this way."

Nomyra nodded. "I saw it while I was . . ."

Her hesitation spoke volumes. She'd been communing with the wizard in the crown. Talia wondered how many times she'd run off with the Key and talked to him.

"Meditating," Nomyra said, picking up her explanation quickly enough. A lifetime of lying must have made it pretty easy to think on her feet. "The giant is nearer the glacier. As long as it doesn't see us, we should be fine." She held her robes in her hand so she wouldn't step on them as she hurried over the gravelly rocks.

Talia shook her head at the priestess's insistence on wearing the impractical robes of her office through the mountains. Finding it easier to let her have her way than to fight, Talia had stopped arguing. "What do we know about giants?"

Dew shrugged. She was concentrating on her ankle too much to elaborate further.

Naul quipped, "Beyond the fact that they're extinct?"

Gregor shifted his pack. "The old sage in my father's nursery spoke of giants. I thought she was being metaphorical. Some sort of comment on the political hierarchy. Now I'm not so certain."

Talia asked, "What did she say?"

"Mostly that they were as tall as mountains with exceptional hearing and sense of smell, but horrific eyesight."

Aleck leaned over at an odd angle to keep his backpack from tipping him backward. He refused to take a smaller load than the rest. "We have many tales of giants, though they were hunted to extinction from the Krimmel range."

Talia perked up. "How?"

The prince shrugged. At least, Talia thought that's what he had meant to do as his bag swayed on his back. "I don't remember hearing any details."

Traneck carried his load much more easily. "They are said to be of living rock and immune to all weapons."

Parnim added, "The tales told to our children claim they're not very smart. Usually, the end of the myth has the characters tricking the giants."

Aleck's beard almost dragged through the gravel, he was angled so far forward. "It was supposed to be a tale about how muscle doesn't always win. I doubt it was based on actual giant traits. Even if you are smaller than your opponent, you still have a chance at victory."

Talia gripped the straps of her bag. "So I guess we know nothing. Great."

A second roar echoed through the valley. The force of the sound itself shook the gravel. The running steps grew louder and more frequent. It was definitely headed their way. The Light lit the world behind them, but the Dark shaded it in front. Talia felt like they were running from safety into danger. They were almost close enough to find that passage.

Talia glanced over her shoulder to get a better idea of how far they'd traveled. "By all the Light touches."

A huge beast with two arms, two legs, and a squarish head

stomped through their overnight camp. Its skin, the same mottled gray, white, and brown of the mountain, with streaks of red, shifted like the bark of the nadph. Talia couldn't tell if it was male or female. She didn't even know if there were male and female giants. The magical held a bundle of woven grass against its chest. Though small compared to the giant, the bundle had to be larger than a frigate.

The beast stomped the boulder that had held Aleck and Jura moments ago to dust. Nyna threw her hand over her mouth to prevent a scream. Talia understood the inclination. Its rectangular nose sniffed the air like a wolf narrowing down its prey. Its square head pivoted on its wide shoulders. Cloudy quartz eyes stared directly at Talia. Her limbs went numb. The image of the giant so easily crushing the boulder with one stomp curdled her blood.

"Run!" she yelled.

Instead of obeying, every party member turned to see what was behind them.

Talia rushed by her frozen companions. "Go, go, go! We have to make the pass."

She cringed as the giant roared in triumph. The rest of the party needed no further encouragement. They took off.

Talia spotted a slit in the mountainside. The giant definitely wouldn't be able to fit through there. It might have been able to punch its way through if it really wanted to get the party that badly, but it would take time and they'd be long gone before then.

"This way," she yelled over the thunderous noise of the running giant.

She ducked as waves of loosened gravel fell from the mountain.

Dew ran at an angle, pushing Talia away from the climbing terrain. "Rockslides quickly turn to avalanches."

Talia nodded, too winded to talk. Dew grew up in the Krimmel Mountain Range. She would know better than most.

Gregor shouted from close to the back, "Faster!"

Her limbs ached. A sharp pained stabbed her side. But Talia

picked up her pace. The winding path through the mountain was just ahead. They'd make it. They had to.

Talia jumped across a small puddle and skidded to a halt. Nyna bumped into her, sending her arms pinwheeling to prevent herself from falling straight into the path of rolling rocks.

"Avalanche." Talia pulled Nyna with her as the group backed up.

The small gravel led a river of larger stones and debris. On top of it all rolled a massive boulder. The thunder of the avalanche drowned out the chasing giant's steps. Aleck pulled on Talia's sleeve and pointed behind them.

The giant had stopped running. In broken Common, it mumbled, "Baby. No more."

A deep moan startled Talia from the avalanche. A giant ripped through the mountainside as if it were no more than beaded curtains.

# CHAPTER TWENTY-SIX

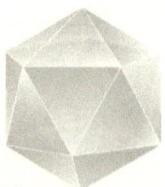

NAUL DROPPED his bag on the ground and pulled his sword loose. Talia did the same, though she wasn't sure how useful a tiny sword would be against a beast that could move through a mountain with such little effort.

Aleck pointed at Rodianiari, who was skirting across the still-shifting avalanche as easily as he might walk along a forest trail. "What is he doing?"

Talia wanted to shout but didn't know how to do so without attracting the focus of the giants. At the moment, they seemed to be distracted with each other.

Ial comforted Jura, who was crying. She must have been hurt.

Talia ordered, "Nyna, check on Jura while we have a lull in the sprinting."

The medicinal guardian's lips twitched, but she went. Talia studied the distance to the crevice. It had seemed so close a few moments ago. Now it was unreachable. She turned to Nomyra. "Suggestions?"

Nomyra grabbed Talia's hands. "A couple members of the party could distract them while the rest of us slip away."

"That sounds like certain death." Talia rubbed her side, forcing out the pain that made itself known every time she inhaled.

"We must all sacrifice for the greater good." Nomyra moved to follow the elf. "Come."

Talia didn't like the way the priestess stared at her.

Dew put a hand on Talia's shoulder. "Umm . . . Talia."

The larger giant ignored the group of tiny people as it moved toward its fellow.

"Now." Talia scrambled to grab her bag and move around the still-crumbling mountainside.

She noticed Ial and Nyna hadn't convinced Jura to move. Talia squeezed the straps on her pack. They didn't have time for theatrics. "Naul, carry her if you have to."

Naul handed his bag to Gregor, who groaned under the extra load. "Maybe I want to carry the pretty mermaid."

Talia rolled her eyes and started forward again.

Jura pushed Naul away and walked toward the giants. Ial rushed after the mermaid who was surprisingly fast on legs. He turned her around. They yelled at each other.

Talia threw her bag on the ground and stomped over to the pair. "We don't have time for this. Those giants will squish us like bugs. Can we fight once we're relatively safe again?"

Jura swung around. Her deep blue eyes flashed rage behind her tears. "Their baby is dead. Can't you feel the emptiness?"

Talia took a closer look at the bundle in the arms of the first giant, whom she could now make out as female. The huge, likely male, beast that had burst from the mountain tilted his head and stroked the frigate-sized rock wrapped in the woven straw.

Now she understood the anguished cries, but she didn't know what she was supposed to do about it. "It's very sad, but we should go."

The mother shook the baby blanket, grunting. The father giant looked down and took a loud whiff. His rocky eye sockets narrowed as he raised his head to the sky and roared, "Elf!"

Talia stepped back and tripped over a stone. Gregor caught her before she could hit the ground.

She looked up at him. "Run?"

He nodded as he pulled her along.

The father took a couple of huge strides and one large bound over the avalanche debris. His bulk smashed into the earth right behind Rodianiari. The force sliced through the surrounding area. Talia's feet slithered from under her as though a carpet had been pulled beneath them. She fell with a crunch as her companions collapsed around her.

All except for Nomyra and Rodianiari. They were so close to the giant's landing, they were flung into the air. The giant reached down with a hand the size of an ox and caught the elf before he could crash to the ground. Nomyra, however, wasn't as lucky. She hit the rocky ground with a sickening crunch.

Nyna screamed and pulled herself off the ground. Ignoring the giant, she rushed to the priestess's side. Gregor helped Talia up.

As Ial ran by, Talia looked at the crevice in the mountain face. They were so close, but it wouldn't do them any good to abandon the elf to his own devices. They couldn't enter the city without him.

Talia rubbed the sweat from her forehead before it could drip into her eyes. Not to mention the guilt she'd feel for the death of another elf. She owed those people a chance at renewed life. She took a deep breath and approached the giant.

Naul put a staying hand on her shoulder.

She shrugged it off. "We have to try and save him." She put a hand on his as it reached for his sword. "I don't think our weapons are going to help."

"Let me get you out of here. Someone else can talk to the giant." Gregor's fear for her touched Talia's heart, but didn't sway her decision.

"We really don't have a choice," she said.

Aleck helped Dew along. Her injured ankle didn't seem to be

holding her weight anymore. "Of course we have a choice. We can help the giant."

Talia brushed dust from her hands. She thought about the glow of her skin when the mini-charging had blanketed the earth. The Bright One, they had called her. She had prayed to the Light to show her a better path than service through marriage, and the Light had answered her. Talia had already made her choice.

She motioned Gregor toward the mountain pass. "Why don't you take the injured through the pass? Without the elf, there's no point in continuing."

Dew smacked Gregor. "Don't you dare."

Talia squinted at Dew's limp. "Those are my orders. You might not be sworn to me anymore, but I'm still in charge of this expedition."

Dew's face reflected hurt. Talia let it pass through her. She would have time for sentimentality later.

As the sun finally reached the top of the mountain wall, the giant's shadow lengthened until it covered the entire area where the party stood.

As Gregor bore Dew's weight, Aleck joined Talia. "I'm not injured. I'm staying with you."

His guards stood on either side, eyes plastered on the giant. They didn't argue with their prince.

She considered sending him away, but doubted he would listen.

The giant roared at Rodianiari, whom he clutched in his grasp. Spittle mixed with sheer force almost bent the elf in half.

From about thirty yards away, which felt much too close, Talia shouted up at the giant. "Hello there."

The grieving father's breath was so harsh, it dragged Talia's hair over her face, then pushed it backward with each exhale. She held her hair back with an arm and squinted up at the giant.

His pink-streaked quartz eyes lacked pupils, but Talia knew he was looking directly at her. "Human."

Talia imagined herself staring down at a beetle. She hoped the giant didn't feel as little for her as she would for the bug. "My name is Talia."

The dwarf prince waved. "I'm Aleck."

The giant blinked, an angry scraping sound followed by dust sifting from his lids. "Dwarf?"

As his guards tensed, Aleck took a step closer. "I am a dwarf. What is your name?" He talked slowly and loudly as though he were conversing with a deaf child who didn't speak Common well.

Rodianiari struggled to free himself from the giant's grip. Talia didn't see the point. She'd watched the giant leap over the massive avalanche like she had the small rivulet. They wouldn't outrun the giant even if the elf managed to free himself.

She glimpsed Ial and Nyna carrying Nomyra to the safety of the pass. Jura followed though she kept looking over her shoulder at the giants, tears glistened in her eyes. Most of them were headed to safety. One less thing to worry about.

Grimly, Talia realized she only needed elven blood. She shook the thought from her head. *No. I'll free Rodianiari. Somehow.*

The giant patted his chest with his free hand. "Bada." He swung his arm toward the mother of his child. "Mim."

Talia nodded her head. "It's an honor to meet you, Bada and Mim."

He ignored Talia as he swung Rodianiari within a few feet of Aleck. The companions tensed, and Naul almost dropped Dew to throw Talia to the ground. She shook her head at his overreaction.

"Elf here. Dwarf move bad elf."

Aleck leaned back but didn't move his feet. "Umm . . . yes, the elf is bad." He looked at Talia for help.

Bada continued. "Bad. Elf no here. Now elf back. Hurt Bamim."

Talia blanched. She shot a look at Rodianiari. The elf growled and a tingling crackled the air.

"Don't you dare." Talia's command shocked Rodianiari. The power in the air dissipated as he crossed his arms instead, obviously not having any trouble breathing.

Mim sat crossed-legged, puddles of water falling from her quartz eyes to the dusty ground. She placed the bundle in her lap and removed the cloth covering her baby. Unlike the ragged nature of its parents, the baby had smooth, polished skin. It looked to Talia more like the statue of a baby than an actual living being.

Aleck lifted his hand as he approached. "May I?"

The grieving mother nodded up and down. "Dwarf help."

The prince cried beside her as he laid his hand on the smooth, still head. "I wish I could."

Talia swung around to Rodianiari. "Did you do this?"

He didn't look at the dead baby. "Babies die. What makes you think I did it? Why would I bother?"

She squinted at the elf with her hand on the hilt of her dagger. Maybe he wasn't worth saving. Just a little blood, right?

At her beckoning, Naul carries Dew closer. She places a gentle hand on the smooth rock of the infant and offers the death prayer.

"When the Stars wish you well, they give you health. When the Stars wish you happy, they give you love. When the Stars with you home, they call to you."

Bada set the elf down next to Talia. He sat next to Mim, pulling her close.

Talia grabbed Rodianiari's arm before he could take off. He started to pull his hand from her grasp until Naul loomed behind him. The elf glared at the large human, but stopped protesting.

Talia's leg tingled as it rubbed against a bag that swung at Rodianiari's hip. She recognized magic as it coursed through her skin. She frowned at the treacherous elf and snatched the bag from his side. Rodianiari's face darkened.

Inside the bag were three large gemstones. She hesitated to touch them, still afraid of encountering a trapped being, but the emerald on her ring hummed and flashed softly.

Dew finished the prayer as Aleck and his guards sang a dirge in sweet harmony.

"The Light calls to you now, sweet Bamim. Go home."

Talia couldn't take the loss. She slipped Windall from her neck and put it on her finger. She had no idea what she was doing, but if giants were magical creatures, maybe she could help with the stored energy in the confiscated gems.

Mim nodded as Talia held a hand up for permission to touch the child. Windall gently glowed as she pressed her hand against the baby's surprisingly pliant forehead. Her second hand grasped an energized gem from the bag.

"Please, Light from above, protector of the innocent, accept this offering from the Bright One. Allow this child to grow with her loving parents. Please let her breathe again."

The familiar tingling flowed through her skin from the bag to her ring. A film of green covered the infant, blowing aside the straw covering. The power soaked into Talia's body, invading her insides with a burning that approached pain. The feeling faded as the stone grew cold. Before the light could go dark, Talia grabbed the next stone and increased the flow.

The baby floated above her mother's lap. Talia climbed onto Mim's ankle to make sure she didn't lose contact. The energy transfer crackled through the hair on Talia's arm. A pink burn, like she would get after a long day on the beach, grew across Talia's skin. She couldn't stop. Not yet. A bump from under the rock-skin surface sent a wave of joy through her. It was working. Bamim's heart was beating — weakly, but it was definitely beating.

Talia grabbed the last gem much more quickly than the first. The flow moved so fast, her muscles vibrated with waves of heat. Her insides were cooking. She had to release it.

The baby giant shook her head, dislodging Talia. She tumbled backward off Mim's ankle. Aleck and Parnim caught her before she could crash into the tiny sharp rocks. The valley seemed to grow dark as Talia's body turned cold from the sudden absence of magic. Too weak to stand, Talia let the dwarves brace her.

Aleck shook her as joy overcame his tears. "Look, Talia. You did it. She's alive."

Bamim cried and squirmed in her mother's arms. She *was* alive. The giants laughed and tickled the little one, turning her cries into giggles.

Mim pointed to the mountain pass. "No more elf."

Aleck nodded. "No more elf."

Talia balanced with one hand on each dwarf's shoulder. "We will deal with him."

She looked back at Rodianiari. He was unmoved.

Naul wiped tears from his eyes as he tossed Talia's bag over his shoulder. "What do you want me to do with him?"

She ignored the question. She had no idea what to do with the destructive elf. "Let's get out of here before the giants change their minds."

# CHAPTER TWENTY-SEVEN

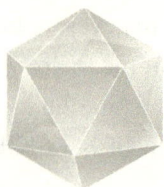

TANIN FIERCELY GRIPPED the wooden oar as the rapids tried to take it from him.

Augusta tucked her body deep into the center of the canoe. "I am still confused as to why this was a good plan." She had to shout above the rushing water that buffeted the vessel with an anxious ferocity.

Rory pushed his oar against a boulder before the front end of the canoe could slam into its unmoving surface. "The dwarves said it was the fastest way to the desert."

In a canoe slightly ahead of them, Orui ducked as a tree branch threatened to knock him into the rushing water. "In the same breath, they said we would be crazy to try it."

Tanin's stomach twisted as the boat turned in a disorienting circle. The flat bottom of the vessel allowed it to bob on the surface with little chance of taking on enough water for it to sink. Which was a good thing since waves of water crashed into rocks and sloshed into the wooden vessel almost constantly.

Ignoring his aching arms, he pushed against the water as if it were a foe on the battlefield. "It was the quickest path. That's all we needed to know."

In the third canoe, Hodan stood to grab a sliding rations bag.

Kettlor grabbed Hodan's tunic before the boy could fall into the water. "Stay still, lad. We can hunt for more food."

Tutor Grayson chanced a look backward to make sure his student was stable. "Not in the desert. We'll need to buy our supplies at the oasis before we set out to cross the barren sand."

Prophet Salvo raised one hand to the cloudy sky. "Lagaw will provide. We must succeed. As long as our hearts are pure and our minds focused, He won't let us fail."

Tanin had faith in Lagaw and that he was on the path to gain His favor. But he didn't believe for an instant that the God of Man would give them anything. They had to earn it.

Salvo's grip on the crossbar with his other hand seemed to prove his point. When they got into the boats, Meerin had insisted on rowing beside her prophet. Tanin had been impressed with her determination. He truly understood why King Juarim wished to marry both women. They balanced each other well. Meerin sat in front, with Orui in back to control the vessel. Tanin couldn't help but sneer at Salvo's silence on the matter. Tanin would never let a woman work instead of him. Salvo might have the ear of Lagaw, but He apparently didn't tell him everything. The God of Man wouldn't allow such weakness in His representative.

The hours dragged on as small waterfalls and jagged rocks next to perfectly smooth ones tried to feed the party to the river. The canoes flowed down one watery branch until it connected to others farther downhill. Two more streams ran into the main flow. The resulting turmoil strained Tanin's already exhausted muscles until he wasn't sure how much farther he could go.

Just as Tanin was about to force a landing, somehow, so they could take a break, the river widened to triple its size. The flow slowed to a nice leisurely pace, like current of the pond in the middle of the Royal Forest. The three canoes coasted in the calmer waters.

Orui slumped down in his seat. "Praise Lagaw. My arms are jelly."

Tanin laughed and dropped his oar in the canoe. He stood in the gently rocking boat to stretch his back. Rory held both sides and counterbalanced naturally as if he had been on the water his whole life. With Lagaw on his side, Tanin wouldn't need the guardians anymore. Rory would make a perfect minister of his new cannon fleet. At least he could always be confident of the weapons guardian's loyalty. Of all his men, Rory never swayed.

Orui clapped oars with Meerin over Salvo's head. "At least we didn't run into any monsters this time."

Hodan was dumping full cups out of his waterlogged canoe. "Unless you count the river itself."

Tanin sat down and took the bailing cup from Augusta. He dunked it into the fresh river water to quench his thirst. The cool liquid soothed his dry throat, which ached with his continued heavy breathing from physical strain.

The princess hung part of her skirt over the side and squeezed a goodly amount of water from it. "I don't think I'll ever be dry again."

Grayson pointed to an easy landing spot for the canoes under a copse of trees. "We could take a break for lunch."

Tanin shook his head. "No reason to now. We have everything we need here. We can let the river guide us for a little bit while we eat and let our muscles recover some."

Augusta shot Tanin a critical look. "There are other needs that are much more difficult for Meerin and I to relieve."

A flush colored Tanin's cheeks as he imagined peeing over the side of the canoe with the girls staring. "To the shore."

Kettlor groaned as he gripped his oar once more. "I'm not sure my hands have the strength."

Orui thrust his oar into the water. His canoe shot forward. "There's no fight in this current. You can handle it." He splashed Kettlor, soaking Hodan instead.

"Hey," the boy cried.

Meerin giggled as she added her paddling to Orui's. "Race you," she dared the other two canoes.

THE SUN HAD DRIVEN AWAY the clouds and dried the inside of the canoes by the time the party made it back onto the water. Tanin had a hard time staying awake as the warmth soaked into his aching muscles.

Augusta had banned all splashing. Her imperious tone brooked no argument, and Tanin let her have her little victory. His men might as well get used to her authority. She would be their queen soon enough, if he had his way.

Grayson dragged his oar through the water to pull even with Tanin. "The current is pulling a bit more aggressively."

Rory nodded. "Maybe the river branches again. The smaller diameter would increase the flow."

Tanin waved off their concerns. "We'll deal with it when it happens. For now, enjoy the rest before we have to fight the river again."

Hodan stood up behind Grayson, swaying easily with the canoe. He pointed excitedly to the shore. "There's someone over there."

Tanin squinted into the tree cover, where he thought he could discern shadows moving around a modest fire. "Probably villagers from this side of the mountain."

Salvo bent over the edge of his canoe, forcing Orui to lean in the opposite direction to compensate. They hadn't capsized a single vessel along the rapids. How ironic if it happened in the middle of the calm.

The prophet focused on the shore. "I feel Ydiny's presence. It tingles through my soul."

Tanin whipped his head toward the shore as the boats moved closer. He paddled backward, trying to stay in one place. With Rory's help, he managed to slow their forward movement to a crawl. The rest of the vessels followed his lead. One after another, they turned in a circle, back upstream, then down again, the movement stabilizing their place compared to the unmoving land.

"Talia." The part whisper, part curse fell from Tanin's lips.

Hodan waved his hands at the party on the shore. "Should we stop?"

Tanin resisted the urge to reach into the adjacent canoe and push the boy overboard. "No," he said instead. He had to remember that Hodan barely knew the princess, though the turmoil she'd caused as she fled the crowning at the Forging Ceremony should have shown the young cultural guardian how dangerous she was.

Rory straightened the canoe to face downstream, pointedly ignoring the shouts coming from shore. A rumbling noise echoed across the water, making it difficult to discern what Talia's party was yelling. Multiple members were waving their arms over their heads in a much-too-enthusiastic manner.

Tutor Grayson hesitated to move forward. "It seems like they really want to tell us something."

Tanin frowned. The current was pulling harder downstream. He chose to concentrate on that instead. The noise and the increased drag suggested they were approaching rapids again. "We'll see them soon enough at Raqmu if Salvo's predictions are accurate. I'd prefer to spend as little time as possible with my treacherous sister until then."

A shout from Meerin interrupted his paddling. "Prince Tanin!"

"What?" Did he really need all these people to break one machine? They'd destroyed the giant clam mechanism just fine on their own.

Rory dug his paddle in as Tanin added his full strength to fight the dragging current and circle upstream a bit. All three canoes circled mostly in place, though with each turn, they ended up a little farther downstream. The current was just too strong to defeat completely.

Meerin's outstretched arm pointed to a soft blue glow from shore. "It's a sign."

Tanin scoffed. "It's not a sign. It's my sister showing off her treacherous blood." But it wasn't Talia. Tanin recognized the long robes and loose pale hair flying in the breeze. "Of course Nomyra is with her." Her hands were the ones glowing as two of Talia's guardians stretched a rope from the void.

Rory tapped the side of the canoe. "It looks like they're trying to snare us. Maybe we should move out of range."

Hodan asked, "Who is the tall man sitting on the stone? I thought I'd met all of Princess Talia's companions."

Tanin shook his head. He could care less who the stranger was. "She likes to pick up strays. It doesn't matter."

Salvo leaned precariously over the side of his boat, forcing Orui to grab his robes again. The prophet's mouth hung open. "An elf. Ydiny sends her minions to stop us."

He stepped over the bar between him and Meerin, who sat in the front of the canoe. Yanking the oar from her hand, Salvo pushed her to the middle seat. He thrust the paddle into the water, jerking the boat forward before Meerin could stabilize herself in the center. With arms flailing, the princess tumbled into the water.

Salvo realized his error and almost dove in after her. Only Orui's quick movements stopped the prophet.

Instead, Salvo gripped the edge of the boat and shouted, "Meerin!"

Augusta held onto her seat as if she were to be thrown in next. She closed her eyes and whispered in prayer. "Please, almighty Lagaw, protect us from our enemies. Provide a safe passage so we can fulfill Your wishes."

Tanin searched over the side for the mechanic. She was the most useful member of the team, with her intimate knowledge of the inner workings of the Machine. A splash from the shore drew Tanin's attention as a large fish tail disappeared under the surface. "That's got to be a huge fish."

Kettlor's face blanched. "We don't know what kind of predators live in these waters."

Orui hesitated in removing his shoes. "Do you think it's safe to go in after her?"

Kettlor shrugged.

Salvo yanked his robe free of Orui's grip. "I will go after her. Lagaw will guide and protect me."

Rory shouted over the increasing roar of the river. "If Lagaw didn't want Meerin in the water, why did He allow her to fall?"

His face beet red, the prophet retorted, "It's a test."

As Tanin considered diving in himself to get this over with and move forward, a human head popped up quite a distance downstream. "There she is." He stopped dragging his oar and let the current move them forward.

Thrusting his oar into the water again, Salvo propelled his and Orui's canoe ahead of the group.

Augusta strained her neck to see around Rory. "That's not her. The hair's the wrong color. And the skin . . ."

The hair was a bright fuchsia, and the skin was covered in pearlescent scales. She breached the water, exposing a dolphin-like tail before arcing back under. Tanin frowned and adjusted his sword belt. "We found our monster."

The canoes caught up with little effort. The water's speed had increased as the width of the river shrank. Talia's group was running along the shore, trying to keep up as they dodged tree roots and treacherous rocks. For some reason, they still carried the rope Nomyra had magicked.

Tanin frowned at the cacophony of water hitting rock. They were definitely heading into another set of rapids. They needed to find Meerin before her body was bashed against a boulder.

Orui yelled over the rapids, "There. It's a mermaid."

Off to the left, the monster swam faster than a cantering horse through the tugging current. Tanin tensed, prepared for a collision. Gripped under the mermaid's arm was an unconscious Meerin.

The mermaid brought the woman right up to the canoe. Orui and Salvo hauled the princess over the side.

The prophet's face wrinkled in concern. He squeezed his

companion and wailed to Lagaw. Meerin coughed and spit up a lungful of water. Tears ran down her face.

The mermaid clapped her hands, easily staying beside the boats without holding onto the wood. "I am glad I was able to help. I am Jura. Now to save you all."

Tanin stared, shocked by her perfect Common. "What do you mean, 'save us'? We're doing just fine on our own."

Tutor Grayson bowed his head to the mermaid. "We are grateful for your actions that rescued our companion."

Hodan looked between the prince and the tutor, unsure where he was supposed to stand. Tanin's face flushed at his doubts. The boy had sworn eternal loyalty to the heir of Tarbin, not some powerless teacher. He'd have to remind the cultural guardian of his oath once they were free of Talia and her negative influence.

Jura untied a rope from around her waist, her scales shining in the sun. Tanin marveled at the living mermaid, until he remembered she was a magical and their goals were opposed.

"We don't need your help." He gestured for Rory to pick up his oar and move forward. He doubted they could outrow her after witnessing her agility in the water. But they could prevent her from tying a rope on the canoes—with what purpose, he couldn't guess.

The current picked up speed as if Lagaw Himself was helping the party escape. Tanin knew he would have to confront his sister sooner rather than later, but it would be on his terms, not hers. His twin's voice rose above the roar. Talia waved her arms from the edge of a boulder downstream.

Tanin blocked her words. He didn't want her to influence his decisions. He would beat her to Raqmu and ensure Lagaw's victory. Talia wouldn't win this time.

He turned at a loud splash from behind, annoyed that someone had fallen out of a canoe again. How had they made it through the rapids without anyone falling overboard? In this more modestly flowing part of the river, everyone was eager to take a swim.

Orui tossed a bucketful of water at Tanin. The shock of the cold water on his sun-toasted body filled the prince with rage. Hodan was talking to the mermaid and pointing at the prince's canoe. She nodded and ducked under the water, the rope in her grasp.

Kettlor clasped his hands around his mouth to help his voice carry. "Waterfall!"

Tanin's anger flared to fear. Downstream, he could see a bloom of mist that blocked the rest of the river. His senses filled with the image of the waterfall at the Golden Palace, with its pillowy spray from the scattered water and the jagged rocks at the bottom. He gripped the canoe's wooden edge.

Luckily, Rory acted quicker. He leaned over the bow and secured the rope Jura handed him. The weapons guardian waved to the shore. Talia shouted something over her shoulder. They wrapped their end around a tree and pulled with the extra leverage. The canoe tipped dangerously to port, then stabilized and moved toward dry ground. Tanin and Rory paddled against the current, trying to aid their progress as much as possible.

Jura swam back to shore, grabbed another coil of rope, and swam back before Tanin's boat had made much headway. Grayson motioned her to the prophet's boat. Orui secured the rope to the bow, just as the river roiled a bit more anxiously.

Tanin's hands on his oar slipped back and forth as his sweaty palms refused to give him a proper grip. Close to shore, he looked back to see Grayson and Kettlor paddling ferociously. The current was so strong at that point, they might as well have held on and hoped for the best. Hodan gripped the wooden sides and stared ahead, frozen.

Tanin cursed. He didn't want to have to break in another cultural guardian before this one was even useful. Between their paddle strokes and the rope, Tanin's boat hit the sandy shore hard enough to skid onto dry land. Tanin jumped out as Rory untied his knot on the bow and tossed the rope to Jura.

Two of Talia's guardians, Naul and Dew, along with a couple of dwarves Tanin didn't recognize, untwisted the anchor rope from the tree to rush downstream for better leverage. Tanin followed. Talia jumped down from her boulder and shouted to him.

He didn't slow down. He could see the edge of the waterfall, a bubbling cauldron before death. The noise was so loud, he couldn't hear anything beyond his heart beating in his ears. The humidity filled his lungs as if he were underwater. The edge of the drop was all smooth, slippery rock, forcing him to slow down and watch his step. He jumped as a hand closed on his shoulder. Rory moved quickly in front of him. Tanin frowned. What was the guardian going to do if he tripped? Be the first one over the cliff?

Tanin stood at the edge of the drop, which was easily twice as tall as the one in the Elven Forest. He could make out the canoe bobbing in the water. His men had given up rowing and were holding on for dear life. Upstream, where the second canoe had landed safely, Salvo, Meerin, and Augusta formed a prayer circle, their hands held to the skies. If Lagaw really wanted them to succeed, now was the time to prove it.

"By the Light, Tanin. We didn't know that was you out there." Talia stood close to him. Her arms twitched.

Tanin swore if she hugged him, he'd toss her in the water. "A mermaid, huh? Where'd you dig her up?" If she'd gone all the way to Kiwa, he couldn't imagine how she had made it to this part of the Eckerd Mountain Range in such a short time. His gaze shot to the sky. "Do you have the dragon with you?" Magic or no, if it would save his guardians, he'd use it.

Talia shook her head. "We'll get them."

Her pale face showed her uncertainty. She had always been a horrible liar. Tanin didn't know how she imagined she could rule.

Orui joined the other rope bearers around a large tree whose roots dangled off the cliff. Tanin wondered if it was strong enough to pull the canoe to the rocky shore. Kettlor, Hodan, and Grayson were ducked inside the canoe as far as they could get. Jura popped up right behind them with the rope in her hand. Even she seemed to be having some trouble with the current.

The rope hit Kettlor in the head. He caught it and tied it to the stern. The crew on shore pulled until it was taut. The canoe twisted in the current, almost capsizing with the sudden change of force.

Tanin closed his eyes and offered a prayer to Lagaw. He'd come through before. If He wanted His will fulfilled, He'd save Tanin's men, wouldn't He?

Augusta screamed, shocking Tanin out of his prayer. He instinctively crouched, one hand on the hilt of his sword. But her scream was from anguish, not fear. Even with the rope fighting the current and Jura swimming backward with all her might, attempting to tug it to safety, the boat was powerless against the giant natural waterfall. Tanin's hand clenched as Kettlor, Grayson, and Hodan flew over the cliff.

# CHAPTER TWENTY-EIGHT

TALIA FELL backward at the sudden slack. She lost sight of the canoe in the mist, but the still-attached rope trailed toward the edge, picking up speed. Gregor stood between the end of the line and the edge. Her heart sank.

"No!" She sprang to her feet and sprinted. She dove at his knees and brought him crashing down. His head cracked against the stone.

Gregor curled into a ball, holding his head. "What was that for? I was just . . ." The whistle of the rope whisking past his head cut him off. If he had remained standing, he'd have been flung over the cliff. He blinked twice, then grabbed Talia's hands. "Thank you."

She concentrated on her breathing, afraid it would stop with him so close. Curse the Dark, she didn't have time for this. Rory crawled up next to her to lean over the cliff face.

Talia scooted out of Gregor's grasp. She felt cold without his touch. That was silly. The ground that was soaked with the frigid mountain water had a lot more to do with the feeling than some ephemeral emotion.

She looked over the edge and found the canoe swinging through the mist that was stirred up from the river. Thank the Light, the rope twisted around the tree still held. All three men clung to the boat.

There was no sign of Jura.

Rory shouted over his shoulder, "They're alive, my Prince."

Tanin leaned over the side, and Talia swore the weapons guardian grabbed hold of his ankle. "How long can they hold on?"

Talia wondered the same thing. She ordered her crew, "Pull them up. Quickly."

Naul grunted, his arms vibrating with the rope. "Easier said than done."

Gregor grabbed the rope closer to the tree as the length expanded with the crawl backward. The tree itself shook as the rope cut into its bark. The swinging vessel strained the stability of the exposed roots. The canoe moved up the cliff slowly. It bounced off the cliff face and jarred the men clinging to it.

Her brother held out his hand to help her stand. She hesitated as her mind imagined him pushing her. She steeled her muscles and accepted Tanin's offer. Talia gripped him a bit tighter than she might have one of her companions. If she went over the edge, he was going with her. How sad, that she couldn't trust her twin, even when she had just saved his life.

Rory crossed to the far side of the scraping rope. "Orui, I'll need help balancing the canoe."

Tanin's medicinal guardian removed his shoes and took up position on the other side.

Nodding in agreement, Rory removed his own. "Good idea."

Tanin leaned toward Talia. "For better grip." He folded his arms and stepped behind his men.

Talia resisted the urge to punch him. "Good thing we happened to be here to save your butts."

The strange man in a long robe spoke from behind Talia. "Lagaw the All-Knowing led you here to ensure our safety and your salvation."

Tanin laughed loud enough for the noise to hang over the roar of the falls. "I'm afraid she's a lost cause. Prophet Salvo, meet Talia Winterlaus, attempted usurper of the Tarbin crown and lover of all things magic."

Her face drained of color.

Salvo's eyes turned dark as his gaze bored into her soul. Talia took an unconscious step back. A hand at her waist stopped her before she could get too close to the edge.

Ial was at her side, though his gaze scanned the misty cliff. "Have you seen Jura?"

Talia's muscles slackened as sadness overtook her anger. "I'm sorry, Ial."

Priestess Nomyra folded her arms, looking more like Tanin's sister than Talia did, and eyed the prophet of a strange god. She looked strong enough, though her gray complexion showed her exhaustion. Talia wondered how this god fit in the game.

Rodianiari pointed to the slowly progressing rope. "Your god doesn't seem intent on saving *all* of you."

Parts of the magically woven rope frayed as the friction of rubbing against the rocks did its damage. Talia jumped in front of Naul to add her strength to the mix. "Hurry. I don't know how much longer this rope will last."

Her palms burned as she pulled in a quickening rhythm. The bits of frayed rope scraped her ungloved hands.

Naul rubbed one bloody hand on his pants, then the other. "How does a magic rope fray, anyway?"

Talia shrugged as much as she could as her bodyweight yanked backward again. She didn't have the breath for words. She hadn't fully recovered from escaping the giants, and here she was, exhausting her efforts again.

The slither of rope was drowned out by the scrape of wood on stone. Rory and Orui gripped either side of the canoe and pulled in unison with the rope crew.

Nothing happened.

Kettlor's voice called out from the mist. "Hurry up. I can't feel my arms."

Rory shouted at Naul, his fellow weapons guardian. "Quit pulling; you're just straining the rope."

As if given permission, a strand of the weave snapped.

Orui dropped flat and reached his hand down. Whatever he said, the words were drowned out by the waterfall. With his feet braced in a crevice of rock, Rory gripped Orui's legs. He leaned back to keep the medicinal guardian from slipping over the edge.

Talia's arms shook with the strain of the rope. "Hurry."

Kettlor's head popped up over Orui's shoulder as he used his companion as a ladder to climb to safety. The husbandry guardian rolled onto his back, panting. Another strand of rope unraveled. The boat fell a few inches.

Ignoring the complaints of his guards, Aleck flattened himself on the other side of the canoe. Ial dropped down and imitated Rory's technique on the dwarf. The boat shifted to the side as a boy climbed up over Aleck's shoulder. It was Tyler's replacement. Talia hadn't been home long enough for her to remember his name.

The rope slipped through Talia's grasp as the weight shifted in the canoe. "Come on. Come on. Come on. We're almost there."

Tanin held the rope next to its knot. "Grab the stern."

Kettlor and Rory grabbed the wooden edge on opposite sides of the boat.

"Pull!" Talia yelled, using the last bit of her strength in unison with her companions.

Everyone pulled simultaneously. The boat tipped horizontally, as if floating. The stern slammed into the granite. Tanin and his guardians pushed it toward the tree as though it were a laden sled. Still precariously over the edge, the last passenger, an old man Talia didn't know at all, scooted over a wooden plank, toward solid ground.

Talia jumped at a crack of splintered wood. At first, she thought it was the stressed tree, and she almost released the rope on instinct. The old oak was battled and bruised, but it still held solid.

"Grayson, jump!" the boy yelled from the edge, where Aleck held him back from leaping into the canoe to help his companion.

The man's foot had broken through the battered bottom of the canoe. "I'm stuck." He yanked harder, which only served to throw him off-balance. He fell heavily against the bow. If his foot hadn't been wedged, he'd have fallen over the cliff.

The force of his body hitting the canoe knocked the boat backward. The rope cinched so hard, it pulled some of the tree roots from their mooring. With a snap, the shredded braiding severed. Talia fell backward at the sudden lack of tension. The other end ripped from Tanin's grip.

Rory and Kettlor backpedaled, but their strength wasn't enough to stop the canoe before they followed it down.

Talia yanked Windall from around her neck and shoved it on her finger. She dove at the end of the rope, letting her instincts take over.

A tingling, almost burning but not painful, traveled from her hand through to her toes. The boat froze. "Come on," she repeated like a mantra.

"She's glowing," said a woman's voice, though Talia didn't recognize whose.

The waterfall faded into the background. The smell of tree sap and burnt rope dissipated. All of Talia's senses beyond the feel of the rope and the attached canoe darkened. Every woven fiber obeyed her command. The air around the vessel fulfilled her wish. The wind itself gathered its force and lifted the boat as easily as a wave on the sea.

Talia rose with it and turned. The people on the cliff scurried out of the way, though Talia only peripherally noticed the movement. Her entire being was focused on the floating vessel. With a sigh, she sat down, cross-legged, setting the boat safely next to the tree.

The rope fell from her hand as her body emptied of all will. The world swam before her in a swirl of sound and color and smells. Talia blinked as a hand landed on her shoulder. She could see it but couldn't feel it. What had happened?

"Talia, are you all right?"

Nyna. It was Nyna. She was so pretty with the light surrounding her.

Talia closed her eyes for just a minute and collapsed into darkness.

# CHAPTER TWENTY-NINE

TALIA SQUEEZED ONE EYE OPEN. A sharp spike stabbed her brain, causing her to curl into a ball. She wrapped her arms around her head. Her right hand, adorned with Windall, felt huge. She pulled it down in front of her face and blinked until the pain in her mind had faded enough that she could focus. Her hand was bandaged in a ball of linen. She couldn't feel details under the wrapping, only a dull throbbing she suspected would turn quite insistent if she moved her hand the wrong way. She hoped she wouldn't have to wield a sword anytime soon.

"Nyna?"

Relief heavy in her voice, Nyna rushed to her side. "Talia. Thank the Light, you're awake. I wasn't sure what else to do."

"What happened?" The image of a waterfall and a canoe hanging over a cliff floated through her mind, only to be drowned out by more pain.

"Naul, help me. Talia's awake." Nyna leaned in with a steaming cup of brewed herbs as the weapons guardian propped Talia up.

The land swirled around her. Talia flung her arms out to steady herself against the uncontrolled movement. She hadn't felt this off-kilter since the one night in the Krimmel Kingdom when the companions had gone a bit overboard at a friendly tavern.

When her sight coalesced into one image, she sipped the tea. "Did we drink last night? I didn't know we had any ale with us." She rubbed her tongue against the back of her teeth. It felt huge.

Naul and Nyna exchanged a concerned look, then focused on the ground.

Talia's face tightened in frustration. She leveraged her body against Naul to get to her feet, then pushed away from him and Nyna. "Okay," she addressed the whole party. "Who wants to tell me what happened and why I can't remember it?"

Nomyra looked up from her steaming cup of tea. "You have a magic hangover." Her skin looked sickly.

Talia wondered if that's what she looked like. "A magic hangover? From what?"

Across the clearing, around a separate fire, a man Talia didn't recognize stood up. "You saved my life when you lifted the canoe."

"I can't . . ." Talia had another flash of memory, a glowing canoe and an obnoxious humming. She lifted her bandaged hand. A soft green shone through the bandages, throbbing with her heartbeat.

Talia turned back to Nomyra. "I don't understand. I used magic to revive the baby, and I didn't have any side effects."

Nomyra accepted more hot water from Parnim. "That's because you channeled magic from the storage gems. A complete waste by the way. Rodianiari is quite upset with their loss."

Talia scrunched her fingers, until pain from her injury forced her to ease up.

Nomyra's pace increased and her face darkened as she continued. "This time, you foolishly pulled the magic from your very blood and almost died in the process."

"You risked your life to save a stranger." This man wore a long robe over his tunic and leggings. If he was some other astropriest here to change her destiny again, she was going to walk away right now.

"No." Nomyra jumped to her feet and stomped forward to

confront Talia. "What you did was risk an entire design that was set in place a thousand years ago to save a nobody on a boat. That is not the sacrifice required of you."

"Hey!" cried a boy Talia couldn't quite see in the dark.

"You are the True Heir. You are the Bright One. *None* of this happens without you. How dare you prioritize your own fear of watching one human die over the well-being of entire races of people!"

Talia straightened her shoulders before they could curve in from the mental attack. Somehow, she doubted Nomyra was worried about other people. "What kind of heir would I be if didn't save those I could?"

"The kind who survives to fulfill her destiny." Nomyra's violent pivot arced her hair and robe in perfect half circles. She stalked into the shadow of the trees. "I'll check on the others."

A rebuttal sat on Talia's lips. Then she realized who was missing. "Where's Ial and Dew?"

Nyna guided Talia to a log by the fire and made her sit down. She was too tired to fight the medicinal guardian. "They went searching for Jura."

Naul threw another log on the fire. "Rodianiari went with them. Something about being able to sense her presence."

Talia gasped. "I remember. She went over the waterfall." The entire event came back to her at once. She gazed up at the cliff face. The surrounding trees filtered the roar of the waterfall, which had faded to a gentler bubbling. "I don't remember descending the cliff."

Naul coughed. "Good. It wasn't very dignified." He rolled his shoulders and cracked his neck.

"Lovely." She groaned. At least no one important had witnessed her flung over her guardian's back.

"Tanin." She yanked her hand away from Nyna before she could complete her inspection.

Her brother's face was lit from underneath by the fire around which his party sat. The creepy effect amplified his look of scorn.

Talia whispered to her companions, suddenly afraid she might be overheard. "Why is he here in the mountains?"

Naul shrugged, looking over his shoulder. "He has business in the desert as well, but he refuses to discuss what kind."

Nyna gently took Talia's hand again to check the bandaging. "He has a prophet with him."

"A prophet?" Talia hadn't heard such a title used in anything except old literature.

"Of Lagaw." Naul stifled a laugh.

Talia shared his amusement. "The mythical god? I thought those were just tales of primitive cultures before we learned the teachings of the Light and Dark."

Nyna didn't seem amused. "And yet they keep popping up. Aleck believes in Thoretick, god of the dwarves. Don't forget the carving of Vinta in Thurrelrun."

Talia considered the implications. "Maybe I should talk to this prophet of Lagaw?"

Nyna directed Talia's gaze with a nod toward the edge of the clearing. "Aleck's talking with him now. He seems friendly enough."

Talia accepted her refilled mug from Naul. Her headache had dissipated but hadn't disappeared. She thought about all the rumors of the mythical gods that had floated through the villages as they made their journey south. Maybe this wasn't the only prophet wandering Tarbin. Though technically, they weren't in Tarbin anymore.

She finished the soothing liquid and set down her mug. "Let's go find out what he's preaching and why he's traveling with my brother."

Tanin jumped up from his seat of scowling and cut her off. "I'm the True Heir, you know. You have no claim on the crown."

Talia reached for the Key at her waist as her guilt over possessing something that wasn't hers ate at her again. She knew he was right. Tanin's concentrated gaze made her let it go and cross her arms, the fold awkward due to the bandage on her hand.

"I only need to borrow it to ensure the Recharging and my role as Bright One. And I *am* the True Heir of Raqmu."

Her confidence felt false, even to her. But she refused to back down with Tanin so aggressive in front of her. Their companions backed each royal twin; the tension rose, just like old times.

"You were but a vessel for the will of Lagaw." The prophet's hands were tucked into his sleeves. "I am the true Bright One."

Aleck chimed in. "Did you not see her all glowy when her magic saved the tutor? She's definitely the Bright One."

Talia's foot tapped the ground to prevent her nerves from forcing her to pace. "The Light guided me to save people in danger."

"Light is only energy manipulated by the great Lagaw to His Purpose. The ancient scrolls tell of its formation." The prophet moved his hands to emphasize each phrase. "Lagaw built the world with oceans and land and sky. He granted His siblings dominion over specific areas of Their choosing. He held reign over all."

The two women at the prophet's side, one in a casual tunic and leggings, the other in an embroidered dress and shawl, lifted their hands to the air. "Praise be to Lagaw."

Talia wanted to ask who the women were, but the prophet wasn't done. At least they weren't wearing robes.

"With His family in the world, Lagaw grew lonely in the dark. He pulled a piece of His soul from His chest and created His Daughter."

"Praise be to Lagaw."

With a tilt of her head, Talia thought for a minute about how the different gods both called the sun Daughter.

The prophet's voice grew louder. "She was welcome company, but she scorched the world, boiling the seas and setting fire to the forests. His siblings complained as all They ruled was destroyed. Lagaw, in His great wisdom, spun His Daughter with a mighty push, assuring that nowhere would receive too much love and wither under her torrent."

Tanin pushed in between the prophet and the well-dressed

woman. To Talia's great surprise, he joined in their chant. "Praise be to Lagaw."

"The night was dark and terrifying for the living of the world. Lagaw's siblings fought for dominance. Ydiny, jealous of Her brother's power, gave Her creations magical gifts with energy She siphoned from the beyond when His Daughter wasn't looking. Vinta, God of the Sea, and Ariat, Goddess of the Sky, warred for dominance of the land."

He dropped his head and folded his hands over his chest. "Lagaw saw Their distress. He cried tears for His creation. The light in His love sprinkled across the night sky, blocking Ydiny from siphoning any more power for Her abominations."

"Praise be to Lagaw." All of Tanin's party joined in the prayer.

Talia was fascinated by the tale but refused to be pulled into the theatrics. They'd obviously done this more than once. No wonder the continent whispered of the return of the old gods. This prophet was good.

He bent his fingers and moved them independently, adding a creepy factor to the magic god. "Ydiny argued with Her brother. He could not take away all that made Her creations breathe. He had given Her dominion over magic, and now He was throwing it away. Lagaw, in His wisdom, judged Ydiny's argument as fair. He found a compromise by creating a Great Conjunction powerful enough to spread magic across the planet. Once every thousand years, the Recharging pours magic into the gemstones that are the very foundation of the mortal realm."

"Praise be to Lagaw." Their voices rose in volume, filling the clearing with reverence. Did Tanin really believe these stories? They'd heard similar versions through plays and poetry since they were kids. Something about this prophet had swayed Tanin to transform fiction into fact.

"But man felt betrayed by their beloved creator. They cried to the other world, 'Why have You neglected us and made magic reign over us?' He laughed at the fear of man. He reached down with His mighty hand and anointed prophets, one from each major kingdom. 'You have your own power here.'"

"Praise be to Lagaw."

Talia suppressed a groan. She was growing tired of gods and their whims and their assigning destinies to people who didn't ask for them.

"Man realized the power He meant was our superior brains, made for invention. He tasked Thoretick, God of Stone, and Wardoan, Goddess of Language, to inspire men. We soon developed architecture, advanced weaponry, effective medicine, and finally machines. All was in balance, until—"

Naul bounced up and down like an eager child. "Can I guess what happens next?"

Talia bit her lip to stop from laughing. Naul hated speeches and morality plays. If he hadn't been in a standoff with Rory, he'd probably be napping by now. She guessed he couldn't take the drama for another second.

The prophet leveled a stern look at Naul.

It didn't faze the weapons guardian. "A traitor human built a Machine to harness the once-in-a-millennium power and greatly increased its capture rate."

Talia rode on the coat of his bravery. "Making the world truly equal by having enough energy to create civilizations of elves, dragons, and mermaids to live alongside humans and dwarves, instead of only a few crushed under them."

Aleck stepped forward. "And now we journey to Raqmu to fix the Machine and restore the balance once more."

Tanin burst through the line of Lagaw followers. "How can you say that?" He pointed at his sister. "You are sworn to protect your people. And yet you're working to revive a long-defeated enemy that will take our land and throw our people into slavery."

Talia waved her bandaged hand at her brother. "They have just as much right to exist as we do. Your prophet just said that Lagaw started the whole charging thing in the first place."

The robed man frowned. "I am not Prince Tanin's exclusively. I am Prophet Salvo, loyal follower of Lagaw and His teachings." He bowed.

The man's proximity calmed Talia's nerves. If that was not magic, then what was?

She returned his bow. "I am Talia, True Heir and Bright One." She introduced her companions, even though they might have already done that while she was sleeping.

Salvo offered introductions for his acolytes, Meerin and Augusta. Talia tilted her head at the proximity between Augusta and Tanin. She hadn't seen him that attentive to a woman while still remaining respectful.

Augusta said, "We might not agree on who holds what title, but we are heading to the same destination, Raqmu."

Talia looked down at Aleck as he looked up at her.

The dwarf spoke first. "Are you suggesting we travel together even though you want to destroy the Machine and we want to repair it?"

Tanin nixed the idea with a gesture of his hand. "No way. It's not happening."

Talia nodded. "On that, we can agree."

The prophet took a deep breath. "Lagaw put you on that shore to save us from the waterfall. The gift you used to save Tutor Grayson *was* granted by Lagaw. Whether or not we agree, you have been touched by Lagaw's hand as I have." Salvo swung his staff so a huge black opal on the top reflected the firelight.

The tingling in Talia's gut couldn't be mistaken. "That jewel is full of magic, isn't it?"

He moved between Talia and her brother, blocking Tanin from her view. "Lagaw does not forbid magic. He only wishes to limit its influence and ensure balance."

Tension forced Talia to roll her shoulders and break his hold on her. She couldn't decide if he was comforting or creepy.

"All our creator asks is that man does not use His given gift of ingenuity to magnify the Recharging to sacrilegious levels. We should not mess with the natural order of things."

Talia tried to search for an argument. It sounded so logical. Tanin's smug expression brought out her aggression. "If building machines is a Lagaw-granted gift, then how can we use it incorrectly? If He didn't want us to build such a contraption, then why did He let us do it?"

"It brings Him pain, but He allows us—"

Ial and Dew broke into the clearing, interrupting the discussion. Held between the two guardians was an unconscious Jura, her tail in place where her land legs should have been.

Dew shook her head at Talia. "She can't change back. She doesn't remember how."

# CHAPTER THIRTY

TALIA HELPED the guardians balance the mermaid on a log by the fire. Jura's pearlescent scales reflected the flames in all directions, like fairies dancing in the trees.

"What happened?" Talia pushed Jura's chin up. Her deep blue eyes were open but nonresponsive.

A faint light flashed through the cloth covering Talia's hand. She forced herself to calm down. Whatever had happened with the canoe had scared her. She didn't want to do that again.

"We don't know," Dew said. "She was swimming figure eights from one side of the river to the other when we found her. Ial had to jump in after her and guide her to shore."

Rodianiari crossed his arms and leaned against a tree, always a little outside of the group. "She has forgotten who she is." He tapped his temple. "I tried to communicate with her, but she sings a song I don't recognize. There is nothing else."

Nyna flipped her bag open and pulled out a cloth, which she dampened in a bucket.

Ial dumped the rest of the water onto the mermaid's tail.

Nyna scowled at him. "I needed that."

Ial shrugged. "Beached dolphins have to stay wet. I thought—"

Dew put a hand on his shoulder. "Naul and I will go get more."

The weapons guardian slung some water bladders over his shoulder. "We'll be right back."

The roar of the waterfall wasn't that far off, but the trees blocked much of the sound. Talia wasn't sure how far the shore was. Jura flapped her fin weakly. Talia hoped it wasn't too far.

Rodianiari bent over the bucket and whispered. The wood crackled and stretched, forcing Ial and Nyna to move aside. Jura's tail fit inside the enlarged basin. The husbandry guardian nodded in appreciation, and then he dumped the last of his water bladder into the small pool, along with any other bit of water he could gather.

Talia wondered if the elf felt guilty for the giant incident. She knew she didn't quite trust him anymore. With Tanin's party so close, she had a lot of people to keep an eye on.

Nomyra paced by the fire, her palpable anger filling the clearing as successfully as the moonlight. "You realize she was our way to Raqmu. Without the mermaid to sense the underground water, we'll never find it. We could roam the desert for decades and never find the city."

With her head in her hands, Talia tried to think of another way. Nomyra was right. Again. They had no map and no clue how to get there without the mermaid.

Hodan shrugged off the hand of his tutor and crept closer. She hadn't seen the new cultural guardian for more than a few hours before she fled her home, which was why she hadn't recognized him at first.

"You have a mermaid? My dad always said—" Hodan stopped after a quick glance at Tanin.

Talia knew Tanin insisted that his guardians forget they ever had a family. Hodan apparently hadn't fully adjusted to the new way of life.

"She has chosen to travel with us to save her people." An idea came to Talia as she studied Tanin's party and realized only humans traveled with him. She left Jura to Nyna and Ial's care. "Tanin, how do you plan on getting into the city?"

Tanin held his hands behind his back and rocked on his heels, so much like their father. *But King Roland isn't my father*, Talia corrected her thoughts. She wondered if she told Tanin, would he feel relieved or angrier?

Her brother's superior tone grated on her nerves. "We have a map." He blinked at her in mock surprise. "Do you mean you've come all this way and you don't know where you're going?"

"We *knew* where we were going, but . . ." She glanced over her shoulder at the amnesiac mermaid. "We've run into a snag."

Prophet Salvo stepped into the light with his women shadows behind him. "Have you then decided to travel with us to learn the Word of Lagaw and His plan for you?"

Nomyra scoffed from the edge of the clearing. "Lagaw isn't real. The Light protects from the Dark, if you know how to read the signs. It is the only warnings we get." Under her breath, she mumbled, "And that's not always enough."

Tanin laughed without mirth. "Your fickle light can't compete with the All-Knowing Lagaw. Prophet Salvo was led by Lagaw's inspiration to a mechanical map powered by magic in the Eckerd library. It has all the current landmasses, oceans, and major cities in constant movement and change."

Aleck leaned forward. "That sounds amazing! I'd really like to see that."

Meerin, the stouter and friendlier acolyte, clapped her hands together. "It had a complicated system of gears, oil lamps, and other elements I couldn't begin to name that all worked toge—"

Augusta sighed loudly to stop her enthusiastic reenactment. "The point is, we have been shown how to get to Raqmu. We need no further assistance."

Prophet Salvo closed his eyes and looked up to the sky. His lips moved silently as Meerin and Augusta mirrored his actions.

Gregor bumped Talia's elbow. "Is he praying?" he whispered.

"It certainly looks like it." Talia closed her eyes too. She didn't feel any tingling. "He's not using magic."

How odd that she could talk about magic so effortlessly when a little over a year ago, she thought it was based on superstition and old myths. Maybe she shouldn't be so quick to judge Salvo's gods. Tanin seemed to buy into the entire idea.

But of course he did. If these gods were real and if what Salvo taught was true, then Talia was the bad guy in this scenario. That played right into Tanin's view of the world.

"Can we see the map?" Talia tried to stay on subject.

"Why?" her brother asked. "Why should we share our information? We have opposite goals, and you have nothing to offer us."

"Except that you won't be able to enter the city at all." It was Talia's turn to laugh. "We don't really need your map. We'll just follow the river. I'm sure Jura will be fine after a bit of a rest."

Meerin stepped in front of Tanin. "What do you mean, we can't enter the city?"

Talia had spoken to one-up Tanin. Now she didn't know if she should say anything. It wouldn't be the first time Tanin had betrayed her after she did all the work.

She took a deep breath and tried to find a way to negotiate with her brother. "There's a dome protecting the entrance, and we . . ." Her thoughts whirled. She couldn't make herself tell him everything. "We know how to open it."

Augusta squinted. "There's always one more thing."

Nomyra's shoulders straightened as she found the upper hand. "It looks to be an addition from after your people moved to the Ngaro Desert. No record of its existence would have traveled with you."

Meerin crossed her arms. "With all the information freely given to us by Lagaw, I know we'll be able to figure it out."

Aleck shook his head. "Not exact—*ow!*"

Parnim had stepped on his foot. "Excuse my clumsiness, my Prince."

Talia thanked her with a look. "It's not a mechanism you can manipulate. It's a shield that requires a very special key to get it open."

Tanin's gaze darted to the Tarbin crown hanging from Talia's belt. "That *key* doesn't belong to you either."

Rory and Kettlor put their hands on their swords. Naul and Gregor did the same.

Talia protected the crown and stepped backward. "This Key is for the Machine, not the shield." *Please, Shining Light above, don't let this come to bloodshed.*

Meerin shook her head. "She's right. Remember?"

Salvo placed a calming hand on Tanin's shoulder. "You saw where the Key is used. There is some other trick to getting into the city."

Augusta sized Talia up. "Or she's lying."

Tanin mocked his sister. "My sister has many talents, but lying isn't one of them. Her brain doesn't move fast enough."

Gregor took a step forward, a growl rumbling in his throat. Talia put a hand on his chest without looking at him. She didn't need her honor protected. She knew her brother was scared and angry. Like always.

Salvo tilted his head at both groups. "Maybe Lagaw brought us together for a reason. Maybe we could work together to get to and enter Raqmu."

Talia didn't like this tentative cooperation, though she wasn't sure what choice she had. "And what happens once we get there?"

Salvo smiled and spread his arms. "We let Lagaw lead the way."

"Praise be to Lagaw."

Again with the chorus; even Tanin's guardians joined in. They'd all bought this prophet's teachings.

Talia didn't see what choice she had. She offered her hand to Tanin. "Allies until Raqmu."

Tanin hovered close; his hand twitched at his side. "Allies until we enter Raqmu."

Talia sighed. "Deal."

He shook her hand a bit aggressively, but she couldn't imagine he'd go back on his promise with all these witnesses. As if reading her thoughts, Tanin scanned the clearing. Plus, she still had the crown.

# CHAPTER THIRTY-ONE

T ANIN PULLED the hood of his robe tighter around his neck. The bitter cold of an early desert sunset chilled him to the core. He missed Tarbin's mild winters. Though Tarbinulus was a port city plagued by constant wind, the ocean stayed warm enough to keep the coldest weather at bay. Out here, the miles and miles of flat sand offered nothing but the occasional oasis to ward off the biting wind.

He complained to Rory. "I know we're supposed to travel by night in the summer so we don't cook in the roasting sun. But in the winter? I could use some of that boiling heat right about now."

Augusta adjusted the back of Tanin's robes to lie straighter. "We need the stars to navigate. They are the constant laid out by Lagaw Himself to aid us with the map He gave us."

Tanin could grow accustomed to her attentions. She was completely at home in the desert environment. Once the ancient city was found and opened, she would be the perfect emissary to navigate its restoration. Once Tanin reclaimed Raqmu as a Tarbin territory, maybe he would move the center of his kingdom to the great city. What better way to show the renewal of Tarbin's greatness than by celebrating with his ancestors? The gorgeous Augusta by his side would only increase his prestige.

That was assuming there was a better way to get to the isolated city than across these desert sands. Hajar Ramliun, the great desert city of modern times, was the last vestige of comfort the group had experienced. And that had been weeks ago.

Meerin scuffed along the loose layer of sand that lay over solid bedrock. "I can't stop thinking about those city people. It was weird that they had total belief in the existence of Raqmu but had no idea where it was and no interest in helping us find it. Did anyone else feel like they were hiding something?"

Salvo shrugged. "The people of Hajar Ramliun have neither the Bright One nor the True Heir. I believe they know where it is, but the prophecy says we will discover it, not be shown the way."

The road had ended a tent city and two oases ago. The party had had to abandon the pack animals and wagons. After over a month of hiking through relatively mild terrain, the landscape turned a monotonous tan, with nothing but the occasional rolling hill to break up the view. Apparently, even the natives thought there wasn't anything of value out this way; there were no settlements and no guides.

Tutor Grayson adjusted Hodan's pack. "Maybe, but they seemed . . . afraid."

A flash of light danced along the sand.

Tanin forced his feet to keep a steady rhythm, though his heart-beat thumped out of control. "Lightning on the ground?"

The arrogant elf gave Tanin a withering look. "That's not lightning. It's magic."

Rodianiari had the same attitude as the first elf Tanin had met. His intolerable nature gave Tanin insight into why Lagaw forbade the Recharging. If this specimen represented the entire elf nation, Tanin had no interest in reinstating their self-righteous magical butts into his world.

Talia's oaf of a weapons guardian lifted his robe like a skirt as he took his huge steps. "Is it supposed to do that?"

The ex–high priestess shook her head. "No, it's not."

With a jump to the side, Talia held the bag holding the crown away from her body as if it had just bitten her.

Nomyra offered to take the flashing bag. "I can funnel any excess magic into the drained gems."

Talia handed the Tarbin crown, Tanin's rightful property, to the treacherous priestess.

Tanin's fists clenched at his sister's naivete. Surely she'd spent enough time with Nomyra to realize she couldn't be trusted. He was amazed he used to find that old woman attractive. After Augusta, Tanin's standard of beauty had risen a few notches.

Salvo joined Tanin. "It's wild magic. Likely strengthened by the mini-charging."

Tanin tensed as the hair on his arms stood up. A few seconds later, a crack of magic crawled along the sand. "Too close for comfort."

Orui swung his staff in a wide circle. "Can it hurt us?"

Augusta nodded and wrapped her arms around her chest. "Oh, yes."

Grayson stopped the staff with a flick of his wrist before it could whack Hodan in the head. "I don't think a piece of wood is going to save us."

Rory consulted the stars and sketched some figures on the ground. Augusta knelt down beside him and compared his math to the map she'd copied from the dwarf library.

His weapons guardian tucked his hands in his belt. "We're almost there, my Prince."

A wave of sand crested over the party. Tanin ducked his head to the side and covered his face with the loose cloth around his neck. Pain filled his chest as sand still managed to invade his lungs. He bent in half and coughed until he could breathe again. He blinked his eyes as he gazed at Talia, who was nothing but a blur.

It wouldn't take much of a distance to obliterate her trail altogether.

As the air cleared and he could breathe again, he jogged to Talia's side. He almost tripped over the stretcher between Ial and Traneck that held the still-comatose mermaid.

A flash of lightning streamed over the heads of the party. Tanin ducked instinctively. In the sudden brightness, Rodianiari's appearance shifted, as though his outside appearance were only a skin covering a much older elf with flowing black hair. He looked like the mad lord that Talia had killed. What had his name been?

Tanin rubbed his eyes as the sky grew dark again. His next glance at the elf showed the same form he'd seen since joining up with Talia. The magic was playing tricks on his mind.

Rory helped Tanin stand straight. "Maybe we should seek some sort of shelter. The weather seems to be worsening. If another sandstorm is on its way, we don't have the same equipment as before."

A horrendous storm of sand had blasted through their camp a couple of weeks before. Luckily, the desert people in the oasis had known what to do, and they had made it through relatively unscathed. Tanin shivered at the thought of getting caught in the open like this if such a storm was building. Maybe this was not the right spot to have his capital.

Salvo walked steadily forward. "We're almost there. Lagaw will protect us. His will is close at hand."

Nomyra held the flashing crown over her head. "I think you're right." As she turned in a circle, the brightness of the gems faded and increased. She moved in the direction of the brightest effect, and the blinking increased even more.

Augusta put a hand on Tanin's elbow, sending warmth tingling through his body. "Lagaw sends us a message."

Tanin squinted at Nomyra. "How do we know it is not Ydiny working through Her emissary?"

Orui shrugged on Tanin's other side. "Who cares? They both want us to get to Raqmu, right?"

Tanin laughed for the first time in days. "You've got a point. Follow my crown. At my coronation, we'll have a grand tale of how it saved us all in the desert by bringing us to the ancient city and giving us the power to destroy the Machine."

Talia scowled. He winked at her. What could she do now? She'd made a deal.

Dew brushed sand from Jura's face. "Let's get a move on, then. We need to find shelter before this storm overwhelms us."

Augusta and Salvo, the two most at home in the blowing sand, climbed to the peak of the next dune with Nomyra and Gregor. As soon as they reached the top, Salvo raised both his arms and waved.

Meerin pressed both hands to the top of her head. "They see Raqmu. We're here." She rushed forward a few steps, then turned back to grab her backpack. "Well, come on. What are you waiting for?"

Her enthusiasm energized Tanin's tired limbs. After all, they were almost done, and he could go back to his father with the full blessing of Lagaw to back him up. It was the start of a new age, and Tanin would be the pinnacle.

He rushed forward, determined to beat Talia to the entrance.

Devoid of dunes, the landscape ahead allowed a view all the way to the horizon. Tanin squinted. He must be missing something.

Orui voiced his doubts. "Am I supposed to see the city?"

Talia pulled her hood down. "I was expecting a large dome."

Tanin turned to Salvo. "What were you waving about? I thought you found the city."

Salvo smiled. "We did. I can feel it down to my core."

Augusta started down the dune. "I admit, I expected something larger, but it has been ten centuries."

Tanin lifted his arms to indicate the empty valley ahead. "Bigger? I don't see—"

A flash of rainbow-colored magic bounced along the valley. In the afterglow, Tanin picked out the outline of a ruins. Columns without roofs and toppled walls spread across the sand. A few smaller dwellings lined the outskirts of what must have been a mighty temple in the ancient past.

Tanin folded his arms in smug satisfaction. "Well, we've done our part. I hope you can do yours."

Talia rubbed her necklace. The dragon charm flashed, then returned to its ordinary tarnished bronze. Tanin wondered if he'd ever get used to the presence of magic. "We're ready."

Tanin hated not knowing what was going on. He signaled for his guardians to close ranks. "Keep an eye on her. Now that we've brought her here, we need to beware of betrayal. Lagaw protect us."

"Praise be to Lagaw," they chorused.

Kettlor motioned toward one of the smaller dwellings that could offer some shelter from the relentless sand. "Maybe we should take cover."

The party moved forward without further discussion.

Lightning flashed across the sky and the ground. Tanin didn't know if that was Lagaw agreeing or Ydiny warning. One way or another, he would succeed.

# CHAPTER THIRTY-TWO

TALIA STARED at the long-dead ruins. "This can't be Raqmu. It's so . . ."

Gregor turned in a circle. "Small?"

The party had survived the sandstorm that blew through the night under the relative cover of small stone buildings. Though sand clung to every inch of Talia's skin, she could at least breathe again.

Nomyra climbed over a toppled column, the Key tucked under her arm. Though the magic lightning had stopped after the storm passed, the crown still blinked in an insistent rhythm. "This is Raqmu. I can feel it tingling through my fingers."

All Talia felt was cold. She shivered in the chill of the early morning air. She couldn't wait until the Light's Daughter warmed her frozen bones, assuming her love could penetrate the layers of cloth and sand. "If this is the city, where is the dome?"

She slipped on a slimy rock and fell to her knees. The cushion provided by her layers of fabric protected her from pain, but not from embarrassment. Ignoring Gregor's offered hand, she pushed up from the ground. Instead of the scratchy sand she had grown accustomed to, a slimy wet mess covered her hands.

She was so shocked, she almost shouted. "Nyna?"

The medicinal guardian rushed to Talia's side, her staff ready. "What's wrong?" She gasped when she saw the green on Talia's upturned hands. She dropped to the stone, practically putting her nose in the slime. "That's moss. How is that growing in the desert?"

Ial stared at a crack between stones on the ground. "There's water here. It's steaming up from below."

Talia rubbed her hands on her robes. She caught sight of Nomyra sneaking around the corner of a roofless building.

Tanin gestured toward the dilapidated structures. "It looks like we didn't need you after all. Maybe you made up the whole dome and key just to trick us into bringing you here."

Talia crossed her arms. "We were working on the information we were given. Maybe your map is wrong and this isn't Raqmu at all."

Tanin laughed. "You're still trusting Nomyra, even though she clings to my crown like she has some claim to it? I know my source is Lagaw blessed and can't be wrong."

Gregor drummed his hand against a fallen carved column without even looking at Tanin. "Where did that prophet and his acolytes go?"

Tanin crossed his arms. "To find the Machine."

Talia snorted. "Well, good luck. It *is* guarded, and you'll never get in."

At least, she really hoped that was true. She couldn't show weakness now.

Aleck kicked some stones that seemed to be part of a crumbling path. "These blocks are enormous. Dwarves wouldn't have moved these."

Traneck knocked on a leaning column, half sunk in the ground. "It would be in much better shape if we had."

Rodianiari held his robes up as if they weren't as full of sand as everyone else's. "After the devastation of the last Recharging, the city was sealed off." He pointed down. "The city is below us. This is nothing but some kind of primitive attempt to mark its location."

He walked forward. His determination made Talia think he knew where he was going. He had, after all, been alive when the last Recharging failed.

Naul walked with careful footsteps around the debris with Dew guiding the way. The stretcher was too awkward to carry through the ruins, so Naul was carrying Jura as easily as a mother would carry an infant. To keep the path ahead clear for Naul's clumsy feet, Dew pushed smaller stones into a crevice. Sparks leaped up from the void.

Talia gasped. "Wait."

She grabbed a larger rock from the broken-up road. Staring down into the darkness, she dropped it. The stone fell a few feet before it bounced off an invisible barrier with a sizzle. It fell back and bounced twice more, sending out circles of blue sparks from where it hit, like a rock skipping along the surface of a pond. The third time, Talia shielded her eyes as the rock exploded into dust, the tiny bits sparkling until there was nothing left.

Gregor picked his way more carefully through the debris. "So, not a shortcut. Got it." He motioned to Tanin. "Unless you want to give it a try?"

Tanin squeezed his fingers around the hilt of his sheathed sword, refusing to acknowledge the sarcasm from his old friend. Talia knew he viewed Gregor's leaving with Talia to assist with her Forging Quest as a traitorous act. Though Gregor had done nothing illegal since Talia had been Tarbin's princess, Talia was sure that Tanin was the one responsible for his ex-friend losing his title.

Her brother rocked back and forth on his heels. "I got us here. Your turn."

She scowled. Wind whipped through the tops of the standing columns, whistling eerily. Talia scanned the brightening sky. Ragaropina had to be close. She had said she'd wait by the sea until Talia called her. Talia had assumed she'd meant the South Sea. Now she really hoped she hadn't gotten it wrong and Ragaropina had been waiting by the northern Ngaro Sea. She didn't think they had enough supplies to wait too long for the dragon's arrival.

Talia followed a rugged path toward the center of the ruins. "There's no sign of Ragaropina. What about the nadph representative? Second Emissary said one would come from the south and follow the river. Since there's no river . . ."

Tanin tossed pebbles into another gap. The flash of the disintegrating stones reflected blue sparks in his eyes. "Seems you're as prepared for this quest as you were the last. When are you going to learn that this is not your place?"

Taking a few calming breaths so she wouldn't push her brother into a gap, Talia chose to ignore him and continue forward. With all she'd seen, she knew she was on the right path. She'd also learned she couldn't control everything. Tanin would learn that lesson someday. For now, Talia needed to get into the city below so she could be rid of him for good. She still possessed the Key, and there was nothing he could do without it.

As she moved along, Talia noticed the ancient settlement, or monument or whatever it was, was laid out in a wheel pattern, with paths leading to the center like spokes. As the sun rose higher in the sky, reliefs carved into the stone stood out more. Some columns looked like they'd beaten flat by sand over time, but some were more protected. She saw curved letters in a language she didn't recognize. Calling her cultural guardian to her side, she pointed out the symbols.

Dew rubbed her fingers along a full column. "It's Veni, the ancient language of the first people. I've never seen it outside of a book. No one has spoken it in centuries."

Hodan giggled. "Maybe you should travel more. For a cultural guardian, there are some large gaps in your knowledge."

Dew clenched and unclenched her fists. Talia recognized her attempt at controlling her temper. Talia used similar techniques to prevent herself from throttling Tanin.

A few yards ahead, Rory coughed. "My Prince."

Talia followed her brother to the central circle of the spoked rings.

On the other side of the carved columns, a black dome, darker than any night she'd ever seen, bulged out from the center of the surrounding obelisks.

Gregor whistled. "I'd say we found the dome."

Nomyra sat cross-legged just out of reach of the shimmering barrier, the crown in her lap and a look of bliss on her face. She blinked her eyes open. "Can't you feel it?"

Talia's emotions had been in such an uproar since the morning meal, she hadn't had time to feel anything. Her brother always did that to her; he sent her normally calm and focused mind into a confusing mess of anger and resentment.

Sand whipped around Talia, forcing her to pull her outer robe around her nose and mouth to breathe. With a hand on her sword, she blinked, trying to determine if a threat approached. A flap of huge wings sent a layer of sand over the dome. The grains flashed over the top and slid to the other side, leaving the surface the same deep black.

Talia dropped her robe as the dust settled, and she stared up at the giant bright-red dragon, who carried the largest tree Talia had ever seen.

# CHAPTER THIRTY-THREE

RAGAROPINA SET the full-grown nadph down close to the shimmering dome. She landed atop a large pillar, which complained with loud cracks but didn't break. Though Talia had flown with the mother of the next generation of dragons to Tarbinulus and then to Astropriest Tower, the majesty of the living legendary creature still formed goosebumps over her skin. Talia grabbed Gregor's hand.

He squeezed her fingers as his face lit up with his crooked smile. A different sort of tingle flowed over the awe inspired by the dragon. This time, Talia didn't let go.

The sun glinted off the dragon's metallic scales. "Are we all gathered?"

Aleck jumped up on a block of limestone to get a better look at the daytime-sleeping nadph. "We are. Though it seems some of us didn't make it in one piece."

Ial took Jura from Naul. Her still-unresponsive form reminded Talia of the sacrifice the magicals were making to save their people.

Ragaropina shook her shimmering muscles. "I don't think they were expecting the all-encompassing desert. The Renquist River used to run from the mountains to Raqmu and continued to the sea.

This drastic change in landscape was not predicted. I spotted them as I approached the city." She leaned toward Talia. "I would not have found you if not for the charm."

Talia released Gregor to study the gigantic nadph. She'd never seen one that tall before. She wondered if they continued to grow their whole lives. If so, he could be old enough to remember the last Recharging. She circled the massive trunk to see if he was still awake. She didn't want to have to wait until nightfall if she didn't have to. She wasn't sure how long the tentative peace between her and her brother would last.

A fairy dropped from his branches, a scowl marring her delicate beauty. Talia suppressed a giggle at the fairy's adorableness. She might look like a cute, tiny thing, but her powerful magic could end Talia.

The fairy landed on Talia's outstretched hand. She pantomimed drinking from a large cup, then turning it upside down and shaking it, like it was unexpectedly empty. Then she swayed back and forth and collapsed. Before Talia could ask if she was okay, the fairy flew upright and gestured to the nadph.

"He's thirsty." Talia's face lit up with understanding, then darkened with frustration. The nadph's roots curled underneath the bulk of the tree and his scratchy leaves painted a more desperate picture. "We're all thirsty. There's water below, if we could only access it."

Rodianiari cut his hand and held it over the shield. "There is only one way to breach the barrier and reach the water." A drip of blood steamed as it hit the black. The entire shield vibrated like liquid in a glass.

Talia nodded. The representatives circled the dome, until they were evenly spaced. She noticed her brother and his companions in the shadows of the obelisks, watching.

Before she could decide whether or not it would hurt, Talia sliced her palm and placed it on the dome. The pain from the cut soothed instantly as the coolness of the dome wrapped around her hand. Her instincts told her to yank her hand out of the gooey substance. She fought the demand of her body and held still.

The elf placed his already bleeding hand on the dome. His image shimmered. For an instance, Talia saw Thilphiliari under the younger elf's skin. She shook the illusion from her head. He was dead, and though her guilt still haunted her, she'd make sure his death hadn't been in vain.

Ragaropina bit her paw and added it to the dome. "It tickles." The dragon giggled, which might have been the oddest thing Talia had ever heard.

Nyna flinched as if it were her own skin she were piercing as she gently sliced Jura's palm. Ial stepped forward so Nyna could press the open wound against the barrier. As her blood mingled with the dome, the surface rose and fell like waves in a storm.

The fairy kissed the extended branch of her nadph companion, drawing forth a gooey sap-like substance. She helped him straighten his branch and add it to the others. Now the dome's waves crested, swelled, and crashed into each other.

"My turn." Aleck accepted a dagger from Parnim and drew his own blood. "Here we go!"

The dome reached out for his hand and sucked it below the surface. The undulating liquid stilled. The entire desert seemed to freeze. No sand blew in Talia's face. No magic crawled along the ground. The Light's Daughter froze low in the sky.

With a loud roar, the dome popped and flung everyone to the ground.

Talia rolled into a ball as her head throbbed in pain and her body vibrated with the presence of strong magic. It took her a moment to realize the rumble in her ears came from outside her body. She forced her eyes open, though tears blurred her vision. She pushed herself to her hands and knees. The ground shook so violently, she didn't think she could stand.

She twisted to her right as someone screamed in fear. Nomyra fell through the crumbling ground, the crown clutched between her panicked fingers. The nadph disappeared through a massive hole in the stone, his fairy flying down after him.

A tall obelisk toppled in front of Talia and cascaded into the abyss below. She scrambled backward.

Gregor skidded to her side. "We have to run!"

She pushed to her feet. In front of her, where the dome used to be, Ragaropina dove through the expanding hole.

Ial clung to Jura with one hand as Nyna tried to pull the two toward solid ground. The blocks beneath Ial were slipping into the abyss, and Nyna refused to let go. All three were gone in an instance.

Gregor pulled Talia farther away from the center of the disturbance, but those stones were shaking and crumbling as well.

"It's no use." She clung to him as the ground leading to safety disappeared.

He held her, his muscles squeezing her body close as if, by sheer force of will, he could keep her safe. His focus darted around the plaza, searching for a safe haven. Talia grabbed his chin and forced him to look at her. A single tear trailed down his cheek. His dark brown eyes were the last thing she wanted to see. And the last thing she wanted to feel was his love.

She rose on her tiptoes, and he curved his back until their lips met. Heat rushed through Talia's body, sparking an intensity she'd never experienced. This was right. Everything about this was right. Why did she fight her feelings? What was the point of sacrificing if there was nothing to sacrifice for?

Gregor pressed against her, hungry, demanding. His passion mirrored her own, and any fear of dying fled, even as the floor crumbled below them.

They clung to each other as they fell.

# CHAPTER THIRTY-FOUR

TALIA AND GREGOR CLUNG to each other, the afterglow of their first kiss morphing into the sheer panic of certain death. A pillar tumbled from the crumbling floor, or ceiling from this new perspective. A stone stele headed straight for the pair.

Gregor pecked her on the lips one last time. Talia tried to think of the perfect words to express everything she'd kept bottled up for months. It wasn't fair. She'd sacrificed her own happiness for her kingdom and now she was going to sacrifice her life for her world. Worst of all, she'd never complete her quest or be with the man she loved.

"You have to push off me. Ready?" Gregor entwined his fingers with hers.

Talia understood his intention as the pillar came at them impossibly fast.

They counted together. "One, two, three." They pushed against each other, hard, forcing their bodies in opposite directions. With a whisk of air, the carved stone missed Talia but nicked Gregor, sending him spinning.

That was when Talia noticed how slowly they were falling. The pillar crashed into the ground, along with paver stones and other pieces of monument, while she floated at a controlled descent. Scouring the air, she saw other figures descending at a rate slower than the debris. Unaccustomed to the dark with merely filtered light, Talia couldn't tell who was who.

She heard chanting and searched for the source. To her right, a spiral staircase with large sweeping stairs of stone and metal climbed from the darkness below to the surface. That was likely the intended method for entering the city. Maybe whatever floating magic was at play had been set up as a backup system? But that wouldn't explain the chanting.

On one of the landings halfway down the stairs, Rodianiari held his hands up, his entire body glowing a soft blue. She couldn't see his lips moving, but the sound was definitely coming from his direction. The magic surrounding his body flickered. For a moment, his hair darkened, and he grew almost a foot. Talia thought he looked remarkably like Thilphiliari. She blinked, and his form returned to the much-younger elf, his blond hair blowing with the force of the magic leaving his body. His power was awe-inspiring. She wondered what a whole city of elves could do if this one elf could slow their entire party's descent.

Almost the whole party. The dragon grasped the nadph in her talons before he could smash into the ground. Jura's tail flapped in the wind as she fell into a large body of water at one end of the cavern. Ial and Nyna tumbled beside her, out of control. Hopefully, the water would temper their fall.

"Aleck?" Talia twisted in midair. She couldn't see him or his guards anywhere. Rubbing her forehead, she scanned the ground. She had about fifteen feet to go, though she wasn't anxious to find the shattered remains of her friend on the desert sand.

The blue light flickered, drawing Talia's attention up. The elf's body flashed to that of the older elf again. At least, Talia thought it did. Rodianiari fell to one knee. His arms crumbled at his sides. The magic flashed in a small explosion as his head hit the stone landing and his voice fell silent.

The ground yanked Talia toward it. She stiffened her muscles and curled up, hoping the sand was thick and soft. When she fell off a horse, she was supposed to roll, but she'd never fallen fifteen feet before. She smashed into the sand on her left side. Pain shot through her as her scabbard sunk into flesh. She attempted a roll, but she didn't have the strength to hold onto her folded legs as pain ripped through her torso. The thin layer of sand acted as an aggravating burn instead of a cushion. She yelled as her palms and knees scraped through the abrasive substance before she brought herself to a stop.

Talia dropped onto her right side, trying to catch her breath. She couldn't fill her lungs without a stabbing pain in her left side. She undid her belt. The sand and her bloody fingers made the unbuckling more complicated than usual. Her scabbard slipped behind her. She rubbed her bruised flesh and sighed in relief when she felt no blood.

"Talia?" Naul's deep voice carried to her.

"I'm here," she said, much softer than she had intended.

The weapons guardian dropped to his knees in front of her. He swiped his forehead, and Talia blinked as droplets splashed her face. Blood poured from Naul's head.

Talia sat up, ignoring the pain in her side. "Sit down," she ordered Naul.

For once, he didn't have to be told twice. "The world spins."

She shouted for Nyna before she remembered the medicinal guardian had plunged into the underground lake. As she tore a long strip from her outer robe, Talia shook as much sand off it as she could. Naul's bleeding scared her more than a little grit in the wound. Moving behind Naul to prop up his swaying body, Talia wrapped the piece around his forehead and pushed on the wound.

Skidding into the clearing, seemingly uninjured, Dew gasped at the sight of all the blood. "Holy Light above, Naul."

The big man blinked at his hands. "Was my skin always this color? Oh, that's a lot of blood." Naul lost it and tumbled forward.

Between Talia holding his forehead and Dew balancing his torso, they were able to keep him upright long enough to tie the piece of cloth tightly around his wound. The bleeding slowed but didn't stop.

Talia took a deep breath, cringing at the pain in her side. She couldn't afford to continue taking short breaths, or she'd be lying beside Naul. "Dew, how's it look?" Talia lifted her undergarment high enough for Dew to check out the injury.

"It looks like you're going to have an impressive bruise in the shape of a sword hilt." Dew helped her straighten out the robe and remove the now torn outer cloak.

"Are you okay?" she asked her cultural guardian.

Sand drifted from Dew's hair as she nodded. "I hit a deeper pile of sand, I think." She tore more long pieces of Talia's cloak and secured one to the already soaked piece on Naul's head. "I'm not sure why we didn't all fall to our deaths, though."

Talia gestured to the landing where the collapsed elf still lay. "Rodianiari saved us. We need to go get him."

Talia jumped as splashing sounded behind her. She stared into the void beyond the jagged light from the hole in the ceiling. The lake seemed to go on forever, like the one around Astropriest Tower. She prayed that Raqmu didn't extend to the other side. If it was underwater, she didn't know what chance they'd have at fulfilling their destinies.

Talia sighed in relief as her companions crawled out of the water. On the shore, Ial squeezed out his soaked robes as Nyna waved at the rest of the party. Now Talia just had to find Gregor and the dwarves.

She waved her guardians over. "Hurry. Naul's hurt, and the last I saw of Gregor, he was spinning out of control in that direction."

Nyna pulled her shoulder bag over her head. It sloshed. "I don't know how we survived that fall. Ial and I are lucky Jura found us and brought us to the surface."

Talia helped Ial untangle his bow from his sopping robes. "Jura's awake? She's okay?"

Ial nodded. "The deep dive must have revived her."

"Elevate his feet before his body goes into shock," Nyna ordered Dew. She dumped the contents of her bag beside Naul. "Jura found us and brought us to the surface. Ial helped me to shore. These robes are much too heavy for swimming."

Talia searched the shore. "Where did Jura go?"

Shrugging, the medicinal guardian shook her herbs and placed them on top of the wet leather of her bag. "She said she had something she had to do and swam off."

Trying not to make too much of the mermaid's disappearance, Talia reassured herself that Jura had served her duty. She was no longer beholden to this quest. She wasn't the Bright One. Talia was. For a moment, Talia wished she could swim off as well.

Nyna picked through a couple of vials. The sand absorbed the excess water, but the liquid had already done its damage. The labels were unintelligible. "I think this is the right one," Nyna said as she uncorked a vial. She sniffed and jerked her head back. "Yep. That's it."

She rubbed it under Naul's nose. He moaned and blinked his eyes open.

Nyna made him look at her. "I need you to stay awake, big man." She gestured to Ial. "Go get me some water, please."

Ial held his hands up in an exaggerated shrug. "With what?"

Dew tossed the husbandry guardian the wooden cup from her bag. "We're going to need to find what supplies we can."

Talia nodded. "I need to find Gregor first." And Tanin. She shouldn't care about him, but he was still her brother. She remembered him drifting down at the same speed she had. He should be okay. Then again, Naul hadn't been.

"I'll come with you." Dew dropped her scabbard and everything else she carried by Nyna.

The cultural guardian was more comfortable with hand-to-hand than any bladed weapon. Talia, however, bent down and pulled her sword from its scabbard. She winced as she straightened, her side reminding her that she was injured.

Nyna glanced up at the sound.

Talia waved off her concern. "I'm fine. Take care of Naul. I'm hoping we won't be bringing you any more patients."

She and Dew searched the fallen stones along the shore, calling for the other party members.

Gregor's head peeked above a cracked horizontal stele. Tingles of relief flooded Talia. Gregor was okay.

"Talia, come quick. I can't get it out." The fear in his voice dropped her mood back into emergency management.

As she and Dew ran as fast as they could through the sucking sand, she shouted, "Can't get what out?"

"The crown." Gregor met Talia at the overturned stone and grabbed her hand. "She must have fallen on it."

Before she could ask who, Gregor dropped to his knees beside the prone form of Priestess Nomyra, who had the Tarbin crown embedded in her chest, up to the jewels.

Dew skidded to a halt and covered her mouth. "Oh, that's horrible."

Talia dropped her sword and fell beside Gregor, the sand grating against her knees registering as no more than an annoyance. "For some reason, I felt like she was immortal."

Gregor squeezed Talia's hand. "She is alive. Look, there's no blood."

Leaning over to put her ear to Nomyra's mouth, Talia caught the faintest breath against her skin. "Blessed by the Light, she is. How is that possible?" She hovered her hands over the smooth underside of the crown that stuck out grotesquely yet cleanly from the priestess's chest. Her joints, from her fingers to her elbows, vibrated with dancing magic.

Talia pulled Dew toward her with a look. "I'm going to go get her. If I'm not out in ten minutes, pull me away."

Before either of her companions could protest, she placed her cut and bleeding hands directly on the surface of the crown.

Her ring flashed before Talia was surrounded by colored mist.

Shouting drew her attention to a mass of swirling fog. She walked through the air, with nothing to put her feet on. Still, she drew closer to the voices and picked out Nomyra and Maitliin flinging insults at each other.

The wizard commanded his descendant to sacrifice.

"Sacrifice what?" Talia interrupted.

The two magic users froze, the silence stilling the rumbling fog.

Nomyra came to her senses first. "Maitliin is insisting on taking over my body and leaving my consciousness in the Key."

Pacing between the two women, Maitliin flung his hands in the air, his cloud-like robes trailing behind his movements. "I know better than anyone how to harness the power of the Machine. I should be given a temporary body to fulfill the prophecy."

Talia clenched her fists. "If you two don't stop arguing, there won't be a body for either of you." She turned to the priestess. "You're dying."

Closing her eyes and crossing her arms over her chest, Nomyra concentrated. Her face loosened from anger to fear. "I can't get out."

Maitliin bent in half, and a maniacal laugh reverberated through the echo chamber. "Soon you will be too weak to fight me."

Anger flushed across Nomyra's face as her fear swelled into fury. "Let me go! I have never been anything but a loyal follower. I have done *everything* you asked of me."

"You have one more duty, my child." The wizard shook his head, unable to talk he was laughing so hard.

The priestess gestured toward Talia. "You should take her body. She's the Bright One and won't survive the Recharging. You could take it as soon as the deed is done."

Maitliin twirled and popped up in front of Talia. His hands gripped her shoulders before she had time to back up. Where his eyes should have been, holes bored deep into Talia's consciousness. She almost collapsed as she stared into the nothing.

How could Nomyra betray her like this? They weren't exactly friends, but she had thought they shared the same goals.

"Enough." A powerful high-pitched voice blew the mist to the side.

The wizard loosened his grip. Talia took advantage of his distraction, knocking his feet out from under him and backing up, though she couldn't conceive of how far would be out of reach in his realm.

Screaming and laughing simultaneously, Maitliin focused on the small figure that had materialized out of the mist. "You can't stop me this time, traitor."

A dwarf, no older than Aleck, swirled into existence dressed in astropriest bright-white robes. Her aura glowed as though she were part-Light herself. She ignored Maitliin and addressed Talia. "You must willingly make your sacrifice. He can't take you."

Talia blinked, staring at Billivin and Nomyra in turn. What had she missed?

Maitliin's head seemed to swell as his anger grew. He rushed the dwarf priestess. She grabbed Talia's hand and used Windall to deflect the mad wizard.

Gliding through the mist with her accustomed grace, Nomyra snatched Talia's hand from Billivin. "We have to get out of here."

Talia balked at her closeness but couldn't shake the feeling that she had missed something. "What did you say about my sacrifice?"

Billivin snapped her fingers. Windall flashed in Nomyra's eye, forcing the woman to back up or be burned.

Talia held her hand away from her body and stared at the dwarf. "Did you do that?"

She nodded. "The priestess was trying to remove your ring. She needs the combined power of both rings to free herself from this prison."

Nomyra brandished Krag. "You're ruining everything, dwarf. After I escaped, I would drag her out from the other side." She turned to Talia. "Regardless of how little you trust me, you know I wish to fulfill the prophecy. I can't do it without the Bright One."

The Krag and Windall rings hummed. The sound vibrated the mist, until the swirling clouds bounced in agitation. The women stared at Maitliin, who waved his arms as though he were directing an orchestra.

"I have him. You have to go." A deep growl reverberated from Billivin as she focused on Maitliin. "I've stored bits of power over the centuries. Squeezing out small amounts as students came to talk with you, always staying out of the way. You thought I posed no danger to you. One day, you'll stop underestimating me."

Her form blurred as she flew toward Maitliin. She barreled into his chest before he could open his eyes.

The mist spread like fog with the sudden halt of vibration. Talia couldn't see beyond her nose. She jumped when Nomyra bumped into her side.

The priestess's hair flew around her head, though there was no wind. She glowed a bright red as she grabbed Talia's ringed hand. "Concentrate," she said. "We can escape together."

Talia pictured the sandy shore, her companions, and the crooked smile of Gregor. She wanted out. She needed to get out. Warmth spread from her fingers to her arm to the rest of her body. A green glow climbed along the same path, engulfing her in a quiet hum.

Nomyra touched the Unity rings.

An explosion of light and sound drowned out all other feeling. Talia's being was sucked through a tube. Her mind swirled, unable to center itself in reality.

In the midst of the confusion, Billivin's voice whispered as clearly as if it were Talia's in her own mind. "Bright Ones, not Bright One. You don't have to do this alone."

# CHAPTER THIRTY-FIVE

Tanin rolled onto his side. Grit clogged his pores, all of them, even the ones covered by layers of cloth. As he sat up, the fine grains streamed from his body like a dry and itchy waterfall. He longed to return to his port home, where the only sand lined the floor of the bay.

Rory slid to a halt in front of his charge. Tanin threw his arms up to protect his face from a fresh onslaught of grit.

"Forgive me, my Prince." The weapons guardian held his hand out to help Tanin stand. "You must come immediately."

Worry creased Tanin's face as he gripped Rory's wrist. Once he was on his feet, his robe felt significantly heavier with the extra layers of sand. His weapons guardian moved away too quickly for Tanin to shake it all off. He pulled the cloth over his head and dropped it at his feet as he followed Rory. "What's going on?"

Kettlor's voice carried over the stone blocks strewn across the courtyard. "I found Orui."

"I have the prince," Rory replied.

Tanin scanned the hole in the ceiling, flabbergasted that he'd fallen from such a height without a single injury. His cheeks flushed as his anger rose. He hated not knowing what was going on. "Don't make me ask again. What's—"

A scream cut him off. Rory and Tanin ran toward the sound. The grit thinned over the pavers, making progress much easier as Tanin turned a tight corner behind Rory.

Tanin grimaced as he caught sight of the blood-soaked ground dented with the body of the prophet. Meerin rocked back and forth, cradling Salvo's head in her lap. Her curly hair was plastered to her head with a combination of blood and sand.

Petting the unconscious man's hand where it was wrapped around his staff, Meerin blinked at Tanin. "He saved me. The prophet used the black opal to mend my cracked skull." She kissed the top of his forehead. "Then he collapsed."

"But we're not done yet. He promised." Tanin couldn't reconcile the death of the prophet before the completion of the prophecy.

Augusta put a gentle hand on Tanin's shoulder. "We must pray."

He hid his surprise. He hadn't seen her approach. "We need Orui."

Kettlor came around a cracked stele with Orui's arm around his shoulder. "I've got him."

"That last step is a doozy." Orui leaned against the husbandry guardian to avoid putting any pressure on his right leg. His face blanched as he caught sight of the prone prophet.

Orui let go of his human crutch and hopped to the unconscious man. He addressed the weeping disciple. "Is this blood yours or his?"

Meerin shook her head as Augusta gently moved her out of the way. "I don't know. I woke up with my head throbbing. Prophet Salvo was glowing a brilliant blue-purple, then he collapsed."

The medicinal guardian pressed two fingers against the prophet's neck. "I feel a pulse, but it's weak." He nipped the man's robe with his dagger and ripped. His hands probed Salvo's discolored abdomen. "I don't see any external bleeding, but this puffy stomach doesn't look good."

Tanin dreaded the answer but guessed the outcome. "Internal bleeding?"

The medicinal guardian wiped his forehead. "There's nothing I can do."

"No!" Meerin screamed. She threw Augusta off and fell beside the prophet. She set the staff over his chest. "Make him better. I beg You, Mighty Lagaw, save the prophet. Take my life in exchange for his."

Augusta grabbed Orui's dagger from the ground and slit her palm. She offered the sharp knife to Meerin, who held up her hand for Augusta to do it. Both disciples placed their freshly bloodied wounds on the staff and their clean ones on Salvo's bare chest. The women muttered a prayer over his body. Tanin found his eyes closing as he added his own to the Great Lagaw.

Nothing happened.

Tanin took the staff, its gem still warm, from the desperate disciples. He couldn't believe that Lagaw would allow the prophet to die now, not when he was so close. "Maybe the magic's used up. We need Talia's or Nomyra's ring."

Kettlor pointed toward the dark lake Tanin had missed in his scramble to follow Rory. "I saw the princess with Dew over there."

Meerin wiped the tears from her cheek as she motioned to Rory. "Give me your robe." When Rory only squinted at her, Meerin waved her hand insistently. "You're the tallest. It will work the best for carrying the prophet."

"Give her the robe," Tanin ordered Rory. Then the prince motioned to Kettlor. "You're with Rory and me. Orui, take the girls and find Hodan and the tutor."

Meerin laid out Rory's robe beside Salvo. "I'm staying with the prophet."

Tanin clenched his fists. He didn't have time to argue, not if he were to save Salvo. "Am I not the True Heir? Have I not been chosen by Lagaw Himself to lead us all into the new era of man?"

With her hands pressed together, Augusta made a slight bow

with her head. "He's right, Meerin. His orders are only surpassed by Prophet Salvo's."

Tanin resisted the urge to kiss her for her loyalty.

Orui used a strip of the prophet's torn robe to bind his own injured ankle. "Let me get this joint secured, and we can be on our way."

Meerin refused to meet Tanin's gaze. She pointed at Kettlor. "You take his shoulders." Then she directed Rory to the prophet's feet. "Just lift him up so Augusta and I can tuck the robe underneath. On the count of three. One, two, three."

The guardians raised Salvo about a foot off the ground. The prophet didn't react to the disturbance. The women worked quickly, straightening the robe under the hovering body.

As Meerin looked unsatisfied no matter how measured the robe lay under the prophet, Augusta took her by the shoulders and backed her up. "You can set him down now."

Kettlor tried to reassure the disciples. "It's not the first time we've had to carry a companion to aid. We won't fail him or you."

Orui put tentative pressure on his bandaged ankle. "Ladies, shall we?" He still limped, but he was able to move without leaning on anyone as he moved away from the lake.

Augusta squeezed Meerin's hand. "Let's find our lost companions. Then we'll head toward the water and get you washed up and presentable for our prophet again."

Looking down at the blood caked on her robe, Meerin acquiesced. She stared as Rory and Kettlor lifted Salvo in the cloth carrier. Her lips moved silently in what Tanin knew would be a prayer.

Maneuvering around fallen stones and making his way toward the water's edge, Tanin noticed the smell of rotten eggs for the first time. He'd experienced the same odor from water in the farmlands when he toured his kingdom. It was one of the reasons he insisted on carrying aquifer water from Tarbinulus. He'd never known anyone who got sick from the foul water, but he couldn't tolerate the flavor.

"Which way, Kettlor?"

The husbandry guardian nodded his head in the direction Tanin was headed. His voice was strained from the weight of carrying Salvo. "Keep heading toward the water until you see a mostly intact obelisk. I saw Talia walking beside it."

Tanin appreciated the slow speed at which they had to move. The ground was hard, with a thin layer of sand in some spots, while others had a thick pile that sucked their feet under. As legendary cities went, he had expected something grander. Stinky water, broken stones, and piles of sand formed a disappointing image.

He heard Talia before he saw her. "Dew, help me pull it out."

Gregor's traitorous voice protested. "Talia, I don't know if—"

"Just do it."

Curious, Tanin moved around a pillar, mostly intact as Kettlor claimed. Nomyra lay on the ground, much as Salvo had but without the blood. Talia, Gregor, and Dew crouched over the priestess.

Before Tanin could come up with a snide remark, Talia yanked something from Nomyra's body with a sickening slurp and tossed it behind her. The metal pinged off the stele and rolled to Tanin's feet. He couldn't hide his shock as he bent down and retrieved his crown.

The crenellations at the top dripped blood onto the Holy Gemstones, which sizzled as they absorbed the liquid. Angry blue light flashed under the surface of each of the five stones.

Gregor berated his future king. "That's not yours yet, my Prince."

Tanin ignored everything around him, focusing solely on the prone prophet as Rory and Kettlor set down their load. The blue glow intensified as the last bits of blood flowed onto the jewels' surfaces. That was when Tanin realized he didn't need his sister. He dropped to his knees and placed the crown, fur lining down, on Salvo's exposed stomach.

Nothing happened. Tanin begged Lagaw to help His servant as he flipped the crown on its side, putting the Holy Gemstones in contact with the prophet's skin.

Somewhere in the back of his mind, he noted Gregor warning Talia, who was yet focused on the unconscious priestess. *Not yet. I have to save him. That's my role in this journey, and I'm not about to fail now.*

Again, nothing happened. As the blue light faded, Tanin knew he was running out of time. In desperation, he flipped the crown upside down.

The crenellated pieces sank into Salvo's flesh. Rory and Kettlor gasped.

Tanin looked up to the heavens and begged his God, "Please, all powerful Lagaw, save Your servant and help me bring You back to Your people."

A bright light flashed from the crown. Tanin covered his eyes to protect them from the intensity. When he could see again, Tarbin's crown rolled to his feet.

"What happened?" Salvo propped himself up on his elbows and wiped blood from his perfectly smooth and uninjured belly.

Tanin picked up the crown and stared into the Holy Diamond. "I —" A face pressed against the surface. It was so tiny, all Tanin could make out was rage. "The Great and All-Powerful Lagaw healed you and brought you back to fulfill your destiny."

Talia spoke from right behind him. "What did you do?"

His body tensing, Tanin clutched the crown protectively. He wasn't about to lose it again. "Not that it's any of your business, but I didn't do anything. The crown flashed at Lagaw's command."

An obedient bulldog, Gregor stood at Talia's side. Tanin wondered how they had ever been friends.

"Give it back." Talia's eyes brimmed with tears.

Smirking at her weakness, Tanin untied his belt and secured the crown to his person. "The Tarbin crown was never yours to begin with. You have no claim over my kingdom or its possessions. This"— he gestured to their ruined surroundings—"is all yours."

He bent down to help Prophet Salvo to his feet. His sister lifted her sword. Tanin ignored her as Kettlor and Rory took up a protective stance between their charge and Talia.

Nomyra called weakly, "Bright One, let them go. We need to talk."

Lifting an eyebrow and daring his sister to act, Tanin waited to see if she'd run to the priestess, the true hider of secrets. Turmoil rolled across her features. Tanin remembered what that was like. He was grateful to know the true God of Man and embraced the peace his faith brought.

In a rare moment of kindness, Tanin spoke to his sister. "You have to have faith in something. Otherwise, you'll always flounder."

Talia's sword arm dropped as the angry flush drained from her face. Tanin turned and made his way back to the rest of his companions. He had a Machine to destroy. Now that he had the Key, nothing could stop him.

# CHAPTER THIRTY-SIX

TALIA BLINKED at the dust her brother kicked up. Her fingers clenched and unclenched as she debated running after him and retrieving the crown by whatever means necessary. She had beat him more than once in the dueling ring. She could do it again.

But her feet refused to move. Tanin wasn't wrong. As the heir to the Tarbin throne, the crown rightfully belonged to him. She only needed it for one more task. She'd arrived at her final destination, only to fail at fulfilling her destiny.

What would happen to the magicals when the Recharging didn't occur? Talia had not only disappointed her father and her kingdom but ensured the destruction of the elves, dragons, nadph, and mermaids. She might be the True Heir of Raqmu, but what good was inheriting the ruins of an ancient city? Who could she help with cracked stones and hidden lakes?

Without the Key, she would never fulfill the role of Bright One, no matter what the prophecy said. Talia squeezed her temples between her thumb and fingers. Something had happened inside the crown. The dwarf priestess had whispered something as Talia escaped, if only she could remember.

A warm hand slipped into hers and squeezed. Her heartbeat slowed, and she calmed down. Unwavering Gregor stood beside her, forcing Talia to quit worrying and move forward.

A roar echoed off the stone walls and carried across the water's surface, magnifying its horrifying effect.

Talia crouched and grabbed her sword from the ground, where she'd dropped it to kneel beside Nomyra. "Was that Ragaropina?"

Dew supported Nomyra as the two rose from the ground. "It better be. I'm not sure we have the energy to fight a beastly threat at the moment."

Nomyra nodded weakly. "It's the dragon. She's distressed. But we need to talk."

Talia didn't have anything to say to the traitor who had tried to give her body to Maitliin. "It's going to have to wait."

With Gregor by her side, Talia waded through the sand to the solid wet shore. Near the opposite wall, Ragaropina stood tall on her back haunches and extended her wings. Something large lay on the ground, but Talia couldn't make out what it was. "She's down the beach. We should see if we can help."

The priestess released Dew when the two hit the stable wet sand. "We have to talk, Bright One."

"Don't call me that!" Talia twisted her ankle, she pivoted so quickly. "I'm not the Bright One. I can't be. I just lost the Key, and my trusted ally has betrayed me."

Nomyra blanched, and her mouth clamped shut.

"Who is my father?" Talia demanded. She didn't want to play Nomyra's games any longer.

Gregor and Dew both looked away. Nomyra shook her robes in a hopeless attempt to rid herself of sand.

Talia ignored their awkward stance. She wanted to know, and she wanted to know now. "Tell me."

The priestess tilted her head, seeming to come to a decision. "My nephew, Seamus."

All the bluster drained from Talia. "Priest Seamus? But he would have been . . ."

"Seventeen." Nomyra folded her hands inside her sleeves as she had many times in her full high priestess attire. Though disheveled, her confidence didn't waver.

Talia tried to emulate the priestess's self-control when all she wanted to do was yell, stomp, and punch somebody. "How did you fool my mother? She said in her letter that both men who came to her looked like my—King Roland."

"The Krag ring provided enough magic to disguise the boy." Nomyra raised an eyebrow. "Once you learn to feel the magic, it's not so difficult to manipulate your surroundings."

"Talia! Thank the Light and Thoretick, you're safe." Aleck's voice shook Talia free of the crippling shock.

With a final glare at Nomyra, Talia said, "We'll deal with this later." Ignoring the burn of her ankle and the ache in her side, Talia rushed down the beach toward the dwarf.

Gregor jogged behind her to catch up. "What happened when you touched the crown?"

She shook her head, the movement tense and jerky. "It's a blur, but I know Nomyra wanted to take all the Recharging power for herself. She had no intention of distributing it to the world."

Dew beat them all to Aleck and embraced him. "How did you survive? Where are your guards?"

Talia rubbed her temples. "Oh, please tell me they're all right. I can't send home more dwarves who sacrificed themselves for a cause that doesn't directly benefit them."

Aleck wrapped his arms around Talia, releasing her as she winced. "Don't say that. We sacrifice to bring the world back to its former glory. That can only benefit us all."

The sincere look on Aleck's face reminded Talia why she struggled through this quest. It had little to do with a vague prophecy written hundreds of years ago and more about people. All the people.

Carrying a huge sack between them, Traneck and Parnim struggled around the corner.

Gregor crossed to help them. "Talia, it's Rodianiari." He took the shoulders of the unconscious elf from Traneck, allowing both dwarves to take his feet.

Talia glanced at the empty landing of the stairs. She'd forgotten about Rodianiari. "Thank you for climbing up and getting him." She patted Aleck on the shoulder.

He kicked a piece of driftwood aside to provide a smooth surface to lay down the prone elf. "Oh, we didn't climb up. We came down the stairs after the floor fell through."

Talia rubbed her temple as she tried to understand what Aleck was intimating. "You what?"

Parnim bowed before Talia. "I am relieved to see you in one piece, Bright One. I saw the separation in the ground and noticed that the taller platform on the other side of the shield was carved out of ground stone instead of placed there from another location."

Traneck continued. "We had just enough time to shuttle the prince to safety when the ground crumbled around us." He flicked a tear before it could hit his beard. "I don't know how any of you survived."

Dew brushed back Rodianiari's light hair. "He saved us."

Remembering the shimmering image of Thilphiliari under the younger elf, Talia murmured, "Most of us." She shot her head up as the image of the dragon carrying the nadph made her realize what she had seen prone on the ground.

A blast of air rushed across the waterfront from a powerful flap of Ragaropina's wings. She shouted, "Let me help, bug!"

Talia motioned for Gregor to pick up the elf. "Can you handle him? I want to make sure the nadph representative is okay. I've never seen one lying on its side before."

He tucked Rodianiari's arm over his shoulder and rolled. The movement gave Gregor enough momentum to get the slight elf onto his shoulders in a secure hold. He nodded at Talia. "I've got him. Go."

She squeezed his elbow, then took the lead. As she got closer to Ragaropina and the horizontal tree, Talia picked out flashes of light dashing between the nadph and the dragon.

Aleck huffed to keep up with Talia. "The fairies aren't happy."

Dew agreed. "They're definitely fighting with the dragon."

The dragon put down her wings, allowing light from above to reveal the extent of the tree's injuries. The browned leaves of the nadph frightened Talia. He hadn't looked well on the surface after his desert journey, but he was in much worse shape now. Ragged scratches the size of dragon talons slashed through the thick trunk. Amber liquid leaked from the wounds. That had to be how Ragaropina had grasped the nadph to prevent him from crashing to the ground.

Covering her mouth at the horror of the new injuries, Talia understood why the fairies were having a fit. "Can I help?"

One set of giant squinting red eyes and many sets of bobbing light globes focused on Talia and began to talk at once.

The dragon's deep voice vibrated the water as she complained. "The fairy pests won't let me carry their master a bit farther to get his roots into the water."

The fairies squeaked unintelligibly but pointed to the many fallen leaves scattered across the sand and the oozing gashes on his trunk.

Talia guessed at a translation. "You don't want Ragaropina to touch him because you're afraid she'll hurt him more."

Coming together and landing in a straight line on one bent branch, the fairies nodded as a group.

His breath ragged from hauling Rodianiari on his own, Gregor plopped the elf on the dry sand a safe distance from the stomping dragon.

Dew braved the angry fairies to get a closer look at the nadph's condition. "I'm no medicinal guardian, but I'd say this tree is going to die if he doesn't get water."

Dropping her wings and her aggression, Ragaropina snaked her head closer to the line of angry fairies. "I promise to be as gentle as possible."

One of the much-smaller winged creatures flew a circle around the dragon's snout. The rest of the fairies formed a perimeter around the wounded bark and held hands. The most beautiful melody Talia had ever heard tickled her magic sense and made her light-headed. The flowing sap slowed to a modest dripping, but the wounds didn't disappear. Two fairies dropped and slid into the sand surrounding the nadph. The rest slowly sat on the bark, seemingly unable to fly anymore.

Dew rubbed one of the enormous branches. The brittle bark crumbled under her touch. She shoved her hands behind her back. "Why didn't the fairies heal his wounds?"

The dragon tried to sneak her tail around a massive branch. She snatched it away as two fairies shocked her scales. "The little beasties consumed much of their life force getting him here alive. If they keep wasting what's left on keeping me away, they'll die."

Talia twirled Windall around her finger as she decided what to do. She remembered how weak she had been after she healed the giant baby and rescued the falling canoe. She didn't know if there was energy left in her ring to heal two magical creatures. Rodianiari looked weak but stable. The nadph appeared near death.

"Let me help." Talia easily opened the recently clotted slash on her palm. Turning the ring to the inside, she spread some of her life's blood on its surface. As the familiar blue built under the green, she placed her hand directly on the open wounds.

The familiar tingling built in her ring finger, spread to her hand, and then rushed through her body until she vibrated with it. Another presence fell in beside her. The outline of Nomyra, her hands next to Talia's, bled through the glow emanating from her hands and penetrating the nadph.

"It's too much for one person." Nomyra closed her eyes and concentrated.

Talia tried to block her doubt of the priestess's intentions as she focused on healing the nadph. She willed the power to build fibers and connect the damaged tissue. She pushed the gaps together, but there wasn't enough fiber. Her ring flashed and darkened. The power source from Nomyra strengthened Talia's weakened ring. More fibers were built with the combined power, and the wounds knitted together to a tight, smooth surface.

The process was similar to healing the giant baby, but Talia had depended on instinct then, practically willing the infant to live. This time, she worked more methodically.

Catching her breath as the magic tried to heal her bruised side, Talia redirected the energy to producing new bark for the recovering tree. With the wounds healed, he needed whatever protection she could provide from the whipping sands. Nomyra frowned and tried to remove her hands. Talia grabbed her wrists and forced the priestess to assist with the final step.

"Almost." Talia's head lightened as if it floated above her body.

Rough vertical bark popped up from the healed skin, leaving not a hint of scarring. With only a few more pieces to go, Talia was pushed from the nadph by a warm snout puffing steam.

Talia glared at Nomyra, who rubbed the finger marks embedded in her wrists. "How dare you push me away before I finished?"

Her hand sparked as she raised it to discipline the priestess. Ragaropina snaked her head down in front of Talia. Her hand went cold as the enormous toothed mouth stared at her, almost nose to nose.

"I pulled you away as you consumed all the energy from your Unity ring and moved on to dispelling your own life force and that of the priestess without even realizing it." Ragaropina sniffed. "Learn to sense your power before you wield it, young one. Your sacrifice is yet to come."

Holding up the hand wielding Windall, Talia studied its surface.

It felt dead. She found no tingling sensation from its closeness. She'd used up all its stored magic, and she had no idea how to recharge it. Catching a glimpse of the shallowly breathing elf, Talia's shoulders sagged with guilt. He had saved her and her companions, and she had wasted the last bit of magic in her possession for cosmetic improvements on a nadph that still looked near death.

Talia rose to her knees and leaned toward the fairies. "Can we help move your friend to the water's edge?"

Aleck cracked his knuckles. "Can't be any harder than rolling granite boulders after an avalanche." He waved his guards over. "Let's give it a go."

Ragaropina put her nose on a large branch. "I'll help," she mumbled, her voice muffled by layers of wood.

The fairies shouted from the bark, but they didn't have the energy for any other action.

The nadph scooted toward the water a few inches.

Shooting her head up, Talia laughed at the dwarves. "I did nothing, and you managed to move him already."

Aleck shook his head. "We hadn't found a good handhold yet. It wasn't us."

Without anyone touching him, the nadph moved forward another foot.

# CHAPTER THIRTY-SEVEN

Everyone froze.

Ragaropina gawked at Talia. "How did you do that?"

"I didn't do anything." She squinted at the dragon. "You must have."

An external tingling tickled the hairs on Talia's arms. Remembering the same feeling from when the elf slowed her descent from the collapse of the roof, she ran to Rodianiari. He was still unconscious.

The nadph slipped a few more feet toward the water's edge. The lake lapped at just the tip of his roots, except for one long, wiggling appendage that sank deeper into the murky water.

Aleck pulled at his beard. "That's a really long root."

Gregor agreed. "Maybe he's doing it himself. You might have healed him enough for some limited mobility."

The lake bubbled and another root shot out of the water and wrapped around the nadph's trunk.

Dew backed up to dryer ground. "That's not a root."

Upon closer inspection, Talia noticed suckers on the one side of each limp, like those on the tentacles of an ocean creature. But this was a lake, not the ocean. It wasn't possible.

"It can't be an octopus." Talia picked up the exhausted fairies before they followed their master into the lake.

Aleck grabbed a knife from his belt and sprinted to the first tentacle that had tangled in the tree roots. The footsteps of his guards echoed behind his. The three dwarves stabbed into the taut appendage.

A huge wave flooded the shore, drenching the companions. A bulbous head the size of a family home breached the water. It made no vocal noise, but its tentacles bashed the surface with a thunderous cacophony.

The deluge of water flowed back to the lake. Its current carried the unconscious Rodianiari toward the beast. Talia dropped the fairies into Dew's arms. "Get them to higher ground."

Gregor dove and caught the elf's foot before he could be washed into the deep.

Ragaropina warned, "Keep your heads down. I've got the slippery beast."

She inhaled with such force that dead leaves and loose sand were kicked up from the ground. A wave of heat hit Talia before the red-and-orange flames flickered toward the water beast.

The octopus dove below the surface of the lake, which had to be incredibly deep at that point despite being only a hundred yards from shore. The bulbous head flew through the boiling surface water and sprayed a torrent at the dragon. The head of the water column steamed as soon as it hit the flames, but that didn't stop it. The sheer volume of liquid overwhelmed Ragaropina, extinguishing her mighty flame. Forced to move before she drowned, the dragon took one mighty leap backward to cough and clear her lungs.

The back of the octopus's head sank into the water as its eyes, situated between the big bladder-like section and the firm bit leading to its legs, focused on the shore. Jura's head bobbed out of the water beside the beast. It didn't seem to notice her as it extended four tentacles at once to grasp the nadph.

Aleck climbed an old statue of a majestic elf that must have been stunning in its day. "Jura!"

Jura waved back and shouted something Talia couldn't make out.

Parnim and Traneck wove around the reaching appendages until they stood near Talia. The octopus dragged the pale tree to the lake. What was supposed to provide life was about to ensure his death.

A jerk flipped the nadph onto a new side. A huge branch knocked Gregor aside. Rodianiari rolled to the base of the tree, where he became tangled in the roots. Before Gregor could free himself, the elf was pulled under the surface with the base of the tree.

"Rodianiari!" Talia shouted. As she sprinted to the shore, the elf dunked below the water's surface. She couldn't let him die after he had saved them.

Parnim and Traneck dragged Gregor free of the clinging branches.

Waving to get Jura's attention, Aleck yelled, "Get the elf!"

The octopus pulled until half of the nadph sank below the surface. The rest of the tree bobbed upright like a buoy.

Naul limped to the party's side then, Nyna and Ial supporting him.

Setting the big man down, the husbandry guardian rushed to Talia's side. "What's happening?"

"I don't know." Talia scanned the water's edge, trying to catch sight of the elf. "But Rodianiari is tangled in the roots of the nadph. I have to get him out."

Ial shook his head. "I'm a much better swimmer." Then he dove into the chaos of tentacles and bubbling water.

As soon as Ial breached the water, the octopus stopped moving. The sudden quiet felt louder than the roaring dragon.

Gregor shook his head in shame. "I'm sorry I lost him."

She squeezed his hand. "It's not your fault."

Jura bobbed on the surface of the water. "Stop! Let him go. He's trying to help." It sounded like she was trying to persuade the water beast to listen.

Nyna climbed a statue that leaned over the water. "I can't see Ial." Her voice shook in panic.

The tentacled beast released his barked prey with a rhythm of pops as each sucker snapped free. Bobbing in the water a couple of times, the nadph flopped over and floated horizontally on the surface.

Nyna pointed near the new scar on the tree. "There he is." Her voice shook. "Ial's not moving." She dove in a gentle curve and swam with a determined stroke to his side.

Talia waded into the shallows. Trusting Nyna to rescue Ial, she hoped to find Rodianiari before he drowned.

Her foot brushed against a slimy surface. She yanked it up as quickly as she could in the dragging water. A sucker was attached to her calf, but it didn't move. Easily plucking it off with the tips of her fingers, Talia wandered why it hadn't attacked.

Gregor splashed beside her. "The beast's not moving."

Talia poked a tentacle with a hesitant toe. The tingle of magic swam up her leg. "It's a magical beast. That explains its size."

"But not why it's suddenly still."

A swirl of gray hair rocked in the waves a few dozen yards from Talia. "Rodianiari. I see him!" She dove for the elf.

Everything moved with the waves, forcing Talia to swim under a floating tentacle, only for it to hit her on the back as the water left the shore. It burned her back, like too much exposure to the Light's Daughter. The magic grew in force. Maybe that's why the beast had stilled. He was powering up somehow for a fresh attack. The thought of an even bigger or stronger octopus, after this one had already stopped a dragon, scared Talia into swimming faster.

Disoriented in the murky water, she swam to the surface to maintain her bearings. She stared in disbelief as a blue light outlined his thin form, piercing the muck in the water. His head moved.

*Oh, good, he's conscious,* Talia thought. "Rodianiari," she called as she switched to a breaststroke to keep sight of him.

She cringed away from a splash to her right. Expecting to have to dodge a reaching tentacle, Talia relaxed when she realized it was Jura jumping and diving in her direction. The mermaid moved through the water with an easy swiftness. Whatever had ailed the mermaid for the desert part of their journey seemed to have healed. Jura once again moved like the healthy young mermaid Talia had first met a few months ago.

Jura reached Rodianiari first. Talia treaded water, waiting to see if she needed help hauling the elf to shore.

Instead, Jura shook his shoulders and yelled at him. "Stop it. He was trying to help."

A blast of light hit Jura in the chest. She flew backward through the water and slammed into the bulbous head. Talia realized then that Jura hadn't been yelling at the octopus earlier.

She been trying to stop the elf.

Rodianiari's head rose above the surface, his hair a tangled mess around him. Talia swam toward him as fast as she could, ignoring the tentacles and other debris in the water. Rodianiari continued to rise until his waist hovered in the air. His entire body shone a bright blue as if he personified the Holy Diamond when it reacted with the right blood. An enormous octopus tentacle rested across his shoulders.

Talia tried to shout as she stroked through the water, but she couldn't catch her breath. She didn't know what was happening. She just knew she had to get to the elf.

Rodianiari squeezed the tentacle. The dull green skin flashed red, then lost all color as it shriveled into a crinkled mess of its former self. Talia circled close enough to touch Rodianiari, but something held her back. Power hung in the air.

The elf shifted position. His eyes stared through Talia. The pupils were huge, and what little white remained was tinted red from burst blood vessels. He pulled the dead limb toward himself. The girth of the beastly octopus threatened to pin Talia between it and the nadph.

Ragaropina bounded into the air with a huge leap, extending her wings to prolong her elevation.

Rodianiari swung around. He whipped a tentacle at the dragon, who angled to the side. The tip ripped into a wing with a flash of lightning.

"You rotten elf, I am not attacking you." Ragaropina whined as drops of blood dripped into the lake. She swooped down in a steep arc and smashed into the water behind the floating nadph. A huge wave crested, topped by the tree. The water dumped him on the shore, far enough up that Dew had to jump out of the way, the fairies clutched against her chest.

The dragon ducked her head under the retreating tsunami and set the nadph right side up. As the water crashed back toward Talia, the current dragged her farther away from shore. Gregor popped his head above the surface, just in time for the water to shove him back under. Talia hadn't even seen him enter.

Another tentacle smacked into Talia's back. She grabbed it like a piece of driftwood for extra buoyancy. The colorless limb offered no support; it was as wrinkled and colorless as the first one Rodianiari touched.

She dropped it and turned onto her back to catch her breath. Every time she rode high on a wave, Talia watched Rodianiari defeat the octopus, one limb at a time. He didn't seem to need her to rescue him.

Gregor popped up next to Talia and wrapped his arm around her shoulder. Her head fell below the surface, and she sputtered as she knocked his arm away.

"Quit trying to save me." She ordered as she stabilized her body, rocking along the surface.

Gregor pushed his hair out of his eyes. "But I thought you waved for my help."

She gestured to the nadph safe and right side up on the shore. "I wanted you to help him."

"Huh. How'd he get up there?"

"The dragon had something to do with it." She twisted in the water and nodded at the elf. "And it looks like Rodianiari is fine and saving us again."

Popping up between Talia and Gregor, Jura shook her head. "No, he's not."

Talia startled back under the surface. She didn't know how many more times her heart could take a shock. Under the water, she watched the blue light emanating from the octopus to the elf. She rose to Jura. "What do you mean?"

"The octopus is a friend. He was so happy to have someone else to talk to, he happily joined me in trying to get the nadph to water before he parched to death." The capable swimmer floated on top of the water at an odd angle.

Talia remembered what Rodianiari had done to the baby giant. "He's draining the octopus, isn't he?"

The mermaid tried to nod, but instead, her eyes closed and she passed out.

Gregor grabbed her waist to keep her afloat. "Talia." He pointed to a deep gash on Jura's abdomen.

"Take her to shore." Talia stroked toward the elf.

Gregor grabbed her arm. "If he's gone mad like—"

"I am not going to awaken the elven nation having to explain why I killed both their representatives. Rodianiari can be saved. He has to be." Talia kissed Gregor's cheek, then pushed him toward shore. "Let Nyna look at Jura's wound. Windall is completely drained."

Without giving him another chance to argue, Talia dove and swam toward the blue light. She popped up at the edge of the huge gap leading to the octopus's stomach. Jura better have been right about the beast's motivations.

"Rodianiari, you look completely regenerated. You can release the octopus now." Talia tried a casual approach.

The elf blinked at her, then pulled more power from the beast. He hovered completely above the water now, only his dangling toes brushing the surface.

Talia reached out a hand to steady herself against the base of a tentacle. Windall brushed the surface and vibrated. The typical tingling morphed into ecstasy. Every nerve in her body demanded more magic. Talia gasped at the overwhelming need that blossomed within her. Her hand grew cold as the energy from that spot faded.

Blinking her eyes open, though she didn't remember closing them, Talia witnessed the mottled lack of color where she had touched the beast. She yanked her hand away. The ring hummed still, but her nerves settled down, giving her back control.

"Stop it, Rodianiari."

He laughed, a dark evil sound that carried across the water and echoed off the walls. "I gave you a taste. Do you not want to join in? I have no crystals. I can't take it all."

Rodianiari vibrated with power, his skin bluish in hue. He dropped down to hover horizontally until his nose was mere inches from Talia's. That's when she knew. He was mad. His look mirrored the one Thilphiliari wore before he attacked her. The longer she stared, the more she realized how much he looked like the elven lord. She stuck her hand through the blue haze. She ignored the water dripping from her clothes as she rose above the water's surface. Something wasn't right.

The magical glow billowed out from Rodianiari, his light hair moving via an invisible stimulant. As Talia pierced the veil, she remembered the other image on the stairs and a flash of dark hair in the desert. Rodianiari's skin floated with the magic. Underneath, Talia hit real skin and long dark hair.

The mirage dropped, and Lord Thilphiliari smiled at Talia

He wasn't dead. Lord Thilphiliari, the elf whom Talia had killed with his own sword to protect herself and her friends, floated beside her. Guilt, then relief, then puzzlement all coursed through her mind in an endless circle.

Adding her other hand, Talia gripped both of the disguised elf's shoulders. She heard her companions calling from the shore. She blocked out their voices. A chill ran through her frame from the wind whipping her drenched body and the knowledge that she had to stop the mad elf. Again.

Thilphiliari laughed and laughed, giddy with magic. "Raqmu has been found. The Recharging is near, and I am ready to save my people. I'm a hero!" His expression darkened as he took note of Talia. "And now I have the Bright One to power it all. You will be drained as you tried to drain me."

Talia whispered to the unstable elf. "Shhh . . . everything will be fine. But first, you have to sleep."

His forehead crinkled and eyes bulged as Talia put Windall to the base of his neck and begged the Light to charge their crystals.

"No. *No!*" Thilphiliari lifted them higher, fighting her hold.

The magic around the two evaporated into the dark of the cavern ceiling. He shifted back and forth, but Talia held tight and concentrated on filling every facet of the ring. She didn't want him at death's door again, but Thilphiliari had to be contained.

"Stop. Please." His voice weakened as the outer elf disguise popped like a bubble, revealing his true form to all, not just Talia.

She held him close in a tight hug. "Sleep."

His eyes closed, and they both plummeted.

# CHAPTER THIRTY-EIGHT

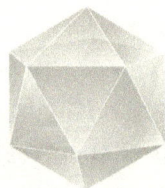

TANIN SLAMMED his body against the wall of a building as light cascaded around the perimeter of the city. He jumped as a strip of brightness flowed under his feet and continued down the thoroughfare. His face flushed in anger as he reached for his sword and tried to find a more defendable spot. His left hand checked the bag tied to his hip. The crenellations of his crown comforted him as he tried to anticipate Talia's next move.

Without a change in pace, Salvo marched straight along the main street. "It is only the lights for when the ceiling is closed. The dragon must have flipped the switch." His gaze flickered to Tanin's side so quickly, the prince thought it might have been his own paranoia. "There's no time to waste."

Hodan jogged beside the prophet. "Shall we find the Machine and destroy it now?"

Salvo slid to a stop. "Destroy?" His eyes rotated back and forth as though he were in a deep sleep, though they remained open.

Augusta put her hands on his shoulders and tried to get him to focus on her. Her hair sifted sand as she moved in close. Her disheveled appearance made her even more appealing. Tanin couldn't help but stop, even in this moment of distress, to stare at her.

Prophet Salvo didn't seem to notice she was there.

Tanin sheathed his sword and gestured Orui to the frozen man. "Can you do something?"

Favoring his injured ankle, the medicinal guardian leaned on his staff and shrugged. The party had not found all their gear, which had left Orui without his complete kit.

At Tanin's frown, he limped toward Salvo anyway. "Let me have a look at him." Orui shouldered his way in front of Augusta.

As if nothing out of the ordinary had happened at all, Salvo blinked twice, lifted his robe, and walked around Orui. Tutor Grayson offered a steadying hand to the wavering medicinal guardian. The rest of the party rushed to keep up with the animated prophet.

His voice sounded the same, but the pace was much quicker. "Yes, yes, destroy the Machine. Well, you see, in order to do that, we need to start it first. When the Recharging is well under way, we'll force a feedback of power that will blow up the whole contraption."

Meerin huffed as she pumped her legs harder than the taller party members. "Is that why you showed us how to fix the Machine? I couldn't figure out why you'd do that if we had to destroy it. Keeping it broken would be a lot simpler than repairing it."

Salvo coughed. "Yes, exactly. We must end its reign for all eternity, or the next conjunction will be another battle."

Tanin shook off the prophet's odd behavior as a relic of his recent injuries. Instead, he concentrated on the streets they were passing. He could have been walking through Hajar Ramliun with the adobe-styled buildings and glassless windows. He wondered if colored cloth had covered the openings when Raqmu was a living city. The unnatural lighting that glimmered from parallel lines on the street and along borders around the ceiling, however, was unlike anything he'd experienced.

Orui's stomach growled, sounding much louder than normal in the empty street.

Kettlor patted him on the shoulder. "Me too, my friend. Me too."

With a roll of her shoulders, Augusta pulled her robe tighter around her body. "Unfortunately, we don't have any provisions. I'm not sure how we are to survive until the Recharging."

After counting his remaining intact arrows, Kettlor strung his bow. "Maybe I can find something lurking in the shadows? We haven't been to a ruins yet that didn't have some sort of residents."

Salvo rubbed his stomach. "Hunger. Yes. I remember now. It's been such a long time."

Rory pulled on Tanin's sleeve. The prince replied with a questioning look. Rory's face crinkled as he gestured with his chin at the prophet. Tanin prayed for Lagaw to calm his weapons guardian's paranoia. He pursed his lips and shook his head with a quick jerk. Rory looked down in acquiescence, but Tanin noticed his muscles were still tensed as if he anticipated a fight.

They came to a crossroads. The magical glow lined both streets, lighting the front of each building. Cracked paint in beige, white, and gray peeled from storefronts and taverns. Made of stone and painted wood, this area of town looked more like Tarbinulus. Broken glass spilled onto the cracked pavement. The shadows made the city look grand and impressive. The light showed its age and destruction.

After a quick glance to the right, Salvo continued straight. "Past the Green Grove stables and one more street, and then . . ."

The prophet swung a quick left down a wide street that made the other entryways seem village-like in comparison. The buildings grew to match the grandeur of the street. In a living city, fancy carriages pulled by well-bred horses would have clopped by, carrying immaculately dressed men and women. The buildings in their bright, luxurious colors spoke of wealth.

Raqmu might have been the jewel of the desert at one point. Now Talia was the True Heir of a dilapidated ruins with nothing left but memories and decay. She would beg to come back to Tarbinulus and serve in whatever capacity Tanin would allow her. The crown bumped his hip as he pivoted. Everything would end the way it had started, with Tanin heir to Tarbin and Talia a political pawn to be used to his advantage.

Augusta squinted up at an elaborately decorated street sign that ran parallel to the grand street the party stood in. She pointed back the way they'd come. "It says this one is Memorial."

Hodan cocked his head at the sign. "It's in Veni."

Tutor Grayson put a hand on the cultural guardian's shoulder. "As it should be. I'm glad we've had a chance to refresh your knowledge of the unused language."

With a fierce yank, Salvo forced open the door of a reddish-pink building.

The painted logo on the sign had peeled over the years. Tanin squinted at the sword that could mean anything without context. "What is this place?"

Salvo rolled his eyes. Tanin's face scrunched at the expression. He'd never seen the prophet so flippant.

The prince raised an eyebrow at Rory, who had tried to point out the change in personality earlier. Shrugging, he acknowledged something was odd. Maybe the prophet hadn't fully recovered from his injuries. With the "watch him" hand signal, Tanin motioned Rory to the prophet's side.

Inside the dilapidated building, Salvo pushed past a swinging door with a creak to get behind the large U-shaped counter. Orui plopped down in a chair and promptly choked on the puff of dust from centuries of neglect. Kettlor opened the door and fanned the debris out with an old pillow.

Rory paused. While deciding whether it was safe to sit, Tanin waved Rory after the prophet. Augusta and Meerin followed close behind.

Orui propped his injured ankle on the counter and sighed. Tanin sat carefully in the chair next to him. He hadn't realized how tired he was until he was off his feet.

Hodan hopped over the counter to get a closer look at the faded signs on the walls. "It looks like some sort of menu with different sizes of the same choices. But it's difficult to make out most of these words."

Pulling a candle from his robe, Grayson patted the rest of his pockets. "Does anyone have a striker?"

A sharp smack of the outside door against its frame forced Tanin alert.

His face completely white, Kettlor held the door closed with a tight grip.

Orui's ankle dropped from the counter with a thud. He threw a piece of leather from the floor at Kettlor. "By the cursed Darkness, why did you do that?" He cringed as he rubbed his injury.

Kettlor peered out the window, one leg braced against the door-frame as if keeping something out. "I—it's not—I can't . . ."

Tanin frowned and forced his way up from the chair that seemed to have sucked him in. The street looked empty; the eerie border light illuminated everything except the shadowed doorways and small alleys.

He nudged Kettlor out of the way and opened the door. Setting the string of his bow, the husbandry guardian moved out in front of the prince. Hodan sensed the protective mode and jumped to his duty. His robes slipped from his shoulders as he freed his muscles, ready for a battle. Positioned on either side of Tanin, the guardians scanned the street for danger.

Tanin held his scabbard but maintained his belief that there was nothing out there. "What did you see, Kettlor?"

"I'm not sure." He pulled an arrow and studied the rooftops across the street.

Orui limped behind the party. "Come on, Ket, you don't slam a door shut in terror unless you saw something."

The husbandry guardian's hands shook at his friend's words. "It was a man's face. I swear I saw a man's face." His voice grew in pitch, and he refused to look anyone in the eye. "A face without a body. It hovered just above the ground on that roof and moved back and forth."

Knocking on his head with a closed fist, Tanin made Kettlor look at him. "Did you hit your head in the fall, or is this just hunger talking?" Tanin knew his husbandry guardian wasn't joking; that was Orui's department. But a severed head flying around was too much for even this world of magic.

"My Prince!" Rory called from inside the shop, his voice laced with an enthusiasm Tanin hadn't heard in a long time.

With a squeeze of Kettlor's shoulder, Tanin reentered the building. Rory dropped an armful of weapons onto the U-shaped counter. Meerin kicked open the door to the back with her own heavy load.

Rory held up a crossbow no bigger than his forearm. "We should all get one of these." Around his wrist, he strapped a leather band that was like a little quiver with slots for the crossbow bolts. "Watch." He flipped a bolt out, cocked the tiny crossbow with it, and fired at a poster on the wall.

Orui ducked too late as the entire shooting process was much too quick to get out of the way. "Man, that thing is faster than anything I've ever seen." He reached up to pry the bolt loose, but it wouldn't budge. "And powerful. It's deep in the brick."

The back door swung open again. Salvo and Augusta pushed through with more weapons.

"What is this place?" Tanin took the load from Augusta. One of the swords in the pile caught his eye.

"Guardian Weapons Depot. These need to be used for the test." Salvo tossed an unstrung longbow to Kettlor. "Tarbin doesn't have a monopoly on guardians. The schools were designed to train guardians and *only* guardians, not noble children without any expectation of serving the greater good. When it was time to equip the specialized to serve their duty, they came here." He tossed a staff to Orui, who caught it with a twirl.

"Nicely balanced." The medicinal guardian nodded, impressed.

The smooth wood had a sharp splinter sticking out beneath an embedded ruby. "It needs some repairs, though."

Salvo laughed. "No, no, no. It is perfect. Prick your finger and drip blood on the ruby."

"But my blood doesn't react with the Holy Gemstones."

"Of course, not. I will activate it, but it has to know who owns it."

Orui frowned but obeyed the prophet and pressed his middle finger into the thorn. With a wince, the medicinal guardian rubbed his finger on the ruby. Salvo motioned for the weapon. He pricked his finger and added his blood to Orui's.

The thorn shook as blue light radiated from the ruby, flashing a purplish glow across the walls of the shop. The wood flowed around the gem until the entirety was enclosed inside and the surface smoothed to a driftwood softness.

Salvo shoved his hands in his robe, his face cracked in an eerie smile. He nodded to Grayson. "You, tutor, try to take the staff."

After wiping his hands on his robe, Grayson reached for the wood.

Raising an eyebrow at Orui, Salvo said, "You must tell the staff if he's friend or foe."

With a glance of skepticism, Orui complied. "Uh . . . don't let him touch you."

Grayson's finger had barely skimmed the surface of the staff when red lightning engulfed his hand. The force flung him against the wall. The tutor shook his head, stunned.

Hodan ran to his teacher. "Are you all right?" He glared as Salvo burst into hysterical laughter.

Tanin noticed Grayson was still breathing, so he chose not to worry about him. He was much more interested in these magical weapons. With these and the cannon-mounted ships, he would easily force the rest of the world to bow to the superiority of Tarbin.

Rory shared his prince's enthusiasm as he balanced swords until he found a pair that seemed to fit. Sunk into the hilt of each was a black opal. Kettlor studied his bow until he found an emerald near the arrow notch.

With a flip of his wrist, Salvo tossed a pair of leather gloves to Hodan.

Catching them without leaving his tutor's side, the cultural guardian inspected the stitching. "They're flexible and firm at the same time. What are they made of?"

Salvo waved the boy closer and cut his finger before answering. "I believe these are salamander."

The activation process mirrored the one with the staff. Tanin covered his eyes so as not to go temporarily blind when the dark returned. When Tanin blinked them open, Hodan held his gloved hands up and flexed his fingers.

Before anyone could react, Salvo grabbed the cultural guardian's hand and placed it flat on the counter. He slammed a hammer onto Hodan's fingers. The boy yelled as his face contorted in shock.

Grayson pulled Hodan back. "What are you doing?"

A huge smile grew on Hodan's face. "Wait, Tutor, look." He took the hammer from Salvo with what should have been his shattered hand. Flipping the weapon in the air, he easily caught it without a single flinch. "I didn't feel a thing. My hand is perfect."

Salvo clapped his hands like a pleased toddler. "There's a set of slippers in here somewhere. See if you can find them while I activate the others."

Hodan and Grayson began searching as Salvo motioned Rory to his side. "These swords will never need sharpening and will cleave through any substance, rock or flesh or grass. We need to find their specialized scabbards, for nothing else can hold them."

After activating Rory's weapons, Salvo moved on to Kettlor. "This bow might be my favorite and will help us out today as we hunt for dinner." He used the blood ritual as he had on the others. When the emerald submerged into the wood, a small plaque replaced it. "This is where you write the symbol for whatever you wish to hunt, and you won't be able to miss."

Kettlor blinked at the odd figure Salvo sketched on the plaque.

The prophet laughed. "There is a whole guide of symbols you'll have to learn. This one is for procapra. There should be a few herds roaming around. They're pretty self-sufficient."

Pulling an untarnished sword from the pile, Tanin weighed it in his hands. With one finger, he balanced the entire weapon just above the cross guard. "It's perfect." He bounced the weapon from one hand to the other. "I'll take this one, but I don't see a gem."

Salvo motioned Tanin closer. He flipped back a hinge on the bottom of the hilt to reveal a sapphire tucked inside. "You have chosen well, Prince Tanin. Once the sword is activated, it will never mar its owner's flesh and will always come when summoned."

Meerin ran her hands through her curls, gripping the ends as she took in the mass of magical weapons on the counters. "I don't understand, Prophet Salvo. I thought we followed Lagaw's teachings and would abandon the world of magic. What is the purpose of these weapons imbued with magic? Is it not sacrilege to use them?"

Scorn flashed across Salvo's face. Though it quickly morphed into the more typical look of quiet understanding, Tanin didn't miss the first emotion.

"Lagaw set the worlds in motion. The alignment of the planets that generates magic is completely natural and as He intended." Salvo placed a hand on his disciple's shoulder. "The Machine that amplifies the natural is evil, not the existence of magic itself."

Meerin hung her head. "I understand, Prophet."

With a whoop, Hodan held up a slipper. "I found one."

# CHAPTER THIRTY-NINE

A WHISPER of leaves and the warmth of the Light's Daughter woke Talia from a deep slumber. Wanting the simple peace to last a little longer, she stretched her arms before opening her eyes. Her forehead crinkled as she detected a hint of brimstone on the wind. The distinct stench of rotten eggs sat under the unusual odor. She thought of abandoned chicken coops and water from the farmlands. Water. Fathoms of darkness and twisted dead tentacles and an elf?

Talia sprang to her elbows and opened her eyes. She couldn't see. Everything was so dark. "Thilphiliari's not dead. We have to stop him."

"She's awake," said a deep voice she didn't recognize as bits of flickering light filtered through branches.

"Second Emissary to New Tarbin?" Talia turned on her side and coughed.

Ragaropina lifted her head, allowing more light to bleed through, producing a kind of dragon halo. She stopped blowing warm air. The brimstone sent faded as Talia's temperature dropped and a shiver ran through her body. The warmth hadn't been from the sun at all but from the gentle breathing of the dragon.

Blinking at her, then the nadph, Talia couldn't understand how the tree was moving when it was still the middle of the day. Talia put an arm over her eyes and fully sat up. "It's so bright."

"In here it is." Ragaropina laughed, puffs of smoke escaping her nose. "Night reigns beyond the city."

The deep voice Talia now knew was the nadph's spoke up. "The lighting tract that runs through the old city still works. Ragaropina remembered how to ignite it." He slid back as his fairy companions danced in his branches, where plump green leaves joined the crunchy brown ones.

"You look so much better. I'm pleased to see you awake." Talia struggled to stand, feeling weak and unpresentable next to the magical beings.

The nadph formed a face out of bark, with a scar visible on the exposed trunk below. "I just needed a good drink and some rest. I feel centuries younger after all the adventure. We've been standing still too long. It's time to move forward."

A hand grabbed Talia's arm to help her to her feet. Dew smiled, tear streaks visible on her face. "Talia, this place is the most beautiful city I've ever seen."

"City?" All Talia could remember was the limestone-strewn floor, a humongous stairway, and a forever-reaching lake. And the elf. "Wait. Was Thilphiliari saved from the lake? We've got to contain him. He's completely mad."

Ragaropina gestured toward an above-ground tomb, where Thilphiliari lay. His dark hair flared around his head, his clothes still dripped, and his skin was unnaturally pale.

Talia's face blanched. "Is he?"

Nomyra handed Talia a warm cup of tea. "He's in a sort of trance engendered by the fairies after I healed the flying pests."

Talia sipped the tea and took in her new surroundings. She didn't remember being moved, but the lake was nowhere in sight. Instead, the sandy ground was covered in tombs of every shape and size, a solid stone ceiling overhead.

Naul stirred a large pot. His head was heavily bandaged, but otherwise he looked no worse for wear. Aleck talked nonstop about something that enthralled him. The rest of her companions were all present, even Jura, who looked like her normal cheerful self.

She squatted and rose to stretch the ache in her leg muscles. The sheer power Talia had used to drain Thilphiliari in the midst of his madness frightened her. She didn't know if anyone could be trusted with so much power.

Ragaropina stretched her neck and wings, garnering Talia's admiration for her beauty. "Before I depart, there is something I must show you."

Talia frowned. "You're leaving before the Recharging?"

The dragon tilted her head in a grandmotherly fashion. "I must get back to my hatchlings. There is no other to greet them when they break into the world."

Aleck brought Talia a hot bowl of soup. "I'd love to see that."

Talia smiled. "As would I." The warm briny soup tasted Light blessed. It had been many hours since she last ate. A chunky bit proved difficult to chew, and Talia blanched. "This isn't the octopus, is it?"

"No," Aleck assured her. "We couldn't eat the beast that was only trying to help our nadph friend on Jura's request."

Dew took the empty bowl and handed Talia a fresh cup of tea. "When Ial and Nyna came back from helping Jura mend the octopus, they brought some fish and some weird sort of mussels."

The steam from the tea warmed Talia's chilled nose as the news warmed her heart. "So it's alive, then?"

The nadph shook as his fairy friends rushed into his branches. "The water beast has agreed to take me home through the underground river."

Talia's eyebrows rose. "You're leaving too?"

"My destiny lies elsewhere. This was but one stop." The tapping of the nadph's roots on the stone floor echoed. "This way, True Heir."

While sipping the soothing tea, Talia took in the graveyard. "Is this all that's left of Raqmu?"

Ornately decorated tombs in every shape and size imaginable lined the walkway that was large enough for a dragon to traverse. Mounted under a cracked marble statue of a fairy, much larger than life, lay a sarcophagus the length and breadth of the nadph walking in front of them. Human-sized tombs dominated, but other sizes filled in with regularity, forming a puzzle of history.

Gregor jogged to catch up. "Impressive, isn't it?"

Talia wiped tea off her upper lip. "It's also depressing." She leaned over one of the tombs to read the inscription. It wasn't in Common, but she thought she recognized the language. "Elven?"

Blowing a bit of sand out of the flowing letters, Dew nodded. "Yes. 'The True Heir Halcianiarian, member of the royal family, beloved husband, beloved father, beloved ruler, brought great fortune to Raqmu when he opened the trade route with Tarbin across the seas.'"

Talia touched the word for her kingdom. "Across the seas? Tarbin did reach far."

Gregor rubbed his finger on another statue, this one of a mermaid with a background of a curling wave. "She was a True Heir as well."

Aleck pointed to one that could have been dwarf sized. "This one is in Dwarven, really old Dwarven. It calls Callick here a True Heir."

Talia looked up at Ragaropina, who rested a wing on a giant tomb. "Is that a dragon True Heir?"

Ragaropina smiled. At least, Talia hoped it was a smile. With her teeth peeking out from behind her lips, the dragon looked threatening.

"Yes. You walk through Memorial Park, the final resting place for all the True Heirs since the founding of Raqmu." She huffed a bit of steam from her nose and swiped an enormous tombstone clean.

Focusing on the odd characters carved into the stone, Dew asked, "What language is that?"

Ragaropina laughed. "The first language, Dragon."

"Dragon?" Dew whispered the word like it was new to her. "I've never seen anything so artistic. Are those letters? Can you teach me?"

"Of course I can, curious one." The dragon preened her chest scales in a show of pride.

Talia wondered at her title and at all those who had shared the name before her. "So the True Heirs don't have to be human. Does Nomyra know that?"

The nadph's bark face shifted to the opposite side of his trunk, making it look like he was walking backward. "The ruler of Raqmu changes based on the needs of the city. The True Heir during the time of the Recharging has always been human."

Nomyra had almost ruined it all. Now Talia's brother was intent on destroying the Machine. She had to convince him to stand down. Would she fight her own twin for the survival of races she hadn't known existed a year ago?

Gregor sneaked his hand into hers. She pulled him closer, absorbing his confidence in her. There was no time for second-guessing. The planets were soon to align, and she had to be ready. She squeezed, then let him go.

"So what am I here to see?" Talia lengthened her stride to walk beside the nadph.

He moved his face to the side, which made Talia a bit dizzy. She focused forward instead of looking at him directly. "More responsibility, I'm afraid."

The nadph moved to the center of the field that had been designed to contain millennia of tombs. "At each Recharging, when surface magic is the strongest, many nadph seedlings sprout from the rejuvenated soil."

He held up a root like a human would hold out a hand. His fairy companions flew down and deposited a seed twice as big as Talia's hand on the gray-brown surface. The nadph used two other tentacle-like roots to bore a hole in the sifting sand.

"The firstborn rises here." With the tenderness of a parent, he placed the seed into the hole and allowed the sand to fall back into place. "She will be born with all the knowledge but none of the experience of the rest of her people."

One of the fairies left her hovering companions and landed on the sand with her legs spread and her hands on her hips.

The nadph chuckled, the rumbling and shaking identical to Second Emissary's. "Yugewmena has volunteered to serve as caretaker of the firstborn. I am not surprised. I believe you know her sister."

Squinting at the still-glowing fairy, Talia recognized the same upturned nose and shiny green hair of Second Emissary's companion. "Philomena?"

"The very same. It seems isolation from the rest of us runs in her family. She will serve the seedling well."

The dragon cleared her throat. "My brood also hatches en masse as the ground saturates with renewed power." She pulled a pouch from underneath a scale on her abdomen. "He will speak his name upon bonding and discover his knowledge as his mind and body mature."

Into her talon, she dumped an elongated stone covered in stunning swirls of yellow and green that seemed to move with the light, not simply reflect it. She pushed the egg partway into the sand beside the strutting fairy. "Yugewmena will guard the hatchling from harm until you have fulfilled your destiny."

The dragon snaked her head toward Talia, who repressed the urge to duck out of the way. Instead, she met the massive beast's gaze.

"You must promise to return here first and check on the new ones before any celebration or rest. They will need you." Ragaropina's eyes narrowed in seriousness. "Without me here to guide him, the hatchling will search for a bond. You will know when he has chosen."

Talia loved nothing better than flying. After donning all the titles she hadn't asked for, she'd gladly accept the role of dragon rider.

A question clouded her joy as she thought of the prone Thilphiliari and the crumbling mer temple. "What about the elves and the merpeople? Who will be there for them?"

Jura straightened from staring at the dragon egg. "After I drop off our friend, I'll head out to our capital city in the Kiwa Sea. My home was but an outpost in the warmer waters of the North Sea."

Ragaropina headed down the corridor. "I will return the elf lord to his kingdom. I'm not sure leaving him to his people in this state is the correct choice, but he has left me few options."

A fairy flew around the nadph, then sat on his bark nose.

The tree touched the spiky tail of the dragon. "If you would bring Thathomila, she could awaken another elf and explain what happened. The elves might understand, or they might not. That will be solved at another time."

With a sway of her horned head, Ragaropina gestured the volunteer to her side. "I would welcome the company on the long journey home."

Parnim scratched her beardless chin as she approached the dragon egg. "This is not a rock, then?"

Talia couldn't tell what answer Parnim was hoping for.

Ragaropina tilted her head toward the dwarf. "It is not simply a rock. Inside, one of my young awaits the magic to hatch into the Light."

Parnim swiveled on her feet so fast, she almost made a full circle. "Prince Aleck, the dragon egg. See the way it swirls with the Light."

Aleck shook his head, his eyes never leaving the dragon egg. "And they will hatch at the moment of the Recharging."

"What am I missing?" Talia asked.

Parnim tossed her pike from hand to hand as if she needed to stab something. "There is an entire collection of these rocks outside the capital."

Aleck added, "And if they are all to hatch when the Recharging occurs . . ."

Talia understood. "You'll be swamped with dragon hatchlings."

Ragaropina dropped onto all four of her talons. "Are you sure there is a clutch of dragon eggs in the Krimmel Mountain Range? I don't know who would have laid them."

Aleck pointed to Ragaropina's egg. "I don't know if they're dragon eggs, but they look an awful lot like that."

Parnim cleared her throat and straightened her shoulders before the dragon. "Since you are to drop the elf before heading home, may I beg a ride to my kingdom on the way? I'll be able to warn my people and protect the young."

Ragaropina nodded solemnly. "It would be my honor, and I will visit as soon as my brood hatches, just in case you need assistance."

The party returned to the entrance chamber of Memorial Park. Parnim hugged Traneck, a bit too long for colleagues, before heading out with Ragaropina.

Talia shook her head, trying to rid her mind of the too-many thoughts rushing around inside. One in particular floated to the surface.

She had to get the Key back and there was only one place Tanin would head. Talia turned to Nomyra. "Where is this Machine?"

# CHAPTER FORTY

ORUI WHISTLED as he walked in a circle, taking in the huge gash in the ceiling above. "I wonder how many desert beasts found their death when they stumbled onto the invisible shield."

Tanin kicked through a substantial pile formed from the steady stream of sand that sifted to the city below. On the other side of the downpour, a field of green swayed among what looked like the remnants of a garden. "Not too many, or the corpses would have blocked the sunlight."

With her hands held up to catch sprinkles of sand as if they were rain, Meerin's face scrunched into her thinking expression. "If sand falls now, why didn't the sand fill in the crack above the shield, essentially blocking all the light and preventing any sort of growth?"

Holding his robes up so they wouldn't drag through the sand, Salvo marched toward a large hexagonal gazebo to the left of what must have been a grand entrance to an immaculate garden when Raqmu was at its prime. "Anything that touched the magical barrier immediately disintegrated into nothing at all."

With a nod, Orui tapped the ground with his new staff. "That explains the lack of corpses."

Meerin agreed.

Kettlor bent over a paw print on what must have been an animal path cutting through the undergrowth. "I wouldn't call it healthy grasslands, but there's certainly something living here."

Tanin squinted over the husbandry guardian's shoulder. "Looks catlike. Is a procapra a cat?"

Placing a hand over his stomach to mute its growling, Orui muttered, "I don't much care what it is. I'm starving."

Hodan inhaled sharply, drawing Tanin's attention. In front of him blinked a goatlike creature with an extended nose and floppy ears. Though it stared right at the cultural guardian, it didn't seem nonplussed by his presence. Another one stepped out of the shadows and uprooted a mouthful of greenery.

Kettlor moved very slowly as he retrieved an arrow from his quiver. "That is a procapra. I've only ever seen drawings, but I'm sure of it. We were taught they were extinct."

Tanin put a hand on his sword as Kettlor readied his bow. "Are they magical? Should Hodan step back?"

The hunter shook his head, then stared down his arrow to aim. As Kettlor's fingers edged back, darts flew from the shadows and kicked up sand around him. Flung off-balance, Kettlor's release sent the arrow flying toward Hodan.

More darts flew at the party from the unknown assailant. Tanin hit the ground as Rory dove on top of him. Grayson slammed into Hodan as two of the small projectiles headed for the boy. The sharp flying weapons embedded in the tutor's side. The arrow from Kettlor's magic bow flew in an impossible arc and pierced one of the fleeing procapras. The beast collapsed as the party raced for the gazebo and what little cover it offered.

Kettlor helped Hodan drag Grayson to the steps.

Tanin clapped Kettlor on the back. "Did you see that? Your arrow still caught the procapra."

"I saw it. It was impossible, but I did see it." Kettlor nocked another arrow as he searched the shadows for their attacker.

Rory pushed insistently on Tanin's shoulder. "Please stay down, my Prince. We don't know what is hunting us out there."

With a scowl, Tanin crouched behind a pillar. The two women stood beside Salvo, who sheltered in the shadows on the far side.

Orui ripped open Grayson's tunic to see his injuries. "What in Lagaw's name are these?"

Grayson screamed as the medicinal guardian poked at one of the barbed shafts. Kettlor scratched his head. "They look like porcupine quills. But they live in forests and don't actually throw them. There has to be contact for them to embed in skin."

A whistling that sounded much like the low notes of a flute rose from the shadows. The procapras froze before crossing the gently flowing stream on the far side of the clearing. The goatlike ungulates rocked gently on their haunches, seemingly soothed by the music.

Prophet Salvo's face lost all color as he collapsed. "Not good. Not good at all. You should have listened to me and gone straight to the Machine."

Orui pointed to thin strands of blue that streaked across Grayson's chest from the puncture wounds. "These barbs are poisoned. I don't have my kit. I can't . . ."

With his breathing so shallow Tanin could hardly see his chest move, Grayson called for his student. "You have to take your place as full cultural guardian to the prince now."

"No. I'm not ready." Hodan looked much younger than his twelve years as he begged his teacher to stay with him, to live. "You can't leave yet."

Grayson coughed up blood, and he grimaced in agony. Tanin had to admire his strength as he took a necklace from around his neck and strung it around Hodan's.

"You have graduated with more experience than any other I've seen. You are ready."

His arms fell to his sides, and his eyes stared blankly ahead. Hodan collapsed onto his chest, sobbing. Orui guided the boy away from the poisoned barbs.

Tanin's lips curled at the show of weakness. Yet he would also miss the tutor. Maybe he could give the boy a moment to mourn before reminding him of his duty.

With a gasp, Augusta grabbed Meerin's arms and dragged her down to the ground next to the prophet. "What is that thing?"

A mythological beast from a time of horror padded out of the shadows with confident dominance. Its tawny body, muscular and lean, was carried on huge cat paws. If it had claws like a normal lion, they would be long enough to slice a man in half with two swipes. Its black tail, full of quills like the ones that had just killed Tutor Grayson, straightened horizontally from its round rump.

As disturbing as those combined characteristics were, none of it made Tanin's skin crawl until the beast turned its fluffy maned head to the light. It didn't feel real. How was it even possible?

It looked like someone had plucked the face of a little old man from his frail body and attached it to the neck of this mighty beast. The image was so disturbing, Tanin didn't know how to react, though every fiber in his being told him to kill it.

# CHAPTER FORTY-ONE

KETTLOR PULLED an arrow from his quiver. "That's what I saw on the roof, pacing back and forth. It must have followed us."

Tanin pulled his sword from its scabbard. "What in the name of the Gods is it?"

Scurrying backward to put more room between it and him, Salvo studied the terrain outside the gazebo. "A manticore. A terrible beast with venomous quills. It sings to soothe its dinner before it tears the prey apart with three rows of teeth."

Tanin and his companions backed into the shadows, everyone tense and anxious.

With an arm draped around Grayson, Hodan growled a whisper. "We can't leave him here."

Augusta twisted Hodan's chin to look him in the eye. "We won't leave him here, but if you don't back up and that thing decides to attack again, his death will have been in vain and his spirit will never forgive you." She lifted the compliant Hodan and lead him toward the rest of the group. "You don't have the right to take away his glory because of your grief."

Tanin rubbed his forehead. Augusta would truly make a great

queen. But the future would have to wait while a monster stalked the present. With a firm grip on his sword hilt, he glanced around to find a more advantageous place to hunker down as they tried to figure out how to kill the beast. He saw nothing beyond wisps of greenery and some tumbled marble statues.

The manticore mewed in the melodic tone from earlier. The cat eyes tucked inside its man face blinked at the gazebo almost lazily.

The black opal on the staff caught the filtered light as Salvo moved his fingers along the wood as though he were playing a pipe flute. "And they're very territorial."

Orui hopped back another step. "What are you doing?"

Tanin swore Salvo was calling the beast toward them. As the human head approached, Tanin knew he would see that grotesque image in his nightmares.

The large chimera approached the party with all the casualness of a midday stroll through the park. Then it roared, a deep, throaty sound. The smell of decayed meat and fresh blood swept the gazebo like a breeze off a slaughterhouse.

Tanin threw his free arm over his mouth as his eyes watered. He brandished his weapon but didn't know how they could get close without risking a quill attack. "We have to disable its tail."

Hodan cracked his knuckles, already wearing the magical gloves. "I'll get it."

Grabbing him by the shoulder, Rory pushed him back before the boy could rush into battle. "No, you won't. Not without a plan."

With another mew, the manticore paced around the gazebo as if plotting its own attack. The party circled under the roof, trying to stay as far away from it as possible without being completely exposed.

Meerin snapped pieces of broken wood from part of a railing. The manticore froze and lifted its tail. The venomous barbs vibrated with a threatening excitement.

Orui grabbed Meerin's hands. "What are you doing? Don't antagonize the manticore."

Kettlor held his bow at the ready. "Hopefully, it'll decide we're not a threat and eat the procapra while we sneak away in the other direction."

Blood rushed to Tanin's head. "No. We're not running away. Are we supposed to look behind our backs every time we venture onto a new street? What if the beast decides to attack when we've almost destroyed the Machine?"

Salvo coughed.

Tanin squinted at him. "Right?"

The prophet lifted an eyebrow at Tanin. "Whatever you think is necessary."

Tanin couldn't shake the feeling that he was hiding something. He'd confront Salvo after they rid themselves of the carnivorous beast hunting them.

"What was your plan, Meerin?"

"I want to watch the mechanism of the quill shooting. I was hoping not to have to sacrifice another friend by throwing pieces of wood instead." Meerin held two bits of gazebo in her hand.

Tanin took a piece from her and tossed it to the right of the manticore. The beast pounced in that direction and flicked his spiked tail, sending a half dozen quills into and around the harmless wood.

Without waiting for permission, Meerin threw the second piece over its tawny back. The manticore jerked its head in the direction of the new assailant and growled out that eerie whistling sound. Instead of twisting its tail to shoot the target from the odd angle, it turned its entire body and shot another round.

The snap of the wood, quickly followed by Meerin's clapping, made Tanin tense, ready to fight.

The disciple shook Tanin's upper arms. Glee danced in her eyes. "It has to face its target to fire. If we can distract it, we can tie down its tail from behind."

Salvo raised an eyebrow at Meerin. "You are quite the smart one, aren't you? That just might work."

Hodan cracked his knuckles. "I'll distract it."

Dodging Rory's reach for his shoulder, Hodan dashed from the back of the gazebo. His determined look changed into surprise as his feet moved faster than seemed possible. He flailed his arms in an attempt to find his balance within the swift movement.

Augusta crossed her arms over her chest. "That could prove useful."

Tanin agreed, until Hodan tripped and skidded to a halt immediately behind the manticore's back legs. The beast whipped around. The disconcerting head of an old man tucked into layers of mane fur morphed into true horror as its mouth opened, revealing three rows of sharklike teeth that reached far enough back that they appeared to go down its throat. Tanin shivered at the thought of being shredded all the way down to the beast's gullet.

A snap from Tanin's right drew his attention just in time to see Kettlor let loose an arrow at the manticore. The projectile arched in an impossible ninety-degree angle and disappeared into the shadows. Tanin thought he heard a bleat from far off.

Kettlor stared at his new bow as if it had bitten him. "By the guidance of the Li—of Lagaw, what just happened?"

Salvo shook his head, eyes dark. "I told you, it can't miss whatever you program it to hit, which at the moment is procapras."

Orui hopped to the steps at the edge of the gazebo. "Hodan, move!" he yelled, waving his arm as if he could drag the boy out of the way by will alone.

Pebbles flew in the air as Hodan scurried so quickly, the manticore pounced on air. Its claws dug into the limestone as if it were mud.

Kettlor shouted at the prophet, "What's the symbol for *manticore*?"

Salvo shrugged. "I don't know. The things had been extinct for centuries before I was born. The mini-charging must have create them anew."

Tired of the bickering, Tanin stomped his foot on the wooden planks. He froze as the entire gazebo shook.

Rory pulled Orui back into the shadows as the manticore turned its focus to them. "Maybe we need more secure cover."

Crouching low to the ground, the manticore stalked toward the party.

Kettlor dropped his bow to the ground and took off his cloak. "Now would be a great time for a distraction, Hodan."

Pulling his dual swords from their magical scabbards, Rory paced down the steps on the opposite side from where the beast approached.

Tanin pushed Orui aside as the guardian tried to stop the prince from following. He wasn't going to miss out on this fight.

Holding his robe up like an ineffective shield, Kettlor yelled for Hodan again.

A trail of kicked-up sand the only evidence of his passing, Hodan slid much more gracefully beside the manticore. He kicked the beast in the side, his added momentum knocking it over.

Kettlor dove off the gazebo steps and wrapped his cloak around the flailing porcupine tail. He rolled to the side too slowly, and the beast's back claws sliced his thigh open.

Righting itself, the manticore focused on its downed attacker.

Tanin hefted his sword, judging its balance. "Let's test this thing out."

He flung the sword with a gentler twist than he would have a smaller dagger. The silver shone in the dappled light as the hilt changed the throwing arc more than he would have liked. Still, the blade hit the manticore's lower leg, embedding itself like an ax thrown at a tree.

The beast cried and limped back from Kettlor.

Rory bounced back and forth on his toes, ready for action. Tanin knew Rory was torn between protecting him and rushing the beast. Leaning heavily on his staff, Orui limped to Kettlor's side. Meerin moved with him, tearing off bits of her robe on the way.

Though Tanin only half believed the sword could return to him, he'd seen the other weapons work as promised. He had to try. Tanin whistled with his hand stretched out as if he were calling his dogs in from the hunt.

The gilded hilt vibrated against the manticore's leg, causing the beast to bite at it. Gripping the blade with its impossible mouth, the manticore ripped the sword from its flesh and spit it out. Blood gushed from the wound, but the injury did little to slow it down. It roared at Orui and Meerin as they approached Kettlor. The robe around its tail held as the beast attempted to use its venomous quills.

Tanin pushed Rory forward. "Go. I can take care of myself."

With a grim determination, Tanin snapped his fingers and whistled for his sword. The blade shook on the ground, then levitated and flew into his grip. Even covered in manticore blood, Tanin thought this weapon was the most beautiful thing he'd ever seen.

Before Rory could reach them, the manticore rushed Kettlor on the ground. Orui held firm as the beast jumped and jabbed his staff into its gut. The tawny fur shone blue as little streams of lightning danced along its surface. The smell of burnt hair mixed with the copper of spilled blood.

Though it was injured, the manticore's momentum still sent it tumbling toward Orui. Hodan barreled into the beast from the side, sending the huge lionlike animal sliding along the pebble-covered limestone. The blue glow disappeared, leaving dark scorch marks on its flesh.

As Hodan tried to stop, his feet slid through the blood that had pooled from the manticore's injury. He rammed right into the manticore, and the two tumbled toward the gazebo. The robe slipped from the manticore's tail in the chaos.

Tanin looked for an opening but couldn't throw his sword again without endangering Hodan. Rory rushed to the steps, and Tanin ran in from the other side. The manticore righted itself before Hodan could find his bearings.

With its terrifying rows of teeth bared, the manticore aimed its injured paw, claws extended, at Hodan, who lay on the ground holding his head. Rory yelled a battle cry and slashed a mighty arc with his right hand. The magical sword sliced through the manticore paw without resistance.

Blood shot out of the wound. The beast curled what was left of its limb against its chest and hopped back a few paces.

Tanin choked on his shout of triumph when the manticore's human face focused on Rory and its newly freed tail came up. Rory's balance was compromised by the clean cut, and he couldn't defend himself. Tanin had to help him.

Rory's left hand lifted over his head as his right continued in the same powerful stroke. The blade cut through one of the gazebo's pillars. The entire gazebo shuddered, and the roof sagged on that end. Salvo and Augusta rushed out of the collapsing protection and right into the threat of the manticore.

The beast swiveled on his hind legs and shot quills in their direction. Augusta shoved Salvo aside. The venomous darts cracked against the ground, except for one. Augusta yelped and dropped to the ground, her arm clutched against her chest.

With a roar that matched the intensity of the manticore, Tanin brandished his blade with both hands and cut off the porcupine tail in one swing. Dodging the falling appendage, he circled the beast to stand over Augusta.

Tanin didn't know how the beast could still move, but it lunged at him with incredible strength. Without enough room to throw his sword, Tanin stood his ground. The beast roared as Hodan once again bounded into it from the side. This time, he pushed the manticore toward the waiting Rory, who dodged the beast at the last minute and took off its head with a single stroke.

Dropping his sword, Tanin knelt beside Augusta. "Let me see your arm."

Tears poured down her face as Augusta showed him the wound. Tanin tore her sleeve to get a better look. The poisonous quill marred her perfect skin, but it wasn't embedded like Grayson's had been.

Augusta took a deep breath, and when she spoke, her voice was solid but weak. "We have to tie the arm off."

Meerin dropped a few pieces of robe on Augusta's lap. "Quickly."

Tanin stared at the folds of fabric. "It's only a flesh wound. She should be fine."

Augusta lifted his chin with her uninjured hand. "I can feel the venom burning. If we don't stop it from spreading, I won't be fine."

Her eyes pierced deeper than his attraction to her beauty. Tanin removed her hand from his chin, which immediately felt cold from her absence. The possible loss of this woman sent chills through his body. He pushed aside what was left of the fabric in her sleeve and tied a secure knot just below her shoulder. Augusta cringed but didn't protest.

Orui's limping gait stopped behind him. "I can't do anything about the poison."

Anger bubbled inside Tanin. What good was it to be king if he was so often powerless? He slammed his fist against the ground. Sharp pain cut through his knuckles, unexpected for contact with a flat surface. He yanked his hand back and saw he'd punched the crown, which sagged from his waist.

"The crown? It healed Salvo. Maybe it could . . ." Tanin tore the satchel in his haste. Ignoring the blood dripping from his hand, he held it out toward Augusta.

Salvo plucked the piece from his slippery grip. "No. It won't work. All of its energy was consumed bringing me back."

Meerin pointed to the black-opal staff. "What about your Lagaw-blessed staff?"

The prophet wiped the nonreactive blood from the Holy Gemstones on the crown. "If there was any magic left, do you not think I would have used it on the manticore?"

Orui put a hand on Tanin's shoulder. "We have to take the arm."

Tanin gasped, then immediately hated himself for the show of weakness. He stood, knocking Orui back.

Rory sheathed one sword in its special scabbard and pointed the other down at the ground, unthreatening but prepared.

Grabbing Hodan by the elbow, Orui pushed him toward the gazebo. "Help me make a fire. It needs to be blazing hot, and quickly."

Though a tear trailed down one cheek, Augusta's face hardened with determination. "It is the logical move."

Tanin had to pull away from her gaze. He felt weak in her presence. Light from the beginning flames lit up the crumpled body of Grayson. He couldn't bear the thought of Augusta's lithe form lying beside the lifeless tutor. He didn't want to lose anyone else.

He nodded at Rory.

# CHAPTER FORTY-TWO

Nᴏᴍʏʀᴀ ᴋɪᴄᴋᴇᴅ the base of the statue. "Either this entire mechanism is new and Maitliin didn't know anything about it, or . . ."

Talia rubbed her forehead. "He left it out so you'd have to consult him again."

The priestess leaned against the base of the bronze statue and crossed her arms. Talia's shoulders slumped as exhaustion overtook every other emotion.

She had expected to find the Machine in the middle of the city. Not a huge statue depicting all the sentient species. The craftsmanship was stunning. A large globe, representing the world, had pieces missing, and the different peoples worked together to put the last bits into place, making the planet whole again. It was a beautiful sentiment, and Talia could appreciate its message. It was exactly what she had been trying to accomplish. But right now, she needed to get to the Machine to make sure it was in working order. Her timeline had gone from lots of room to move around to everything should be done already.

Pointing to an inscription under the supposed mechanism for

opening the chamber below, Gregor motioned Dew over. "What does this say?"

Nomyra jumped from her defeated position to see for herself. "What did I miss?"

The cultural guardian squinted in the dim light. "I believe it says, 'The Machine will obey the Bright Ones, together or not at all. Prove your worth, and all will be restored.' Why does everything have to be so cryptic?"

Shaking her head, Nomyra corrected Dew. "It says Bright One."

Dew sighed. "No, it doesn't. It's plural. Think about the 'together' line. It wouldn't make any sense if it was a single person doing it together."

The last words Billivin said before Talia freed herself from the crown came back. "It is plural. That's what everyone since Giddeona in the Astropriest Tower has been trying to tell me. This is not a do-it-on-your-own kind of quest. It never has been." She gestured to the whole party, including the dwarves. "We're a team. Are you with us?"

Aleck grabbed Traneck's spear and stuck it in the center of the party, both dwarves still holding it. "To Team Bright Ones."

The weight of the title on Talia's shoulders that she had felt since the astropriests first dumped it there lightened, as her friends helped her lift it. She grabbed the spear just above Aleck's hand. This quest wasn't her last. She didn't have to sacrifice her life to save the magicals.

Gregor smiled and piled in next to her, quickly followed by the guardians. All eyes turned to Nomyra.

The priestess kneaded her hands, her face etched with indecision. "I've always been on my own."

Talia shrugged. "You still can be. Or you can join a group."

Two steps forward and a squeeze in between Gregor and Nyna put Nomyra within arm's reach of the spear. The entire party held its breath. Even Nomyra seemed to stop breathing as her hand twitched. She stared at Talia, who gave her a gentle nod.

Nomyra gripped the spear and whispered, "To Team Bright Ones."

The group shouted at once, "To Team Bright Ones!"

Before releasing the spear, Talia spoke the words to the group's frequent prayer. Her companions joined in by the third word. "For the Light despite the Dark, we will shine in knowledge to fight the shadow of doubt."

Stepping back from the spear, Talia held Gregor's gaze a moment longer than she intended. He really did have the most beautiful eyes. "So do you think you and Naul could give the mechanism a look? I know there wasn't a ton of such things at the dwarven school, but I do remember there being an advanced class I wasn't qualified to take."

Naul rubbed his head. "If the priestess can't figure it out . . ."

With a supportive squeeze of his elbow, Talia encouraged Naul forward. "She's an expert at interpreting the *Stars'* movements, not *making* objects move."

Nomyra tilted her head in acquiescence.

*That's a change,* Talia thought. *Usually the priestess would do whatever she could to hide a gap in her knowledge.*

Dew plopped down and flipped open the book with the impossible title she'd received from Giddeona. "I'll see if I can find anything in here. I was so busy studying the Machine, I didn't see much in the way of other mechanisms."

Aleck jogged after Naul and Gregor. "I might be able to help. Maybe it's similar to the mechanism we use to open and close our main gates."

Talia remembered the odd apparatus that used rock counterweights to open an underground chamber. After spending a couple of days in front of what had turned out to be a false door, Talia understood the ingenuity of the Krimmel Dwarves. Hopefully, that knowledge would come in handy. She still didn't know what condition the Machine would be in when they finally uncovered it.

Turning to Nomyra, she asked, "How do we make the Machine work without the Key?"

The priestess shook her head. "We don't."

Nyna mirrored Talia's crossed-arm stance. "Prince Tanin is unlikely to give it up without a fight."

Talia rubbed her eyes. "There has to be a way."

The ground grumbled and shifted under Talia's feet. "Not again." She braced herself to run before she could fall. That was not an experience she wished to repeat.

Before she could tell which way was safer, the ground fell silent. A cheer from the statue drew her attention.

Gregor's wavy head bounced up and down as he waved Talia over. She rushed to his side.

He bowed and indicated an opening in the stone. A stairwell twisted below the statue and into darkness. "After you, Bright One."

With a huge smile, Talia pecked him on the lips. "You did it."

Aleck patted the big man. "Actually, Naul figured it out."

Gregor blushed. "We mostly asked dumb questions until he realized which parts were supposed to be pulled and which pushed."

Naul rubbed his head as his cheeks flushed pink. "I just played with a few things until it made sense."

With a flourished bow, Talia stepped to the side of the entry. "Then, Guardian Naul, I believe you've earned the right to go first."

He smiled. "I would be honored."

Dew whispered a bit too loudly to Talia, "This way, if he trips, he won't take us all down with him."

Waving off Dew's warning, Naul stood tall and marched down the first step. "I am as graceful as a—" He slipped on the third step and caught himself on the edge before he could fall any farther. He coughed to clear his throat. "Umm . . . be careful. It's slippery with all the sand."

They laughed as they filed in behind the weapons guardian.

Talia moved carefully behind Nyna as the dim blue light changed to complete blackness under the surface. "We don't happen to have any torches with us, do we?"

The sound of cloth rubbing stone came from directly behind

Talia. Nomyra said, "There should be light around the ceiling, like in Memorial Park. You can light it with the magic from Windall."

Talia twirled the emerald on her finger. "How?"

The priestess took Talia's hand and placed it on a smooth surface bordered by rough-hewn stone. Windall flashed as the silver made contact.

Her voice pitched lower, Nomyra chanted. "I beg of you, Light, show me the way."

Talia added her voice to Nomyra's. Her hand tingled, and the green gem brightened. She continued to chant as a pulse vibrated through the smooth surface. Her hand warmed as though she gripped a mug of tea. Before the burn could grow unbearable, the strip flashed a soft blue. It flowed like water down the incline and around a corner. Based on the glow, the room at the end of the stairs had to be quite large.

No more than a couple of inches from Talia's face, Nomyra offered Talia an awkward smile. Even though the priestess was technically her great aunt, her constant betrayal had made it impossible for Talia to feel any familial affection for the woman. She pulled her hand from Nomyra's grip as the priestess dropped her gaze to the stairs at her feet.

Noticing the rest of the party staring at her, Talia felt trapped on the narrow stairwell. She pushed past Nyna to get down the steps quicker. In her rush, she slammed into Gregor, just off the bottom stoop. His warm arms wrapped around her shaking body before she could trip over her own feet. Her anger immediately calmed at his touch. She could get used to this.

Naul's voice broke the spell. "I didn't open the door on my own. Maybe it's meant for you."

Aleck's laugh drew Talia to move around the rest of the line to see what they were talking about.

"No, you figured it out." The dwarf pointed at a large hammer suspended in some sort of energy field in the opening between the bottom landing and the large room on the other side.

A vine-like rope lashed a dark-stained wooden staff as thick as Talia's arm to the V-shaped center of the shining metal head. Runes carved into the metal flashed in a rhythm very much like a heartbeat. Words floated in the miasma that held the hammer in place.

Gregor leaned close to the hammer.

Talia pushed him back a step. "Be careful." She wanted to know what the words said before she let anyone touch it. "Dew? Can you come down here?"

Nyna stepped up a stair to allow Dew room to reach the landing.

The cultural guardian squinted at the oddly floating words. "For the Guardian of Sword and Stone, you have breached the opening and won passage to the next test." As Dew read, the words scrolled as if they could hear her voice. "Eckick, hewn by Thoretick himself, is for you to wield to aid your journey as you serve as Bright One alongside the True Heir."

Traneck gasped. "It cannot be. Eckick is a legend of an age past. Could it possibly have been in Raqmu all this time?"

Aleck jumped up and down. "I can't see the runes. You'll have to grab it for me, Naul. The runes will verify its identity."

With a crack of his knuckles, Naul reached forward. He sprang his hand back before it could breach the barrier. "What if Gregor is the guardian of sword and stone the weird ghost words are referring to?"

Gregor waved away the suggestion. "You're the True Heir's guardian. I'm more of a . . ." His gaze bored into Talia's soul. "Fan."

Talia grew uncomfortable under Gregor's scrutiny. She pushed Naul forward. "It's for you. I know it is."

The weapons guardian cracked his knuckles and his neck. He reached into the glowing field. "It tingles." As soon as his hand closed over the polished wood handle, the field flashed dark. His hand fell a few inches as he adjusted to the full weight of the magical weapon.

Aleck grabbed Naul's elbow, pulling the hammer down to where he could see the illuminated runes. "I can't read it, but it's definitely the same style as the runes on the cover of the King's

Tomb, which are also said to be carved by the mighty Thoretick himself."

Traneck wiped a tear from his eye. "Legend says the Hammer of Thoretick always hits its target with exactly the desired amount of force. Whether you are nailing a roof shingle or crushing an enemy's skull, this is the only tool you'll need."

Naul shifted the weapon from one hand to the other. "Let's hope I get to test it on a nail before a person."

With the hammer out of the way, a warm breeze blew from the larger cavern. The rest of the party made it down the stairs. Everyone stood at the edge of the opening.

The tension of the group beat behind Talia's temples. She looked to Nomyra. "Do we know what's next?"

The priestess rubbed her hands on her robes. "I know how to work the Machine, with the Key, of course. I didn't know about the mechanism above, so I don't know what other surprises lay below. According to the plans Maitliin chose to share with me, there was nothing under here but the Machine itself."

Dew rubbed her hands together. "So either he didn't know or he held back on purpose."

With a glance into the room beyond, Gregor commented, "It seems that precautions were placed after that greedy wizard over-played his hand."

Wiping a hand across her sweating forehead, Talia walked under the arched entryway. "I guess we'll have to trust ourselves to figure it out."

The blue light bordered the top of the large cavern, a smooth element in a rough-hewn environment. Cones of crystalized stone hung from the ceiling and dripped onto the sand below.

Turning in circles as he stared up, Aleck pulled at his beard. "I don't think I've ever seen a cave with stalactites and no stalagmites."

Traneck kicked at the sand underfoot. "Or so much loose sand. Usually, there's enough flooding to wash the small bits away."

The dwarf prince nodded in agreement.

A large shadowed apparatus sat near the center, but a barrier of layered concentric circles surrounded it. Something was odd about the stacked circles.

Talia walked forward to get a better look. "Maybe it has something to do with the Machine. Who knows what residual magic was left behind?" Her heart skipped a beat as a click, like the snapping of a stick, sounded under her boot.

Ial grabbed her and pulled her back as a line opened in the sand, spanning the entire width of the room. Leaves as long as Talia was tall, with finger-like variegations, sprung up from the widening gap.

Nyna took Talia's hand as the plants swayed in the still air. "I suppose I shouldn't be surprised by moving plants after all we've seen, but . . ."

Talia squeezed her companion's hand. "Me too."

Ial said, "This must be your trial, Nyna, medicinal guardian, keeper of the plants. What do we do?"

Naul leaned on the handle of his new hammer. "Maybe that's why I was given this beauty?"

Nyna crossed in front of Naul before he could move forward and whack the obstruction. "Don't get too close. If this is what I think it is . . ." She kicked off her shoe and tossed it into the middle of the plants.

A large bulb burst through the crack in the ground. Its jaw opened wide, exposing jagged, grasping teeth and a smooth fleshy inside. It snapped the shoe from the tallest leaf, tearing a bit of the greenery. With a loud gulp, the plant swallowed the leather. The outline of the crushed leather stretched the thin stem without much effort. Two more heads popped up on either side of the swallowing one. They bumped into each other, unseeing, then slipped back under the ground.

Talia couldn't believe what she had seen. "Why would a people who want me to Recharge the planet make it impossible to do so?" She fought the urge to throw her shoe at the blasted thing.

Yanking her bag off her shoulder, Nyna squatted and flipped the flap open. She pulled out the fire starter and handed it to Naul. "Will you please grab one of those torches by the statue and bring it down?"

He nodded. "I'll be right back. Don't have any fun without me."

Talia gestured to Dew.

The cultural guardian shouted at the jogging Naul. "I'm coming with you."

Nyna took off her other shoe and dug her toes into the sand. "It's called a biting weed." She picked up small stones. "We need stones about this size."

Talia searched for ones bigger than her fist. She didn't know what they were for, but doing something felt better than just standing there fuming. "Such an innocuous name for such a huge beast of a plant."

The medicinal guardian removed her outer robe and tore it into strips. She pulled a jar from her bag. "Well, the ones I'm used to are no bigger than a dandelion. They eat insects and sometimes small frogs if they get too close. You just have to watch out for them when you're hiking because they hide their biting bits below the leaves in a pocket and only come out when the hairs on the leaves are agitated."

Tossing the rocks in the air and catching them, Talia judged their weight, guessing how far she could throw them. "I'm guessing we can't just walk through, then."

After rubbing the paste from the jar on the cloth, she tied it around the end of her staff. "Not when they're this closely packed together. Their teeth suck for chewing, but they'll slice right through the skin of your calf if you're unlucky enough to get too close. At this size, they could probably—"

Gregor whistled. "Bite us in half."

With a roll of her shoulders, Talia prepared for whatever was next. She had faith in Nyna. "Tell me what to do."

"Right." Nyna held her staff by the end, with the clothed end angled forward. "When Naul has the torch, you're going to toss a rock at the center of a group."

"Got it." Talia piled the few she had gathered by her feet.

Aleck judged the small pile. "Traneck and I will find more."

Naul and Dew jogged back with the flaming torch.

Talia aimed at what she hoped was a grouping. It was hard to tell with the plants in a long line and their leaves all tangled together. "Get ready, Naul."

Before he could ask any questions, she threw her first stone. It slid right along a leaf, agitating every hair on the way down.

Ial clapped. "Great shot."

Nyna shook her head. "Wait. Not yet."

A head shot up like before and snapped at the air. Naul rushed forward with the lit torch.

Nyna yelled. "Don't get close yet. The fire will only—"

With a huge reach, Naul touched the head searching for its meal. The bulb squirmed backward as the flames lit its petals and emitted a piercing screech. Talia dropped the rock she had prepared to throw next and covered her ears against the painful pitch. Every head from each individual weed flew up simultaneously. They pointed their sightless faces toward the screaming bulb. Before Naul had a chance to move, they opened their mouths and spit out a sticky viscous fluid. The outpour doused the flame and soaked the weapons guardian. He fell backward like timber. Gregor rushed forward and caught him by the shoulders. Dew grabbed the torch in a roll to avoid the snap of an angry head.

The relief brought on by the silencing of the initial screech faded as Talia watched the bulbs snap viciously. Their necks stretched and their reach increased. Talia ran to Gregor and helped him drag Naul farther away.

At a safe distance, Talia dropped Naul with a groan. Her hands were covered in the sticky goop. "What is this?"

Nyna pushed her out of the way. "He can't breathe."

Talia kicked herself for not noticing that Naul was turning blue. Nyna grabbed a clean cloth and wiped the sticky resin from his mouth and nose. She smacked his face with more anger than Talia had ever seen from the medicinal guardian.

Her voice reflected her fury. "Wake up, Naul. Come on. You can't give up before you've used that fancy new hammer."

With a great inhale, Naul sat straight up. "What in the cursed Dark was that?"

Nyna dug through her bag with quick desperate strokes. "You were supposed to wait until I had drugged the head with the cream. It would have gone into a coma-like state, and *then* we could burn it." She yanked a single vial out of her pack. "Now if only I had a few gallons of this. I didn't travel prepared to take down a forest of flesh-eating plants."

Nomyra took the small container from Nyna. "I could replicate them with a touch of help."

Talia knew she wanted to borrow Windall. She held her hand out. "I'll try." She didn't want to give up her ring. She'd already handed the Key to a power-hungry relative. Fighting to get back something else that was inherently hers sounded like a nightmare.

With a shrug, Nomyra put it delicately in her palm. "May the Light guide the magic. Multiplying an object is a very different skill from lighting a room or healing a body."

The last thing Talia wanted was for the woman to touch her again, but what choice did she have. "Fine. Show me."

The twinkle in Nomyra's eyes reminded Talia of an addict. Not as desperate as Thilphiliari had appeared, but definitely longing for the feel of magic in her veins.

Nomyra pulled Talia's unadorned hand flat and gestured to Nyna. "Every time a vial appears, grab it so the next one has some-where to go."

The medicinal guardian studied the aggressive bulbs. "I'll need about a dozen."

Nomyra nodded as she moved behind Talia and pressed her body and hands against her niece.

Talia cringed, feeling like she was no more than an instrument for Nomyra's magic, a human-sized Krag ring. But anything was better than giving this woman her only touch of magic.

Nomyra's voice intimately whispered against her ear. "Think of the object you're holding. Feel its weight and its slightly chill temperature and the way the liquid inside vibrates with the beating of your heart. Extend your consciousness around its elemental makeup and pull from Windall."

The sensation of floating enveloped Talia as she wrapped herself around the vial, though her hand remained splayed. The emerald shone with a fierce light. The power flowed through her, not Nomyra. She had to remember that the next time she felt insecure. She had the power. Nomyra couldn't take that strength from her if Talia didn't offer it.

"Take all that energy and focus it at your empty hand. Everything you felt, from the smoothness of the glass to the viscosity of the liquid, replicate it with the magic."

Talia's core vibrated with the energy. She thought about the curve of the vial's neck and the brittle cork holding the liquid inside. "Now another," she whispered to herself.

A weight fell into her second hand. Though she knew that was the goal, she still dropped the vial in surprise. Luckily, Nyna was paying attention and caught it.

With a sniff, Nyna's eyes widened. "That's it. It's the oil I need." She pointed to Gregor. "Go light a few more torches if you can find them. With the biting weed on high alert, I'm not sure how long the chemical will keep them calm."

Talia picked up Gregor and Aleck with her peripheral vision jogging toward the entrance, but she quickly lost interest as power from the ring built up again and she replicated another one. She could get used to this. No one would ever have to go hungry again.

Time had no meaning as Talia replicated one vial after another. Flashes of Nyna handing out vials and spreading out torches danced through her field of visual, but none of it sunk in. Nothing registered beyond the tingling of her body and the repeated weight of a new vial in her hand.

A violent shake of her shoulders brought her out of her trancelike state. The magic faded from her body and drained into the ring. It felt lighter as the vibrations ceased.

"Now!" a voice shouted. It sounded like Nyna, except much more forceful than Talia had ever heard her before.

Soft yet strong arms lifted her from the ground and guided her farther back from the line of snapping heads. Glancing over her shoulder at Nomyra's hand, Talia shook the priestess off. She didn't need her assistance.

Her legs buckled without the extra support. Apparently, she did need some help. Copying small vials took more energy than she would have imagined.

As her hand groped for support to avoid falling face-first into the sand, she felt something sticky. She yanked her hand away.

Naul grabbed her hands as she tumbled sideways. "It's just me. I haven't had time to wash the plant goo off."

Talia relaxed against the weapons guardian, goo and all. "I should help."

Chuckling at her, Naul put a sticky arm around her shoulder. "You helped plenty. Watch."

Talia found it difficult to focus on the line of greenery, as if she'd been up for hours drinking. The tinkling of shattered glass sang across the chamber, then everything grew quiet. Until the bulbs stopped moving, Talia hadn't realized how much noise they'd been making. Now each mouth hung from its stalk, jaw opened loosely.

Nyna's thin figure held a torch high as she approached one. She set the toothy beast aflame. None of the other prone heads moved. "Good. They're out. Light them quickly. I'm not sure how long that small amount will work."

The rest of the torch-armed companions ran along the line. Each head burst into flame as if a formal candle-lighting ceremony had commenced.

Talia leaned against Naul to stand. "Nyna, you've done it. That's amazing."

Gregor helped Naul to his feet. "We've got to find you a bath, my friend."

After accepting Eckick from Aleck, Naul leaned on its long handle. "I could do with a nap as well."

Talia agreed. "I'm feeling pretty worn out myself."

The medicinal guardian took Talia's chin in her hand and stared into her eyes. Talia tried to push her off but couldn't find enough strength to make it stick.

With a jab of her chin toward Nomyra, Nyna asked, "What did you do to her?"

The priestess tucked her arms in her robes. "I showed her how to use her magic. Replication takes a good deal of energy. She'll be fine after a short rest."

The warmth from the line of fire calmed to a comfortable level as the leaves crumbled to ash. A blue dome, much like the one that had encased Naul's hammer, shimmered to life in the center of the dead plants.

Talia turned Nyna around and pointed. "Looks like you did it."

She shook her head. "We did it."

Leaning on her heavily, Talia forced Nyna to approach the levitating corked bottle. "We might have all helped, but you showed us how. If that hammer was meant for Naul, then whatever this is was meant for you."

Dew read the words that floated in the ether. "For the Guardian of Medicine and Justice, you have defeated the dionea and won passage to the next test. This syrup will counteract any venom, poison, or illness, but only once per person. Use this never-emptying source to aid your journey as you serve as Bright One alongside the True Heir."

Nyna's hand shook as she reached through the mist and grasped the bottle. She held it against her chest. The blue field faded, darkening the area.

Aleck stepped across the still-smoking plants to the other side. "I can't wait to tell my people of this journey."

After Dew and Nyna helped her cross the line, Talia pushed them away. "I really need a moment before we go on." Talia tilted her head as a thick layer of smoke moved along the ground. For a moment, she thought the coils had eyes. "I definitely need a rest. That smoke just blinked at me."

Sand kicked up at Talia's feet as Ial slid to a stop beside her. "Talia, that's not smoke."

The top layer of the circular barrier around the center of the room rose up on a long neck. A forked tongue flickered from a wide mouth as two yellow eyes stared down at the intruders.

Talia's head felt light as all her blood drained to her feet. "Is that a snake?"

Ial shook his head. "Worse. It's a naga."

The room grew black as Talia lost her fight to stay conscious.

# CHAPTER FORTY-THREE

T<small>ALIA</small>."

She brushed off the shaking hands. "A little bit longer."

"Bless the Light, she's talking."

With a sigh of resignation, Talia sat up. She grabbed her head as it threatened to tumble off her shoulders. "What happened?"

Nyna pried her eyes open. "Producing the potions drained you."

Talia raised her hands. Her right was adorned with Windall, though she felt little from its presence.

When Nyna got up, a huge shadow of coils hissed along the far wall. Talia's heart jumped as she pushed herself to her feet, grabbing for her sword. "The snake? Where is it?"

Gregor held her elbow as Talia's quick movements threw off her balance. "Ial wants to know if he can keep it."

Talia's mouth fell open. None of this made any sense. "How hard did I hit my head?"

Naul motioned to the center of the room. "Not as hard as Ial, apparently."

Tired of the innuendo, Talia pushed Gregor away and marched toward her husbandry guardian.

Ial was talking to the layers of coils in front of him. "It's okay, little beastie. She looks mean, but she won't bite."

Talia folded her arms, trying to look angry when all she really felt was embarrassment for missing the slaying of the snake. "I might bite if there were anything left to fight."

At the sound of her voice, a pointed head the size of a boat rose up from the center of the coils. It arched its neck and stuck out its tongue.

Talia didn't hesitate this time and whipped out her sword. "I was kidding. Feel free to kill monsters with or without me."

Ial held up his hands, one of which was covered in what looked like a falconry glove. "Shhh . . . I know she sounds mean, but you look scary. Give her a minute." He backed up toward the beast, keeping his body in between it and Talia.

"What are you doing? That thing could swallow you." Talia lifted her sword.

The snake head slid behind Ial. Talia twisted her wrist, flipping her sword in a circle.

Dew grabbed her sword arm. "Hold up, Talia. The naga is nothing more than a big puppy. Ial's got it under control."

Talia stared at Dew, then Ial. "Have you gone mad? Or am I still dreaming?"

The snake peeked out from behind the perceived safety of the husbandry guardian's body. It nuzzled Ial's hand, and he scratched under its chin like he would a cat.

Ial reached his hand out for Talia as Dew guided her forward. She looked across the chamber at Gregor. He shook his head and held up a hand. Apparently, he wasn't into the whole the-giant-snake-is-friendly bit, either. But Ial seemed so confident. Did she trust her companions or not?

Before she could change her mind, she sheathed her sword and walked through the sand to Ial. He took her hand and placed it gently on the snake's nose. Her entire body shook as warm air blew across her arm from the nasal slits.

Talia rubbed across the scales in a circular pattern, encouraged by Ial. She could discern each scale edge, but the connection was much smoother than she would have imagined. "Incredible."

Aleck joined her as she backed up a few paces. "This big guy slithering around down here explains the lack of stalagmites sticking up from the ground. His girth alone would crumble any kind of formation before it had a chance to fully solidify."

With a flip of his wrist, Ial motioned for the snake to move aside. "I'm much more worried about what he was eating down here. It must be massive to keep him alive."

Gregor jumped out of the way as the snake uncoiled and moved toward the wall he stood against. Its triangle-shaped head disappeared inside a tunnel Talia hadn't noticed.

As the rest of the body followed, Gregor walked over to Aleck and Talia and shook out his limbs. "No snakes. I'm pretty sure I wrote that into my contract."

*He's afraid of snakes. Interesting.* Talia would have to remember that if she ever needed to get back at him for something.

Ial held up the falconer's glove. "This should come in handy. It would have been perfect with the griffon."

The leather looked properly worn but not as old as it must have been after being stored in this deserted city for centuries.

"What does it do?" Talia asked.

Ial's face lit up as he turned his gloved hand from side to side in front of his face. "I can talk to animals."

Dew closed her eyes as if reading something in her head. "For the Guardian of Husbandry and Hunting, you have won over the naga and earned your spot. This falconry glove will allow you a means of communication with all nonsentient animals. Use this tool to aid your journey as you serve as Bright One alongside the True Heir."

Naul squeezed Dew's head with his huge palm. "Your brain is something to behold."

She knocked him off with a twist, but her smile spoke of how proud she was of her memory.

Nomyra sat cross-legged on the sand. "Your brain shall be truly tested, Cultural Guardian. I've never seen this writing before. And the Machine lies beneath."

Concern marred Dew's face. "It *is* my turn."

The companions followed her to a circular metal plate that remained remarkably clean despite sitting lower than the surrounding sand. Its entire surface shone in the unnatural blue light. Colorful depictions of humans and animals drawn in unique poses spiraled from the inside to the outside, or from the outside to the inside; Talia couldn't tell which. Not a speck of dirt, dust, snake scales, or animal droppings of any kind marred the pristine figures.

Gregor whistled. The single sound encompassed Talia's awe and frustration.

Dew plopped down next to Nomyra. "I've never seen anything like this."

With raised eyebrows, Nomyra simply rocked her head up and down repeatedly.

Placing a hand on Dew's shoulder, Talia asked. "How can we help?"

The cultural guardian sighed. "I'm not sure you can."

A loud gurgling drew everyone's attention. Naul sheepishly put a hand over his stomach.

Traneck stomped his spear against the ground with a muffled thump due to the cushioning sand. "We have been at this for hours and missed the midday meal. We should prepare food while our companion deciphers the final clue."

Dew jumped to her feet and hugged the dwarf guard. "Yes, yes, please. I need the peace and quiet to think, and some food will help my legendary brain work better."

Backing up, a bit off-balance, Traneck bumped into Aleck, who caught him before he could hit the ground. "Exactly," he mumbled before fleeing toward the stairs.

Aleck laughed. "He's not accustomed to attention from a pretty girl. I should probably go help."

Naul, Nyna, and Ial saluted Dew on their way out. Gregor stayed behind beside Talia.

"Are you sure you don't want help?" Talia asked.

Dew squeezed Talia's upper arm. "You were pretty good with the hand-to-hand combat in school, but the languages never seemed to grasp your interest."

With a blush, Talia had to agree. She had always preferred the more active lessons. Lowering her voice, she motioned to Nomyra's back. "Are you okay being alone with . . ."

Glancing over her shoulder, Dew considered her options. "She wants to get to the Machine as much as we do. I can't imagine she would harm the effort in any way."

"We'll be right upstairs if you need us."

Gregor offered. "I'll bring you both food once it's sorted out."

Dew had already stopped listening as her focus returned to the mysterious message.

Fatigue cascaded over Talia. Gregor seemed to sense her change in energy and put his arm around her waist. Talia allowed him to help her toward the stairs. She leaned her head on his shoulder, enjoying the natural musk of his body. She had never understood why so many noblemen insisted on dunking their clothes in strong perfumes.

"Talia." Nyna's voice echoed down the stairwell.

She pushed Gregor away before anyone else could see them so intimately entangled. He hid the hurt in his eyes, but Talia caught it. Curse the Dark for making this so difficult. People fall in love all the time, and it's never so complicated. Why did everything in Talia's life have to come with a prophecy and a set of rules?

Nyna's footsteps beat on the stone steps. She grabbed the wall to avoid from running into them. "Talia, hurry. Your brother is here."

Adrenaline reinvigorated Talia's worn-out body. She reached for her sword and pushed past Nyna.

When she reached the surface, her hand gripped the hilt so tightly it throbbed. Her fear wouldn't let her loosen up. Contemplating Tanin's motivations for approaching her at this moment had her in an almost panic. She had to confront him eventually. It might as well happen now before they got the Machine up and running.

Her fingers loosened their grip as she took in Tanin's ragged group. "What happened?"

Covered in sweat, her brother set Augusta down at the base of the statue. At least, Talia thought it was Augusta. Her normally shiny skin had faded to a splotchy green tint. She didn't move, and Talia wondered if she was still alive.

Nyna examined the unconscious disciple. "Her breathing is dangerously shallow, and her limbs have gone cold. Where is Orui?" Peeking under the robe for an injury, she exposed the armless shoulder. She covered her face with a gasp.

Talia's hands drooped to her sides. "What happened, Tanin?"

Her brother pleaded in a tone foreign to Talia. "You have to heal her. Please."

She had to question whether this was her brother at all. She remembered how callously he'd described Tyler's death. Tanin had only known Augusta a few months, while Tyler had grown up with him.

She reached into Windall with her mind. It didn't respond. "I don't think I can regrow her arm." The words sounded so wrong, Talia fought the urge to rinse them down with a swig from Naul's hidden flask.

A deep sigh from behind her caused Talia to step to the side. Orui leaned heavily on Hodan. He didn't look much better than Augusta did, color-wise. He limped, but he seemed to have all his limbs in place.

The medicinal guardian pushed against Hodan's shoulder to stand up straight. "We thought we could stop the venom by removing the arm, but it flowed too quickly. I can't help her."

Hodan's sweet boyish face was marred with deep lines and dark bruises. His bloodshot eyes attested to much crying.

Resisting the urge to give the boy a hug, Talia wondered why his tutor wasn't by his side. "Where's Grayson?"

A dam broke in Hodan, and tears streamed down his face. "He's . . . the manticore . . . it was so fast."

Talia could barely understand him through his sobs. "A manticore?"

From the ground, Tanin shouted, "Yes, a manticore! Another magical beast that you so desperately want to save. It killed Tutor Grayson. And Augusta is next if you don't help her."

The grief in her brother's tone moved Talia. "Nyna, do you think that new vial will cure the venom?"

The medicinal guardian dug in her bag and pulled out the small glass container. "The floating words said it would cure anything. It could all be a bunch of horse manure, or it could work."

Talia startled as Prophet Salvo leaned over Tanin, the crown blatantly clutched in his fingers. She knew what she had to do, even though it filled her with self-loathing.

Reaching over to Nyna, she plucked the magic elixir from her hands. "We'll heal her, but only if you hand over the crown."

Salvo clutched the crown closer to his chest and took a step back.

Tanin jumped to his feet, his fists clenched at his side and his face throbbing the deepest red. "Are you joking? You would let an innocent woman die because of your own pride? I thought I was the callous twin." His right hand clutched his hilt. "We share the same parents. Apparently, we have more in common than I suspected."

Her hands shook as she almost gave the bottle back to Nyna. It was time to tell him. "Just give me the crown for the Recharging. I promise I'll return it afterward. It's not mine to keep, anyway. I'm not the True Heir to Tarbin."

She swallowed so hard, she thought it echoed in the complete silence of the staring crowd. She felt herself accepting, for the first time, her destiny. "We shared a womb with our mother, but we don't share a father. You are the only legitimate heir to Tarbin." She lifted her hands to the ruins of a once-grand city. "I am True Heir to what's left of Raqmu. I only need the Tarbin crown to complete the Recharging, then you can return home, triumphant and unchallenged. The crown *is* yours."

Tanin's breathing slowed as the information sank in. Talia knew the range of emotions he struggled with as he tried to reach a decision. She'd been juggling the same ones for months.

Nyna tugged on Talia's tunic. Her eyes pleaded with Talia to just give her the vial. On the ground at their feet, Augusta's body convulsed. Talia begged the Light to give her a few more minutes. To not let one more death be on her conscience. She was trying to save an entire world. Yet if Augusta died, Talia would never forgive herself.

As she was about to hand the vial to Nyna, Tanin turned to Salvo with his hand out. The prophet hesitated. Rory bumped into his back, his hands on his sword hilts. Salvo tensed, but then he plastered a weak smile on his face and handed it over. Without looking at her, Tanin tossed the crown to Talia, then dropped to Augusta's side.

Talia caught it with one hand and dropped the antivenin into Nyna's with the other. The gold felt cold and lifeless. She shivered as she tucked it into the bag on her hip.

Murmuring "Manticore" repeatedly, Nyna lifted a dropper full of luminescent fluid. It shifted colors a few times before settling on a reddish brown. Tanin pried open Augusta's lips, and Nyna squeezed the elixir into her mouth. The convulsions stopped abruptly.

Everyone in the plaza crowded closer. Talia prayed to the Light that the sudden stillness was a sign of healing, not death.

Nyna sealed the vial and tucked it back in her bag. She pried back Augusta's eyelids and flattened her ear against Augusta's chest.

Sitting back on her heels, Nyna squeezed Tanin's hand. "Her breathing is steady, and her heartbeat is strong. I think it worked."

Tanin stared at Nyna's hand for a blink, then tore his away. "Orui."

"It worked," Talia said as she helped Nyna moved out of Orui's way. "As handy as that vial is, I hope we don't have need of it often."

Nyna wrapped an arm around Talia's waist. "It won't work on Augusta again, either way."

After a quick examination, Orui reported to Tanin. "She seems to be asleep now. Her heartbeat and breathing are steady. She doesn't have a fever, and her skin is the proper color." He looked up at Nyna. "Whatever was in that vial worked."

Tanin wiped his face before jumping to his feet. If Talia didn't know better, she'd have thought he had actually shed a tear of relief.

With a great sniff, Talia's brother faced her. "Are you truly giving up all rights to the Tarbin crown?"

She threw her hands out. "I have no rights. I don't have Tarbin royal blood. My father is in the line of the Machine guardians, the True Heir's line. You have Father's—" She coughed to clear a sudden blockage. "King Roland's. You have King Roland's blood, making you the uncontested heir to the Tarbin crown."

Tanin rubbed his forehead. "Assuming all this is true, where does that leave us and this quest?"

Talia gestured to the ruins surrounding them. "I have to do is best for Raqmu and its ancient residents, *all* sentient beings, magical and mundane. I have to make sure the Recharging happens."

Her brother straightened his back and met her focus. "And I have to do what is best for Tarbin. Amplified wild magic awakening who knows what—such as the sea beast that attacked Tarbinulus Harbor—is just too dangerous. Magic will get a boost. It's all part of Lagaw's design. Prophet Salvo has taught me much about how the Gods work and what They desire from us. Maybe if you listened to what he had to say instead of brushing it off immediately . . ." He ran a hand down his face. "You're a citizen of Tarbin. How can you disregard the safety and security of its people?"

Talia shook her head. "What about the entire civilization of elves, locked in tree tombs to survive the magic famine? They deserve to live just as much as we do. The merpeople, hidden under the seafloor, need the Machine to amplify enough energy to power their existence. Maybe, if none of these people suffered, I might agree with you. But they're already there and they've already waited a thousand years. It's time to put right what once went wrong."

Stomping his foot on the ground as he routinely had as a child, Tanin took a step toward Talia. "And what of our people? What of humans? What will the magicals do when they once again subjugate our race?" He turned to Aleck. "And what of your people? You will be just as much a victim of the marauding magicals as we humans. How can you support her in this madness?"

Prince Aleck tilted his head, considering Tanin's warning. "Dwarves, humans, nadph, merpeople, and elves all lived in harmony for millennia. Working together, we built this grand city and discovered so much about how the world works and how to help each other grow and progress. My people, the Krimmel Dwarves, look forward to reuniting with the great sentients. We've all been asleep, not just the magicals."

Tanin clenched his fists, about to dive into another argument, when Dew popped up from the underground trials.

"I did it. I figured it out. It wasn't a language at all. It was the steps of a carefully choreographed dance." She held up a circlet of shining silver. "The floating words gave me this and told me it would translate any spoken word as long as I'm wearing it."

Dew pushed it down on her curls and smiled at Talia. Her face fell as she noticed the dour expressions on everyone else's.

Talia stared at her brother. "So what will it be?"

# CHAPTER FORTY-FOUR

NOMYRA PAUSED in front of the door to the Library. The priestess had studied the map of Raqmu since before she could read. She knew every building, every alleyway, and every secret.

But she no longer knew where she belonged or why she was here. With the Stars hidden by the city dome, Nomyra had only one option: her sister.

She shuddered at the thought of asking Giddeona for anything. This was all her fault. If she hadn't meddled in Nomyra's laid-out plan, everything would have been on schedule. Now everything was out of control and hung in the air like steam after a summer rain, blocking Nomyra from seeing what lay ahead.

The encounter with Maitliin in the crown had left Nomyra shaken. She had worshipped him, respected his power, trusted his knowledge and motivation. Yet the whole time, he hadn't wanted to charge the Great Diamond for the responsible use of the astropriests. The long-dead wizard had desired all the power for himself in a new body he claimed: hers.

That hadn't been part of the plan. No wonder the dwarf priestess had thwarted him all those years ago. One man should never have all that power. She might not be as all-inclusive as Talia, but even Nomyra knew that.

With a hand planted firmly on the door, Nomyra waved the Krag ring in a star pattern over the stained-glass window. Even drained of power, the Library would recognize the Unity ring.

The door popped open. As the true location of the Library, Raqmu had the grandest entrance. The ceiling stepped up from the doorway to the grand room beyond. The ever-climbing layers made the visitor feel smaller and smaller as she entered the repository of centuries of knowledge.

Nomyra sucked in her breath as she allowed the grandeur of her forefathers to penetrate her. The stained glass shone from the inside as if little lights had been melted into its form. She saw images of constellations, as well as the old gods.

With each of the five Planets displayed in a different bright color that matched one of the Holy Gemstones, an image of the Great Conjunction to bring about the Recharging sat in the center of the ceiling. Since the Library didn't allow anyone to leave except through the door they had entered and no one had set foot in Raqmu in centuries, Nomyra had never seen this part.

The conglomeration of old gods and light-dark worship made Nomyra think. Had the two always been acquainted with one another? Were they supposed to be one religion, twisted together to make a complicated whole? If so, what had happened to the gods over the years? Where had they gone when the Dark interfered in the lives of mortals?

She rubbed her flushing cheeks. She didn't have the luxury of anger. In a few weeks, the Recharging would occur. She had thought she'd be ready. She'd believed she had fulfilled her destiny, the purpose of the Highwind line. Now, Nomyra struggled with the very definition, and she searched for her sister to answer the big questions.

Crossing into the main branch that was accessible from every location, the room darkened, lit only by the familiar soft blue glow. Her first memory, from when she still toddled across the floor after her sister, took place in the Library. Her father, Grand Astropriest of the Tower, had sat both sisters down and told them their destiny: to fix what Maitliin had broken by funneling the Recharging energy into the Great Diamond under the city.

He had always tossed aside his long hair when he regaled his children. Nomyra pictured him pulling at the white strands when they caught in his jewelry. The locks would flow around his shoulders like each strand vied for the center of attention. The candles on the wall had framed his angular face, so like her sister's, emphasizing the chin and shadowing the eyes. His voice had sounded so loud in the little cove by the fireplace, his words full of import.

It wasn't until years later that Nomyra had realized the destiny was meant only for Giddeona. Nomyra had been a spare, an extra just in case. After their mother's death, Giddeona had abandoned the cause. Her father had bemoaned the future, having lost all hope. Nomyra had donned the robes and stepped up to clear the Highwind name. She had waited for the praise and support of her father, which never came.

"Giddeona." Nomyra knew she was in here. She could feel her sister's heartbeat. "Is that why you abandoned your calling? You knew the whole time what Maitliin had planned."

"I tried to warn you." Giddeona's shaky voice, so like their mother's, brought Nomyra back to happier times. Her older sister waited in the commons. She must have known Nomyra would come as well. After all these years, they were still connected.

Nomyra had locked up the Library after her father gave up on the cause. She hadn't been among the collection since. Seeing the full shelves and the familiar blue lighting brought back fond memories. "Do you remember when we used to play hide-and-seek in here?"

Giddeona's light laughter, sounding much too young for one who looked so old, tickled Nomyra's heart. "I remember Mother creating tablet after tablet of searches for us, and we'd scour book after book until we found the answers."

Nomyra laid a hand on the back of the crooked chair their mother had sat in as the girls scampered through the dusty aisles. "We climbed every shelf and separated the most-used books into piles for easier reach."

A puff of dust flitted into the air as Giddeona tapped a neglected volume. "She'd sit there with a cloth over her nose so she could breathe."

"Until she didn't." After a pause, Nomyra sat in the chair and crossed her legs.

Giddeona stared at the wall over her sister's head. "We didn't know she was sick."

"She didn't want us to know." Nomyra tucked her hands into her robe sleeves.

"You're a lot like her, you know." Giddeona squatted by a pile of books. "You refuse to show any weakness."

Nomyra's anger flared. "I didn't have a choice. You left. You abandoned your duty. I had to take over, or the Highwind name would have been a disgrace for another thousand years."

"A disgraced name." With a contemptuous wave, Giddeona frowned, her face caving into itself. "Mere letters have no bearing on this world or how it works. We are insignificant."

Nomyra kicked the chair as she jumped to her feet. "We all know how you feel. When you walked away, you dropped it like baggage you couldn't stand to carry around. Instead, you took on the Feltwith moniker. That was the maid's name!"

"There's nothing wrong with the maid. She took good care of us for many years."

Clenching her fists, Nomyra glared at her sister. "Father never recovered from your betrayal."

"Probably for the best. All he did was repeat lies told to him without any consideration for the fallout." Giddeona ran her hands over her face with a groan. "Mother made us read these books for a reason. She wanted us to see the bigger picture. Her body gave out before it truly sank in. It took me years to see through Father's hate and find Mother's love."

With a complete loss of self-control, Nomyra screamed, "You never loved anything!"

Giddeona grabbed her little sister's shoulders. "I love you."

She fought the grip as tears streamed down her face. "That's a lie. You left. You left me to shoulder the responsibility. You left me to find the True Heir and to anoint the Bright One."

"I left you to choose your own fate." Giddeona guided Nomyra to the fireplace corner their father had frequented. A modest cot with a small pillow and a cotton blanket sat beside a wobbly round table piled with books and a small gem-powered lantern. "But I never abandoned you."

Nomyra wiped the tears from her cheeks. She'd avoided this place for years, content with the resources her father had provided. She hadn't been able to face the memories of her youth. A pile of paper caught her eye.

A tiny desk with an awkward two-legged stool held the paper, most of it full of tiny writing. Empty ink jars littered the area. Destroyed quills stuck out of drawers at all angles.

Giddeona rubbed her hands together as she crouched in front of a larger pile on the floor, covered in cobwebs. She wiggled a finger by a small black spider that was no bigger than her thumbnail. The arachnid scurried away.

Nomyra pulled a sheet off the top of the desk. It was definitely Giddeona's handwriting, but more frantic than she remembered it. With a tentative look at her sister, Nomyra wondered if she'd gone mad. She might not have any answers at all.

Then Nomyra saw her name. "What is this?"

Her sister smiled and motioned for her to sit on the cot.

Nomyra ignored her, too distracted by the page in her hand. It described the fight with the beast in the lake in Raqmu.

She tossed the page to the ground and shot to her feet. "You figured out how to do it. You can exit the Library through any door, can't you? This is a miracle brought by the Light itself. It changes everything."

Possibilities flowed through Nomyra's mind like a whole new world had opened up to her.

"Oh, no, no, no, Myra. Don't think of such things. I had to sacrifice. I had to . . ." Giddeona's eyes darkened with hidden terrors.

Nomyra found herself afraid to ask for the details, but the possibilities of entering in one city and exiting in another were too enticing to dismiss.

Giddeona grabbed her sister's shoulders again and pulled her so close, their noses touched. Nomyra noticed the lines around her older sister's eyes and mouth, the paper-thin quality of her skin, and dark spots that should have been on a woman much older than she was.

"What happened?"

"Nothing I didn't choose. But that is the point. I chose." Giddeona squeezed Nomyra's shoulders. "Destiny is something we determine for ourselves. It is not set forth by the stars or the gods or our parents. You determine your own fate. You can be influenced. You can be tricked. But only you can decide."

She pushed Nomyra down onto the cot and sat beside her. She picked up the crumbled piece of paper. "I have been watching you, and I have been recording." She gestured to the huge stack beside the desk. "Talia and Tanin too, and a few others. That Aleck has so much potential."

Nomyra shook her head. She was wandering off again.

Giddeona grabbed her chin. "You have choices. List them."

"That's why I searched you out. I need you to tell me." Nomyra scuffed her feet against the floor.

"You don't need anyone to tell you. You know."

Nomyra tucked her arms into her sleeves. Her whole life, she had demanded control, all the while feeling helpless to stray from the path. Could she actually choose her own way?

"I can charge the Great Diamond."

Giddeona nodded. "That is one option. Your blood should work as well as Talia's. It is the same, almost."

"But I would die, and who would ensure the power goes to the tower?"

Giddeona jerked her head away at Nomyra's questioning glance. "Don't look at me. I won't help those self-important elitists."

"But you said I could choose."

"Yes, oh yes, I did. And so you can. But I don't have to agree with you." Giddeona left the cot and leaned against her desk.

Nomyra's eyes narrowed. "I could help Talia Recharge the planet, allowing the magic to go wild."

"Yes, another option."

"But then Talia would die." Nomyra felt guilty about not telling Talia the truth. After Talia had saved her from Maitliin, Nomyra had understood the girl's ability to sacrifice. If she'd been prepared from the beginning, maybe she would have been emotionally set for the inevitable ending. She had been so happy when she found out her guardians could be Bright Ones too. But only Talia's blood would work. And the Machine demanded it all.

"She doesn't have to die as long as she doesn't do it alone." A dragging sound interrupted her explanation.

Giddeona clapped her hands in excitement. "And here it is."

Nomyra swung her feet up off the ground and gathered her robes in her hands as a group of spiders, which must have numbered in the hundreds, came around the bookshelf carrying a scroll. Her skin crawled, though the tiny hairy legs weren't anywhere close enough to touch her.

Giddeona took the rolled parchment from her eight-legged friends and made some sort of sign with her pinky finger. The group scurried off in different directions, disappearing into the shadows before Nomyra could plop a book on them and squish the lot.

Laughing at Nomyra's reaction, Giddeona slid the scroll into her sister's arms. "The original Machine was not designed to multiply the magical charge of the natural conjunction. It was created to imbue a bit of that power into humans and dwarves so we could manipulate matter the way the magicals can. Without that touch of the divine, we are incapable of any magical talent."

Nomyra's mind reeled with the new information. She unrolled the paper and scanned the language. It was in Veni, but the letters were shaped a bit differently. "This is old, really old."

Squeezing her sister's shoulder again, Giddeona smiled. "You didn't have all the facts, and now you do."

Nomyra blinked at her sister. "How long have you known the truth?"

"I still don't know everything." Giddeona guided her sister toward the entrance. "Plus, the truth depends on who is telling it. You must gather the facts, everything you can find and everything you can experience, and then decide for yourself."

Nomyra pulled her sister over the threshold into the Raqmu entrance chamber. "You can travel through the doors. Come with me."

Giddeona's face lit with the reflected light of the unnaturally shiny stained glass. "It gets more spectacular every time I see it."

"Gid, we can do this together." Nomyra took her sister's hand.

The excitement drained from Giddeona's face. She looked deflated and tired. "I wish I could, but I cannot."

For some reason, Nomyra understood. "You made your choice."

A slight upturn of her lips emphasized her wrinkles but lightened her eyes. "Yes, Myra. And now you must make yours."

Nomyra embraced her sister for the first time in decades.

# CHAPTER FORTY-FIVE

More out of habit than hunger, Tanin shoved another bite of smoked procapra into his mouth. Salvo had convinced both parties that they had to work together to get the Machine running. They'd be able to make their final decisions afterward.

Tanin didn't like it, and he hated that he had relinquished his crown so easily. Next to him, Augusta squeezed his elbow. Her color was still pale, but she was in good spirits considering the sacrifice she'd made for the cause she believed in so fervently. He couldn't regret doing whatever he must to make sure she was by his side. By the way she returned his longing gaze, Tanin knew Augusta felt the same.

He'd deal with the wrath of her betrothed later. King Juarim would owe Tanin for succeeding in strengthening his resurgent religion. Tanin would use that to sway him into letting Augusta make her own binding choice.

He pushed a strand of hair off her face. She had trouble adjusting herself with only one arm. Even with the missing limb, Augusta's beauty shone brighter than the afternoon sun through the cracks in the ceiling. She would make a glorious queen. Her imperfection would stand as proof of the evil of magic.

He took her bowl and his own to the wash basin where Dew and Hodan were cleaning up the remnants of the meal. The boy hadn't left Dew's side since she came up from the lower chamber. Tanin hadn't had time to talk to Hodan privately. When he did, he would ask Hodan to get his hands on that circlet. It would come in handy as they traveled home after their triumph. Everyone they met would have to be taught the glory of Lagaw and how humans would reignite their destiny to rise above all other races.

Across the plaza, a robed figure marched toward the central statue. Tanin moved around the glow of the fire to get a better look and almost tumbled over Orui.

The prince grumbled. "Could you give me a little space? I know Rory threatened to cut off your ears if you lost sight of me for an instant while he's busy working on the mechanism for the roof, but if I step on you one more time, I'm going to break your other ankle."

Orui didn't respond to his charge's complaint. "It can't be Kettlor or Ial. There's no way they made it to Grayson's body and back so quickly."

With a sigh, Tanin shielded his eyes from the light above to peer into the murky darkness between the rows of stadium seats. "I think it's just one person."

"It's Priestess Nomyra," Dew called from the wash basin. "She likes to come and go as she pleases."

Tanin dropped his hand and turned away in contempt. "This entire fiasco is that woman's fault. If she hadn't messed with the natural order, this city would still be buried, the Machine would never be functional, and the world would just charge naturally, the way Lagaw intended."

Orui tapped his makeshift cane on the ground. "You make a good point."

For the first time in months, Tanin questioned Salvo's teachings.

"The prophet always said we had to destroy the Machine so no one could Recharge the planet in excess."

When Augusta called for Tanin to help her up, he recognized the same twinkle of doubt in her expression. Her hair flew around her face, much more wild than normal. "So why are we repairing it? I thought it made sense at the time, but now I'm not so sure."

Gripping her hand, Tanin started toward the stairs. A scrape vibrated the ground below his feet. Remembering the feeling of falling into nothing, Tanin hurried Augusta backward. "Away from the center."

She followed him but kept focused on the stairs leading down. "Meerin and the prophet are down there."

Orui limped after them. "They're probably causing this racket. If the ceiling falls on their heads, it'll be their own doing."

As quickly as it started, the grinding vibration stopped.

Dew wiped her hands on a ragged towel. "Maybe they realized we were standing up here and it was a bad time to open the gates?"

Before Tanin's breathing could return to normal, a much angrier grinding came from the ceiling above. He squeezed Augusta's hand, unsure if he should run for the cover of the underground or take his chances and make for the bleachers.

Augusta pulled back. "Wait. Look."

Above the statue, a perfectly circular hole expanded from a small one in the ceiling. It grew as the pieces twisted. Centuries of dust fell, forming a fog of debris. Tanin released Augusta to pull cloth over his mouth so he could breathe.

With a flick of a bedroll, Hodan tossed a thin blanket over Tanin and Augusta. The prince helped her hold it over her head to protect her from being inundated by soil but still allow her to see the majesty of the stunningly open sky.

Gregor sprinted up the stairs.

Tanin left Orui with Augusta to see what was going on. "Is everything okay?"

His ex-friend looked like his old self, with shining eyes and a toothy grin. "They sent me to make sure. It looks right to me." Gregor waved dust from the air in a vain attempt to clear his line of sight. "We accidentally started to move the floor before the ceiling was out of the way. No sense raising the dais if it's just going to ram into the rock above."

Tanin understood now why the ground had rumbled first. "I don't think it's stone. Look how it's sliding into those crevices on the edge of the dome."

Bits of debris peeled off from the screeching metal as it slid into the pockets.

Gregor dropped a familiar hand on Tanin's shoulder. "How did they forge such strong, thin sheets? I really hope all that knowledge is in this city somewhere."

Angry at his comfortable familiarity, Tanin shoved Gregor's hand off. "It seems Talia is staying and since you threw your fate in with hers, you'll have plenty of time to explore."

He meant every bit of his spiteful words, though the prospect of the advanced knowledge hidden in this city intrigued him. He'd have to find some spies to keep an eye on what they discovered. Any sort of technology was the purview of Lagaw and intended for his disciples, not the blasphemers focused on Ydiny's magic.

Gregor tucked his hands in his pockets and rocked back and forth on his heels. "I'm sorry. I thought we had reached some sort of middle ground."

Tanin's eyes narrowed at the friend he had once shared everything with. "There's never been such a thing. You chose Talia's treachery over your best friend's legitimate claims. You can't come back from that."

With a heavy sigh, Gregor tilted his head toward the stairs. "We're about to pull the Machine up from the depths. Talia told me to ask if you'd want to witness it."

After gesturing Augusta to his side, Tanin adjusted his sword belt. He hadn't told Talia about their new weapons. If push came to shove, Tanin's party would have a definite advantage. "Let's go."

Dew called from the wash station. "I'll wait here for Kettlor and Ial and—"

Hodan stared off to a far corner of the city. "Me too."

Tanin could guess what he was feeling. He had Orui by his side and they were joining Rory, so it shouldn't be an issue. "Fine," he said.

Gregor warned them, "You might want to move the encampment back as well. If we're guessing correctly, this entire statue will be pulled into the ground and the center of the plaza will open, much like the ceiling just did. And we're not sure how big the hole will be."

Dew shoved her chin at Nomyra, who was almost within hearing distance. "I'll make the priestess help us."

Gregor moved out of the way as Aleck and Traneck made their way down the stairs.

Tanin passed Gregor to join the rest of the party already descending the stairs, Augusta's hand held protectively in his. He couldn't care less about the politics of his sister and that priestess of a false religion. He had his own questions for his prophet, and he needed answers. He wouldn't get those wasting time up here.

The eerie blue light that had lit the above chamber before the ceiling opened flooded the underground chamber. Tanin helped Augusta over a scorched gap in the floor. Gregor didn't seem to be bothered by it. Tanin didn't want to seem weak, so he didn't ask any questions. The group stopped at a large hole in the ground that looked like a miniature version of the opened archway above.

Gregor hopped down to a ladder. "It's darker down here, but once we activate the statue, the Daughter's light will aid our repairs."

Tanin moved to follow him but stopped at a tug from Augusta. Her pale face stared at the dwarves, who were easily descending the ladder. One shoulder twitched without the weight of her arm. He realized why she had stopped. "You can't climb a ladder, can you? I didn't think . . ."

She forced water from her eyes with a determined blink.

He crouched in front of her. "Climb on my back. I'll take you down."

The shake of her head was so subtle, Tanin thought he'd imagined it. Until Augusta walked around him to the edge. "I can do this. Our Lord Lagaw demands it of me, and I am eager to comply."

Tanin stood, awaiting her next move. She grabbed the bottom of her robe and skirts and awkwardly tucked them into her tight belt.

Momentarily distracted by her muscular yet softly feminine legs, Tanin started forward when she waved at him a second time.

"Tell me how I can help," he insisted.

With a bit of a wobble, Augusta managed to get to her knees. "Guide me over the edge. I can take it from there."

Tanin swung onto the ladder. He anchored one arm around a rung and reached his other toward her dainty feet. She extended one down, and he guided it to a stable rung. Shaking a bit as she shifted her foot for stability, Augusta slipped her second leg over the edge. Tanin couldn't imagine how uneasy she felt, yet she progressed without a word of complaint. They would have strong children to rule Tarbin.

After adjusting his stabilizing arm to grip the ankle she already had on a rung, Tanin helped Augusta find the same spot with her second foot. "You've got it. Now take the next step."

He moved down two rungs and waited for her to crest the edge. With her upper chest flattened on the ground above and her feet stuck on the rung below, she hesitated. "I'm not sure how to transition."

Without hesitation, Tanin climbed up a couple of steps until his feet were on a rung just below hers. He pressed his body firmly against hers, stabilizing her against the metal ladder. "I will protect you until you get your grip."

Augusta's huge brown eyes met Tanin's bright blue ones. He felt her frozen muscles flex as her jaw set in the determined look Tanin found so enticing.

"I trust you," she said out loud, as if she were reassuring him as well as herself.

She wiggled her torso between Tanin and the ladder. Her robe slid up her body as it caught on the ground. She didn't have an extra hand to push it down, and Tanin wasn't about to slow her progress by loosening his grip. For some reason, Tanin felt compelled to look away as her undergarments were exposed. It wasn't like he'd never seen a girl's under things or that he didn't long to see Augusta's. It was something else he'd never felt for a woman: respect.

She finally scooted into place and secured her hand on the top rung. "I'm good." She sounded out of breath.

Tanin also felt out of breath, but it had nothing to do with physical exertion. He loosened his grip and climbed down, careful not to disrupt Augusta's stability.

His heart raced at the implication. "I'll stay right below you. You set the pace."

Augusta closed her eyes in what Tanin recognized as a silent prayer. "I am ready."

She gripped the side of the ladder and slid her hand down as she moved one foot at a time to the next rung down. Continuing in a steady, almost hypnotic pace, they made it the fifty feet down with no major difficulty.

Tanin lifted Augusta and spun her around. He stopped with her body pressed against his. Their noses touched. He breathed in her scent, earthy with a hint of vanilla. Augusta licked her lips as Tanin wove his hand through the hair on her neck.

Meerin's voice broke the spell. "Augusta, you made it. Good."

Tanin reluctantly released the princess.

Her fellow acolyte didn't seem to have noticed anything out of the ordinary. "I wasn't sure if you'd be feeling up to it. You've worked as hard for this as I have. You should be here to see Lagaw's plan come to fruition."

Tanin swallowed heavily, his hands cold. His doubts returned. "About that plan, are we sure we need to initiate the Recharging?

Why can't we just take pieces out of the Machine until it won't work anymore? Wouldn't that be more effective?"

Meerin dismissed Tanin's complaints with a wave of her hands. "Lagaw wants us to destroy the Machine in a big explosion. It's a much more dramatic idea than just making it not work. Think of the legends. We'll convert so many people this way."

Augusta stopped messing with her robe and looked up at Tanin. "It would be a dramatic demonstration. Prophet Salvo always knows how to gain the attention and worship of a crowd for the glory of Lagaw."

Tanin had to admit, the Machine bursting into pieces in the middle of the Recharging would make for one heck of a story. Too bad his father wouldn't be here to witness his triumph. "Maybe that could work. How much does Talia know?"

Meerin led Tanin and Augusta down an incline to the Machine chamber. "I'm not sure. She's not sharing anything with us."

Tanin smirked. "Of course not."

As his eyes adjusted to the darker interior, a monstrosity formed itself out of the gloom. Gears and tubes twisted in odd angles around a large funnel-like contraption. Sparks flew as Naul smashed something with a hammer. Meerin clambered up a ladder next to Naul.

Tanin couldn't make any sense of the chaotic Machine. He sidled up to his sister, who looked just as baffled as he felt. "So these twisted bits of metal and coil are what has tormented us for the last year?"

For a second, Talia's shoulders loosened. "It seems ridiculous that one device could change the world so drastically."

Nomyra whipped into the room then, her dramatic flair in full swing. She stopped abruptly in front of Talia and Tanin, her robes swishing around her like waves breaking on a rocky shore. "What happens here in a couple of weeks has little to do with that thing and everything to do with the people who wish to manipulate it."

Tanin and Talia crossed their arms at the same time. He could feel his twin's distaste for the priestess as it so perfectly mirrored his own.

On a platform over their heads, Gregor snapped his fingers. "We're ready, Talia."

"Do it." Talia pointed at the transition between the rough stone and the smooth tiled surface of the floor. "We should probably move closer to be safe. We're not really sure how secure this lift will be after a thousand years."

Before Tanin could ask what was about to happen, Gregor used this body weight to pull down on a long lever. The ground shuttered. Tanin half crouched to maintain his balance. He reached for Augusta, but she shrugged him off. He scoffed at her stubbornness but let her have her way. This time. They weren't married yet. She could risk her life if she so desired.

Even though Tanin tried to be cold about the possibility of further injury to Augusta, he remained close by, just in case.

A chilly breeze blew down from above. Tanin watched the floor part, much like the ceiling had. *If something works, don't fix it.* Apparently, the ancient Raqmu preferred spiral openings.

The platform jerked upward. The sudden movement dropped Tanin to his knees. He caught Augusta before her head could hit the ground.

Rory shouted from the Machine's platform. "My Prince, I'm coming." He clung to the railing wisely placed around the raised apparatus.

Tanin wasn't sure he wanted only Talia's crew monitoring the Machine. "I'm fine. Stay there."

An earsplitting screech stabbed Tanin's senses. What kind of beast would make such a noise? "What have you awakened?" he yelled at his sister, who was on her knees next to him.

Talia reached for her sword, then released it with a laugh. "Nothing, Tanin. It's just an old counterweight, like the chains on the portcullis of the castle."

Tanin pivoted in his crouch to see behind him. The statue that had dominated the center of the plaza moved down through centuries of cobwebs and neglect. Its shaky descent matched the rise of the Machine. Tanin's anger morphed to fascination.

As the platform approached the level of the paved plaza, its movement slowed. With one final shudder, it stopped, perfectly even with where the statue had been moments before. The only sign that anything had happened was the sand sifting through cracks between the platform and the plaza.

"Don't move until I lock it down." Meerin climbed along the outside of the device, from handhold to handhold, to another platform lower than the main one. She pushed, arms straight out with her head tucked down, on a horizontal lever. After the first squeak of movement, it seemed to move much more easily. A loud click echoed through the tiles.

Meerin stood up and rubbed her hands on her tunic. "Done."

Augusta pulled at Tanin's sleeve as he regained his feet. He reached his hand down to help her up.

"No." She pushed him away as she rose. "Look." She pointed to the bleachers surrounding the plaza.

People, lots of them, were crowding the outskirts.

Tanin exchanged a knowing smile with Augusta. "We have our audience."

# CHAPTER FORTY-SIX

TALIA FOLLOWED her brother's gaze. The Light's Daughter brightened the city closer to what must have been its original majesty. The crumbling rooftops and the ragged streets truly foretold the work ahead of her. After the Recharging, she wouldn't have anything else to do. She'd give Tanin the crown he coveted and try to restore as much of Raqmu's dignity as she could, along with her own.

Dew rushed to her side. "Talia, that was incredible to witness. And we weren't the only ones watching."

Naul hopped down the last few rungs of the ladder from the platform. "It was even more exciting to ride."

Drawing her companions together, Talia gestured to their incoming visitors. "What do we do about them?"

Naul whistled.

Up on the platform, Gregor cocked his hip. "Were you whistling at me, sir?"

With a curt laugh, Naul shook the ladder. "Sure was. Now come down here so I can show my affection."

Talia rolled her shoulders. She wanted to laugh, but she knew, as

Tanin gathered his men to plan Light knows what, that these new arrivals would be another responsibility she'd have to handle.

The priestess joined Talia's gathering. "They've come to witness the Recharging as it was foretold. You saw how they reacted in Hajar Ramliun. It seems the desert dwellers remembered, even as most of Tarbin forgot."

A crowd of people marched down the main thoroughfare toward the plaza. Their voices rose in song, the tune floating through the air in an eerie echo. Talia couldn't decide if it was encouraging or disturbing.

Shock set in as Talia realized she'd have to find places for all these people, at the very least for the next few days. She didn't have time to organize anything. What happened if there was a fight? She wanted to rule and truly believed herself capable of the task, but not now. She had too much on her list already.

"We have to turn them around. It's not safe. There could be another manticore or who knows what other dangers. This city has been abandoned for centuries. The buildings could collapse with the slightest nudge." She pulled at her hair, forcing it behind her ears. "And what of the plaza seating? If it collapses and injures these people, I'll never forgive myself."

Nomyra shook her head. "They would not miss the Recharging."

Dew pulled the tiara from her satchel and pushed it onto her curls. "I've been wanting to try this thing out." Dew turned to Talia. "Shall we?"

Talia clenched and unclenched her fists. If she were to rule this city, she should be the one greeting its first visitors.

Still on the platform above, Gregor called down, "Want some company?"

Talia's first instinct was to tell him no. She didn't need anyone. His huge smile sent a shiver down Talia's spine. Maybe not, but she definitely *wanted* someone. "Yes, I'd love some company."

His confidence in her tingled along her skin like magic from Windall. Maybe, just maybe, she didn't have to do this alone.

Her brother smirked, killing her good mood. "Rory and Meerin will make sure the Machine is ready."

"I'm sure they're capable." Talia looked away before she got in another fight. She couldn't leave the instrument of the Recharging with the people who wanted it to fail. "Naul, will you please stay?"

Naul swung his hammer into the makeshift sling he'd fashioned and switched places with Gregor. "I've got this."

"I know you do." Talia twisted her hair up into a bun on top of her head.

Aleck put a hand on Traneck's shoulder. "We'll stay too."

Traneck's gaze followed Meerin as she sneaked around to the back of the apparatus. "We'll keep an eye on things."

Talia shook hands with both dwarves. "Your experience will be much appreciated."

With a focused stride, Talia headed toward the stands with Gregor, Dew, and Nyna.

Nomyra jogged to keep up with Talia. "I have to speak to you. I discovered something about the Bright Ones in the Library."

Dew pushed in between Talia and Nomyra. "The Library? There's one here?"

"*The* one is here." Nomyra's eyes shone just as brightly as Dew's.

Talia watched Augusta tag along behind the group. "That's all very exciting, but we might want to keep any discoveries to ourselves for the moment." She scanned Nomyra's disappointed expression for any sign of subterfuge. Talia hated that she couldn't trust the people who had the most knowledge about her destiny.

With a nod of acknowledgment, Nomyra moved behind Talia, tucking the scroll she held under her robe.

As Talia approached the moving lines of people, she realized how immense her task had become.

How would she get them food or clean up their waste? She really hoped she wouldn't have to deal with any of these mundane issues until she settled the whole Recharging business. Apparently, everyday life continued for most. She envied their simplistic lives.

An unnatural quiet rolled through the crowd, cascading from the front to the back in an almost choreographed fashion. Talia felt every eye on her. She rubbed her hands on her hips, trying to mop up the sweat that had popped up on her palms. She wasn't afraid to speak in front of crowds. It had been part of her training as a royal princess. But she'd always represented her father or Tarbin as her kingdom. She'd never spoken on her own behalf. What if she sounded as scared as she felt? What if they didn't listen to her? Panic jumbled her thoughts into a mess of images with no organization.

Talia jumped as Nomyra's voice broke through the silence. "People of the desert."

Dew elbowed Talia and pointed to her translator tiara. Talia nodded permission for her guardian to repeat their words. She hadn't seen the magical gift in action yet. The novelty distracted her from her anxiety.

After a slight bump into Nomyra to get her attention, Dew spoke with equal conviction. Talia heard the same words in Common from Dew's mouth. In what still sounded like Dew's voice, four different phrases echoed across the crowd. Two of them were completely unfamiliar; one was Common; the last was one of the dialects Talia recognized as the rolling language of Hajar Ramliun.

A raised eyebrow was Nomyra's only reaction to the new toy. "I, High Priestess Nomyra, interpreter of the Stars and follower of the Light, have the honor of introducing the True Heir of Raqmu, Talia Highwind, formally of Tarbin."

As Dew's tiara shared the translation across the gathering, each group cheered as their language rang through the tiara.

"Your True Heir will ensure the success of the Recharging; the Bright Ones will not fail."

Talia exchanged a look with Gregor. Nomyra had said "Bright Ones," plural. What had changed?

The people stomped, clapped, and generally hooted. The racket stirred up the dust on the seating and filled the air with a thin mist yet again.

Talia coughed as a breath of dirty air clogged her lungs. The crowd once again grew quiet. Before, they had been looking at the group of people approaching them. Now, every set of eyes stared directly at her. Some in the back had climbed onto the bleachers to get a better view. Many young children sat on parents' shoulders. The crowd had grown so silent, it felt like everyone held their breath.

It was time for Talia to set the tone.

Nomyra touched the crown and Talia's throat. "They should hear your voice." She whispered a prayer to the Light, and Talia's tongue tingled.

Suddenly terrified, Talia whispered, "I don't know what to say."

Her voice rang above the audience noise, quieting them. Her cheeks burned with embarrassment as she scowled at Nomyra, but she dared not reprimand her. She needed to think fast.

Gregor held both her hands. His face replaced the gawking audience for a brief welcome second. "Yes, you do. Let your heart handle this one."

Her knees shook, and her chest ached. Self-conscious for the first time in weeks, Talia straightened her robes. She wished she'd had time to tidy up first. She drew courage from the bedraggled faces of the people who had made the same long desert trek as she with nothing more than hope for the Recharging.

"Welcome to Raqmu, the ancient gem of the desert."

Dew repeated her words; this time, only three languages rang out.

"I'm proud to stand here as True Heir and am prepared to do whatever is necessary to Recharge our world and reignite the ruins of a once-progressive society. I could do none of this without my companions, the Bright Ones, who have suffered with me, through failure and redemption, through heartache and triumph. We welcome you, who have chosen to join us as witnesses, into our fold."

She smiled at Gregor as a brilliant idea struck her. "I appoint Gregor Rivenwood the Marshal of Raqmu. Please come to him if you are in need of anything."

The color drained from Gregor's face. "I'm what now?"

Talia waved her hand at her throat. Nomyra quickly brushed her throat, then nodded.

With a smile so big it hurt her cheeks, Talia brought Gregor close. "You wanted a new position and a new title. I've just given you one." This time, she got to squeeze his hand for encouragement. "You ran your father's lands for years. A few stragglers in a deserted city are going to be easy."

The priestess tilted her head, seeming to understand. "I would be willing to stay and answer any questions they have. I should remember enough of the desert tongue to communicate basic needs. Plus, many likely speak Common."

Augusta stepped forward. "I also will stay and offer the visitors comfort."

The offer confused Talia. "Are you sure you're up to it? You're not fully healed." Her voice softened when she realized that maybe she shouldn't bring it up.

The noblewoman pulled her robe tighter around her mutilated shoulder. "The sacrifice to my God only strengthens me. These people are in need of shelter and water. Lagaw, the Caring, would want me to see to their needs."

Now Talia understood. Augusta wanted to stay and initiate the visitors to her god. Talia should have thought of that immediately. That's what they'd been doing the entire time they crossed the continent. Talia refused to be threatened by an old belief reborn. After the Recharging, they would all know for sure which religion reigned supreme. For now, she would let Augusta speak of her god. If she stayed out here, Talia would have one less person to watch while repairing the Machine.

"As you wish," Talia offered to Augusta. She watched a line form in front of Gregor. "Dew, maybe you should stay, just in case."

Her cultural guardian patted her on the shoulder. "It will be taken care of."

As they walked back to the Machine, the crowd clapped and

hooted again. Talia pivoted on her heels to soak in their belief in her. She wished she could store it away for a later time. She still didn't know how she would handle Tanin's desire to destroy the Machine while she tried to restore the planet. That problem had to be solved.

# CHAPTER FORTY-SEVEN

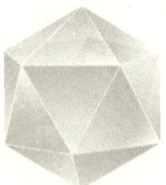

THE MACHINE SPARKLED in the dimming light as the sunset and the Raqmu blue brightened the perimeter of the plaza. For the last few weeks, Talia's and Tanin's people had worked together to get the mechanisms in perfect working order. Each piece had been polished and tested. Talia was confident it would function properly when the time came.

The reinforced stadium seating, safe thanks to Gregor's attention, vibrated with the energy of the crowd. A contingent from Hajar Ramliun had arrived three days before with supplies and Giant Eagle emissaries. She had expected the visitors to be disappointed with the crumbling city they held in such high esteem. Instead, they viewed the ancient Raqmu with reverence and eagerly dove into repairing and restoring its monuments.

Talia shook her arms, draped in a clean tunic. One of the desert families had tailored the tunic and leggings. Her entire party had received gifts of new garments, which they were all grateful for. Talia hoped she didn't get blood all over it. She'd gotten pretty good at pricking her finger, but Nomyra said the Machine would require more than just a drop.

Somehow, her guardians were supposed to participate in the ceremony, but no one quite knew how. They'd run out of time, and they were just going to have to wing it.

After adjusting the crown on her belt, Talia checked her dagger. She'd never had an audience this large when activating the Holy Gemstones, not even the first time with the Krimmel Dwarves. Had that only been two years ago? It felt like a lifetime.

As the sky darkened and the first Stars winked to life, Talia climbed the ladder to her designated platform. The basin to hold her blood for the Recharging was much larger than she had envisioned. She put her hand on the container. The cylinder was fully a hand and a half tall and as round as a dinner plate. To fill it would take every ounce of blood in her body. She knew she had to sacrifice for the people of the world, but she hadn't thought her life was on the line.

Gregor pulled her hand from the glass and wrapped both of his around it. "Nomyra assured us that you don't need to fill the container. The planetary conjunction will send energy through the Machine, which will focus it and send it into the core of the world. It should only need a sample of blood."

Talia squeezed his hands, then pulled hers from his grip. She didn't want the people watching to think her weak. "I know. It's just that there's something Salvo is hiding, and I can't figure out what it is. He's been different since we've been in Raqmu."

With a nod, Gregor leaned against the railing overlooking the vast plaza. "Would it make you feel better if I kept an eye on him?"

"Actually, it would." Talia gestured toward Nomyra. "I'm also not convinced that she's on the up and up. I'm trying to trust her, but a lifetime of treachery and manipulation is hard to just forget."

At that moment, Nomyra met Talia's gaze. Sometimes, Talia wondered if the priestess had some sort of tracker on her, like a fairy in Talia's clothing who sent Nomyra messages. She seemed to know uncannily when Talia thought about her. It didn't lead to the building of trust; even if Talia knew intellectually that it was paranoia on her part, she couldn't shake the feeling. Even after Nomyra had told her that she didn't have to do this alone, that it wasn't all her. She only had to initiate the Machine. Then she could pull back, and it would still work as her companions manned the rest of the mechanism.

Gregor kissed Talia on the cheek before she could stop him. Warmth spread through her from the simple peck. After denying her feelings for the nobleman for so long, her heart lightened as she embraced them. When this was all done, they'd rule the city together and life would be able to find a new normal. Between her companions, Gregor, and Aleck, Talia saw true hope. She just had to survive this one big moment, then everything else would fall into place.

Gregor leaped from the platform to the ladder and shimmied his way to the ground to talk with Salvo and Meerin. The engineer's face glowed, even with oil smeared on her cheeks. Too bad Talia couldn't convince her to stay and help. She had a true gift for these apparatuses. If the ruins they'd explored over the past couple of months were any indication, Talia could use someone like her to help put the city back together.

Dew lightly climbed the ladder to stand next to Talia. "We're here. Ial had to convince Naga to leave his hidey-hole. We don't know how safe the chamber below will be when the Recharging happens."

The ringing of huge feet on the metal of the platform announced Naul's arrival. "I think the darn thing didn't want to leave Ial's side. I've never seen such a beast act so puppylike."

With an adjustment of her shoulder bag, Nyna joined the crew. "It would be cute if it weren't for those fierce fangs and nausea-inducing breath."

Ial called from the ladder, "Seriously? After waking up next to Naul all these years, you complain of the snake's breath?"

Talia's smile was so wide, it made her face ache. She wouldn't trade the feeling for any other. To her right and left were her truest friends, her real companions, who had all agreed to accompany her into this unknown endeavor. She embraced the well-being that calmed the worry to a slight whisper. No matter what happened today, she would know that she had done everything she could to return the world to its prior magical state. Along the way, Talia knew she had embodied love instead of hate, and that was the legacy she wanted to leave.

Tanin laughed below. The affection he lavished on Augusta was something new to Talia. She'd never seen him so happy and so giving to another human being. Maybe this quest had done him good as well. Brought him out of his dark motives and into a world of hope. She didn't know if it was his new faith in Lagaw or his love for Augusta or a combination of the two, but Talia was grateful for the change.

Noticing her looking at him, Tanin winked at his sister.

And just like that, Talia's doubt returned. "He's definitely up to something."

Nyna pulled her hair out of her face with a ribbon. "He swears that Lagaw will ensure their victory. That they don't have to do a thing."

Naul brushed off her concern. "What can he do at this point? The Machine is functioning perfectly. Side by side, Rory and I went through each cog and every lever. No one had access to it without someone from the other team joining them. He didn't have a chance to set up any kind of sabotage."

His protests eased Talia's worry. He was right. There was no way Tanin could have done anything that her companions wouldn't have seen. Plus, he had spent much of the last couple of days with Augusta, preaching to the people.

"Of course, you're right." She turned back to the panel. "The waiting has my mind wandering to all the things that could go wrong."

Nyna dusted some sand off the side panels where she was to stand during the Recharging. "I still don't understand what we're supposed to do up here."

Dew shrugged. "Giddeona's scroll said the Bright Ones were to assist the True Heir as the Recharging progressed. And in the end, our children would inherit the Bright One title until the end of our lines."

Naul nudged her playfully. "Thanks, Dew. It's all clear now."

Talia's fingers circled the gear where the Key fit. Finally, its rough crenellated top made sense. While other crowns had nice arches and lots of filigree in intricate patterns, the Tarbin crown always had perfectly squared projections. The Key to the entire mechanism was a fancy gear. The Holy Gemstones acted as an energy source once her blood activated it.

Talia remembered all the times it had soaked up her blood and emitted energy. This time, the blood would flow across the gems as the crown spun in the mechanism. During the test yesterday, the Machine had groaned to life with just a taste of her blood.

The sound of the roaring crowd still filled Talia's ears. The last squeaky bits had revealed themselves, allowing Meerin and Naul to wax the protesting parts. Luckily, the travelers had carried enough wax in the form of candles to complete the job.

Nomyra called from below, "The Planets have shown themselves through the Dark. Be ready. You will know when."

Talia looked up at the five bright dots directly over the opening in the roof. The closer they got, the more the air seemed to vibrate with power. As it had at Astropriest Tower a year ago when she had learned of her Bright One title, Talia's skin began to glow.

Dew covered her mouth in awe. "It's happening."

Grasping hands with her companions, Talia offered a prayer. "To the Dark, please allow the power of centuries to reinvigorate the magical races on this planet. To the Light, guide us on this path of rejuvenation and allow the Recharging to occur as prophesied."

As a last-minute thought, she offered one more prayer. "To Lagaw, Thoretick, Ydiny, and any other god who's listening, please allow our mission to succeed. We act out of care for all the creatures of this world."

A blanket of peace washed over her nerves. She didn't know

which source it came from, but she used the temporary calm to focus her mind. Pulling the bejeweled crown from its bag on her hip, she held it up for the watching crowd. She might not have Nomyra's flare, but she wanted the witnesses to have something to remember.

The gems flashed intermittently as the power in the air flowed in and out of the facets.

When only a tiny gap existed between the Planets, the air buzzed. The palpable magic filled the air, like humidity after a rain. Talia's fingers burned with the exposure. That was what Nomyra had meant when she said Talia would know when to start the Machine.

She flipped the crown upside down and pushed it into its spot. On the ground, Meerin and Aleck turned the lever to start the movement of the gears. The Machine groaned into action, vibrating the platform. Everything worked as it had earlier.

Talia peered through the metal mesh to Aleck underneath. He held a fist over his head as the signal that everything looked good. She wondered if that was where Billivin had stood vigil for Maitliin before he betrayed her. This time, the dwarf had nothing to worry about.

She chanced a glance at Gregor, but he didn't stand below with Salvo anymore. She didn't see either of them anywhere. Gregor had promised to keep an eye on the prophet. She had to trust that that was what he was doing. Talia had her own task.

She held up her knife, allowing it to glint in the Light from the Planets. The crowd aahed, which quickly evolved into a chorus of inspirational tones. Talia soaked up their reverence. As the song rose in volume, so did the magic in the air. The influx of power made Talia feel like she was floating.

The Planets snapped into place like the last pieces of a puzzle. Magic danced in the plaza like lightning bugs. If Talia hadn't known what was happening, she'd have been terrified. The buzzing overwhelmed the singing crowd and dominated Talia's senses. She used every bit of her determination to focus, when all she wanted to do was dance in the euphoric feeling.

With a swift movement, she sliced her palm and plastered her bleeding hand to the dome in the center of the crown gear. Ecstasy flooded her body. Her glowing blood flowed over the gems and into the container.

A loud snap shocked her. On the designated watch spots for the Bright Ones, four rounded domes popped out of the panels. Before Talia could ask what it meant, the energy distributed through the air coalesced into one tight beam, seemingly shooting down from the conjunction itself. The Recharging was happening. Talia had succeeded.

The concentrated energy shot through the center of the Machine. The entire thing rocked violently, forcing Talia to hold on with her other hand to prevent her blood donation from slipping off the gear.

Talia picked up shouting underneath her, but she couldn't discern whether it was a warning or excitement. Her Bright Ones, her trusted companions, stood by her side. She trusted them to keep her safe while she fulfilled her role. She stared at the jar her blood dripped into. Nomyra had assured her she would know when it was time to stop feeding the Machine.

The beam pulsed at the same rate as Talia's heart. She could feel both through her hand, where it was pressed on the cold metal. She was surprised staring at the blue stream didn't blind her. It didn't even hurt. Whichever god had orchestrated this feat was truly magnificent.

The pulsing of the beam grew erratic. The brilliance dimmed as Talia started to feel light-headed. She heard mumbling and a tug at her arm. She blinked at the container and realized that she was giving too much blood. With a yank of her hand, Talia freed herself from the Machine. The beam fractured into pieces.

Talia collapsed as she lost sense of up and down.

Dew caught her before she could smash her head into the railing. "You did it. Talia, you succeeded with the Recharging."

"Did I?" Talia tried to focus her mind, but she felt so weak. "Water?"

Nyna pressed a water bladder to her lips. "That was something to see."

Blinking at the Planets above, Talia knew something didn't feel right. They were still coalesced as one big globe, the five making one. "I missed something."

Nomyra's head popped over the floor of the platform. "Did you see him? Are you okay?"

Maitliin. Talia hadn't seen Maitliin or Billivin in the crown. That was more than she had ever fed it, and she hadn't seen another soul. "No. I didn't see him. Maybe the magic was so powerful, he couldn't fight his way through?"

At that moment, she spotted Prophet Salvo climbing out of the large opening where the magic beam had cascaded. Where was Gregor? The prophet held his hands over his head. His look of triumph couldn't be mistaken.

Tanin shouted from the ground. "What are you so happy about? It worked. The Recharging happened."

Augusta pressed tight against the prince. "I don't understand. He said there would be a great explosion."

Anger fueled Talia as she gained her feet. "What are you talking about?"

Sprawled on the ground with one of Rory's swords at his throat, Gregor spoke through clenched teeth, fury warping his face. "I'm sorry, Talia. They jumped me, and Salvo took off."

Salvo's laugh emptied into the night sky, where the Planets drifted a little farther apart, though they still appeared to be one large light in the sky.

Nomyra gasped. "It can't be."

Lit from below, the prophet's face distorted into a creepy mask. "You fool, I would never destroy this beautiful creation. Your prophet doesn't understand the gift that it is. Without this invention, humans wouldn't be able to use magic at all. I found a way to control who can access the magic. Now I have all the power *and* all the technology. You want a world of human domination? *This* is how you do it."

Talia's mind spun with his words. "I don't want that kind of world. That's not what we're fighting for."

Tanin shouted at the prophet, "You swore that the Machine had to be stopped in the middle of the Recharging. The magical races are dead and should stay that way."

With that same laugh, which Talia found familiar though not like the prophet, Salvo continued, "The elves will never awaken, and the merpeople will drown in their watery tombs. Dragon eggs will hatch stillborn, and the nadph will truly burn. The dark ages are over. The age of enlightened man has begun."

Nomyra tossed a rock at the platform to gain Talia's attention. "Can't you see? It's him. I don't know how, but it's Maitliin." The priestess rushed to the elevated ladder.

Talia grabbed the railing; otherwise, she might have collapsed. "The crown seemed to save Salvo, but maybe it didn't. Maybe Maitliin took over his body as he tried with Nomyra."

Salvo-Maitliin stared down at Talia. "And you. You should thank me. To have the planet itself Recharged would take *all* your life's blood. When I was crowned True Heir and Bright One, I discovered the truth of my fate. They intended to sacrifice me for the magicals."

As Nyna wrapped her bloodied hand, Talia studied the level of the container. It was only a quarter full. "But the Recharging happened, and I'm fine. I don't understand."

Sitting on top of the still-rumbling Machine, Salvo-Maitliin rubbed the surface like a favorite pet. "The Recharging didn't happen as intended, silly girl. You should have been consulting with me as Nomyra had. I told her to let me speak with you, but she refused. I could have cleared up all the confusion. She seemed to think you would object."

Aleck called from the levered mechanism that sat catty-corner to Talia's platform. "What do you mean the Recharging didn't occur? We saw it happen."

Salvo-Maitliin scoffed at the dwarf. "Go back to your stones, primitive. I hooked the Machine to a giant diamond under the ground. The thirsty jewel has sat empty for a thousand years. I have fed it, and the magic will be for me and my disciples alone."

Meerin pounded on the Machine. "No. The magic was to die. Lagaw demands it so."

She pulled out a tool and undid a screw holding a panel in place. Before she could damage the inner workings, Salvo-Maitliin shot a fireball from his palm. It exploded, flinging Aleck and Meerin from the Machine.

Augusta yelled and ran to her unconscious friend. Traneck knelt by Aleck. He didn't seem responsive.

Fury washed over Talia's shock. Her body shimmered as magic from the air coalesced around her. She shot her hands at Maitliin. A wave of magic smashed into him and swept him over the edge into the hollow middle of the Machine.

Naul whistled. "I'm not sure why the True Heir needs guardians if she can do that."

Dew asked, "If all the magic is in a diamond, what do we do now?"

Talia had other questions. "Why did Maitliin believe he'd have to sacrifice his life for the Recharging to occur?"

Arriving at the platform, Nomyra pointed to the jar. "I believed as much as well. That the True Heir must drain her entire magical blood into the Machine to feed the full Recharging. But that paper from Giddeona said the Bright Ones can also contribute. I just don't know how."

Talia took in the mostly empty jar and the moving Planets. She feared they were wasting time. "There's still time. I just need to feed it what I have."

Ial grabbed her wrist and shook his head.

Nyna stood tall next to him. "He's right. You don't have to sacrifice your life. You've done enough already."

Naul rubbed his sweating head. "The Machine is hooked to the diamond, right? What good would it do anyway?"

Her face bright and eager, Nomyra held an open hand to Talia.

"Let me fix it. Maitliin taught me everything about this blasted Machine. I was supposed to hook up the diamond while he was stuck in the crown. But he's still down there, and I'll need extra firepower."

Windall flashed on Talia's hand as if it agreed with the priestess. At this point, Talia didn't have a choice. No one else had been tutored by the evil wizard. She had to trust Nomyra. Talia closed her eyes as she slipped the Unity ring from her finger.

Nomyra slipped the ring onto the hand opposite the Krag ring, which also vibrated with renewed power. "I won't fail you," she called as she climbed the ladder to the top of the Machine and slipped into the opening.

"Hurry," Talia said as she looked up at the conjunction. The perfectly round connection looked to have a bit of a nose on one end as one Planet moved away from the others. "There's not much time."

Dew rolled her hand across the sacrificial opening in the middle of the rotating crown. "Only one hand will fit here."

Naul cracked his knuckles and tried to lift the cover of the container of liquid. "It doesn't move."

As her companions tried to work out a solution, Talia watched the Planets. It was happening too quickly. They wouldn't be able to solve this in time. She scanned for Gregor on the ground. She didn't even try to stop the tears from flowing as she met his eyes for the last time.

He leaned against Rory's blade. "Talia? What's going on?" Gregor kicked his captor's feet out from underneath him and rushed the platform.

"It's now or never." Talia unwound her wrapped hand and prayed that Nomyra was able to disconnect the underground diamond. She couldn't let the elves, merpeople, nadph, and dragons die off because one human wanted to monopolize all the power.

With a quick squeeze, the wound reopened. Before she could change her mind, Talia pressed her hand to the offering dome. Her blood flowed easily along the surface and across the crown. She could hear it dripping into the jar over the whirling of the Machine.

The dew drops of magic spread out through the air coalesced once again into a tight beam.

As before, the panels on either side of the crown snapped open. Through her teary vision, Talia watched her companions arguing, but she couldn't hear anything over the roar of the magical beam. Ial tried to pull her from the Machine, but it wouldn't let her go without her permission. And she wasn't giving it.

Though she stood beside them, Talia felt like she was observing her companions from a distance. Naul pointed to one of the open panels. Each guardian moved to stand in front of an exposed dome. Nyna held her hand to Ial, who sliced it neatly down the middle. She pushed her hand onto the surface, followed by Ial on the next one. Dew and Naul mirrored their actions on the other side of Talia.

With all five of them attached to the Machine, the beam brightened until Talia felt as if the Light's Daughter stood beside her. Yet there was no heat, only Light. An explosion underground rocked the Machine. Talia braced her legs against the movement.

Able to focus again, Talia sized up the flow into the jar. Blood lapped near the top. The energy stream widened and dimmed as the Planets drifted farther apart

"Please be enough," Talia whispered, a prayer for the reconciliation of past evils by her family and other rulers who thought only of their own power.

Her skin glowed again. Her body and mind lightened as she realized she didn't have to die. Her blood might have been needed to start the Machine, but her faithful guardians, tested and proven, were destined to join the efforts.

Nyna gasped and held up her free hand. It shone like Talia's skin. The same was happening with Ial, Naul, and Dew. The guardians who stood by her side and who had agreed to sacrifice their own well-being to save her life glowed with magic.

"Not yet," Talia said, answering Dew's questioning look. As she looked up to judge the movement of the Planets, a bout of dizziness caused her stomach to clench. She closed her eyes and returned her head to pointing straight ahead. She counted her blessings. She might be weak from blood loss, but her heart still beat. She would be here when the magicals awakened.

At that moment, Talia felt like she could overcome anything.

The beam flashed one last time. Then darkness spread across the plaza.

# CHAPTER FORTY-EIGHT

TALIA REMOVED her hand from the dome. She sat down immediately as her limbs shook with fatigue. After everything that had just happened, she didn't want to fall down like an injured animal. She felt weak but invigorated. She'd succeeded. The planet was Recharged and the magicals saved.

Ial and Nyna sat down beside her. Dew and Naul joined them on the other side. Each held their sliced hand against their chest as if some secret choreographer instructed them.

The air around the Machine was bereft of magic floating visibly. But Talia could feel the buzz. She thought of her companion's glowing skin. Reaching behind her without standing, Talia pried the crown from its immobile gear. The Machine shook as it stopped turning.

She placed the Key in her lap and gestured to her guardians. "Touch it. I need to know if you can feel it."

Dew hovered her hand above the Ruby. Ial leaned in with his hand over the Black Opal. Nyna joined him over the Sapphire. Finally, Naul shakily approached the Emerald. That left the central

Holy Diamond for Talia. They pressed the gems at the same time with their still open wounds.

The world dissolved as Talia's mind tumbled into the crown. The familiar swirls of color surrounded her as her companions popped into focus, forming a circle.

Elation tickled Talia's skin, an entirely different kind of magic. "You can all do it now. Your blood is like mine."

Nyna studied her hands, the mist cascading over her movements. "You're saying we have magic. I could heal with a touch of my hand?"

In the center of their circle, the dwarf wizardess who had saved Nomyra and Talia coalesced out of the mist. "Oh, yes, dear Bright One, and so much more, though it's more complicated than just touching." She beamed with true joy. "This is but the first step, newly anointed Bright Ones. Thwarting Maitliin is no easy task; I would know."

Talia wanted more. "That's enough with the cryptic talk. What do we do next?"

Billivin giggled and tucked her hands into her robes, much like Nomyra always had. "I am Wizardess Billivin of the Mountain Dwarves. I was sent as a guide to the Recharging a millennium ago. When I discovered that the rulers of Raqmu expected Maitliin to sacrifice himself to ensure the Recharging, I had to tell him. I thought he would pull out or demand the required mundane guardians to aid him."

Her face darkened. "I didn't realize his true plans until the moment of the Recharging. On my last inspection of the Machine, I found his connection to the enormous diamond. I rushed to the surface too late to stop the beam. In our struggle, we broke something, and the Machine stopped moving. As we fought to fix it, our souls were trapped in the Key."

She snapped her fingers. Talia blinked and found that they were all outside the crown. Billivin hovered above them, her ghostly form outlined coldly in the Dark.

"Only later did we discover that the Recharging had failed and the world had collapsed into war and chaos as they fumbled to recover from such a blow."

As if sensing her presence, Maitliin slid down a panel from the top of the Machine to the platform. "You witch! You thwarted my plans again. How?" His feet slammed into the metal grating.

Talia bounced, but her hand remained on the crown. Her guardians looked to her, but she wasn't sure what to do.

Billivin squatted within the circle and seemed to look at all five humans at once. "Set me free. Set me free so I can take Maitliin with me. Our time has passed. It's yours now. Fix what I couldn't."

A pull of power from the open wound on Talia's hand was sucked into the Holy Diamond. Billivin's image sharpened until it was almost opaque, and her floating form touched the platform.

Billivin stood tall in front of Maitliin. "One man was not meant to have all the power."

Through tight lungs, Talia squeaked out, "How do we free you?"

"My spirit is tethered to the crown. Look and you will see it. The combined power of the Bright Ones can sever it."

A thin channel of fog rose from each crenellation of the crown to form a rope wrapped around Billivin's bare feet. "I see it."

Talia had trouble focusing her mind. She'd lost a lot of blood today, and her body was weakening. She once again turned to her guardians. "Concentrate on the tether. We need to pull it from the crown."

Ial reach out his hand.

Dew slapped it back. "With your mind. If we could just pull it, she could free herself."

Talia commanded her fellow Bright Ones, "The Holy Diamond first."

All eyes moved to the glowing stone peeking through Talia's fingers. She didn't know what everyone else pictured, but Talia envisioned her mother's sewing scissors. The vision was so vivid, she felt the cold metal in her fingers. She clipped slowly until the tether sprang into Billivin's foot. The bit left around the gem dissipated into the air.

Nyna giggled.

Talia hoped that wasn't from blood loss. "Keep going. The Holy Ruby next."

They moved around the circle, severing one tether after another. With the final separation, Talia yanked her hand off the crown.

The wizard Maitliin, still in Salvo's body, grabbed the Key from Talia's lap. He focused on the dwarf wizardess. "How did you get free?"

The dwarf priestess smiled. "The Bright Ones fulfilled more than one prophecy on this night."

Maitliin backed into the railing, clutching the crown to his chest like a safety blanket. "I won't go back."

With her eyes downcast, Billivin looked sad, almost regretful. "I'm not going to put you back. It's time to move on and face the Dark."

"No!" Maitliin pulled power from the Key and flung a lightning bolt at Billivin.

She tossed it aside with a sweep of her hand. "You cannot harm me any longer."

A sneer morphed the usually peaceful demeanor of the prophet's face. Talia couldn't believe she hadn't recognized the change from the minute of possession. She might not have agreed with Salvo's beliefs, but she couldn't fault his motivations for a peaceful world.

Maitliin yelled at Billivin, "Maybe not, but I can trap you inside the crown again. You will not drag me into the ether. I have not served my purpose yet."

He scraped his hands on the crown's crenellations and streaked blood across the gems in one smooth movement. After whispering foreign words, the top of the crown opened into nowhere like the hungry maw of a beast. The swirling colors from the other side made a whirlpool of crackling lightning.

No wind whipped past Talia. Whatever was being kicked up was not on the same plane of existence as she. Billivin, however, turned to flee as her ethereal robes pulled from her ghost form, floating toward the hungry crown.

Talia used her last bit of adrenaline to crawl to Maitliin. She tried to wrest the crown from his grip, but in her weakened state, she didn't have the oomph to get it done. After everything Billivin had done for the world, Talia couldn't let her get trapped again. She grabbed hands with Ial and Naul, who took Nyna's and Dew's, until they formed a circle with Talia facing Maitliin.

Magical droplets dispersed through the air gathered around the circle. The companions found themselves hovering above the platform.

The power invigorated Talia. "Return the crown, Maitliin. Your time has passed. A new era has begun."

The wind drowned out his egotistical laugh, but Talia saw the refusal on his face. Billivin screamed as her form flew toward the gaping maw of the crown. Talia pulled from her friends and focused a flash of lightning into the center of the whirlwind. The magic portal snapped closed with an audible click. The sudden quiet echoed more profusely than the wind had.

Maitliin growled and stomped his foot. "You can't stop me forever. I've done nothing but plan my return for centuries."

Talia lost the connection to her friends and fell flat in utter exhaustion. "I'm sorry they tricked you, but what you did punished a world full of innocent magical creatures."

Billivin rushed the wizard, but he threw up a barrier she couldn't seem to penetrate.

"No one was innocent to the treachery." Maitliin twisted his hand around the crown to reignite the whirlwind. "Now sit still while I decide what to do with you. I might not be able to control all the renewed magic, but I can certainly control a great deal of the population, especially in this prophet's body."

Talia filled her lungs with air and forced her muscles to move one more time. "That body is not yours."

With an awkward roll, Talia kicked his legs out from under him. Maitliin's torso slammed against the railing. He managed to stay upright by releasing a hand from the crown and balancing himself. His face distorted in anger.

He pointed a hand at Nyna. "I'm through with your disobedience. You've just lost a guardian." Lightning shot from his fingers.

Nyna screamed as the smell of burning flesh filled the air.

Adrenaline pumped through Talia's veins as she screamed, "No!" Her exhaustion fell away as she thought of nothing but saving Nyna. She flung herself at him, ramming her shoulder into his gut. The magic lightning dissipated as Maitliin doubled in half. Talia reached for the crown in his outstretched hand. He spun away from her grasp and pushed himself backward.

Talia lunged as he rammed into the railing. "That's not yours."

Maitliin rushed toward the ladder. Billivin leaped forward. Talia tripped as her sluggish feet draped the platform. Her forward movement hit Maitliin high on his shoulders. His arms pinwheeled as he leaned precariously over the railing. Talia grabbed the crown from a flailing hand and tossed it to Ial.

Talia took a moment to smile and enjoy her triumph, when she felt a tug at her belt.

Dew yelled, "No!"

Turning tightly, Talia grimaced as Maitliin dove at her with her own dagger.

Billivin sucked in the last droplets of wild energy and bounced off the platform with supernatural strength. She rammed into the plunging knife with such momentum, both dwarf and wizard flew over the railing.

# CHAPTER FORTY-NINE

TALIA CRINGED at the crushing sound of Maitliin's head against the paved plaza. Billivin's ethereal body fell into the flesh and disappeared.

Augusta screamed and rushed to Salvo's body.

Bent over her prophet's crushed form, Augusta yelled at Talia, "What have you done?"

Meerin appeared from the other side of the apparatus and joined Augusta's wailings. Talia didn't know how to tell them that Salvo had been dead from the moment the crown touched him. It had never healed him at all. Maitliin had taken his body.

A ghostly mist rose from Salvo's still form. Tanin grabbed Augusta and backed her up from the prophet. The fog bulged and popped until Billivin's dwarf shape became clear.

"Come, wizard. Your time has gone. It is their turn now."

As her elongated arms flowed from Salvo, they pulled more vapor with them that slowly took the form of Maitliin. He seemed deflated, weak. Without a bit of struggle, he allowed Billivin to wrap him in her arms.

The dwarf sorcerous smiled up at the raised platform as Meerin drug Salvo's body away from the ghostly figures. "His pain will not hurt another living soul," she said, her voice fading as her form dimmed. "Thank you for succeeding where I failed."

Then the misty forms swirled like the portal in the Key. Their forms commingled into no separation could be made between the two. In a rush of wind, they flew through the opening in the ceiling toward the Stars above.

Talia gripped the railing as she squinted at the disappearing forms. Where were they going? How did they know which way to go?

Dew tapped her on the shoulder. "Talia, look."

On the ground below, Prophet Salvo's head rested in Meerin's lap while Augusta and Tanin kneeled at his side. Unbelievably, Salvo lived. She couldn't hear what he was saying but Meerin and Augusta sobbed openly as he touched each of their cheeks. Finally, he turned to Tanin.

Her brother, always defiant to any authority but his own, bowed his head and kissed the prophet's hand. Talia's chest tightened at his pain. She didn't agree with Salvo's teachings, but she hadn't intended their quarrel to end like this.

Salvo's shaking hands held Tanin on either side of his head and pulled him down where the prophet kissed him on the forehead. Then he pressed his hand on the place he kissed and mouthed more words.

Talia moved to the stairs. Her body still vibrated from the influx of magic. Maybe she could save him.

Though she didn't notice Gregor climb the ladder, he must have for he put his strong arms on her shoulders and held her still. "They don't want our help."

She knew he was right, but everything hurt and she needed to help someone to make it go away.

Before Talia made up her mind, Meerin wailed into the night sky. Augusta collapsed against Tanin, her body convulsing in grief. The prophet's body laid between his disciples, lifeless.

Tanin's arms squeezed Augusta. His glare, however, enveloped Talia with more anger than she'd ever seen, even from Maitliin.

Talia couldn't guess what he was thinking, but she knew to the depths of her soul, that Tanin no longer considered her a sister. She had now lost her entire family while trying to do the right thing.

She tensed as footsteps clopped down the upper ladder from the central opening of the Machine. She turned as Nomyra reached the platform.

Nomyra's face was unreadable. "He's gone, isn't he?"

Dried blood streaked the priestess's hands and the front of her robes. Talia nodded once as she tried to decide if the blood was Nomyra's or someone else's.

When Nomyra didn't say anything else, Talia ignored her presence. She supposed she got what she deserved. After all, she wasn't a Winterlaus by birth. The Light had re-aligned Talia's life to its original intention. What did it want from her now? What was next?

Nyna wrapped her bleeding hand as she instructed Gregor to tear more cloth for her to tend to everyone else's. Talia took the Key from Ial so he could be tended to.

As she held the now cold metal, Talia could feel the power of the stones and somehow knew she didn't need to bleed on them for the magic to recognize her commands. Everything was more present, stronger.

She took Naul's injured hand. With a pull through her weakened body, Talia conducted a healing warmth through her skin to his gash. The bleeding stopped, and the skin stitched together.

Naul's arm shook. "That tickles."

Talia's limbs felt strong and light at the same time. Her motivation grew as her hope blossomed. "Come to me." She motioned to the rest of her guardians, whom she healed one at a time.

Power flowed through every fiber of her soul. Everything seemed possible in that one moment. She smiled at her companions, whose blissful faces mirrored Talia's rapture.

The Great Awakening was at hand. The magicals would rejoin a world they had helped found. Peace and prosperity would be shared by all sentient life. The euphoria and immense power made Talia imagine all the things she could fix in the world, all the things she could make fair. Surely her sacrifice was minor compared to the healing of an entire world. She had to cling to that.

Talia moved in for a group hug. "For the Light despite the Dark, we will shine in knowledge to fight the shadow of doubt."

Gregor squeezed her hand. "What's next?"

Talia shrugged. She'd been so scared of failing, she'd never considered what to do if she succeeded.

Dew pulled back from the circle and pointed at the crowds pouring from the stands and heading toward the center. "I don't know how many of those people are going to stay, but it looks like they're approaching to hear a word from their True Heir."

# CHAPTER FIFTY

TALIA HAD no idea what to tell the expectant faces below the plat-form. She gripped the railing Maitliin had tumbled over. Augusta and Meerin wailed, while Tanin stared at Talia with such animosity, she was grateful she didn't stand beside him.

No, she definitely couldn't address the crowd right now. She had completed her destiny as Bright One. True Heir could wait until she had settled things with her brother. With a glance at her companions, she pointed to Dew.

"Can you talk to them, please?" Talia's eyes fell on Tanin's below. "I have a few more things to deal with."

Gregor tried to stop her. "But Talia..."

"No, Gregor, I have to do this."

Dew straightened the tiara in her curls. "Of course, and I should say—?"

Talia watched as some of the witnesses fell to their knees beside Salvo's corpse and others touched the Machine with as much rever-ence. "Tell them the Recharging worked. That those who wish to stay in peace are welcome. Any who wish to leave are free to go."

Before Talia climbed the ladder down, she held a hand out to

Nomyra. The priestess knew what she wanted immediately. She pulled Windall from her finger and placed it on Talia's palm. Talia thought about demanding Krag too. Taking inventory of the broken priestess, Talia decided to let her keep her status symbol. For now.

Until Talia's foot hit solid ground, she hadn't realized how wobbly the platform was. She moved out of the way as Ial and Nyna clomped down close behind.

Gregor wrapped her in his muscular arms and held her so close, she almost couldn't breathe. It felt so good, she'd almost rather have suffocated than abandoned his embrace.

"Are you sure?" he asked. "We could sneak around back and run away. You've done everything you set out to do."

She enjoyed the vision of her and Gregor lost in the woods, enjoying each other's company. Only for a moment though. Talia had always obeyed her duties. She couldn't abandon her responsibilities as True Heir, even if she wasn't quite sure what they entailed.

Talia reluctantly pulled away from his embrace. "I'm sure."

The two tumbled into the side of the Machine as the ground shook with an angry force almost as violent as when the beam from the conjunction had charged the world. The dark sky above showed a line of energy radiating from the moving planets. They didn't look like they were aligned anymore. What was happening?

Gregor whispered in Talia's ear. "What's happening?"

She reluctantly unfolded herself from his comforting hold. "I have no idea."

Ial pointed at a constellation the beam seemed to travel through. "It's far west of us."

The crowd moaned in fear and fell to their knees. A piece of sheeting fell from the Machine and hit the ground on the other side of Tanin and his companions. Tanin looked at his sister as if she were responsible. How could he still think such thoughts of her? After all they'd been through.

As quickly as it had started, the ground grew silent. Aleck limped over to Talia, leaning heavily on Traneck.

His face was lit with glee even though blood caked the back of his head. "You did it, Talia. I'm so proud of you." He practically fell into her as he wrapped his arms around her waist in a tight hug.

Talia gripped him just as tightly. "I have something for you." She put her fingers on the crown on either side of the Holy Diamond. With a whisper of permission, the Key released the gem into her palm. She handed it to Prince Aleck.

Tears drained into his beard as he held the Holy Gemstone with both hands. "My father will be so surprised. I told him you were going to give it back, but he didn't believe me."

"I can't send you home like that, now can I?" Talia cupped a hand over Aleck's head and begged the Light to heal his wounds. Her palm warmed, and a gentle blue light enveloped the dwarf's injured scalp.

Aleck brushed his hand across the new flesh, running his fingers through his clean hair. "Amazing. That skill could really come in handy."

Talia wiped sweat from her brow. "It takes quite a bit out of the magic user. I'm not sure it's always such a clever move."

Traneck bowed. "You are a generous and honorable True Heir, Talia. The Krimmel will surely work with you as you rebuild this glorious city."

Talia returned his bow. "I look forward to our continued relationship."

She smiled as she pulled Traneck in for a hug. The dwarf leaned in for a whole second before he pushed away.

With his guardians in tow, Tanin marched toward Talia. "I'll take the Tarbin crown now before you kill the rest of us with your obscene displays of power."

Talia agreed. "Of course, my brother. Just a second." She pulled the Holy Ruby off with a silent prayer for release.

Tanin put a hand on his sword hilt. "What are you doing?"

She ignored his anger and handed the gem to Gregor, who tucked it into a pocket. "I promised you the crown." Talia pried off the Holy

Emerald with ease. "I didn't say you could have the Holy Gemstones. They belong to the races sworn to protect them." She went after the Holy Black Opal next.

"You have no right." Tanin fumed before Talia. If Aleck, Ial, and Nyna hadn't blocked his way, he probably would have outright attacked his sister.

Talia embraced her newfound power. Tanin was not going to intimidate her this time. She knew she was doing the right thing and didn't need his, or anyone else's, approval. "For centuries, the Tarbin crown was mounted with substitute jewels. I'm returning the symbol the way it was handed to Tarbin to begin with."

After giving the Holy Sapphire to Gregor, Talia held the crown up. It looked pathetic without the sparkle of the gems, fake or real. She thought of her father's face when he saw the empty gold and blood-stained padding. They might not be related biologically, but she knew he had done the best he could, and she didn't want him to look any less in front of his people, who until very recently had also been her people.

She closed her eyes and held the crown out as she begged the Light to guide her magic. Windall flashed, but she didn't need its power. Her blood tingled with magic. The energy flowed from the ground itself, like water from a spring. All she had to do was focus it.

Picturing the sparkle of each jewel in their goose-egg shape and size, Talia wove magic to fill the spaces on the crown. Blue haze billowed around the crown and her hands. She renewed the cloth to a silky sheen. With the vision of her brother's head in mind, she shaped the cushion to perfectly embrace his full head of hair. All drops of blood disappeared from the gold of the Key itself. The magic buffed it to a blinding gleam. Somehow, Talia knew it would remain that shiny and fingerprint free without any work from the royal servants.

She concentrated on the gems. She didn't want glass replicas, like the fake diamond Nomyra had dramatically broken at the beginning of this crazy journey. She wished her birth kingdom to be honored with the real thing. The mist swirled in tiny whirlpools among tiny whirlpools at each empty gem mount. Her will forced the facets to form and the color to gleam in exactly the right shade. The mist dissipated in an ethereal breeze, revealing the stunning gems underneath.

Talia sighed as she released the leftover magic into the stone beneath her feet. Slack-jawed, Tanin didn't move.

With a gentle push to Ial's shoulder, Talia moved around him to stand in front of her brother. "The Tarbin crown is renewed. As True Heir of Raqmu, I welcome a friendly and mutually beneficial relationship with my birth kingdom."

Tanin released his sword hilt and stepped forward. "I don't know what kind of relationship we'll have going forward."

Talia put the crown on Tanin's head. "It looks good on you, Brother. We might not see eye to eye on many things, but I do think you've changed on this journey."

He stood taller with the symbol of royalty, then he took it off. "I'm not king yet."

Talia tilted her head in acknowledgment. "But you will be soon enough." With a sweeping motion, she gestured at the city and the gathered people. "I have no idea what my legacy will be here."

Augusta tucked under Tanin's arm, fury in her eyes aimed at Talia. "Prince Tanin's legacy will be to bring the word of Lagaw, the God of the people, to all of Tarbin and Ngaro and then the world. Your Ydiny might have won the battle, but she won't win the war."

Talia balked at the suggestion that she worshipped the goddess of magic. "That's one thing I can promise. We will welcome all beliefs and all cultural practices as long as they don't infringe on the rights of any other. Raqmu was founded on education, exploration, and inclusion. This is the world I wish to recreate."

Meerin broke into the conversation. "There is no truth beyond Lagaw's wish for mankind. All other gods are inferior and must take their place accordingly." She pointed to the covered body. "Prophet Salvo died for this belief, and we will honor his sacrifice by continuing his work."

Talia looked up as Dew began her speech. "We would offer him an honored spot in Memorial Park."

Kettlor and Rory lifted the prophet's body. The crowd parted, forming an aisle for them to pass undisturbed. Hodan and Orui waited for their prince.

Tanin cocked his head, his eyes squinted. "What do you want?"

"I will never challenge your throne. I have no blood right." Talia rubbed her elbows. "But please don't tell Fath—King Roland. He will blame Mother, and it wasn't her fault."

Tanin seemed to consider all she had to say. "Fine."

Without further discussion, Tanin took Augusta's hand and marched after Prophet Salvo's body.

At the end of Dew's speech, which Talia hadn't heard a word of, the desert people lifted their voices as one in a melancholy song.

Not all of the fathered stayed to sing though. A good portion followed Tanin and his procession to Memorial Park.

Talia didn't want to worry about the division in her newly minted Raqmu. She leaned against Gregor and joined in at the repeated chorus. One way or another, this was her home now. She should learn some of the customs.

# CHAPTER FIFTY-ONE

THE REMAINING GATHERED TURNED to Talia as her brother walked away. Talia thought about attending the funeral of Prophet Salvo, but she wasn't sure she'd be welcome. Plus, he had talked of a world divided, and she wanted to live in a world united.

Dew motioned for Talia to join her on the elevated platform. "They wish to hear from you."

Aleck and Traneck shimmied over the rungs ahead of the humans.

With a heavy sigh, Talia took her time climbing up the ladder as she searched for the proper words. She'd won. The Recharging had occurred, and the Great Awakening would cascade across the world. She had thought she'd feel relief, at least for a moment. Instead, the true burden of rebuilding a city in ruins weighed on her shoulders.

Above the patiently waiting crowd, Talia gripped the railing and appraised their expectant faces. What could she say to set the tone?

A hand fell on her shoulder. Gregor nodded, his complete confidence in her bolstering her belief. Dew stood to her left, while the rest of the Bright Ones formed a semicircle behind the True Heir.

Aleck and Traneck stood to the side, but they both nodded to her in encouragement.

The tips of Talia's lips twitched. She wasn't alone. There were multiple shoulders to spread the responsibility across. Talia knew what to say.

"Welcome to the new age. You are all witnesses to the return of balance in our world. Raqmu will be a place of unity and inclusion. No matter your beliefs or your needs, there is a place for you here if you wish to stay." She cleared her throat to disguise the tears that tried to clog it. "But know this. If you wish to exclude anyone for their race, for their mundane or magical status, for their worship of the old gods, for their belief in the Light and the Dark, for their outright lack of faith, then this is not the city for you. Raqmu will be a symbol in the desert, of progress and hope and a connection to all the elements of existence. Together, we will make it so and lead the world to this new reality."

Murmurs broke out among the listeners as the translations echoed across the plaza. Talia hoped enough would be willing to try this new kind of kingdom. She hadn't sacrificed her future or that of her companions in order to strengthen barriers. She wished to unite, not divide.

Dew shouted, "The Bright Ones of Raqmu are ready to serve. Who is with us?"

A cheer erupted in the crowd. Aleck held up his hands. "To Team Bright Ones!"

A chorus of voices joined his chant. "To Team Bright Ones!"

The audience seemed to sense the end of the ceremony. They dispersed without any further orders.

From behind, Gregor wrapped his arms tightly around Talia's chest. "You did it."

"*We* did it," she corrected him. Unwilling to push him off, staring eyes or not, she leaned into his warmth.

He laughed. The joyous sound washed over Talia. She turned in his arms, grabbed the back of his head, and brought him to her lips.

Her skin tingled, and her stomach fluttered. This time, it wasn't from magic. She didn't have time to get lost in the feeling, though Gregor's eyes reflected the intensity she felt.

"Later," she whispered, a finger on his welcoming lips.

Gregor's breathy "soon" shook Talia almost as much as the Recharging had.

Reaching her hands out for the rest of her companions, she had to shout to be heard above the bustling voices exploring the Machine below. "Are you ready for this?"

Aleck backed out of the circle, but Nyna grabbed his hand and brought him in. "You're part of this too."

Naul leaned in. "I'm up for another adventure, but can we rebuild the tavern first? I'm thirsty."

Ial punched him on the arm, his expression agreeing with his large friend.

Exchanging looks with her companions, Talia confirmed a consensus. "So, the tavern first. I'm sure one of these tribes knows how to make some powerful drink."

Naul's stomach growled.

Talia's heart heaved, but she swallowed her tears. No more crying. She had stuff to do. "I agree, Naul. All great ceremonies are followed by feasts."

"Attention!" Talia threw her hands up, but no one heard her above the ambient noise of rustling feet and murmuring conversation.

Dew yelled out attention which was translated and amplified by the tiara. The crowd quieted down and returned their focus to the platform.

Talia continued, "For my first act as True Heir, I declare tomorrow Meet-Your-Neighbors Day. We will meet in the plaza. Everyone bring a dish to share, and we'll get to know each other and the skills we all bring to the table."

The crowd cheered as Talia made her way back to solid ground. It was time to establish a base of operations. A whiff from under her arms scrunched her nose. And a bath would be quite welcome.

Naul brandished his hammer as a man in heavy robes approached. The stranger bowed repeatedly and mumbled in a language Talia didn't recognize. A family lined up behind him, a teenage girl behind them.

Talia touched Naul's arm. "I'm pretty sure they just want to shake my hand."

Gregor nodded. "I've worked with many of them for a couple of weeks now. I've seen no animosity."

Talia squeezed Gregor's hand. She was anxious for them to be alone, but she knew she had a responsibility to these people first. "If these are to be the citizens of Raqmu, then the True Heir must serve them. I will start by shaking their hands."

Naul sidestepped but stayed close.

Talia smiled at her ever-protective guardian. "You know, you're officially not my guardian anymore, Bright One."

He guffawed. "Well, until we train new guards, you're going to have to live with me doing my old job."

Nyna stood on Talia's other side. "Me too."

Ial and Dew casually walked down the quickly forming line. Talia knew they were searching for weapons or suspicious behavior. She would have to find replacements soon. She had a feeling her ex-guardians were going to be busy with new jobs as they rebuilt this city.

Talia shook hands until all the faces blurred together. She'd never been so happy or so tired. As the last of the people moved out of the plaza, Talia leaned against the Machine.

Gregor tucked his arm in her elbow. "So, True Heir, are you ready for some much-needed shut-eye?"

She leaned her head against his shoulder. "Yes, please. I was starving a minute ago. Now all I want to do is sleep."

He kissed her on the forehead and pulled her upright. "Let's go, then."

Talia sighed. "Not just yet. We have a baby nadph and baby dragon to check on."

Talia took a moment to stare at the Stars above. The Planets still shone like beacons of hope, though all five were now spread out across the Dark expanse. They wouldn't perfectly line up for another millennium.

Hopefully, her children would be more prepared than she had been.

# CHAPTER FIFTY-TWO

ALANNA STARBURST TAPPED her knees in an agitated rhythm. Her elaborately applied makeup had long-ago smeared, and her immaculately straightened hair had puffed out into its usual uncontainable mess. She pushed a strand of deep black behind the tip of her pointed ear as she agitated her amethyst gem on its silver chain. Something was wrong.

Yet everything had gone exactly as planned. The grand Machine had danced with the power of the conjunction and the land sang with renewed magic. Her people had survived the long drought and were ready to power all the technology they'd been sitting on for centuries.

But something still dug at Alanna. Her advisors insisted that the first beam that had lit the night sky was but a precursor to the main event. But the ground had vibrated under Alanna with an unmistakable influx of magic. She had no doubts about that. What other civilization could possibly both have known of and been prepared for the planetary conjunction? All other races were too primitive to manipulate the natural world, remaining slaves to it.

Alanna scratched between the ears of her familiar, Dog. The

large gray square-jawed canine sat by her side, closer than normal. She knew he could sense her unease.

She frowned at a jingle of bells on her door. Dog barked in the low gruff voice that would scare away anyone who dared disturb his mistress without her permission.

"It is I, Racheia, your loyal servant, Supremacy. I have your hot tea and am ready to prepare you for bed."

With a high-pitched yap of familiarity, Dog padded to the door and sat expectantly. Racheia brought him a special treat every night. Sometimes, Alanna thought her familiar loved Racheia best.

Usually just as happy to see her doting handmaiden, Alanna couldn't calm her mind enough to consider sleep. She opened the door and allowed Racheia and the rest of the entourage into her room. They carried basins of steaming water to wash her face and decorative combs to groom her hair. The routine annoyed her this evening.

She motioned to her mirror-mounted vanity. "Leave everything here. I'll be back shortly."

Alanna grabbed her shawl from the hook by the door and rushed out before Racheia could stop her. Dog hesitated, having not received his treat yet. As Alanna turned the corner and headed down the stairs, the loyal beast barked and ran to catch up.

She waved at the guards as she pushed her way through the front doors of the Supreme Quarters and into the carefully cultivated lawn.

A terrified expression marred the face of the Officer of the Night. Alanna knew the guard would send for the Archivist.

Alanna smiled at her stolen bit of freedom as she sprinted across the tightly cropped grass to the stone enclosure of the Temple Complex. The public area was never locked, and she knew she could enter whenever she wished. But if she wanted to talk to the Supremacies alone, she'd have to hurry.

Cutting through the middle of the courtyard, she jumped over Contemplative Bench and balanced along the edge of Ponder Fountain to get to the second set of doors. She slowed her breathing and pointed a finger at Dog. He sat immediately and hung his head. No animals were allowed in the sanctuary, familiars or otherwise.

Alanna put both hands on the door handles. After pressing her forehead to the space in between the two doors, she whispered her request for admittance. "Please allow me to consult the past in order to ensure the future."

The doors recognized her plea with a snap. Alanna pushed them open and entered the darkened room. The mechanism closed on its own behind her, and the lock snapped back into place.

Though the only way to open the door, Alanna still felt a little thrill at using forbidden magic. That kind of energy had to be used through stones that powered machines. If a person used magic through thoughts and desires alone, that person would lose a part of their soul. If they used too much, their soul would drain with the magic, leaving nothing but an empty husk.

Alanna shivered at the thought, but knew that this minor use would cause her no harm.

The first time Alanna had been granted entrance, almost seven years ago, she had been blown away by the stunning beauty of a chamber few would ever see. Only the sitting Supremacy, the Archivist, and the Council of Etten were permitted entrance.

The only source of light emanated from a giant glass box in the center of the room, large enough to hold a large pond of water. A calm of wisdom and experience washed over Alanna. She knelt on the elaborate carpet surrounding the enclosure, whose contents swirled in a never-ending dance. With her hands folded in her lap, she waited to be acknowledged.

The spirits in the mist were much more active than normal. The influx of energy should have affected them. It all made sense. Alanna truly hoped that they knew what that first beam meant. As much as the council tried to reassure her, Alanna could feel that something big had happened. Something she had to work into her governance. After all, Alanna hadn't won the Supremacy by trusting what she was told and going with the flow.

A pale face formed just behind the glass. "Your instincts guide you well, as usual."

Another misty form cascaded over the first. "The old kingdom has awakened."

A burst of hair took shape around a wispy indistinct face. "Tarbin wishes to claim its prior glory."

As the old souls always did, they fell one after another on top of each other, communicating as a group. The voices and features changed rapidly.

"The Recharging occurred as prophesied."

"We Enlightened are not the only ones with knowledge."

"Though ours is greater."

Alanna suppressed a smile at the gruff voice of her predecessor. She missed her time with him and always listened for his advice above everyone else's.

The prior Supremacy's soul waved the others away. His slightly bent form and bald head pressed against the glass. Supremacy Richlieu's arthritically deformed hands traced symbols in the air as he channeled the thoughts of the others flowing behind him. "You were right to come to us. The council might want to ignore the happenings of the old kingdom of Tarbin. But Tarbin has a power of their own, and we cannot allow them to conquer us. It's time to open our borders to ensure our continued survival. Their way can never be our way, but we cannot hide here as our resources dwindle. We must ensure that Tarbin's rise does not mean Etten's fall."

Alanna pressed her hands against the glass before Richlieu's ethereal form. "Thank you, Supremacy. I will do my research and learn all I can of this Tarbin."

Dog's growling bark warned Alanna of the approaching Archivist. He hated when she came in here alone. His role was to write down all that happened within these walls.

She jumped to her feet and ran to the chamber doors. She flung the doors inward as soon as the lock snapped open.

Archivist Tloonin stumbled over the threshold. "Supremacy Alanna, I would have come at your merest suggestion."

"I know, Archivist, but I had to do this on my own. I will fill you in later. I promise." She bounded over the bench, Dog hopping excitedly beside her.

Alanna knew what the next step was. She could go back to behaving like the leader of her kingdom now that she had direction. She hated the in-between, the not-knowing. As soon as the home star arose in the morning, she would hit the library and learn all she could. It was time for the Enlightened to build ships again. Tarbin awaited.

# ACKNOWLEDGMENTS

So many people to thank. I'll start with my critique group: Ann, Maurine, Annette, Louis, Diane, and Sydney. Your practiced eyes and critical minds helped improve this work one chapter at a time. Thank you. I should also give a shout out to Red Robin, Sabrina in particular, who tolerates us every Wednesday night. We found our home.

Inklings Publishing has been instrumental in getting my career on track. Thank you, Fern, for your continued support. Tod, as always, you rocked the editing and I don't know what I'd do without you.

To the patient readers who have waited for this novel for a year longer than you should have, I owe you everything.

My family, especially my always supportive husband, get extra kudos. This book took longer than it should have and never once did anyone suggest I give up. My dad, my husband, my son, and my daughter worked together to keep me motivated and lent me more encouragement than I deserved. I can't imagine this life without them.

Kelly Lynn Colby is a writer of all things fantasy. Whenever she tries to create a mundane story, a dragon pops in to take over. She eventually stopped fighting and caved to the magic. The dragons must have known something she didn't, because her debut novel, *Tarbin's True Heir*, won a bronze medal in the IPPYs for fantasy. You can find her work in the Recharging series as well as numerous short stories in anthology collections. Look for her new paranormal thriller series Emergence, with first book *The Collector*, set to release in September 2020.

If you want to be the first to learn of new releases and giveaways from Kelly, download this free story and join her newsletter here.

Newsletter QR code

facebook.com/kcolbywrites

twitter.com/kcolbywrites

instagram.com/kcolbywrites

ALSO BY KELLY LYNN COLBY

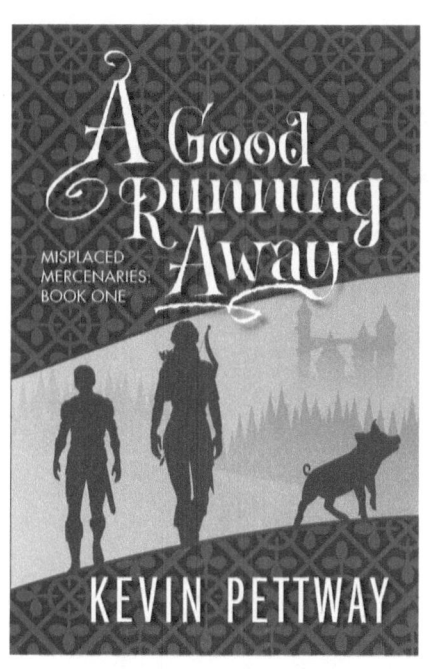

www.ingramcontent.com/pod-product-compliance
Lightning Source LLC
Chambersburg PA
CBHW032200180726
48284CB00001B/122